SECRETS OF MARY CELESTE

STEVE DAHILL

Jumpmaster Press
Birmingham, AL

Copyright

Edited by: Ghia Truesdale
Artwork: Generated by Midjourney
Cartography: Jude Dahill

Library Cataloging Data
Names: Dahill, Steve, (Steve Dahill)
Title: *Secrets of Mary Celeste* / Steve Dahill
5.5 in. × 8.5 in. (13.97 cm × 21.59 cm)
Description: Jumpmaster Press™ digital eBook & paperback edition | Alabama: Jumpmaster Press™, 2018 - 2023. Alabaster, AL 35007 info@jumpmasterpress.com

Summary: When the *Mary Celeste* is found adrift off the Azores Islands, Mary Celeste Briggs' devoted son, Alexander is unaware that his own father absconded with the entire family fortune, now lost at sea. The teenager hires a smuggler to rescue his family. Through nefarious backchannels, the cruel smuggler captain is privy to the fortune, and aims to steal it. Will his lonely daughter help Alexander Briggs outwit the smuggler in a desperate race to find his missing family before they perish?

ISBN-13: 978-1-958448-86-1 (eBook) | 978-1-958448-25-0 (paperback)

1. Historical Fiction 2. Maritime Fiction 3. Mary Celeste 4. Ghost Ship 5. Unsolved Mystery 6. 19th Century Fiction 7. Age of Sail

Printed in the United States of America

SECRETS
OF MARY
CELESTE

STEVE DAHILL

For Cathy, Jude, Katie,
and Maura, with my love

In the 19th century the sailing ship *Mary Celeste* was found drifting in the middle of the ocean by a passing vessel. She was not damaged nor was her valuable cargo disturbed. Her crew, however, including the captain, his wife, and their young daughter had all vanished without a trace.

The mystery of the *Mary Celeste* has never been solved.

Until now.

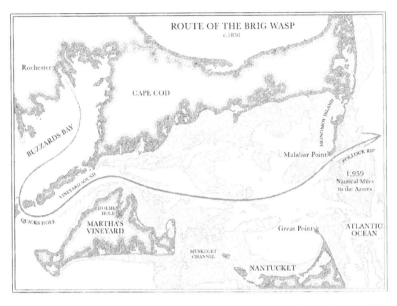

ROUTE OF THE BRIG WASP
c.1830

Rochester

CAPE COD

BUZZARDS BAY

MONOMOY ISLAND

Malabar Point

POLLOCK RIP

1,959
Nautical Miles
to the Azores

VINEYARD SOUND

QUICKS HOLE

HOLMES HOLE

MARTHA'S
VINEYARD

Great Point

ATLANTIC
OCEAN

MUSKEGET
CHANNEL

NANTUCKET

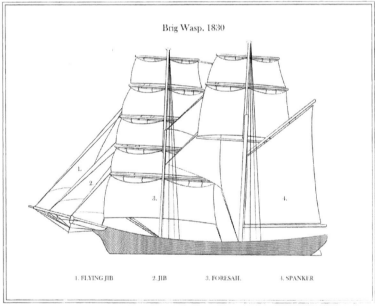

Brig Wasp. 1830

1.

2.

3.

4.

1. FLYING JIB   2. JIB   3. FORESAIL   4. SPANKER

Artwork and Cartography, Jude Dahill

1832

A cold rain stung the lookout's cheeks as gale-driven spindrift flooded his weary eyes. The young sailor's frozen hands clung precariously to the mast peak of the British ship *Halifax* as it rocked violently in a confused sea of massive, white-whipped breaking waves. Max Hardy glanced at the ratlines below him hoping to see his replacement climbing up; he wished to be safely 150 feet below in his warm berth.

Suddenly a glimpse of white emerged from the low-hanging clouds. Was that a sail looming a mere 500 feet ahead? Max could not discern a defined shape as the apparition disappeared into the rain. Was it a ship hurtling toward *Halifax* or did his eyes play tricks? Max stared toward the vague spot where the threat might reappear. A strong burst of wind parted the clouds momentarily he blinked twice and swiped streaming water from his eyes. There! Where at first a Leviathan appeared to rise from the deep, a black hull emerged bearing down on *Halifax* as if running from a rabid pursuer.

"On deck! Larboard bow—a ship!" bellowed the youth.

Lurching closer the encroaching vessel came, wild and unkempt: her sails shredded, her rigging drooping in tangled heaps. Lying dangerously low in the water, her hull crashed into the gray waves like an overburdened packhorse struggling for one last step. Her deck was awash with green seawater. But at the wheel, climbing her shrouds, or manning her sheets and halyards he saw not a single crewman.

"Sail-ho!" the lad screamed. "She's on top of us!" *Why wasn't Halifax turning away?*

The young seaman scanned the deck far below. At his warnings the watch had burst into confused activity. The first mate made quick calculations how best to escape and called for the captain. Others who rushed to the alarm from dreary sleep waited for commands. Through the flying white water and a steady rain, every man aboard recognized the impending danger of two ships on a collision course. The tense crew hung on the ship's larboard rail. Commands to avoid catastrophe had not been given and the men stared hard at the captain when at last he climbed on deck.

A burly middle-aged man with a loose, white beard covering his neck like a scarf, stood the captain. His stout frame was wrapped in a sealskin coat, his ancient cap pulled tight to the howl of the night. He looked up, over, and astern. In over 40 years at sea, Captain James Breton had rarely been so utterly undecided.

Peering through a brass telescope, Captain Breton made a cursory sweep of the ocean. He confirmed the crew's apprehension was not misplaced superstition. Nor was the lookout's warning drunken incompetence. Max had called it right. But how was this possible? Another ship sailing at *Halifax* in mid-damn-ocean? Had the other's lookout not seen *Halifax*? Captain Breton noted his taut storm sails were about to split. But if he did not change course immediately the hard-charging phantom ship would ram *Halifax* amidships. Yet if he turned away too sharply *Halifax* would fall off to leeward and founder as colossal waves broke over her beam end and she must go down. A row of men looked to him: turn away or attempt to cross the stranger's bow? *If I choose wrong, I and thirty-two men will perish.*

"Any sign of crew?" Captain Breton cried to the man aloft through calloused, cupped hands. Even during wars in His Majesty's service, he had never asked such a fateful question. Thankfully, his lookout answered with conviction. "None, Sir!"

An unmanned ship will stay her course, reasoned Captain Breton.

"We shall wear ship! Helm-down! Loosen fore stay'sls and hoist the flying jib." *Halifax* began a sharp turn away from steep waves breaking against the gunnels. The ship risked capsizing, but Breton had no choice.

"Captain, we'll lose the jib," complained the first mate.

"Damn it—DO IT!"

The crew jumped. Captain Breton timed his maneuver so that as *Halifax* rose on the crest of a breaking wave, the three helmsmen turned the wheel and *Halifax* slid down the backside. Rising from a trough her bow shot airborne and crashed hard, buried deep into green, cold ocean water. Men on deck clung to lines and tackle. Only a web of storm netting strung along the bulwarks protected men not holding fast from going over the side.

Staring intently to larboard Breton's hopes rose. The ghost ship remained on a steady course as *Halifax* turned away. *But will we clear her bow?* He tried to gauge the speed of the two intersecting ships: no, *Halifax* needed more separation—he must find additional speed. Again, the captain looked up, back, and around, as his bushy head jerked about on weary shoulders. *Damn it! We don't have room.* The two ships closed.

"Raise the spanker! All hands hoist—NOW!" As he watched the crew raise the gaff and the expansive sail catch a gust, he felt as powerless as a trapped mackerel dangling from a finely barbed hook.

The crew got the spanker up and its sheet trimmed the same moment a wave pushed *Halifax* far over onto her starboard side. Her lower spar tips sliced through the roiling water; terrified men clung to masts and rails. For a moment outside of time the ship creaked and wallowed. *If a breaking wave crests now, we'll go over for certain,* the captain thought. "Ease spanker sheets!" he bellowed. The ship slowed with his desperate command. Her long keel caught undisturbed, solid water and righted. The next roller in the sequence caught her stern square, her bow down. *Halifax* made the turn.

A moment before the encroaching ship had been aimed at *Halifax* amidships. After Captain Breton's desperate turn down and away, her bow now pointed at *Halifax's* aft quarter where only the captain and three hearty men at the wheel remained. The two ships continued to close: one driving fast downwind, the other turning hard away, and only a scant 100 feet apart. Breton glanced over his shoulder at the waves to his right. He convinced himself the swells looked smaller than a moment before.

"Helm-down, twenty degrees! Quickly—more ease on the spanker sheets!" He planned to turn the ship away from the wind at an even deeper angle, gain speed driven by the seas and propel the ship to safety if her hatches held and she remained upright. Wind, waves, and the momentum from their new direction should create a narrow gap between the two hulls.

Suddenly the stranger's jib boom snagged a line attached to a mizzen spar run through a double block at *Halifax's* stern. The captain grabbed a ready ax and swung with all his strength. In two angry strokes he severed the line. *Halifax* staggered momentarily yet continued her escape down the next wave's backside. Miraculously the two hulls, only 30 feet apart, did not crash together. Instead, the mystery ship silently slipped past *Halifax's* stern. Breton would have cursed their people, had any stood on deck. But the passing ship appeared as empty of life as a forgotten graveyard in an abandoned village.

Captain Breton bent over and inhaled great gulps of air. He did not care men standing nearest him on the quarterdeck had witnessed their famously heartless captain's moment of fear.

10

Halifax was improbably safe and could continue on her former course. His eyes, however, remained locked on the passing ship. His emotions veered from his initial terror to a loathing of her people. Quickly however, greed triumphed. Although unmanned, the dead ship appeared seaworthy, sailing to its doom without witnesses. He had come close to death many times before when cannon spat hot fire and jagged splinters had ripped through his thighs. But the pain of battle paled compared to the terror of the unknown. Despite the wind whistling through the ship's rigging like tensioned harp strings, the nearing dawn and lifting sky to the west heralded a quiet day ahead. The noises of the passing gale sounded to the old naval officer like the echo from a sea-battle's last furtive shot. Not a man spoke.

Captain James Breton of the East India Company merchant ship *Halifax* had embarked from Antigua two weeks earlier bound for London. A Dutch schooner encountered after three days of sailing NNE warned him to watch for Tripoli raiders southwest of the Azores. *Had these raiders captured this ship and then abandoned it?* Wars on the Continent were over. Bonaparte long dead. Privateers no longer hunting enemy merchant ships had been repurposed for the prosperous, illegal triangular trade and would likely ignore defenseless brigs like *Halifax* transporting only copper nails from Massachusetts, West Indies fruit, and raw Georgia cotton. *So, what happened to this ship?* Breton watched as she slid past his stern about to disappear.

The stranger was brig-rigged: two masts with every sail hoisted, ripped, and useless. *What careless master kept his sails full with a storm approaching?* Breton's glass had dropped for two days running; every ship in the mid-Atlantic knew a SW blow approached. He watched as the ghost ship sailed down the steep waves. Her bow disappeared into foam then breached like a humpback as torrents of cold white water washed over her decks, through the scuppers and returned to the sea. Without crew working sheets and braces and no one at her wheel the ship ran feral before the wind. He noted her deck hatches were torn open; sea water would eventually fill the hold and sink her.

After the phantom cleared *Halifax's stern* Captain Breton turned his focus to other possibilities.

"Mr. Levy, drop the spanker. We shall come about."

His crew jumped to trim two storm sails as her wheel spun. *Halifax* followed the stranger. *When the winds abate, we'll board her.* For an hour the two ships wallowed a few hundred feet apart. *Halifax* struggled to sail slower while the other vessel fought to stay afloat. She was so low in the water Breton feared she would go down before they could board.

"Captain, if no one's at her pumps she can't live long…" First mate Levy offered the unnecessary observation every man was thinking. Breton growled.

Halifax's third watch ended. Tired men were piped to a cold morning meal of water-soaked hardtack, bacon, and ale. As the fog began to dissipate the sun broke through. The crew revived with full stomachs anticipated the possibility of filling their pockets on account of this unusual discovery. The gale hurried east. The waves, however, remained large: green, heavy rollers formed one thousand miles away in the western North Atlantic. Soon the winds would turn NNE and the seas calm as the day warmed in the late-summer sun.

The captain gave new orders: put *Halifax* close alongside the stranger.

Was it disease or pirates, Breton wondered? It did not matter; her people were certainly dead. And James Breton, with an unexpected opportunity to claim an abandoned merchant ship— an extraordinarily valuable prize—was not about to forfeit a fortune worrying about those unfortunates. Yet he feared unknown dangers might lurk aboard the strange brig; perhaps a dying defender or a stranded pirate lay wounded, armed with a musket. Or the ship carried the rampant cholera plague. Breton assembled a small boarding party and warned his boys not to touch any bodies, living or dead.

"Flags, Mr. Levy?" he asked his cautious but competent first mate. Once a midshipman in the King's Navy who failed his Lieutenant's examination, Stephen Levy had followed his former captain through 20 years of peacetime voyages in the mundane merchant service. There they had plied the West Indies trade aboard slovenly ships such as *Halifax*, vessels fat and high in their stern, straight at their prow, and prone to wobbling in even moderate seas; in a storm she was hard to handle, even worse for those suffering below deck in dark, airless, and cramped spaces. *Halifax* was an ancient ship of 500 tons, three masts, and 37 crewmen hailing from as many different countries as she had made landfall.

"Remnants only, Captain. American I believe," the first mate guessed.

"We shall have a look. Mr. Levy, arm yourself. Sammy, take two men with me. Lower the gig." To the helm he ordered, "Hove-to!" He raised his large head, craned his bushy neck, and with cupped hands blasted a commendation to the lookout who had saved the ship, "Mr. Hardy, an extra tot of rum for 'ya tonight—but holler if you see any sails!" Breton did not want witnesses.

Every man on *Halifax* understood a ship that discovered a derelict vessel at sea could come to own her outright. Despite how the abandoned ship's crew met their death (likely disease was the deck's conjecture) *Halifax's* crew were of the same mind as their captain: boarding and taking the ghost ship was worth any risk. Life at sea was hard and every man aboard dreamed of a cottage or a tavern ashore. Absconding with someone else's hard-earned wealth was a tradition each man of *Halifax* would welcome if given the opportunity. On rocky coasts, organized gangs scouted storm-wrecks tossed on a lee shore, combed over debris thrown onto reefs and rocks, and scavenged cargo scattered along isolated beaches. Other more despicable mooncussers took it further and lit false beacons to lure ships desperately searching for a safe harbor to a rocky death on a black night. But out in open ocean, to come upon an abandoned, seaworthy vessel was as rare a discovery as catching an albatross with a butterfly net. *Halifax*'s crew could claim a prize more valuable than wages from 50 long ocean voyages. Each sailor would receive a percentage of her auction price—enough to buy a comfortable retirement ashore or a month of gambling, drinking, and debauchery in port. Either way, this abandoned ship if successfully salvaged, returned to a European port, and sold at auction, would transform their squalid lives. And so, the crew watched with special care as Levy and three able-bodies rowed the ship's 20-foot longboat across heavy seas to the wallowing brig. If the boarding party met armed resistance, every *Halifax* man was prepared to defend their captain with pikes, axes, pistols, and knives. Like their British captain, many in the crew were seasoned former Royal Navy men hungry for prize money, hard seamen willing to risk dying in the taking. They had learned to turn a Nelsonian blind eye to the necessary means applied.

Keen to understand the mysterious cause of their good fortune, the men aboard the drenched longboat finally reached the abandoned ship's sides. First to board, Sammy leaned over and read the tidy scroll below the stern rail.

"*Mary Celeste. Rochester,*" he yelled.

Captain Breton nodded. *Some Yankee bastard will be missing her.* Climbing aboard he sniffed at a stale odor. It surprised him. He had expected the stench of decay. "Mr. Levy, you and Sammy go below forward. Find something."

Levy gulped, tightened his grip on his pistol, and descended a steep hatch ladder. Near the wheel, Captain Breton cautiously stepped down a companion ladder leading aft to the master's quarters. There in a tight, tidy cabin he was astonished at what he found: on the captain's table sat a scattered dinner set with three plates of expensive china, silver spoons, and a tureen. Three heavy cups and a serving ladle lay on the table along its protective lip. A pot of dead flies and weevils revealed remnants of what had been a hearty broth of summer vegetables. Dried scraps of ribs from a pig clung to the plates of fine Staffordshire porcelain, now chipped and cracked from the storm's violence. Breton was forced to admit this Yankee scoundrel set a respectable table. Whatever had taken place on this ship interrupted the end of a bountiful meal. *Was the food poisoned?* He looked around the cabin, carefully inspecting the cots and cupboards. *If so, where are their bodies?* In the small, dark cabin, Captain Breton picked up a plate and sniffed—the food was old but not rank. He smelled a spilled mug: hops still pungent though stale. The setting divulged no signs of violence, discharged guns, bloody knives, wrecked furniture, or broken bottles. There were no blood stains on the floor. The people here had calmly interrupted their meal and then, for unfathomable reasons, abandoned ship. He noted a panel oil painting on the cabin wall: *"Emma Briggs"* was inscribed in the gold-tinted frame, below the frame the word *"Mary"*. He recalled the name of a privateering ship he had chased for months during the largely forgotten war with America in 1814: a fast brig named *Rattlesnake*, owned by a slave trader whose daughter's beauty was only overshadowed by her cunning. She had married a clever and ambitious privateer officer and together built a great trading firm. *In Rochester.* The husband's name was Briggs. *Mr. and Mrs. Briggs*, mused Breton, *have somehow gone missing from their fine ship.* Breton climbed back to the deck. He examined *Mary Celeste's* ravaged sails and ruptured running rigging. His first mate reappeared at about the same time.

"Mr. Levy, get five more boys over here and take down what's left of her sails. Hoist a working jib and a mains'l then hove-to in case the wind picks up. Put Sammy on her wheel and set a fore-staysail for steerage. Keep close abeam *Halifax.*"

Stephen Levy was surprised Captain Breton did not ask what he had discovered forward.

"Nothing unusual below, Captain. Cots all empty and a mid-day meal was left all about. No one down there. No bodies neither. Only rats and a few angry cats."

Fever? Captain Breton thought, barely listening. *Cholera, malaria, or dengue followed by madness? Did they jump overboard?* He knelt on the deck and inspected what might be blood. *Murdered? Was there a battle with North African corsairs? Or a mutiny? If so, what happened to the mutineers?* He saw no evidence the crew of *Mary Celeste* had been sick. The people ate a customary meal and then abandoned a perfectly sound ship.

"Captain, the hold's full," Mr. Levy continued, "...casks of oils and vinegars, spices, molasses, saltpeter, barrels of alcohol, and sugar. A strange smell, sir. Reminds me of spirits but nothing's been disturbed. A few casks leaked. She's got four feet in the bilge. We'll need to man her pumps..."

The brig *Mary Celeste* appeared a seaworthy vessel in good repair, of recent build, carrying valuable cargo, but neither living souls nor rotting corpses remained. Captain Breton walked aft and looked at her wake. He wondered if he should retrace *Mary Celeste's* course and look northeast for signs of her crew, perhaps captive on another ship. But *Halifax* had not sighted any other sails during the last two watches; no ships had passed from south or west. After quickly figuring the value of the cargo and the ship he decided against searching for her possible owners. He remembered his painful losses in '14 against these Yankee scum; he felt disinclined to solve a mystery or rescue these imprudent people. In the vastness of the Atlantic Ocean a missing crew certainly meant a dead crew. He would sail the two ships for the nearest port—the Azores—and claim her as salvage. His petition would go to a court in London. He was confident the British court would rule for an ex-Naval captain whose ignoble fall should not erase 20 years of bloody service fighting for the King.

After many violent years of war, followed by unemployment ashore coupled with the loss of the family estate to taxes, Captain

James Breton was left without family when his only kin had been killed before his eyes by an American privateer in the year '14. Suddenly presented with a path to remake his fortune, he could also restore his name. As he paused to savor the moment, he absently gazed toward *Mary Celeste's* stern davits and noted something curious he had missed. The empty, sterile scene on her deck had provided an incomplete puzzle. But now he had one possible piece, and he could fill in the rest. Captain Breton decided against the action a more curious man would take and climbed back into the longboat for the short row back to *Halifax*.

"The damned fools," he muttered in disbelief.

Rochester Village, Massachusetts. Briggs and Sons Shipyard.

A sharp crack broke through the morning's quiet and echoed against the work sheds. To Alex Briggs it sounded like a musket fired over a saltmarsh although he suspected the cause. He heard men screaming in pain from inside the work-shed where he had toiled earlier in the morning. *Damn it—the jack-stands.* Alex sprinted through the wide sliding doors and saw the stands supporting a heavy, 32-foot workboat had collapsed, no match for its massive weight. Three men caulking its seams with cotton and hammers were trapped beneath.

Two of the men screamed for someone to lift the boat off their legs, one hideously bent backwards, its snapped bones protruding through heavy overalls. Pools of blood darkened the dirt floor. A third man struggled to free his neck caught under the gunnels: his face hidden, his cries for help fading. His powerful arms pushed pitilessly against gravity's onslaught in a futile effort to free himself.

"What happened?" Hal Pierson yelled as he ran into the shed close behind Alex. "Thomas Larkin—Shed Six, bring men! Fast! Now! You, Briggs! Run yonder to Shed Four!"

Alex saw only one of three jack-stands holding the boat remained upright supporting the stern. If it too collapsed the three trapped men would be crushed with the boat's full weight. As he ran toward the injured men, he heard another sharp crack. The workboat teetered.

"We don't have time Hal!" cried Alex. "We need to raise the boat before the stand snaps!"

"I'm in charge! Do what I say—run, get more men!"

"I'll rig a hoist!" He scurried off ignoring the shed-boss. Alex knew every inch of these buildings he had been exploring since he was a small boy. "They'll bleed to death while we argue!" He shouted over his shoulder.

Hal stared at the owner's obdurate son, a fair-haired troublemaker, not fully grown, but too big and strong for him to bully like the other young workers.

Glancing up at the oak beams supporting the shed's roof, Alex Briggs ordered, "Block and tackle there!" Feeling a queasy burp in his stomach he hesitated for a moment but recovered in time. Alex preferred to stay on the ground while on land, on the deck while at sea. He pointed to two workers who had scrambled into the shed. "Give me a stout line, no five-eighths, hanging up yonder. Quick now!" He directed the workers to run the line under and around the fallen boat while he rigged a hoist with two pulleys to the roof beam—a six-to-one purchase. Was it enough? Alex grabbed the rope's bitter end and scrambled up the seams in the rough-hewn timber walls. He tied a sailor's bowline around a cross beam while hanging from it supported by a bent arm as if furling a sail on one of his father's ships. "Heave!" he shouted.

The two men pulled on the hoist and the collapsed boat moved—but not enough. The worker whose head was caught continued to bleed and choke, a jagged splinter protruding from his neck. Alex heard him gag. He needed more men to heave or an additional block and tackle. He dropped to the floor and grabbed two more blocks to connect to the hoist, but the ropes did not reach each other—short by two inches! *Damn!*

"Help me!" Alex cried, nearly defeated by the small miscalculation.

The two struggling workers who held the entire weight of the half-raised workboat began to falter. Hal Pearson stood imperiously and watched Alex Briggs attempt to tie the ropes. *Owner's son. So sure of yourself.* He remembered the scorn Alex had leveled at him earlier in the week correcting him in front of the yard manager. Hal enjoyed watching Alex panic now indifferent to the suffering of his own men.

A third yardman ran into the shed. Seeing the untenable situation, he intuitively heaved on the tensioned line attached to the boat giving Alex enough slack to tie a simple hitch to secure the two sets of blocks. The rescuers armed with a 12-to-one purchase—five times the lifting power—bent to the task.

"Heave!" Alex screamed, "Again!" He and three men pulled.

The workboat rose a foot off the ground. Hal, shamed by his earlier inaction, finally took hold of the injured workers' arms and shoulders, and slid them out. Their legs were crushed, and they stifled great sobbing bursts. However, the man whose neck was caught no longer stirred. Newly arrived rescuers gently slid the unconscious man from under the raised workboat. They wrapped shirts around his bloody neck and pressed hands to stanch the wound. A cart appeared and they rushed all three men to the village's elderly doctor.

Stealing a guilty glance back at the failed stands Alex thought he should best slip away. But a younger boy, Thomas Larkin, who had helped Alex set up the stands earlier in the day, rushed into the shed followed by Mr. H.R. Sterns, the domineering yard manager of Briggs and Sons Shipyard.

"Why'd the stands fail, Hal? Eh?" Mr. Sterns demanded fast surveying the scene.

"Cuz them boys used th'old stands, not the new ones like I told'em." Hal pointed to Alex and Thomas.

Mr. Sterns turned to the boy and the owner's son. "That so?" He only asked the smaller boy for a confession. Thomas, an anxious lad of 16 who had never caused trouble, an honest, diligent boy, was the eldest child of a mate aboard the overdue

Mary Celeste. Panicked, he looked at Mr. Sterns first and then at Alex. Neither lad spoke. "Did you set up the wrong stands?" Mr. Sterns pressed. "Out with it boy!"

Thomas clutched his hat between bunched fingers. An answer was required, and Alex made no attempt to contribute. Like earlier in the morning when it had been easier to grab the nearby, older stands, ignoring Hal's clear instructions to use the new ones, it was easier now to remain silent.

"Yes, sir. A mistake an' we know it. Won't be doing it again sir," Thomas Larkin replied.

Mr. Sterns turned to a head-down Alex Briggs. "Master Briggs, you and Thomas have caused damage and broken gear. Those two men caught under got their legs hurt bad. They won't be working for months. And the other man lost blood. I pray he'll return after a few days of rest."

"I'll work every Sunday Mr. Sterns, and make it up," replied Thomas, shamefaced. "My mother needs my wages until my father returns with *Mary Celeste*." Thomas pleaded and glanced to his older friend for support.

Sterns could see he would get nothing more out of either boy, one too eager to bow low, the other anxious to be away. He turned his full attention on the lad he could not censure.

"…Ah yes, *Mary Celeste*," Sterns said. "Master Briggs, your brother sent me to collect you. He has news." Sterns pointed. "He's in your father's office."

"About *Celeste*?" Thomas interjected. He looked at Alex for hope. Both their fathers were overdue at sea aboard the ship; they shared a common bond and a common fear.

"Not sure," Sterns answered honestly though somewhat absently. To Alex he continued, "Hard to read your brother, Alex. If he's got bad news, he's remarkably spirited…"

Alex bounded out of the shed, glad to escape the collapsed boat, the bloody floor, and the needy looks of Thomas Larkin. Scurrying toward his father's office like a hungry Labrador retriever, Alex Briggs jumped over stacks of blocks, tackle, and lumber, and nimbly rounded several sheds. Winded, he flew through the open door to his father's office. Pushing a chair out of his way he slid to a stop on the polished floors. He stood before his elder brother, Ezekiel Briggs, a scant four years his senior who had commandeered their father's desk in Captain Briggs' absence.

"Do we have news of *Celeste*... of Father... Mother?" Alex panted, leaning against the large walnut desk.

"What was the commotion about?" Ezekiel Briggs did not bother to look up from the papers he had hastily assembled upon his brother's frantic approach.

"A workboat collapsed. Tell me!" Alex spat out, "What of—?"

"And how did this calamity come to pass?" Ezekiel's eyes rose to his brother's face giving away nothing.

"The stands were old and rotted. Do we have news Ezekiel?"

"Very well. I will speak to Mr. Sterns. We must determine who was at fault."

"It was no one's fault. Damn you, brother, what about the ship?"

"You know I do not condone vulgarity." The brothers' locked eyes. "Our family is not coming home," Ezekiel finally revealed.

"*Mary Celeste*? Was she found?" cried Alex nearly in tears.

"It seems we're orphans now." Ezekiel answered without expression or emotion.

"Lost?" Alex stammered. "Or, or—?"

"*Found*, actually."

Alex could not believe he detected mirth in his brother's narrow eyes. He cringed. "What word of Father and Mother? Lizzy?"

After a moment's hesitation, Ezekiel handed Alex a letter on brittle parchment, apparently dried after having become wet. "It came by the post moments ago from a Boston packet, just arrived from the Azores."

Alex grabbed it and read. The Portuguese authorities in San Miguel *regretted to inform E. Brigg their flagship* Mary Celeste *has been found drifting in the Atlantic Ocean southwest of the Azores Islands. Her crew was not found to be on board.* Whether they were alive or dead, the Portuguese did not say. If they had a theory regarding the whereabouts of *Mary Celeste's* crew, they did not share it.

Alex read the letter twice, turned it over, read it again and looked up, his eyes slightly brighter than seconds before. "It doesn't say anything about where the crew might have gone! They could be ashore or rescued and taken aboard a passing ship. We have to find them!"

"You think Father would abandon the ship with Mother and Lizzy on board? For no good reason forego the cargo and his strongbox—" Ezekiel stopped abruptly realizing he had said too much. His younger brother was known for his wits and might realize Ezekiel's focus was more about what was *on* the ship, than *who*, unlikely as it must be, might have survived. Alex took his eyes off the letter and stared with disbelief at Ezekiel. Over the weeks since his father had sailed away Alex observed Ezekiel's mood had shifted from sullen, dour, and timid, to nervous agitation. And now sitting in his father's elegant office with imported furniture, lush Persian carpets, and vases and prints from the Far East, Ezekiel appeared unusually calm, more arrogant. If such a thing is possible after receiving such disastrous news, Ezekiel displayed neither sorrow nor surprise. "The letter says nothing about the ship's boats. They might have rowed to shore!" suggested Alex hopefully.

"From the middle of the ocean? I don't think so," Ezekiel reasoned.

It had stung Alex his father left him behind to suffer Ezekiel's petty whims. *How could Father insert Ezekiel as director of the shipyard when he doesn't know a keel from a crosstree?* Earlier in the morning, Ezekiel had assigned Alex the arduous task of scraping dried barnacles off a work boat's bottom then turn it up on stands for other men to caulk and paint. Last week he had been tasked to paint a schooner's entire topside in the late summer sun until his fair skin peeled away like old varnish.

Since *Mary Celeste* cast off her dock lines weeks earlier Alex had fought to recall Captain Briggs' exact parting words. His father's rushed instructions had flowed incoherently, rasped through increasingly violent fits of coughing as he uttered vague warnings and cryptic explanations of a financial calamity and a hastily arranged voyage. These strange events taking place Alex must accept without question, explanations will come. Even so, minutes later Alex's restless brain had already forgotten most of the instructions remembering only his father's sad eyes. The captain did not explain why his youngest son must stay behind while Alex's mother and sister sailed with him. He recalled the handkerchiefs his mother kept discretely at hand to minister to his father's endless bloody coughing fits through the recent hot summer nights. Yet this did not explain why his sister earned a berth on *Mary Celeste* while he, eight years her senior, did not. In the weeks since the *Mary Celeste* abruptly sailed away Alex had been indolent, ignoring his studies, hiding from his tutors, and barely finding enough energy to fish for bass migrating south in the outgoing September tides. And today he again had ignored the instructions of the feeble-minded shed-boss: old stands, new stands, what was the difference? Mere wooden jack-stands, whether old or new, were equally inadequate for the waterlogged, heavy oak workboat. It should have been careened onto its side and supported with sturdy staves and cross beams; this Alex had tried to explain to Hal Pierson who remained indifferent to the warning.

Alex dropped his argument, noting Ezekiel's startled look at his younger brother's lucid suggestion.

To remain useful Alex must keep his naïve hopes alive, Ezekiel thought. *Mary Celeste's* crew might have somehow survived, though unlikely. Ezekiel quickly countered Alex's optimism with affected sarcasm, "Father would not abandon ship in the middle of the ocean unless she was *sinking. Obviously, Celeste* didn't *sink.*"

Alex bristled from his brother's belittling tone and tacked when at another time he would have plowed straight ahead into a heated argument. "We need a ship, Ezekiel. What about the topsail schooner careening by South Wharf, the *Thomas H.*?" Alex suggested.

"*Thomas H.'s* re-fit won't be ready for weeks. Plus, we haven't a captain in port until Harding returns with the *Emma.* We'll need to wait—"

"No, Ezekiel. We must sail on the next tide."

"We could hire *Wasp.* Captain Gant?" Ezekiel offered. His thin lips barely moved. He had heard Captain Gant's fortunes were at an ebb these past months. Ezekiel had learned the smuggler and notorious former privateer had loaded his speedy offshore brig with rum at an inopportune time; since the spring the price of whiskey had soared instead—a cheaper shot favored by the thirsty immigrants and mill workers in Lowell, Haverhill, and Fall River. Gant had gambled wrong. He should be amenable to a charter with a guaranteed profit.

"No," Alex retorted angrily and stared out the window. "We must find another."

Rochester Harbor, crowded tight with small craft and coastal fishing schooners, had only one ocean-going ship in port, a brig tied to a nearby wharf: Captain Quartus Gant's unkempt though lightning-fast *Wasp,* a ship Alex Briggs considered offensive to the natural sea.

"Why not *Wasp?* She's dependable. Always returns," Ezekiel reasoned. "And profitable."

"You know why," Alex retorted. As always, his older brother displayed his intense focus on money—the cause and effect of every action he took.

"I know her reputation. So what if she's lost a few boys over the side?"

"She doesn't *lose* boys. *Wasp* is old and decrepit." Alex stewed.

"Why do you care? You won't be going aloft on a charter."

"Her captain's a right bastard. He keeps rusted shackles below. You know what those are for. Father warned me to stay clear of *Wasp*."

Ezekiel reeled him in. "We have a choice then, it seems." He drew his long fingers to his lips. "Wait a few weeks until we can provision one of our inbound ships. Or charter *Wasp* if you want to leave on tomorrow's tide."

Alex recalled infamous stories about *Wasp*: her violent captain, an insidious, foul mate, and a ship as ravaged as her smuggling and slaving reputation. Young men new to the sea sailed on *Wasp* once and never again. Those were the lucky ones. But looking out to the crowded harbor of only small boats, Alex finally came to reason that time was more his enemy than a captain who cursed.

"Ezekiel…" Alex looked at his brother. "…we don't have a choice—hire *Wasp*." He took a few deep breaths. "She has crew. Her bottom's dirty but she's fast off the wind. We could reach the Azores in two or three weeks." He watched his brother's eyes but saw no indication he agreed. "I'll search the islands closest to where they found *Celeste*," Alex continued, sounding more confident than he felt. "Ezekiel, hire *Wasp*'s captain today while I ride to New Bedford. I'll borrow a current table for the Azores from a Portuguese whaler Father knows. I'll ship out on *Wasp* and lead the search. If she weighs anchor on the morning tide with a full press of canvas, we have a chance."

Ezekiel appeared neither ready to acquiesce nor bemoan the extreme risks and high costs to charter a ship with an empty cargo hold. Instead, he asked what Alex considered a disturbing and curious question, "Before I decide… Alex, have you received any correspondence from Father since he left Rochester?"

"No. Why?" Alex shifted his weight impatiently.

"I thought he might have shared his plans about the purpose of *Celeste's* voyage."

"The last time I spoke to father was August."

"What did he tell you?"

Alex thought back to the day on the pier when his father had hugged him farewell and whispered in his ear... *new partners in Spain, shipbuilders in Italy, bankers in London.* Alex remembered only bits and pieces. *I will return before spring. Mind your studies and remain ashore. Be obedient to your older brother but avoid his new associates. I am sorry to say I am quite ill. I need Mother's care and she will not leave Lizzy behind. I fear for our family's future so I must act with great haste.* Alex looked around his father's office—to the charts on the walls, the blackboard with outdated tide tables his father had meticulously kept current, to the shelves with tidy ships' logs in chronological order. *I have to find them. Nothing else matters.*

"He told me to keep a sharp eye on the men overhauling the *Emma*," Alex replied.

Ezekiel's frown indicated his dissatisfaction at the answer. With great difficulty Alex kept his angry thoughts to himself. He would not tell Ezekiel anything his father told him, more important now since he was sure Ezekiel had not received similar instructions.

"Your rescue plan... I shall think about it. We shall talk at evening meal."

Alex resisted an urge to argue. *What's there to think about? Our family's lost—not a damned carpenter!* Alex often let his fiery temper loose against his brother. Combative with the boys in the yard, furious with his tutors who kept him captured inside on a glorious early fall morning, Alex was said to be a frivolous young man, never sitting still, impetuous, and too often rude. Some days Alex felt his chest would split apart like a log on a chopping block. His father cautioned him to control his outbursts lest he suffer the reputation of a rich man's son turned sour against the world. Alex stood and left. *Arguing will not save my family. Perhaps Ezekiel only needs a little time.* He skulked out of his father's office and reasoned his brother, despite a complete lack of empathy or any evidence of filial affection, surely would do everything in his power to rescue their lost parents and young sister.

Alex Briggs was wrong.

E zekiel Briggs watched his brother depart and sat back in his father's office, a mariner's room reflecting its owner's perspicacious attention to ocean trade by fast sailing ships. In one corner, dusty after weeks of lax maintenance, stood a globe marked with the world's trade routes: tested courses avoiding shoals, rock-strewn channels, and profit-draining doldrums. Above it on a paneled wall rested a chalkboard with the daily tabulations of Rochester Harbor's flood and ebb currents with the corresponding low and high-water levels. They had not been updated in the weeks since Captain Briggs had suddenly and mysteriously weighed anchor leaving Ezekiel in charge. Across the window stood the captain's substantial desk built with rare woods imported from Batavia during his years in the Canton poppy trade. His desk boasted rare walnut hardwoods, oiled and varnished to a high sheen. Not long before the desk had held tidy stacks of orders, invoices, and ships' manifests: the orders of the day for a prosperous, global trading house. Ezekiel used it now for storage.

Sitting more comfortably at the desk than his father would have approved, Ezekiel ignored its disorder. Tall and angular with a sour temperament, Ezekiel Briggs was cursed with a large head teetering tentatively on a spindly neck. He favored ill-fitting suits a minister ensconced in a parish of rich widows might wear. His clothes were imported and expensive however—of the finest threads with bright brass buttons he unconsciously rubbed when his nerves faltered. Ezekiel was proud of his well-kept hair, fine-clipped nails, and rich, thick sideburns that crept lower after every shave, threatening to mask the remainder of his lusterless face. Ezekiel by trade and training was an accountant with a nose for profit and not a shipbuilder in any sense. In fact, his new role managing the family business was incongruous with his entire life and his contentious relationship with his father.

Unlike Captain Briggs and his younger brother Alexander, Ezekiel Briggs professed no affinity for the ocean or sailing ships and made little attempt to convince his father otherwise. Nor did he demonstrate any particular capacity for shipbuilding. He was familiar with masts and hulls of course, ships he saw every day of his life, but how they found their way across the seas powered solely by wind was a science that escaped him. Nevertheless, Ezekiel had an aptitude for commerce, only he preferred making money *from* money, a far less risky occupation than hauling fragile cargoes on leaky ships vulnerable to sticky fingers, shipwrecks, and exorbitant tariffs.

Despite trepidations of the risks to the family's reputation, he had become increasingly interested in the opportunities presented by one seagoing trade; a duplicitous business avoided by most firms but embraced by a few ship-owners Ezekiel admired —mostly Providence and Newport men. Those shrewd investors, as he considered himself, required only a single upfront infusion of capital, a fast ship, mute crewmen and heartless captains with a sharp eye for price and availability. Finally freed from his father's misguided objections he felt an overpowering urge to set his own plans in motion. *Fortunes are not amassed through patience.*

Ezekiel recalled a conversation from the day after *Mary Celeste* weighed anchor. He had his moment in charge, and he intended to make the most of it. He had summoned to his office one of the yardmen known to hammer straight and true.

"Mister Briggs? I come as you asked for."

"Ashley Brown it is?"

"That's what my missus calls me when she's spittin' mad, sir. Ash is good," Ash Brown said with a guarded smile.

"Ash then. I'm told you've sailed the middle passage."

Ash Brown stared, his eyes wide, his lips suddenly dry. He wet them. "Could be."

"Answer a few questions. I'm not judging you. You were a master's mate." Ezekiel had eyed the former sailor in his forties whose callused, crooked hands were strangling what once had been a hat. "How many voyages did you make, on what was it called, *Whitecap*, from Bristol?"

"It's been many seasons past, sir—"

"Six? Ten?"

"Ah, closer to twenty. I have a large family, my brother's, too…"

"Yes, I understand need. The trade— it has three legs, thus *triangular trade*?"

"Aye, one investment, three returns, sir."

"Who puts up the initial capital?"

Ashly Brown had asked to sit. He took a corner chair and sank into it like a weary fish resigned to the net.

"Men from the city. Providence, sir."

"Your first leg, what was the cargo?"

"Mostly rum, Mister Briggs. Good, strong Newport rum. *Whitecap* was a fast ship though past her time. A brig rig when canvased full she'd make over ten knots, sir. Faster with the wind abaft the beam."

"Did these Providence men show their faces?"

"Never sir. Only their solicitors and money men came to inspect our manifest."

"And you sailed to London?"

"More so to Antwerp, Lisbon, sometimes Leghorn. We sold the rum for ten dollars a barrel. It was a good take. Silver, some gold coins they paid us."

"Go on."

"Our master hid the coin below, and we sailed south past Tenerife to the coast."

"Africa. Freetown?"

"Aye and Whydah. For the cargo. They was housed in cages, sir, along the river. The place was teaming with cages. Sick folk most, underfed and very unhappy. Some had been caged for weeks, some longer. The traders there felt no compulsion to feed'em anything but a bit of gruel and water. The dead were dumped in the river. We mostly moored upwind."

"How many to a ship?"

"We had us a diagram for guidance—like stackin' logs on a lumber run. The cargo lay head to foot tight together in rows along the lower deck. Some were shackled—big ones, angry ones. The women and children were mixed in. They lay there flat, crying and cursing. And no privy, sir. The stench was awful. Whips flew until we got the hatches locked tight. I recon each deck had two hundred. Two decks of'em."

"And you sailed to the Indies?" Ezekiel asked as he made tabulations on a notepad.

"Aye, along the middle passage. It's got reliable wind and misses the doldrums. To the Indies or to the Carolinas. Sometimes Georgia where they paid us more. We offloaded the ones who survived—"

"What was the spoilage, per voyage?"

"Ten a day. Twenty if we got becalmed. Some trips we lost all the women and young'uns within a day or two."

"And once in port?"

"We'd drive'em out with our cutlasses and whips, sir. The ones who were alive but couldn't walk we'd drag down the piers where they were taken to a pen of sorts, to see if on land they'd come to their senses and earn a price."

"The captain pocketed a second profit, correct?"

"He did, sir. Gold he demanded. Gold he got. He put it with the first bag, took some coin to buy new cargo. After we deloused the ship and washed her down, we loaded for New York or Boston."

"What kind of cargo?" Ezekiel had already done the calculations of the profit from the rum-run and the middle passage and felt a surge of excitement he had not felt for many months.

"Whatever's in demand up North here, usually molasses. We got up to fifty distillers in Newport alone. They're all hungry for the sticky residue. Sometimes we'd load raw cane, and the distillers would boil it down themselves. People gotta drink."

"Any other cargo?"

"Cotton, for sure. Great bales of the stuff. The ship filled to the gunnels. We'd have a sweet ride home, almost sweet enough to forget the middle passage." But Ash Brown never forgot the middle passage. The horrors of the splashes over the side, at night and at dawn when the reckoning came from below: *Take her, she's gone. Take my dead child, my son, my mother.* He didn't need to know the language to understand the misery. Up and over. Day after day.

From his associates in Newport Ezekiel knew the price paid for barrels of West Indies molasses, a paltry expense compared to the profit of distilled, full-proof rum sold to Europe. One ship. One investment. Three legs. Two bags of gold and a ship filled with cheap raw materials harvested by slave labor to be sold at extraordinary profit.

Although New England's God-fearing citizens looked askance at the Beacon Hill merchants who kept African slaves among their liveried household servants, these same church goers coveted the massive fortunes those merchants built from New England's active triangular slave trade. Albion's seed, descendants of the second sons of England who would inherit neither title nor wealth, had come to America and built great institutions—universities, banks, and trading firms—with the triangular trade's blood money. Ezekiel Briggs could taste the gold: suddenly freed from his father's oppressive dominance, he was eager to drink from the fountain.

Although the English Puritans and their descendants like Captain Ben Briggs did not blush from running blockades and the occasional nighttime smuggling sorties on isolated beaches, Ben forbid his 10 ships to ply the triangular trade.

My father... what a hypocrite! Cargo is cargo, Ezekiel had convinced himself.

To Ash Brown Ezekiel had asked, "Your Captain retired a very wealthy man."

"He did, your honor. He built the largest house in Manchester and bought three brigs and two schooners."

"And what of his investors?"

"Well, to be honest, sir, none of those money men admit to their investments. They'd be shunned at church and town, though I can tell you the people admire their fine homes in Providence and Beacon Hill. One of them has funded a new college on a hill in Providence. He's a well-respected man but no one's ever heard him admit where his first competence come from. No sir, the Providence men ain't never heard the cries of the middle passage. They never smelled the stink or heard the splashes."

"But you did."

"Aye. It keeps me up and—"

"That is all I require. Good day."

Sequestered in his stuffy office toiling over ledgers, Ezekiel for many years had waited impatiently for an opportunity to manage the Company in a modern, efficient manner. The Company owned fast brigs and schooners, employed men hardened to the cold realities of the sea and the waxing and waning of tribal conflicts. Yet his father repeatedly had said *no.* Now things had changed; Ezekiel now had a freedom he had never expected, and his father off-shore not able to way-lay his next moves.

In April Captain Briggs, the sole owner of their prosperous business, had collapsed suddenly and without fanfare ceded operation of the business to his eldest son. Ezekiel had admitted to himself that this was odd; if Captain Briggs felt any confidence, warmth, or affection toward Ezekiel, he hid it. Instead, the captain layered criticisms, tart observations, and frequent promptings for Ezekiel's need for improvement. This was counterbalanced by his mother who doled out sympathy in her knowing, yet hesitant manner as if she had erred somehow in his development.

His younger brother Alex on the other hand had received a gentleman's education. Alex relished history and the ancients and enthusiastically took to tutored lessons in Greek and Latin. *'Those elite studies,'* his father had chided Ezekiel, *'won't help you track the tons of goods we'll ship this year.'* Captain Briggs credited Ezekiel only on his accounting acumen, but the faint praise did nothing to replace the void Ezekiel felt in a life empty of filial affection. He lived a lonely life under a disapproving father. Where and when the opportunity availed itself, he promised he would strike out on his own.

Ezekiel and Captain Briggs almost came to blows arguing over the opportunities and risks of the triangular trade. Eventually they reached an uneasy compromise: instead of the objectionable voyages to Africa, they borrowed enormous sums from eager, generous investors. So infused, Ezekiel speculated heavily in cotton. Unfortunately, prices had plummeted, and a recession followed losing the Hammond Company the capital Captain Briggs had earmarked for expanded trade. Now Ezekiel faced his folly, debt repayment at exorbitant rates that would soon come due.

The ensuing disagreement between father and son turned acrimonious. Ezekiel's greed and stupidity, his father threw at him, had lost their entire investment and placed the family's fortune at risk. The captain admitted he had pledged significant collateral to fund his son's failed scheme; Ezekiel could not deny it. His ledgers showed the unmistakable severity of their new debts. It was odd, however; his father did not explore ideas how to relieve the debt nor did he discuss how they might still expand their business. Ezekiel had hoped his father in desperation might reconsider the triangular trade.

Instead, soon thereafter and without notice, Captain Briggs sailed away on the family's newest and most valuable brig, the speedy *Mary Celeste* with Ezekiel's mother, young sister Elizabeth, and 20 Rochester men. Ezekiel found himself alone in charge of the firm, unmonitored except for his suspicious younger brother's watchful eyes. Ezekiel received from his father no explanation for this unplanned voyage, no instructions for the management of the firm's financial health in his absence, and no timetable for the ship's return. Ezekiel reasonably assumed *Celeste's* unexpected voyage was local, perhaps to Castine or Brooklyn. But weeks passed. *Mary Celeste's* whereabouts remained unknown. Ezekiel's rigid composure began to rattle like a frail wind-swept door. Their local bank accounts were dwindling, and despite his tabulations, he was unclear how much accumulated riches existed. If his ledgers were correct and despite the considerable new debt, he factored the Briggs family was among the wealthiest merchants in New England.

And so, he decided to verify for himself the exact balances of the Briggs family fortune with an eye to putting them to better use. A few days after the mysterious departure of the *Mary Celeste*, Ezekiel made his monthly trek to their New Bedford bank to withdraw cash for supplies, payroll, and new sails for a schooner. To his shock, he was told his father had visited days before disembarking and withdrawn over $575,000 in cash, Federal Notes, stocks, and bonds. The Briggs and Sons' accounts were all but empty.

In panic, Ezekiel rode to Boston by coach and discovered the same travesty with the bank holding Briggs' bullion and silver in iron vaults. Briggs and Sons' accounts had been stripped dry by their owner. And worse, he discovered new mortgages had been issued on company sheds, docks, ships, and land; even their gracious home on Water Street was leveraged. As payments on these loans became due Ezekiel could do nothing but beg for extensions from the creditors, wait for a court's unfavorable decision, and face ruin.

Day after day since his father's departure on *Mary Celeste* Ezekiel had sat in the office, morose and distracted, issuing unenthusiastic direction to the men in his charge. Until a cloudy morning one week prior, leaving the family house he noticed a letter on the parlor table. Oddly it was addressed to Alexander who did not have a habit of correspondence and unlikely knew anyone outside the south coast. He recognized poorly disguised handwriting and a postmark from New York City where *Mary Celeste* often loaded cargo before a long voyage. Ezekiel tore open the letter and read it twice.

Hunkered beneath the brig *Wasp's* low cabin ceiling, Captain Quartus Gant sat behind an old tobacco-stained table he used for charts and meals. A large, thick man, Captain Gant wore a heavy black beard neatly trimmed on his cheeks and neck. His dark facial hairs were peppered with white as if individually selected by an artist's delicate strokes. Gant's deliberate choice of a gentleman's apparel was unusual for a sea captain and disguised his massive strength and brutal physicality. On merchant ships most officers wore rough, loose cotton or woolen pants and heavy work-shirts under thick tarpaulin jackets or oilskins. Captain Gant, however, dressed as if dining at the finest hotel in New York. He preferred expensive silk dress shirts and tight, black ties, tailored, creased woolen trousers, and a vest under a long, black formal coat with elegant beaver lapels.

Captain Gant congratulated himself. Bartering five barrels of rum to create an invented position in the post office for his nephew had been a profitable investment. Purloined information the wily captain needed to underprice Briggs' confidential trade contracts came steadily. And now today—with news of an abandoned ship and a missing crew—everything has changed: he must sail east to steal Brigg's unguarded fortune. At least the battle would be joined over a distant horizon where his activities would be masked, and upon an ocean he called home. His former friend believed he had tacked away from Gant's trap. Briggs might have succeeded, but the damn fool fell off his own deck!

With a sour taste in his mouth Gant recalled years ago when he, Ben Briggs, and the former Emma Hammond, now Mrs. Ebenezer Briggs, had stolen a privateer's amassed fortune that, before his eyes, had slipped beneath the waves. Logic told him the three had thus been forever deprived of a life of ease. Soon thereafter, however, the other two—suddenly inseparable day and night—had mysteriously prospered: building new ships in new yards. Briggs and Sons consequently grew to a level of prosperity only surpassed by the feigned righteousness of the newly married couple. Gant had been left with only a fast brig and a savaged heart—his sole recompense for agreeing to their tenuous fellowship. Sailing away to a lonely smuggler's life, he held a deep-set suspicion the two had played him for a fool. For 20 years he had tried to piece together the missing parts, but it always came out the same: Ben Briggs and Emma Hammond married and prospered while he spent his nights with a pistol under his pillow. After too many sleepless nights, he concluded that from the very beginning embrace and Briggs' first hearty hand-clasp, the two had recruited him as expendable man of action, a man not afraid of the bloody side of larceny, a man not afraid to look death in the eye. Unable to reverse the couple's obvious double-cross, Gant instead devised a methodical campaign to exact his revenge.

Gant had a nose for truth. In their younger years Briggs had been as much a privateer and smuggler as he, only less brazen in his technique and more focused on hiding their untoward activities: blockade running, sorties in the night and outright theft. Gant suspected Briggs continued to make the triangular run whenever he found himself stretched. And she, the former mistress of Newport's renowned Great Hill estate, was no more a church-going matron than was Gant a peacemaking Quaker. He had learned a painful lesson trading dances with her. He found her duplicitous as a snake; a woman who had a taste for gold and an unfailing sense of her own self-preservation. He thought he knew her. But he had been wrong about her, about them both: Briggs, a once-cherished brother-in-arms, Emma, a passionate lover, the only soul able to soothe his inner demons. He came to loath the hypocrites they had become.

Thus, Quartus Gant had made it his life's ambition to see Ben and Emma Briggs strewn on the rocks, their respected aura stove-in, weakened like strakes upon a lonely beach. He dreamed of their bones washed clean by a torrent of tides bleaching their ribs white, left to the gulls and the beachcombers. Bit by small bit, in increments not noticed by either Briggs or the woman, he had therefore arranged for invisible partners—slave ship investors who profited from Gant's voyages to the African west coast and in his debt—to amass a great quantity of Briggs and Sons' outstanding financial obligations. Both Ezekiel Briggs, who bragged about his can't-fail cotton investments, and his father Ben, anxious for easy-money loans, fell hard for Gant's scheme.

"And they agreed?"

Weeks earlier, Gant had questioned the scurrilous confidence man from Providence. A man Gant had employed for the better part of 10 years who delivered what Gant sent and returned with promises of fellowship to a devious, profitable course of action to bring down the lead trading house in Southern New England.

"Yes, Captain. On the second week of whatever month you select."

"All the obligations, the ships, the yard?

"Yes, all. As we agreed to in the spring. Notices hand-delivered by the county constable will be placed in Captain Briggs' hands."

"And the timeframe?" Gant wished he could speed time forward, relive it, enjoying his triumph again and again.

"Sixty days is typical for repayment, according to the notes' terms and conditions. I would expect forbearance, however. Captain Briggs has been a worthy client for many years."

"Worthy my ass, he's a thief and a liar. I'm the only client you need to worry about. So, by end of the year...."

"We will have foreclosed on all Briggs' properties."

"Including ships?"

"That is correct. We only await your assent to begin the proceedings."

Gant had considered it for a long minute while the smoke from his pipe filled the airless cabin and his companion had wiped his eyes with a greasy end of his scarf.

"Do it."

Briggs and his business would collapse in full view of the world. At Gant's direction, Ben Briggs would find his former pliable investors and lenders unbending and unsympathetic. And she, the proper and fashionable woman, would be scorned in the village and town, ruined in the face of financial and moral duplicity. Her fortune—having been built on the backs of slaves—forfeited, her sins exposed to the world. Impoverished, shunned, and disgraced she would never again be able to show her face at service or in any of the captains' fine homes along the coast. Never again would she receive invitations to the balls she so enjoyed in Boston and New York when the high season arrived and she and her man escaped Rochester for weeks at a time, spending, swilling, and devouring the tastes of America's nascent mercantile aristocracy. Her friends, New England's leading merchant families, had learned to deny (or to conveniently forget) their wealth's sordid origins. Unsavory acts of theft, smuggling, and slaving had, over many years, morphed into respectable trading businesses accepted by polite society, inclusion into which the Briggses so assiduously devoted their adult lives. Many of New England's trading families had followed the same route from squalor to parlor. However, if Gant got his way, the Briggses would stand convicted for the sins of the many.

And after years of secret deals, of profits steered to the right palms and into the right accounts, Gant thought he had succeeded. But one anonymous Hammond and Sons creditor, despite careful, secret arrangements made among the Providence men, had evidently sent word to Captain Ben Briggs about the impending general action. From whence the warning came was unclear, whether from a friend of Briggs, a sympathetic creditor, or an anxious banker hoping to abscond with his blood money in advance of the bloodbath. What happened took the money men and Gant by surprise: Briggs had moved with frantic speed, stockpiling his ample fortune, disappearing down Buzzards Bay on his flagship.

Gant's ploy had been foiled, but he did not despair. He knew the hunter must simply delve deeper into the glen. Today's new information that the *Mary Celeste* had been found afloat devoid of her master, combined with the earlier purloined intelligence of Briggs' hastily-amassed fortune, began to crystalize into an even bolder plan. With vigorous determination to right every wrong life had set against him, Gant would re-take the fortune Briggs and the woman had kept for themselves. How exactly they deceived him he might never learn. With his nephew's help the prior week, he had learned *what* Briggs had hidden aboard the *Mary Celeste*. The *where,* exactly, he must learn.

Gant's twitching fingers fished his pockets. He found a small porcelain locket his wife had given to him before his last voyage, before her untimely death. "*It's only something small,*" Claire had whispered that night as they lay together despite her advanced condition, "*to keep us always close.*" He rubbed it recalling the April day he had returned to find his daughter hysterical, pointing to fresh graves, explaining she had failed to arrest her mother's hemorrhaging. He wondered if his wife had had a premonition this small gift would be her last; she was wont to offer trinkets. He placed it deep into his cabin's desk drawer. Gant's grief had turned to anger toward the daughter he blamed. He had left the girl with clear instructions whom to summon. Yet for reasons still unexplained, no one had come. And as weeks turned to months his anger festered and rose every time the girl smiled like her mother or walked in her familiar Cork County sway, an eye over the shoulder, a smile to the wind.

Ezekiel discovered the depth of his father's antipathy toward him when he first read his father's letter—intended only for Alex's eyes. It became clear that his father planned for Alex to eventually run their company while Ezekiel would return to his stuffy attic office. Alex might be actively aligned against him or—because Ezekiel had intercepted the captain's letter—be totally unaware of his father's vile intentions. Either way Captain Briggs had revealed what happened to the Briggs and Company assets, its gold, cash, and bonds: the old man took their entire fortune aboard *Mary Celeste*.

Abandoned by his parents, not part of the family future, Ezekiel stood alone dreading his father's return. And then today with their agent's astounding missive informing Ezekiel their flagship was found floating and undamaged, her cargo safe but her crew mysteriously missing, everything took on new meaning. Suddenly the stark reality of his father's letter that Alex would never read completed the picture. His next steps were suddenly as clear as tabulations in a neat column. Captain Briggs had carefully planned for everything except what has come to pass: *My father is dead,* Ezekiel thought, *but our ship and family fortune have fortuitously survived.* Ezekiel enjoyed the irony: he who had been kept in the dark now knew everything. Alex the anointed heir, nothing.

For the first time in his 22 years Ezekiel Briggs felt like a free man. His control over the company would soon be permanent. He could move into a large inland house away from the damp harbor, reshape his father's company into a modern, profit-minded enterprise, and finance voyages along the middle passage. *Beacon Hill elites will nod and tip their tall hats as I ride past in my new carriage and four.* Someday he would hold a private service for the memory of his parents and sister, but not today. This was a time for private celebration.

Not a man to revel long in good tidings, Ezekiel sobered to the reality of what he must do next. To retrieve the ship, either he or a trusted director must present their claim to the authorities holding their ship under quarantine. Ezekiel dared not walk down a floating dock never mind sail across the ocean, so whom could he trust to arrange for the ship's return? Alexander was the obvious choice, but had he received another letter or warning from their father?

From a young age, his brother had often sailed with Captain Briggs. Ezekiel grudgingly pictured the two sharing stories near a warm coal fire in a ship's cozy cabin, while he was left at home, his nose in his books. Alex might be part and parcel to his father's plans or innocently unaware. To charge him with the responsibility to return their ship involved risk, but so did any other alternative. Alex it must be.

His brother was not Ezekiel's only threat. His father had divulged yet another secret in his letter: a trusted worker, name unknown except for the initials "*T.S.*" had built an impenetrable compartment on the ship where a strongbox packed tight with the family's money was hidden. His father wrote Alex could trust "*T.S.*" to reveal to Alex—and only Alex—where to find the strongbox.

And so, Ezekiel had frantically searched the company's employment rolls for a Thomas Sullivan, or a Thaddeus Stillman, or a Timothy Saltonstall. But no worker in the Briggs and Sons yard had initials "*T*" and "*S*". And now with *Mary Celeste* found and Alex ready to sail off to the rescue on the next favorable tide, this worker who knew the Briggs family's deepest secret represented a massive exposure.

Frustrated, he threw the list aside and studied the project manifest instead: what yardmen prepared *Mary Celeste* for her voyage? He circled a man's name who had the skills and access but recalled his face and rejected it. Another name was a more likely... but Ezekiel was running out of time. *Celeste* had been found. His brother's fervent rescue plans were fast underway. *If my father is dead his plans must die with him.* A lowly yard worker who knew about the Briggs family's hidden gold was an unnecessary and unacceptable threat. He decided he would accept the risk of sending Alex to retrieve the ship. He could not afford, however, this yard-man to walk free about the village.

Ezekiel looked at the workman's name he had selected. If he had guessed wrong, he would reduce his complicit link to the necessary action by employing the services of Manny G., a man skilled at minimizing risks.

Manny G. dropped a small pouch with proceeds from the previous night's crawl onto Ezekiel's desk clutter. The heavy-set brute with thick lips and cold, dead eyes prowled New Bedford's docks and waterside shacks banging on doors on behalf of Mr. Ezekiel Briggs' largess, now overdue. His technique was simple and effective: a fist driven to the gut or a sharp blade held tight to the throat. A broken arm did not have the same effect however, as pinky fingers slowly crushed in an iron vice; these were working men, immigrants. If they couldn't work, they couldn't pay.

"Come in. Shut both doors—tight. Look at this name." Manny read the scrap of paper slowly and returned it. "Do you know him?" Ezekiel demanded.

"I seen his face."

"He's threatened me. I should go to our constable but... I prefer your methods."

"Hmmm." Manny fidgeted, his hands inside his trouser pockets.

"He's demanding a great deal of money. I have done nothing wrong. So, I would like you to approach him in the dark, when he's alone. Encourage him to leave Rochester—forever. Perhaps he suffers an accident? You decide. But first I need him to tell you where he built a hidden compartment below deck on the *Mary Celeste*. I need to know exactly where this compartment can be found. Make sure he tells you and return here."

"And after...?"

"I told you. He's blackmailing me. Our Constable would lock him away."

"So, you want me to—"

"Apply the same justice as would the Commonwealth." Ezekiel deliberately calculated a generous supply of silver coins from a desk drawer. "I need an answer." Manny's ill-tempered gaze stared back at Ezekiel for a time before he counted his payment. Each coin made a sharp clink as it landed on the desk. "Return no later than six tomorrow morning. We have a ship sailing on the tide. I must have his answer before then. I'll pay you an equal sum when you return."

Manny grunted brusquely and turned. Ezekiel's cold stare fell at the back of his skull to no effect. Manny shook the bag and shut the outer office door with more energy than necessary. Ezekiel stared at the door and decided he needed to find a new enforcer. *With age a conscience grows.*

Ezekiel returned to the challenge of chartering a ship. It must be a sturdy vessel able to rapidly cross the ocean in autumn and return before winter. *Wasp* was not ideal but would serve. She had a privateer's speed and room for a transport crew—if their claim for *Celeste* was successful—enough sailors to deliver both ships home. But Ezekiel's difficulty would be to induce *Wasp's* seedy owner to agree to a long and arduous voyage where blood might spill, a voyage devoid of the usual smuggling profits. The man Ezekiel must convince to agree to a dangerous voyage was a fierce competitor, his father's enemy, a threat to their business and no friend to Ezekiel. If Ezekiel was forced into a supplicant's role, he would suffer one of Gant's customary explosive confrontations.

It had been a hectic morning with the life-changing news of *Celeste*, the bloody commotion in the shed, Alex's moody reaction, and finally Manny G.'s insolence. Ezekiel felt a nervous tingle run down his arm and he shook his wrists. He needed calm and time to think of how to approach the *Wasp's* master. If he failed to arrange for *Wasp* to carry Alex to the Azores, he would never recover *Mary Celeste* and his father's strongbox. His fingers unconsciously tapped on the gleaming walnut desk and his nervous frame began to shake. He glanced out the open office's doors where a looming figure approached.

Captain Gant took the last two steps in a single stride and burst into Ben Briggs' sanctum without the pretense of a knock. His hard-soled boots resonated with deliberate emphasis on the polished floors. Gant had avoided this room for many years but was never a man to turn away from the opportunity to profit from another's misfortune. Like he had done his entire life he hid personal attachments or any display of affection and remained indifferent to the cruelties other men suffered.

"Ezekiel," Gant said in a flat, indecipherable way.

"Captain," replied Ezekiel who offered Gant a clammy sponge-like hand offset by bony white fingers.

Gant ignored the outstretched hand and chose a seat.

"It could be yours now. All of it." Gant's short, weighted words shook Ezekiel's fragile confidence. Ezekiel's gaze froze, as stiff as his high collar and necktie, but he wisely let the captain continue. "And *Celeste* taken back." Gant concluded.

Word traveled fast, thought Ezekiel. "I am familiar with the law, Captain Gant. *Mary Celeste* has been declared a shipwreck. She's claimed by an English merchantman, *Halifax* of Whitby. She's anchored in San Miguel awaiting a ruling on salvage."

"I see. Any sign of your family?" *Clearly not a quick-wit like his father.* Captain Gant was surprised Ezekiel did not react to his opening remark.

"None."

"A dreadful loss."

"Yes, dreadful." Ezekiel looked vacantly at Gant whose black chair slid closer. After an uncomfortable silence, Ezekiel said. "What do you mean 'taken back'?"

The captain reached for his pipe, lit it and blew a cloud in Ezekiel's general direction as he smiled but did not immediately answer.

Ezekiel, like most ship owners along the New England coast, knew Quartus Gant traded at night when clouds were thick and prices were negotiated under watch of armed men brought to a secret rendezvous. Rumor had it Gant's ship sailed faster than any coastal brig or schooner in Massachusetts' waters despite his indifference to her maintenance. The brig's crew were unsavory seamen who did not grimace at the sight of blood or recoil at the threat of prison.

"Ezekiel, you'll need to make a counterclaim in Sao Miguel. The Portuguese port-warden will petition the court. You'll need silver… or *other* means of persuasion. Your family's lost—not your ship."

"Will *Halifax's* claim hold?"

"You won't know 'til you make a counterclaim. Or… we cut her out."

"Steal my own ship?" Ezekiel squirmed. "My responsibilities keep me in Rochester."

Gant smiled through the smoke and released a soft chuckle. Both men wanted the ship but only one was willing to cross an ocean and fight for it. Gant presented his bait, hesitating as if searching for a new idea. "Perhaps there's another way. Your brother. Alexander? He could represent Briggs and Sons. I'll take him aboard *Wasp*. He makes the claim on your behalf. If it's granted, we'll sail *Celeste* home before the final harvest."

"And if the court rejects our claim?" Ezekiel feigned calmness but felt excited recognizing he could lead the smuggler by the nose.

"I'll cut her out. Let the courts haggle. I'll deliver *Celeste* back to Massachusetts' waters before they know her anchors were stowed."

"So, you'll return my ship—?"

"And your brother!"

"…and my brother. What will this charter cost me?"

"Half."

"Half of *what*?" Ezekiel asked.

"Briggs and Sons," replied Gant.

"You're mad! I will pay you handsomely for the return of *Mary Celeste*. But my company is not for sale!"

"*Your* company?" Gant asked as if he was suddenly confused with unexpected information. He continued, "I hear things at the courthouse. Part of my business. I understand as originally drawn-up, *before this last* voyage, your father's will stipulated when he died Briggs and Sons would be split into two equal shares."

True enough. "You said, '*before*'...?" Ezekiel muttered in disgust wondering, *How is it our private affairs become common knowledge of every scab with a dollar for bribes?*

"*Before* your father left on *this* voyage. *Before* last month. You should inquire about changes he made to his will. I hear they may concern you." Gant sounded sincere, almost sympathetic.

"How so?" Ezekiel whispered.

"Don't just take it from me. Ask your solicitor. You'll learn upon certification of Ben Briggs' death, Briggs and Son's reverts to a single shareholder." Gant ignored Ezekiel's insouciant sneer. "And *you're* not the shareholder."

It did not take Ezekiel long to realize how Gant knew the details of Captain Briggs' will. What shook him was the purported change in it. The older man set his hook. "And since your father most certainly has drowned, your continued management of this firm hangs on the reading of his new will."

Ezekiel's gut heaved. His earlier paranoia about his brother and father's alliance against him was suddenly settled in his mind: Alex was a threat to Ezekiel's future, position, and wealth. In a moment of clarity, the answer to all his problems fused into a single determined action.

"Captain Gant," Ezekiel spoke with reinvigorated authority. "I agree to hire you and your ship to return *Mary Celeste. And* her cargo. *Everything* on board. If you fail to recover the ship by legal means, assist my brother to get on board and retrieve precious family items—trinkets, my father's papers, mementos. Bring all these back to me. For your service I will issue stock valued at ten percent of Briggs and Sons." Ezekiel hesitated and Gant sat with what appeared to be a smile forming. When Gant did not immediately ascent, assuming they had an agreement, Ezekiel pushed ahead. "And I have one last condition: my brother embarks with you... but does not return."

"Forty."

"Then our business is finished! I am busy today, Captain Gant," Ezekiel raised his voice with affected impatience.

"And if I told the village that you would barter your brother's life for a mere ten percent..." Gant's voice remained measured as his lips curled into a smile.

"No one would believe you," came Ezekiel's reply.

"Your brother will," Gant reasoned.

"I don't want him hurt... only left behind... somewhere." Ezekiel weakened. "He'll find his way home."

Aye, he'll find his way and beat you to a pulp, Gant smirked, bemused at the thought. Aloud he advised, "Best you be traveling when he returns." Captain Gant let the threat and its painful ramifications hang in the smoky air before he continued, "Forty percent. Once you and I become partners, there'll be nothing left for him here. I'll prepare papers showing your father agreed to our new agreement before he ran off." A wily smirk blanketed Gant's face.

"Forgery?"

"I have the means."

"And my father's revised will?"

"I understand from my cousin Prescott probate records in the Plymouth County courthouse are criminally disorganized." Gant paused. "Despite the clutter, young Prescott *might* be able to dig up a copy of your father's original testament."

Ezekiel stalled nervously and asked, "Can your crew take *Mary Celeste* from the Portuguese? She has a twelve-pound canon."

Gant had seen the long gun set up on *Celeste's* foredeck to counter pirates. Though it was not powerful enough to shoot 'through and through' a hull and sink *Wasp,* carefully aimed, it could damage *Wasp's* sails and lines. He did not underestimate the task of cutting out a defended ship in a foreign port. "My boys will cut her out," Gant reassured. "Forty."

"And my brother?"

"Lost someplace. Safe but destitute."

"Eventually he'll return—"

"Where no records will support his fantasies," Gant replied confidently.

"For twenty percent, we have an agreement…"

Gant erupted from his chair and pounded his powerful fist on the walnut desk. Papers flew. "For twenty percent," he shouted, "you have a *problem*! I'll speak to Alexander this hour about his *thieving* brother who should be a *grieving* brother!"

Ezekiel found a surprising calm driven by his long simmering jealously. He considered his father's deceit and abandonment. He remembered nights watching young Alex on his father's lap reading by firelight—fantastic histories of battles, knights, and royal heroes. Ezekiel had only needed a few moments of guidance and a dose of affection but instead watched his mother's quiet preference for the carefree, younger child. Now his future was on a dirt path to poverty unless he could recover the strongbox. Everything of value the Briggs family owned was locked in the damned strongbox hidden on *Mary Celeste* an ocean away. Without those-funds Briggs and Sons would find itself insolvent before winter. *Captain Gant, you can have your forty percent—of nothing.*

Ezekiel sighed. "Forty percent. Agreed. Time is our enemy. When can *Wasp* sail?"

The slow grin residing on Gant's lips as the conversation veered to his way of thinking now slowly dissipated. Ezekiel had acquiesced too quickly. *What's he hiding?* Gant deliberated in silence. He would get this agreement in writing with a witness before morning. On returning from the Azores his daughter would carefully examine Briggs' company ledgers and bank accounts. He stared at Ezekiel sitting on the edge of his chair behind a dead man's desk.

"Let me hear it clear. You say, 'Recover my ship. Return my mother's doilies, my sister's bonnets, and my dear, departed papa's desk papers. But leave behind my beloved brother?'" Gant leaned over the desk. "Did I get it right?"

"I think my conditions for the charter were clear," Ezekiel murmured, looking away.

Gant smiled broadly. He enjoyed watching Ezekiel shrink. He pitied the young man's pathetic weakness though appreciated his utter lack of conscience—a trait he admired.

"*Wasp* must load water casks, salted-beef, and cod overnight. I have a Weweantic packet arriving with provisions at dawn. Give your brother a signed claim for the *Celeste* to present to the Portuguese. Instruct him to obey. I run a tight ship. I hear he speaks his mind."

Ezekiel nodded absently. "If our claim doesn't work…"

"It will if your brother follows my lead. But if his smarts fail us, my boys won't. We'll cut her out, though I can't guarantee her condition."

"As long as she's floating."

Gant had what he came for, even more. Ben Briggs had fallen from fortune. His Missus, Emma had once captured Gant's heart. The likelihood his former lover had died left him strangely empty; only faded memories remained of soft dawns and parted curtains. Gant struggled to return to the present: Alex Briggs might not be as pliable as his older sibling.

"The boy will want to learn his family's fate." Gant said as Ezekiel nodded. "And you don't?" Gant goaded.

Ezekiel ignored the question and tapped the desk with one of his white fingers. Gant watched Ezekiel curiously, recognizing a familiar image, like a mirror steamed by a morning's shave. He stared hard at Ezekiel until the final instructions brought him back.

"Return *Mary Celeste* to Rochester, Captain Gant. I shall tell Alex we agreed to search for the crew at your discretion as conditions allow, of course. He'll stay useful if we give him hope. But if he proves troublesome… he has no love for climbing aloft." Ezekiel looked out the window at the men in the yard: Captain Briggs' men. Their families had sent sons and brothers aboard *Mary Celeste*. They would need an honorable accounting of the tragedy. Ezekiel must demonstrate he did everything possible to find their missing people. "My instructions to you are to search diligently for the crew," Ezekiel said. "For one week. Return both ships before November." Ezekiel looked out his doors and held tight to his desk forcing his fingers to stop their tapping. "Bring the ship home... but leave my brother—"

Gant stood and interrupted, "...somewhere. Aye."

Ezekiel did not respond. In the heavy silence agreement had been reached. Gant lumbered out the heavy doors and felt like an accomplished privateersman when cannon fired as he climbed aboard a helpless prize. His heavy footsteps resonated along Briggs' stone path leading to the docks. As he ambled from Captain Ben Briggs' office, it occurred to him all the misery and misfortune in his life led back to the man who built this office. But after today, Gant's fortune would rise with tides of retribution.

Aye, I'll leave his boy somewhere. Anywhere is somewhere, ain't it?

Massachusetts' long south coast shoreline was peppered with fishing villages, ship-building yards, and burgeoning fleets of graceful packets and lumpy whalers who reached every corner of the earth. Wealth had come steadily to the barons who lived in these ports, captained the ships, and tallied each voyage's ample profits in their counting houses. They built fine homes with simple white clapboard façades edged with classical, revival-style column reliefs. The largest, most expensive of these sea captains' homes were set back from the noise, odors, and wind-swept conditions along the harbor's immediate edges, the busy province of fishing shacks, chandleries, rope walks, and sail lofts.

Captain Ben Briggs followed tradition and built a stately three storied revival home in the Greek-design larger than any other in the lower village. He purchased the side lots of his three nearest neighbors for enough room for an oversized footprint and the home's many rooms. The Briggs manor sat near to their shipyard for a short walk, but far enough away to offer some respite from the bustle and constant interruptions.

Evening meal at Number 10 Water Street was served each night on delicate English porcelain on top of fine lace from Ireland. Ornately carved walnut chairs and a grand oval dining table were imported from Midlands' craftsmen. The Briggs brothers, unused to dinners without their missing parents and sister, sat stiffly across from each other in the formal dining room and would have sat further apart had they been able to reach their plates.

"Mr. Sterns told me about the incident." Ezekiel studied his food refusing to look at his brother. "You and Thomas Larkin ignored Hal's instructions."

Alex was anxious to talk about the rescue plan. He blocked the bloody images of the trapped men and gave no forethought to his flippant answer.

"So what?" *Why bring this up?* Alex snorted to himself. *The men are only alive because of my hoist.*

"As I suspected. I told Mr. Sterns to sack Mr. Larkin."

"That's unfair! Thomas provides for his family. His father's also on *Celeste*—"

"It is done. He must learn to take direction from the men in charge. The question remains, will *you*?"

Alex clutched his fist under the table. He should own up to his mistake and beg for a changed edict for Thomas. But that's what Ezekiel wanted and would give him the advantage. Instead, he sulked. After a few bites in silence Ezekiel finally got to the *Mary Celeste*.

"I hired *Wasp*," Ezekiel said casually as he wiped his chin. Alex waited. "Captain Gant has agreed to take you as a passenger. You will sail to the Azores and petition the Portuguese to release *Mary Celeste*. If necessary, submit a claim to London. We will more likely receive a positive decision if the owner's son makes our claim in person. Captain Gant will bring a delivery crew to sail her home. Our other options appear more difficult... perhaps dangerous... so obey him. You're representing me as Managing Director and of course Father *in absentia*. Which means—"

"I study Latin," Alex retorted.

"Don't be coarse with me." Ezekiel rose to the snub.

Alex glowered at his older brother. The two looked nothing alike, once beyond their spindly architecture of wild arms and legs. Long and lean, Alex appeared a bit too skinny for his mother's cook and Mrs. Hawley the housekeeper's comfort, but his stomach and arms were as hard as a mast. *"He will grow sturdy like his father,"* Mrs. Hawley had often predicted. His blond hair shone lighter now from a summer of sun as he never wore a hat. A hint of chin stubble and sideburn wisps thickened each week; he had only recently taken a razor to his face. A nose perpetually sun-burned centered two blue-green eyes always searching, missing nothing. The yard bosses labeled him argumentative, over-active, and easily distracted. They viewed him as a rich man's son who thought he knew everything: how to rig a ship to point 10 degrees higher, how many coats to paint a rail to withstand the winter's salt air, how much ballast to shift for improved speed in a following sea churned by a foul current. The yard men most loyal to his father remarked Alex's brash, often foolish actions might eventually catch up with him—as early this morning they almost had. He was known to run blindly into danger and opportunity alike. Alex often won running races during yard festivities where he either won by a torso or ended face down in the dirt after a mad leap to the finish line. Despite his youthful blind bravado, Alex avoided climbing aloft where the masts and yards swayed in confused mayhem in a gale and inexperienced landsmen were known to fall like wet autumn leaves. On most of their voyages together his father kept him grounded on deck, but when called to duty to lend a hand in a tight spot or sudden gale, Alex did not duck his responsibilities and climbed with the balance of the best topmen. After, he would rush to the security of his berth, however. Men said Alex Briggs neither sought nor understood the safety of the middle ground.

Alex counted few youths as friends; none were particularly close. He usually ignored the village girls who smiled in his direction. In his precious free time, he sailed across the bay with a chum or fished alone in the rips. Only out on the saltwater did he relax, dreaming of the day when he would steer his own ship. His father had promised him a command, perhaps a topsail schooner or a fast coastal brig like the *Mary Celeste*. He day-dreamed about building his own fleet: tall, beautiful ships to out-sail any ship on the ocean. Today however, with the arrival of the agent's devastating news, Alex Briggs' dreams and ambitions would be delayed—possibly forever. Thereby, he determined that, before his life could have a future, he must overcome all obstacles and find the lost crew.

Alex ignored the uninspired plate of steamed cod and boiled potatoes in front of him. He also ignored his brother's admonition. Pleased Ezekiel had hired a ship, despite the rumors of her difficult master, Alex remained angry.

"Damn your talk about the rotting ship, Ezekiel! We're sailing to rescue our family."

"And where do you think you will find them? *Swimming? Celeste* was adrift and abandoned. They're gone—wake up."

Alex had stopped listening. "The letter didn't say anything about her longboats. They might have made it to shore."

"Let us assume you find her boats gone. What will you do?"

"Look..." Alex took a small, neat ledger from his jacket pocket. "I rode to New Bedford this afternoon. A Portuguese whaler who sailed with us last spring wrote a rough current table for the islands..." Alex showed Ezekiel a set of numbers copied in small script with ebb and flood currents, high and low waters, depths and current directions east, west, north, and south for the Azores archipelago. Ezekiel gave it a cursory glance. "Once I plot from where *Celeste* was first sighted, I can calculate drift, current, and tidal motion. I can map-out where a rowed boat might have landed."

In heavy fog, Alex had often sailed through Quick's Hole between Buzzards Bay and Vineyard Sound dodging submerged ledges and menacing rocks. He knew the local New England current tables from memory. He and a pal, Charlie Eldridge, sold copies of the tables they calculated and scribed to merchant ships anchored in Tarpaulin Cove on Naushon Island waiting for the currents to turn fair in Vineyard Sound. These numerical tables, indicating the rate of moving water pulled by the forces of the earth's rotation, were as legible to Alex Briggs as the words of the New Testament to an evangelical scholar.

"Your plan..." said Ezekiel, his unbridled scorn palpable, "...is to search *every* beach in *every* cove on *every* island and sand spit in the entire Azores Island chain?" Ezekiel expected a likewise testy answer.

Instead, Alex bit his lip and took a breath. *Too much rides on tonight.* He spoke slowly, surprising himself with a calm response to his brother's taunt. "I will find Father, Mother, and Lizzy. Or at least I'll learn what happened. A lot of time has passed... but you and I need to know."

Ezekiel sat quietly for a long minute and chewed. Alex was not blind to his brother's ambition or his fights with their father. But the lives of 20 people and the future of their company depended on the decisions made at this night's meal. Alex assumed he and his brother would find a way to work together— even if their motivations were as different as canvas and silk.

"One week." Ezekiel's tone was low, conciliatory. "I shall instruct Captain Gant to search landings you select. But you must do something for me in return."

In order to save our parents' lives I <u>owe</u> you something? Alex thought as his eyes narrowed. *Ezekiel must have had this request prepared.* Alex fought hard not to curse. He nodded.

"Father built a cleverly hidden compartment on *Celeste* to secure his papers, logbooks, business correspondence, and personal items. On this trip he also took ledgers, bills, and invoices from my office. A petty amount of currency—nothing of value except for my accounting purposes. You know how fastidious Father is. He keeps these in his seachest—a strongbox. Find his strongbox and return it to me."

Alex shifted and looked at the fish turned cold on his plate. "You'll get the damned ship and everything in it," he said to his boned filet.

Without emotion Ezekiel pressed on. "Of course. But if our claim fails, you must ask to board her so as to retrieve a few personal items: tell them bonnets, porcelains, what nots. But retrieve *all* Father's papers. What I'm looking for will be stored in his chest. Better yet, bring his *entire* seachest home along with the knick-knacks from Mother and Lizzy. But don't allow anyone to inspect the chest. Father wouldn't want a competitor reading his private correspondence."

Anxious to be away, Alex stirred his fish into a mushy broth with his fork. "I don't know where Father hid his strongbox."

"I don't believe you. You've climbed all through *Mary Celeste*. You know every nail and plank. You'll find it." Ezekiel grabbed his fork holding a thin piece of cod tail. He raised it like a sword and slammed it down on the table. But the three slender prongs were no match for Mrs. Hawley's soggy, poached masterpiece.

Ezekiel stared at Alex then looked down. Alex smirked but quickly sobered and reflected on his brother's intense interest in the seachest, more important than family or crew. He remained silent and tried to discern the truth.

Ezekiel filled an empty goblet with fresh Wareham ale and ambled into the next stage, hoping to trap the boy in either an easily discernable lie or a misstep. "I received a letter from Father before he left New York." Ezekiel said while he dabbed his lap with a linen napkin. "I got the impression he intended to write to you as well. Yet you say you got no messages or *messenger* of any kind?" Ezekiel's fingers played on the table's imaginary keyboard.

"I did not." Alex grew annoyed with the incessant tapping. "What did Father write? Did he describe his cargo or his intended course? Do you know anything to help me find them?"

"Will you swear an oath you have not heard from Father since he left Rochester?"

"I have not! What are *you* not telling *me*?"

The two Briggs brothers glowered at each other across the table.

"I believe you. I'm not hiding anything," Ezekiel finally said as if he owed Alex no further explanation and expected, like his father, to have the final word. "We must work together and help Captain Gant bring *Celeste* home and with luck return our family safely with her. But I must have your agreement: even if we lose our claim for *Celeste*, you *must* return the strongbox to me. Otherwise, I will not pay Captain Gant for an extended search. I must know I can trust you."

Alex hesitated. He had a ship, a crew, and the semblance of a rescue plan. *Where does trust come into play?*

"His papers, his strongbox—they're all yours." He paused then gestured emphatically with the Portuguese current tables. "And I'll bring *Celeste* home. But tell Gant he doesn't get paid unless he searches where I say."

Ezekiel finished his peas and washed them down with a gulp of the ale beginning to finally calm his extremities. He belched.

"Captain Gant commands *Wasp* on charter from Briggs and Sons. As a Company director you share responsibility for our family's well-being and property. I will instruct him to assist you." Ezekiel expected Alex to thank him. Instead, Alex sat with arms crossed. Ezekiel continued, "I will tell Captain Gant what we agreed to. Oh, and once you're aboard *Mary Celeste* I may be able to help you locate Father's strongbox. He would have cleverly hidden it in a locker to protect it from pirates or thieves. I'm waiting for word from one of our carpenters who built it."

"Who?"

"From father's friend—you know...?" Ezekiel left the unknown name to float in the evening air. Reluctantly, and after a pause a bit past comfortable he completed his own sentence, "Mr. *'T.S.'*"

Poker-faced, Alex recognized the game. He shrugged and shook his head.

Ezekiel's dour expression revealed to Alex his brother's clumsy ambush had failed. He studied his brother as if to land a counter punch in a game of glove-slap. Ezekiel's designs on the future meant nothing to Alex Briggs. Craftsmen, strongboxes, and hidden compartments were sideshows but apparently the only things Ezekiel cared about. Alex tracked Ezekiel's darting eyes barely disguising his growing anger. *Liar*, thought Alex fearing more what his brother was *not* revealing.

"No matter. Stay alert for my message tomorrow. Prepare a bag. You are representing our company to foreign port officials. Bring an evening jacket and a gentleman's hat. Tomorrow's tide turns at seven."

In his haste to get away Alex pushed his chair back and it squealed with a cat's screech. In Rochester's inner harbor Alex knew tomorrow's flood would not turn until seven-sixteen. Ten minutes later it would turn in the outer channel: at Centerpiece Shoal at the harbor approach, at seven thirty-five. Alex left the table hungry, disgusted with the food he could barely swallow and with a brother who lied with the ease of slime that grows on the bottom of a keel.

"Ezekiel…" Alex asked, "…have you any message for Father, Mother, and Lizzy?"

Ezekiel Briggs wiped his chin and lips. For a brief moment a distant memory of a woman's gentle voice rang in his ears, and he hesitated. But the cruelty of his life and his resolve to improve it drew him inevitably to his decided course of action. He stood like a bishop rising at the altar. "My love, of course…" He looked down at his brother for the last time. "Please convey to them my love."

Boots and bare feet pounded over Captain Gant's head as the crew prepared to cast off. He rubbed his temples and replayed again what he must do. *The boy knows,* he reminded himself. If a bloodless attempt failed, he'd cut her out. But if protected under a Portuguese battery of long guns the taking of the *Mary Celeste* would require stealth. And risk his blood. Therefore, the boy first.

Quartus Gant suspected scant few people knew where Briggs had placed his money on the ship. One of course, was Ben Briggs' youngest—now conveniently under his boot. Once offshore he would effect an inquisition upon Mr. Alexander Briggs.

For offshore inquisitions requiring muscle without a conscience, Gant owned the fealty of Gregor Raca, a slow, lazy brute from a backwater wasteland who for five years had sailed as first mate on *Wasp*. The mate remained loyal to Gant as a hungry hound heels before his trainer. Through *Wasp's* many violent voyages he ably controlled crews of disparate drunks, scoundrels, and thieves. *We must continue to feed the beast*, Gant reminded himself even when Raca strayed into abject depravity.

Captain Gant understood fear and balanced scorn with promises when it came to the length of Raca's tether. Both men shared a silent understanding how a crewman's fear of an officer's rage is a powerful motivator for accepting dirty work high on a mast during an icy winter gale. They also knew fear was their most powerful tool for revealing hidden truths.

As a hated enforcer well-known along the coast, Gant knew Raca could break this son of a rich man when the time came. The boy would lead Gant to the strongbox. If not, Gant faced a potentially deadly brawl and Portuguese guns. *If blood is to spill, best it not be mine*, Gant determined.

On board his ship Captain Gant reigned absolute lord and master with total dominance over every soul aboard. Once a ship disappeared over the horizon and beyond the reach of civilized communities and their laws, ship masters like Quartus Gant ruled with a Roman Emperor's authority over life and death. Offshore a captain might be kindly and familiar with his crew or a cruel despot. A wooden sailing ship on a lonely ocean might be a comfortable community of kindred adventurers or a deadly prison with no escape.

Wasp, once a fine, respected brig with an enviable record for speed and dash had been subjected to years of the tedious commodities trade—coal, lumber, salt cod, and nails. But it was also one of the fastest ships on the Atlantic coast, able to outrun frigates and customs cutters alike. With the notorious Gant as her longtime master and a crew of the worst dregs of New England aboard as a misfit crew, *Wasp* delivered profits to her investors but misery or worse for those unlucky first-time landsmen who came aboard.

Despite Wasp's unsavory reputation, Gant paid fair wages, so lonely men and farm boys yearning for adventure were willing to sign on. And because Gant delivered steady profits to his investors, he had seldom been at a loss for men to work *Wasp's* sails or clamber over her sides on a foul night.

Gant paused before he went on deck. He held a precious document his daughter had prepared—a counterclaim addressed to Portuguese authorities signed by Ezekiel Briggs demanding *Mary Celeste's* immediate release. On board as a passenger, her owner's son Alexander Briggs would legitimize their claim. And if the boy's reputation for verbal acuity failed, Captain Gant brought enough experienced hard men to overpower any guards on the quarantined ship. For extra security, an ace in his hand, he possessed an agreement signed hours before which upon his return granted him a minority ownership in the prosperous Briggs and Sons trading company. *A fair day's smuggling indeed*, the captain told himself.

"Isaiah, drink." His wife's cool hand soothed his forehead; her other hand helped him sip fresh chicken broth. Isaiah Cooper felt weak not debilitated. Saved from slavery by a man they honored, he knew he faced poverty if he could not return to his job at the shipyard, a happy life in Rochester at risk of being dashed like a quahog shell upon a rock.

Isaiah had lost a great deal of blood when the workboat fell on his neck. Had he been trapped longer he might have bled to death. Vaguely, he remembered Alex Briggs' voice yelling and a commotion.

"How…" He tried to rise. Maisy Cooper held him down. "…did they…?"

"The Briggs boy," she said. "The younger. Rigged a hoist. Two in fact. He moved fast, thank the Lord, or our children would be goin' hungry."

Isaiah smiled through his pain. A third attempt righted him, a fourth raised his powerful legs and brought his feet to the floor. He steadied himself against his knees; his eyes cleared, and he noticed the concern in his wife's face.

"What?" he whispered.

"They told me… *if* you survived… there was no more work for you." She looked down at her hands.

"Who said this?"

"Hal. The shed-boss. Said you're too old and feeble to keep you on."

Isaiah sighed. "It's Ezekiel Briggs, ain't it? The past year…" His voice trailed off. His mind raced. Ever since Captain Ben Briggs placed his eldest son in charge, the Briggs' yard was no longer the congenial, secure workplace it had been for decades. Isaiah needed a new job.

"What news of *Mary Celeste*? I heard shouting."

"She was found, Isaiah. Drifting… Not a soul aboard." The news shocked him. Kind Captain Briggs who employed him for these many comfortable years was dead? He wiped unabashed tears with his bloody sleeve. A ship found at sea without crew meant only one thing. "Cap'n Gant's *Wasp* leaves on tomorrow's tide, Isaiah. Young Master Briggs has gone aboard to search for Captain Briggs, his Missus, and their daughter t'bring'em all home." Her eyes darkened at the thought of Gant.

"Admirable, but folly," murmured Isaiah. He did not trust Gant to undertake an honest charter. "Somethin' else is in the wind." The townsfolk spoke openly of Gant's smuggling. Isaiah knew he was guilty of worse.

"Captain Briggs wouldn't want his boy aboard *Wasp*," Maisy intoned.

"True. *Wasp*'ll be needin' crew," muttered Isaiah.

"Yes, for sure." Aghast, she exclaimed as her husband struggled to move his feet, "What're you doing? In the name of the Lord, lie down!"

Isaiah had already made up his mind. Although weak and despite his injured neck, now deftly stitched and bandaged by his wife, he knew he too must sign aboard *Wasp*.

"We need the money, Maisy." He held her reassuringly. "I'll get an advance for you'n the babies. I can ship out and return before winter."

"Crazy man!" she scorned then choked on a sob. "You can't climb riggin's no more! And they'll already got a carpenter."

"I can cook."

"Says *who*? You burn my kettles black. You pluck a chicken and I'm spitting feathers all night! You're stupid *and* delirious. Lie back down!"

"Their cook... Peter Betts... I seen him stagger outta *Cock'n Bull* on East Wareham Road every day when I come home." Isaiah counted out silver coins, running a tally in his head. "Tell my brother, I need Mr. Betts to enjoy himself tonight."

"Betts'll miss the morning tide—" Maisy had run to the end game.

"He must. Here's enough to buy whiskey so he falls down." He filled her palm with coin. "Will you do that?"

"Think of your children, Isaiah. Think of me? Must you do this?"

"The yard has no work for me. I'm needed on *Wasp*." Isaiah thought on what he must do. He knew Captain Gant and there was nothing to admire. Two years ago, Gant had returned from Nova Scotia—loaded down with beaver pelts and sealskins—but with fewer crewmen. One lad had been beaten to death by Gant's first mate—a vicious man with a temper as quick as his kick. Another sailor's brain was crushed, and after three days of suffering died having screamed for hours in great pain. Two other men had been flogged, an outlawed punishment but still a favored discipline on slavers and the meanest-run merchantmen. Another boy whom Gant had whipped perished of gangrene and fever since no surgeon sailed on *Wasp*. Other sailors had fallen from Wasp's weakened yardarms in storms when Gant pushed the ship beyond her limits. Word was Gant had made no attempt to come about and retrieve the drowning seamen from the ocean. Although a skilled navigator, Quartus Gant was neither admired nor respected. Only his cruel mate, Raca, a few well-paid thugs, and a dutiful daughter remained with him. Isaiah asked again, "Maisy, will you ask my brother to buy drinks? Make sure Betts misses the morning tide."

"I will." Maisy had been married to this man a long time; Isaiah and the good Captain Briggs had saved her from the depraved misery of slavery. Isaiah was determined and his plan was a good one—cooks ate well and had their own sleeping berth. He might come back in better health. "But if you don't come back?"

"I will." He kissed her. "Quickly now to my brother. I will say farewell to our children and pack my duffle."

Isaiah watched Maisy hurry away as requested and wondered if he would see her face again in this life. He fell back, exhausted and felt the throbbing in his neck. His physical strength and determined fortitude that had served him so well in his youth when he had survived unpardonable abuse now must again keep him alive so the boy may live as well. How he would survive an ocean voyage in such a weakened state he did not know. But he must try. He owed Captain Ben Briggs a great debt. *After this voyage*, Isaiah wondered, *will my debt be repaid?*

Manny G. stared at a shadow newly formed from a distant tree trunk and felt for his knife. He came upon his target where he had expected to find him—walking alone down a dark path with a sea bag slung over his shoulder. Manny knew the man but had not spoken to him or shared a room in a tavern or in a work-shed. He thought of what he must do. He grabbed his knife from his great coat pocket.

Their conversation was brief. A word? Do you know the *Celeste*? I have been asked to inquire about work you did on board. You don't have time? Nor I, so best we talk fast and go on our way. No, I do not say who sent me. I will have my answers. You have carpenter skills, yes? When did you work on *Celeste*? A compartment? No! I will not make way. I stand. I will have your blood if I don't get what I need. Tell me about *Celeste*! I'll cut your b---s off you dog, tell me now, no, you cannot... what... you cur—!

The other man's knife appeared in the mist. Taken by surprise, Manny G. had not expected anyone to counter his aggression with a force as deadly as his own. The sea bag dropped, and the two men fell into fighting stances. Each soon saw the other had engaged in knife battles before. The two fighters were strong, fast, determined, and skilled. Blades swept back and forth in near darkness. One of Manny's lunges caught something, and he heard a rip as his victim's shirt gave way to the long blade. He thrust again but missed and tripped on a small rock, turning in time to block a punch. He stabbed fast at an arm with intent to drive past his elbow into his heart. He saw his opponent was fighting to defend and get away, fighting to hurt but not to kill: an opponent with strength and skill who apparently fought with a knife in either hand coupled with a callused fist balancing his attack. Manny smiled, however, relishing his own lethal intent giving him a decided advantage.

He turned and threw his arm and blade forward, this one a feint while his left hand reached to grab his opponent's arm from inside, preventing an attack with his knife hand. But he had not expected a punch which was fast and met Manny's chin with the power of two men. Dazed, Manny fell back, stepping away in fury and pain. The other tried to step around him, prepared to run. Manny knew he could not keep pace and made a desperate last attempt at getting what he needed. Tell me what I must know, and I will not kill you! I will let you disappear into the night, but I must know... Another blow, from the back side of the other's knife cracked Manny's turned cheek and Ezekiel's man knew this was no longer a fight about secret compartments: he was fighting for his life. He looked into the eyes of a killer: no quarter, no mercy, no more questions. They fell on each other like two starving dogs devouring bones. Tumbling onto the path, punching and scratching, each tried to get his knife blade into a lethal position—under a rib, into a stomach, across a tendon, into an eye. They each tried and failed, tried again. Their heads butted and Manny began to rip anything he could catch with his teeth.

He knew he had an advantage with his weight suddenly on top. Manny G. began to press his knife against his victim's neck and as he did, he lost sight of the other's blade. Out of the darkness came a knife hidden behind their entangled arms—a knife not part of Manny's plan, a knife not factored in his payment, a knife sharper than his own and as well used—cut into Manny's skin, severed his arteries and breathing passages slicing deep to the bone across the breadth of his thick neck.

The sun squinted over the eastern shore of Rochester Harbor. From the foredeck, the *Wasp's* first mate watched a large black man approach. Behind Mr. Raca, a tall young woman in a blue bonnet stood tentatively holding a clipboard, making note of provisions and crew coming aboard.

"Taking on crew?" Isaiah Cooper asked Gregor Raca in a steady voice.

"Aye. Lookin' fer able-bodies. Your neck?" barked Raca. "What happened?"

"A burn, sir, from my last voyage. Kettle overturned—not by *my* hand, mind you."

Raca scowled. "You a cook?"

"Aye, sir."

"I need able-bodies." Raca snorted. "Got a cook."

"I'm better."

"Hah, don't doubt it." Mr. Raca gestured to another crewman. "Has Betts showed his ugly arse yet?" A head shook. The first mate turned his narrow eyes to Isaiah. "Be here when the clock tower strikes seven. If Betts don't show, you're aboard. Yer name?"

"Cooper," Isaiah said proudly. "Isaiah Cooper of Freetown." Raca froze for a moment remembering a squalid African prison-port. Isaiah, used to the confusion, quickly added "The village near New Bedford, sir." Raca nodded and motioned to the girl who scribbled a note.

As the tide was about to turn, *Wasp's* former cook, Peter Betts lay unconscious behind the *Cock'n Bull* outhouse where the barkeep dumped him hours before. *Wasp* would go to sea with a new cook.

Isaiah Cooper came aboard gingerly, and looked into a cold galley with its unfamiliar tools. His hand touched the painful wound on his neck. He felt for his small, sharp sailor's knife and took a deep breath. He knew he had not enough strength to fight a deadly match, but the knife felt reassuring, nevertheless. Determined to eat well on this voyage he would try to sleep often, ever with an eye open. He must regain his strength for lethal confrontations he was sure would come. *For Captain Briggs*, he reminded himself. *For the good Captain.*

Willy Harrison's first voyage on *Wasp* came about by an invitation hard to refuse. For weeks his cousin and closest companion from childhood, Pierce Harrison, had encouraged Willy to abandon the local shipyard and sign aboard *Wasp*. Suddenly on this morning of a hastily arranged rescue voyage for a lost crew, Willy appeared in need of a berth. Pierce had been long time crew on *Wasp* and although he could not recommend with enthusiasm life aboard the ship or the first mate, wages were good. *Wasp's* voyages typically ran short, and its commerce transacted under a midnight's darkness. Sailors who could keep their eyes sharp, fists ready and mouths shut received bonus pay on *Wasp's* near-shore "cold" voyages. A healthy pay-off looked good to Willy. Pierce had taken a wife, a girl from Bourne, and put her up in a cottage by the Wareham River. Willy too had a girl. He longed to do the same.

Not yet halfway through his third decade, Willy Harrison shared a close resemblance with his cousin Pierce: both young men displayed a farmer's bulk of biceps and shoulders—a strength passed down from generations of Harrison men bent to the strain of clearing acres of rocks and stumps necessary to cultivate New England's sparse fields. But the Harrison cousins had turned from the taxing farming existence to find freedom and sure wages at sea. Willy had learned carpentry and so offered these skills when ashore between voyages to the many ship-building yards along the bay's long coast. His cousin, tall like Willy, dark haired and brawny but without Willy's deep-set temper and lust for bar-fights, stayed offshore more than not. Today the Harrison cousins would cast off on their second voyage together, though for Willy his first under the smuggler Gant.

Willy enjoyed a reputation as a skilled worker, clever with tools, machines, and weapons—especially deadly with his long knife. With it he carved blocks of wood into intricate designs. He could hit a bullseye from 50 paces at the harvest fair or conclude drunken arguments with the knife in either hand. He kept the knife sharp and near when he slept. Knives spoke to him and spoke for him when his tongue failed; knives were a language he understood—shapely, tuned, and bright like a girl's smile; but when angry his blade cut deep and viciously—a raging bull freed. Willy smiled often—too often some said—but friends, including cousin Pierce, knew behind his smile hid an explosive temper. The sharp end of a knife he called 'Red' often spoke for him after taverns let out, and the scar on his left cheek proved he had not always ducked fast enough.

Whereas their long gait, thick arms, and earthy dark complexions came from the Harrison side of the family, the cousin's outlook on life varied greatly. Pierce Harrison seldom smiled with Willy's ease. His oblique face displayed a quizzical expression most days, neither objecting to a conversation's direction nor openly going along. More often he waited to see which way the wind blew. So he was mighty relieved Willy had joined *Wasp's* rough and raucous crew; Willy would watch his back.

"Sun's just risin' and you already got the bit in yer teeth, huh?" He and Pierce stowed their duffle bags in the forecastle below and forward. "So, I'm guessin' you don't need much encouragement this time, eh?" Pierce asked his cousin.

"What do y' mean?"

"Thought you been likin' workin' in the Briggs' yard?"

"Carpentry's fine for a single man. Bess is threatening to go off with a storekeeper from Fall River if I don't get her out of her mother's house." Willy looked ashore for unusual activity. Hesitant about a rescue mission without stolen bounty he nevertheless wanted to sail away.

"I told you Bess'd be trouble, ha! And then you got drunk and threatened her brother with your bloody knife? What's wrong with you today—you and Red been fight'n?" Pierce asked.

"Who said anything about fight'n—wha'd'y' hear?" Willy looked around. Pierce smiled. Willy took a different path. "I won't be needing Red on this trip. We only got a quick over-and-back, right?" Willy asked as he patted Red hidden deep in his trousers strapped to his thigh.

The cousins climbed on deck to help other able-bodies load barrels of salted cod.

"Nothing set up I can reckon'. Raca ain't sayin'," said Pierce in a hushed voice, "But Captain's more about our passenger— you know Captain Briggs' youn'un?"

"The tall lad? Heard he's a bit uppity but a good seaman," Willy replied casually. "Only seen him in passing."

"Well, Mr. Upitty's on board as charter-master. We're off to find *Celeste's* lost crew. What do you think about *that*, eh? A ghost ship with everyone dead. We'll find'em all stiff down below, I wager. Poison or disease, you watch, it'll be ugly." Pierce shuddered at the thought. He turned and looked kindly at his younger cousin. "An' what you got *there*—?" Pierce gestured at a bandana Willy had tied tight around his neck. "You ain't one to scratch yourself shavin'."

Pushing the bandana higher, Willy muttered, "Make no account of it, will ya?"

"As you'll have it, cousin", Pierce Harrison smiled. As children Willy had always protected Pierce from village bullies. And after two profitable voyages Pierce had become more and more afraid of Wasp's first mate and his increasingly brutal tactics forcing men and boys to bend to his will. Pierce preferred the path of comfort over confrontation but knew his cousin had a different outlook. Pierce was relieved he was aboard, and lowered his voice, "Raca told me to tell you, do as he says, and there'll be bounty in the November run to Block Island. He'll cut you in for a share. But on this trip, there'll be no arguin' and no fight'n. Keep Red hidden in your belt. And no eyes for the captain's daughter neither. Ha, do it and Raca will cut your b---s off!"

Willy would have no trouble keeping out of Raca's way. Although the first mate's brutality was well known, Willy feared no man. Nevertheless, he did not want to bring any attention to himself. The girl aboard would not be a problem either. He had a girl, and she was trouble enough. In the next moment, however, when Captain Gant's daughter appeared on deck, Will noticed she had grown into a stunning young woman since he had last seen her. The Gant girl's loose, long cedar-colored locks flew momentarily in the rising breeze, framing a smile that reflected the sunrise. She quickly gathered the escaped hair into her bonnet and her eyes found his. He tipped his cap and admired her openly. Without modesty, she looked back and returned a bright smile. He let his eyes follow her discretely as she turned slowly and crossed the deck. He continued loading crates and shifted his position to keep her in his line of sight as she stepped gracefully toward the bow. His languid view, however, was suddenly intercepted by the menacing glare of *Wasp's* first mate Gregor Raca.

Alex Briggs packed a canvas sea bag with a heavy sealskin jacket and overalls, a woolen coat and trousers, a hat, mittens, and cotton linens. He left his formal dinner attire and a high hat carefully stretched out on his bed for Ezekiel, a childish but satisfying act of rebellion. He put on soft boots with strong laces and warm linings stitched in Taunton factories: boots with sturdy but pliable soles to hold ratline on a cold night even though he did not expect to go aloft. As he left his house and took in the sight of the harbor and *Wasp's* tall masts he looked up and felt uneasy.

The brig *Wasp* had a rig of two unusually tall masts, four square sails on both her foremast and mainmast, a gaff-rigged spanker on her main and two jibs on her bow. Formerly the ship had been a dashing armed privateer during the 1812 war with Britain, her soaring rig and sharp entry delivering unmatched speed that ensured prizes for her owners, while escaping fast pursuing British frigates and cutters. But since her new owner changed her name from *Rattlesnake* to *Wasp*, she had fallen into disrepair and disrepute, an unheralded cargo vessel full of unsavory companions bent on ill-intent and pillage. Alex noted each of her sails about to be loosed from their halyards and spars, each with a purpose: large square sails for when wind blew from aft or abeam balanced with a spanker on her main, staysails between masts, and jibs on the bow to help drive the ship closer to the wind. When first built in Newburyport, *Wasp* was fast— quick to turn and able to steer high allowing for shorter, faster, more profitable voyages. Her cannon from privateer days were long ago sold for scrap yet she remained an angry predator with armed and dangerous crewmen. Her sharp-curved bow threw thousands of gallons of water onto her deck as she charged hard and fast through rough waters making for a wet ride in a heavy sea. Experienced crewmen knew to hold fast during these dips into green water. But a new crewman might wash overboard unless he anticipated the ocean's usual rhythms and prepared in advance for collisions of water and wood. In a storm, *Wasp* was stable due to a wide beam amidships and a flat stern, and so ably carried large North Atlantic swells. But as she aged, the brig's ongoing maintenance and critical preventative repairs sadly lagged. She could sail fast with grace and speed when all her sails were set and trimmed but her yardarms holding her heavy canvas sails were cracked, lines controlling them old and stretched. The ship's wooden hull begged for new planks and fresh paint. Rot had set in alongside mold growing on deck. On this crisp morning the sad-looking brig *Wasp* sat at the town wharf waiting for the tide to lift her high enough to back out with a pilot boat's help into Rochester's main channel. The tide rose and the sun began to warm the day.

Alex stepped onto a narrow, creaking gang plank, climbed aboard and immediately came face-to-face with Captain Quartus Gant. Smuggler. Slaver. Privateer. Despite his unsavory reputation Alex Briggs knew from his father the man was once one of the most capable sailing masters in America.

"Good day," said Alex, lost in his rescue plans. Then he added, "Captain"—but not fast enough. Gant took it as intended insolence and uttered a low growl. They had never met before, and Gant said nothing. He walked away in silence. *Doesn't he know who I am?* thought Alex.

Alex turned to see the first mate he remembered as a worker in his father's yard years ago. Gregor Raca had been dismissed for one too many brawls. On the main deck the mate was abusing new arrivals, boys fresh from Carver and Wareham farms.

"These lines gotta coil without twists and hung up proper like and outta the way, right?" Raca turned to Alex and said, "Ahh, Master Briggs, I see you're *finally* here. You almost missed our tide. I'll need to teach you how to read the tables, right? Stow your bag near my berth. Follow me, sharply now." They went below. Alex dropped his bag and coats and climbed back on deck.

Captain Gant approached and spoke to Alex this time. "You and I shall speak once we clear Pollock Rip. Stay clear until then."

"A warm welcome indeed, Captain." Alex forced a smile to tame the bite of his remark.

"I'll take no insolence. I got instructions from your *brother*," Gant threatened. Alex wondered what they were. "You'll do as I say," Gant continued the open-ended threat. Alex nodded and looked away at the pretty young woman who joined them. "My daughter Pricilla sails with me. Pay her no mind."

Alex's nod meant he heard Gant not yet deciding whether to comply or not. Gant glowered. Alex had known Pricilla Gant most of his life. As children in a small village, he sometimes saw her from across a road or in a classroom where they endured Sunday lessons. He could not remember ever having spoken to her. Nor did he think she had ever once looked in his direction kindly or otherwise. His friends called her stiff, but Alex thought that verdict unfair. She seemed a confident girl, perhaps a bit to herself. After her mother died this past spring, she probably hadn't time for friends or school he guessed.

"Pricilla." Gant motioned to her. She wore a comfortable, sky-blue day skirt with a white cotton blouse tied tight to her neck. Her blue bonnet rode unsteady over a bundle of defiant hair yearning to surf in the morning's rising breeze. Her father beckoned without warmth. "This here's Alexander Briggs.

79

Seems his folks have gone missing. We're settin' out to bring'em home."

Pricilla glanced at Alex and smiled briefly. "Welcome aboard, Mr. Briggs."

After an awkward moment staring at each other, Alex turned back to Gant. "We'll conduct a thorough search, right Captain? My brother assured me you committed to one week." He looked at Captain Gant urgently and back to Pricilla. She nodded with a short smile as if she had overheard an earlier conversation. Alex was embarrassed by the young woman's nod. *Of course, silly boy,* Pricilla's face seemed to imply, *whatever you say.* He flashed a look of anger. *Does she know something I don't know?* Gant said nothing. "Right?" Alex looked sternly at Captain Gant.

"I'm paid to search for one week. *One.*" Gant did not sound particularly committed. Alex swallowed hard.

"Good day, Mr. Briggs." Pricilla turned fast and her skirt swirled more than necessary and brushed onto Alex's legs. "Papa, evening meal will be at sunset. We have a new cook, though he suffers from a bit of fatigue and needs my help. I expect we'll be clear Monomoy and Pollock by then." She had factored their speed and course confidently having calculated the day's wind, tides, and currents. *Wasp's* planned course and expected speed for their first 40 miles gave her just enough time to help prepare and cook a hot meal for 20 hungry men.

Gant grunted and watched his daughter walk away. In addition to sewing and washing his clothes and preparing meals, the girl helped him navigate. She was at ease aboard a ship. He found her studying a tide table a week ago under a candle; she remembered what he taught her, lessons he had intended for a son. The girl grasped a command of *Wasp*'s sails and ropes like a rated able-body sailor and managed their cargo manifests and his personal and trade correspondence. Pricilla could read a barometer and forecast the weather; she knew how to navigate using the ship's charts, sextant, and chronometer.

Years ago, Gant had agreed with Claire to give Pricilla an elementary education in the convent school in New Bedford. His daughter prized this education, and it served him well when she accompanied him on short summer voyages during which she tabulated both a route through shoals and landed prices for the contraband carried over the rail late at night. It was only after her mother's death, six months earlier, had Pricilla Gant become cautious and reticent. And then, without any explanation, Gant had abruptly cut off her education. They argued. Gant no longer looked at her with even the pretense of kindness. Worse, the more she matured, the more Pricilla mirrored her late mother's womanly attractiveness. Gant became angrier with Pricilla even as the memories of the painful loss of his wife drifted slowly into his dreams. Seeing his daughter reminded him of all he had lost in his life. He often chided her in front of the crew although surprisingly not yet today with a wealthy passenger on board. This was their first ocean voyage together since the night he had expected so much more of her. The night his world turned black.

Gant turned his back on Alex and watched Pricilla. With clipboard in hand, she eyed every cask of salted food and fresh water that crewmen rolled onto the deck. She glided effortlessly across *Wasp's* uneven, crowded planks amidst the confusion of a deck packed with men, live poultry, and salted provisions. Gant recognized in her his own natural affinity for a ships' rocking motion balanced with the calm poise of her dazzling mother. But rather than leave him in comfort of Claire's memory, his daughter reminded him of his failings and lost chances. Captain Quartus Gant came to the voyage boiling like a cauldron of the hot coal tar spread for protection upon the ships' shrouds and spars. Tar: wet, hot and black as night.

An hour before daylight, Ezekiel Briggs awoke to the irritating sound of clanging pots in the pantry. *Wasp,* docked nearby, would soon cast off. He did not feel it necessary to wish his brother a successful voyage. With no further interest in talking again to Captain Gant, Ezekiel sent a heavy purse to him after a demand received at first light. Mrs. Hawley brought coffee, hot and bitter. He added a large spoonful of expensive refined sugar. Before she left the room, Ezekiel detained her with an anxious hand. *Manny was never late.*

"Have we seen Manny G. yet, Mrs. Hawley?"

"He's not come around. No post either, Mr. E."

"Mrs. Hawley, tell Abe to look out along Wareham Road and paths coming from East Rochester. Be quick and tell him to run. We have a ship leaving soon. I need Manny G."

"Yes, Master Briggs."

Time passed slowly and the coffee drilled a hole in his stomach like an auger through wet pine. He read yesterday's newspaper from New Bedford. From his father's office he could see *Wasp* with her lines cast off and lashed onto her pilot boat, four men with sturdy oars. She would back out shortly with Alex and his hopes aboard. Still no word from Manny.

"Master E.!" Mrs. Hawley rushed in. "Sir, Abe found Manny G. He's dead!"

"What?"

"Yes, Abe found him laying by Eastern Creek his throat cut deep from ear-to-ear! His head nearly off…"

Ezekiel couldn't breathe. *Only a very dangerous man could kill Manny G. Where was he?* He looked out his window as *Wasp* passed the wharves of Briggs and Sons heading to sea. Ezekiel realized his brother must find their father's hidden strongbox by himself. Perhaps he should have admitted the extraordinary value inside the chest. Would it have made a difference if he had explained the family's future financial viability was at stake? Alex would die trying to find their lost family, but would he even casually search for the strongbox?

Mrs. Hawley had been talking for some time before Ezekiel caught a fragment, "...and Master Ezekiel, should I tell the constable?"

Ezekiel looked up absently. "No. This has nothing to do with us."

Daylight advanced. Rochester's protected harbor sparkled on a warm morning below the brilliant painted blue mirror of a cloudless sky. Thick glades of pines to the north and east balanced boulders lining the shore. The land sloped to where thick eel grass bordered sand. Sheltered fishing shacks lined the beaches and long granite and wooden piers jutted out into the serene harbor waters packed with fishing skiffs protected from autumn gales by a mid-harbor island. Wealth and prosperity blossomed in Rochester because of this natural protection, a deep anchorage, and rising bluffs blessing the moored vessels with security and peace.

A pilot boat towed *Wasp* into the deeper channel where crew hoisted a staysail to make her way to the bay. Alex craned his neck to look at *Wasp's* foremast peak above her four foremast yardarms. Offshore, he avoided looking up when heavy seas rolled the decks side-to-side, and his stomach heaved. For the first two days of every voyage it was the same—miserable retching and headaches. He was happy he would not have to climb *Wasp's* masts on this trip, a dangerous business aloft. On deck Captain Briggs preferred Alex stay near the helm.

Like all men new to Briggs and Sons ships, Captain Briggs counseled his youngest son to 'never trust your balance' and always 'keep three points of your body in contact with the ship'. A sudden wave might throw a sailor off a yardarm and knock him to the deck dead. Or worse, a man might fall overboard into an ocean so cold his heart stopped beating before his gasping lungs filled with sea water. And even if a sailor survived his tumble into deep ocean water, his head would quickly disappear amid competing whitecaps and waves making it impossible to see him from the deck of a ship sailing away. One slip or mistimed step high on a ship's mast was almost always fatal. Alex was one of the few sailors who had learned to swim. Most sailors shrugged at the thought: if you went overboard, swimming about only prolonged the agony of certain death.

Alex felt alone in the world as he stood at *Wasp*'s forward rail. He did not trust the ship, but it was *Wasp* or nothing. He looked around the deck and noted its un-seaworthy condition. No Briggs vessel would leave port in such a deplorable state. He hoped it could survive the Atlantic.

As *Wasp* disembarked, Alex waved at a few workers from his father's yard who stood dockside. News of yesterday's overturned workboat and Alex's quick action had passed among them and the shopkeepers in Rochester Village. Many waved and called him by name with affection; a few followed the sea-bound motion of the ship along the pier and shouted him good luck to find the missing crew. Mothers, fathers, and sweethearts of the lost men waved with high hopes despite heavy hearts. Their affectionate accolades toward Alex did not go unseen by *Wasp*'s captain or his curious daughter. She had overheard excited talk about an accident in the Briggs shipyard and a quick-thinking young man.

As the ship sailed out of the harbor, Alex avoided Captain Gant and Raca. The first mate shouted unnecessary instructions to crewmen who seemed not to be listening. The impeccably dressed Captain Gant remained silent at the wheel with an ever-present pipe clutched in his teeth. He grimaced as *Wasp*'s crew slowly hoisted the yardarms into position, let loose the sails, and trimmed the sheets tight after an interminable period during which the sails flapped. Alex suspected Gant's seedy crew had other more valued skills.

He gazed past the stern as Rochester disappeared. Men and boys with Raca up their arses hoisted *Wasp's* main topsail and topgallant and tensioned the jib sheets. The breeze filled as they passed Mattapoisett Neck and headed southwest toward the Elizabeth Islands. As he wondered when he would see this shore again, Alex noted a clean, faint smell of meadow flowers from windward.

"I'm always sad leaving home." Pricilla Gant's voice came from behind him. "I'm sorry about your parents and sister—"

"They may be alive." Alex had not heard Pricilla approach and so interrupted her more sharply than he intended.

Like Ezekiel, the young woman had jumped to a foregone outcome. *Why does no one believe I can save them?* He turned to face her vivid deep green eyes striking him like a strong gust of wind. He noted a carefully tied blue ribbon in her respectable bonnet. The precious satin flourish had not been there when he boarded earlier. He thought he should make note of it, perhaps return her generous smile. Alex glanced away however, resisting this reprieve from his growing melancholy.

"Alexander, we shall be many weeks together at sea—"

"Just *Alex*." Again, he cut her off.

She ignored his rudeness. "*Alex*, I heard—"

Alex responded immediately, "What did you hear?"

Pricilla deftly ignored the edge in his voice. "…about what you did in the yard yesterday." A small smile played at the corners of her mouth.

Alex was not sure if she was referring to his role causing the accident or its successful outcome. Embarrassed, he turned away and mumbled, "A few workers were hurt. It wasn't my fault." He leaned further over the rail and inspected silent seaweed. He did not know how to talk to this girl. *My word how her eyes shine!*

Pricilla frowned. "My father has taught me a great deal about the ocean—" She suddenly stopped; her words sounded awkward and affected. She feared she might begin to cry. Instead, she swallowed hard and perked up. "I was hoping you and I could be friends," she said as pleasantly and directly as a young woman can say to a young man. Alex did not know what to say. *It shouldn't be difficult! She has recently lost her mother. Say something kind!*

He waited a moment too long. She moved on. "Well, you certainly don't talk very much," Pricilla spoke over her shoulder as she turned away in a rush her hands tight by her side restraining her skirt. "I will let you be. Papa told me to remind you to report to his cabin after we clear Pollack Rip."

"I don't need reminding," Alex retorted as she left him. He gripped the rail and watched a solitary gull keep pace. *Wasp's* sharp bow dug into building waves and sailed deep into Buzzard's Bay where spray wet her fore deck and her rigging hummed in a low, somber tone.

For 200 years, ships sailed from New England to Europe carrying the wealth of America's fertile continent: beaver furs for rich gentry, hard oak and soft pine lumber for shipbuilding, Deer Island granite for buildings, dried corn, salted beef and cod for European cities' growing hungry masses. But a voyage across thousands of miles of open ocean was slow and dangerous. Storms far out to sea ravaged ships and passengers.

Near shore was more hazardous by far: shoals, rips, rocks, and sandbars surrounded every southern New England island and cape including the Elizabeth's, Martha's Vineyard, Nantucket, and Monomoy at Cape Cod's southern tip. Alex had sailed these treacherous waters since he was a boy in his Padanaram-built catboat *Sea Smoke,* which he named for the fog rising from harbor waters on a cold winter morning. As *Wasp* began her long voyage, he paid close attention to her intended route: would Gant sail directly through the Woods Hole cut and risk its currents and rocks, or sail southwest transiting the wider Quicks Hole, a further but safer opening to the Atlantic? He looked aft. Gant steered southwest. He inched *Wasp* higher, and Alex saw Quicks Hole off the larboard bow. As the ship tacked an hour later and entered the cut, he noted *Wasp* turned sluggish as her new and inexperienced men slowly hauled her wind to change direction. The *Wasp* was a sloppy ship he realized, her crew lazy, poorly trained, and indifferent to sailing's finer points. She could not sail safely through the narrow Woods Hole cut or any other dangerous passage. Alex shuddered thinking about the North Atlantic Ocean. In November.

The wind increased to a steady breeze. With all sails set on two masts, she made fast time sailing past the golden bluffs of Martha's Vineyard and they were deep into Nantucket Sound when afternoon skies dimmed. Another hour later and they spied Nantucket to starboard, sailed north of Point Rip and passed south of the Monomoy beaches through an ever-shifting channel of soft sand bordering rocks and rips. After Monomoy, only Pollock Rip blocked their route to open waters and the Atlantic.

Alex's father had recounted one night as they sat in a cozy saloon how Pollock Rip's wild motions prevented early English settlers from reaching their intended New York landing: *Mayflower,* despite many desperate tacks, could not make headway south or west against Cape Cod's foul currents. The ship, an ungainly vessel, packed tight with sick and desperate settlers, had neither a deep keel nor a rig powerful enough for hard upwind sailing in such a raucous sea. And so, she retreated northerly to a quiet bay protected by the arm of Cape Cod. There, first in a barren cove devoid of game or fresh water, then soon after in Plymouth, they made a permanent landing and settled. Rochester Village, 20 miles south and bordering warmer, game-filled waters and shore, was founded 10 years later. The Briggs clan had emigrated from England's Midlands soon after and felt lucky to have found a new life of freedom and possibilities on the bountiful southern New England coast.

Alex watched two sailors struggle at the wheel as *Wasp* approached Pollock Rip. As currents pushed underwater ocean rivers between rocks and shoals on the bottom, torrents of water escaped and broke the surface, crashing in a wild world of breaking white waves without any obvious or visible cause. A ship caught unawares in a violent rip's furious fissures surrounding the exposed east coast of Cape Cod might slide sideways and founder without any nearby rescue to be found.

The passage was fraught with danger and Gant did not take his eyes off his horizon. He scanned for newly forming breakers. With luck the wind would hold long enough for *Wasp* to stay well south of Pollock Rip yet comfortably clear Nantucket's outermost sand bars to the south sticking out like tentacles of a giant sea squid. Alex had sailed through this channel back in June with his father on *Mary Celeste*. Captain Briggs had steered further south than the course chosen this morning by Captain Gant. Alex recalled his father's warnings about raging spring storms that for days drove sand into what had been a deeper passage. Accustomed to navigating and communicating with helmsmen aboard his father's ships, Alex studied Gant with increasing concern. Observation had been part of his education and he had been encouraged to speak his mind. He presumed the same was expected of him on any vessel, including Gant's.

"Captain Gant, your charts don't show it but—" Alex stopped short in the wake of Gant's glare. The captain looked south for his Great Point bearing and quickly back to his compass fix. Alex continued cautiously, "A half mile further south has depth to forty—"

"Mr. Raca!" Gant bellowed. Raca raced over and stood before Alex who backed off and moved awkwardly nearer the rail.

Gant kept his course north—too far north.

A sailor dropped a lead weight every 20 seconds and relayed the depth in fathoms to the captain. "Six and one," He reported. "Seven... Five now!" One fathom represented six feet of water depth at low tide. It was near low tide. *Wasp* was sailing in only 30 feet of water. Dry and empty, *Wasp* drew 20 feet. They were neither dry nor empty. "...Four!"

The narrow channel was becoming shallower every few feet. Anxious eyes looked north. Had *Wasp* crept too close to Pollock Rip? Even though the visible breakers remained hundreds of yards north, *Wasp* had less than five feet of water under her keel. If she grounded here, she would be swept by the current onto the rips, turned on her beam, crushed, and torn apart. Lifeboats would not survive the breaking waves.

"Down ten degrees! NOW!" Gant cried as the helmsman swung his wheel violently until their compass read 10 degrees more to the southeast. All sheets were eased in unison. *Wasp* headed southerly.

"Four... Three and one!"

"Trim all sails. Fast now!" Gant cried as men frantically obeyed. "All ships' crew to leeward! Lean over! FAR over!" he roared.

Alex ran forward screaming at Captain Gant, "If you trim, we'll head up *into* the shallows!"

Captain Gant ignored him.

"Three men on the wheel! Keep her down!"

Wasp ached to sail higher into the direction of the wind and the looming shallows. But Gant forced the wheel over, the rudder down. By doing so, the ship heeled onto her side—near broaching. With crew weight to leeward, her wheel down and sails trimmed hard, *Wasp* was out of balance, her sails stalled and so no longer driving the ship forward. But as she heeled over onto her side, her keel rose higher, away from the bottom. The ebb current was at its peak and pushed the ship nearly sideways at three knots in the direction of open ocean and deeper water.

"Three and five, sir..."

The crew waited for impact. If the ship hit the bottom, she would stand firm, her masts crash down. No one dared speak. Each man gripped the nearest sturdy line and measured his pathway to the nearest ship's boat. Alex swung uneasily on a tight halyard; he felt the keel scraping bottom. Grounding was near certain.

"Three!" *Wasp* should be hard aground. "Three!" Again, nothing happened. "...Five-Oh... Six... Ten!!" For 30 seconds, not a sound was heard except rushing water. "Ten again!"

"Ease! Ease all." Gant cried. "Come up five degrees, slowly. Depth? *Depth*!! I want depth every ten seconds you rat!"

"Still at ten, Captain. No change…"

"Ease foresail. Helm, up another five."

"Twelve now, Sir!"

The ship clear, her people breathed again. A few smiled and patted their neighbor on the shoulder. *Wasp* had found deep water. In the six months since Gant had last sailed here, spring gales had shifted sand from Nauset beaches into this narrow channel. But by sailing *Wasp* nearly on her side for 200 yards Captain Gant had reduced her draft by five feet. And by timing their transit to coincide with a strong easterly current *Wasp* had safely crossed the rip—although barely. Gant nodded to Pricilla who looked up from the cabin below clutching her charts and current table.

Alex held onto a brace as Gant approached and grabbed his shoulders. "Never again! Not a *WORD* outta you while I'm steering. Understand me?" Alex nodded. He was right about their course but wrong to question Captain Gant's clever maneuver. "One hour. My cabin. Did you get my message?"

"Yes, she, ah, told me…"

Gant stomped away. Alex glanced aft; with currents abated a single crewman could manage the helm. A faint image of crashing waves was yet visible northwest; Cape Cod and Chatham were far astern, Rochester long passed. They had quit Massachusetts' waters; ahead lay the vast and lonely North Atlantic Ocean. *Wasp* sailed fast to the east carrying joyless people into an uncertain darkness.

Alex hoped to find Pricilla in her father's cabin. His tongue had failed him before; he planned to express a more considerate condolence at his first opportunity. On entering the captain's cabin—more a storage locker than a proper officer's cabin with barely enough headroom for a grown man—he found only Captain Gant and Raca eating at a small table. There was no seat for him. He stood while they ripped into legs of chicken, washed down with ale. He wondered if they saw him in the dim light. Given Gant's last instruction, Alex remained mum. Finally, his mouth full, Gant looked up.

"Do you understand I control *everything* on this ship? I sail her. I provision her. I own the lives of every soul on board." Alex kept silent. "Your father's captains may need your observations. But not on my ship. Here you've got no role. You do nothing. You say nothing. You watch and obey. You're a passenger, nothing more. More worthless to me than a sack of horse dung. You hear?"

"Aye... Captain."

"Now, who's this '*T.S.*'?" Gant changed direction so fast Alex stumbled. Gant dropped a half-eaten leg of meat onto his plate. He spoke slowly, with angry pauses. "Who... is... '*T.S.*'?"

"I don't know anyone with those initials." *Curiously, Ezekiel had asked the same.*

"Your father keeps a seachest aboard *Mary Celeste*. Where's he keep it?"

So, both Gant and Ezekiel want something in father's strongbox—yet Ezekiel didn't know Gant knows about it.

"I don't know."

Gant looked at Raca who scraped his chair back abruptly and walked over to Alex. Without warning Raca's huge fist buried hard into the boy's gut. As Alex collapsed Raca hit him again with a powerful forearm—a violent uppercut into Alex's mouth and face. Alex fell hard to the floor, bleeding. His front tooth cut into his bottom lip and loosened. He could not breathe.

"I'll ask again boy. Who's this '*T.S.*' fellow?" Gant continued eating as Raca stood over Alex cowering on the floor. Alex choked, his hands clinched in a ball, his eyes on fire. Gant finished a mouthful and continued, "Tom? Thaddeus? Timothy?

Spear? Saltonstall? Smith? Who goes by '*T.S.*'"? A friend of your father? An employee?"

Alex's mind raced, his mouth and stomach roaring with hurt. "Does he sail on a Briggs vessel? Is he one of the new hands come aboard *Wasp*? Tell me or Mr. Raca will beat your rich boy's face until it looks like bluefish guts!"

Unable to talk Alex froze. With a nod from Gant, Raca swung his hard-toed boot into Alex's cheek—sending him sprawling head-first against the cabin wall. The blows felt nothing like he had ever known. Sharp fishhooks embedded into his palm, bruised shins while climbing masts, sickness' retching and nausea was nothing compared to these knock-backs intended to bring agony.

Alex staggered to his feet. "I have no idea what you're talking about… when my brother—"

Gant cut in. "It's your *brother* who's askin', boy! Claims *you* got an accomplice—someone goes by '*T.S.*' Believes you and '*T.S.*' know where Captain Briggs hides his valuables onboard *Celeste*. Ezekiel thinks you're lying about what you know. He's asked Mr. Raca and me to learn the truth." Raca poised for another blow. Gant set down his meal, stood, and walked over to Alex. Staring down at the bloodied heap halfway standing holding his stomach, Gant's nostrils flared like a bull poised to charge. "Ezekiel hired us to return a certain item from its hiding place." The captain hesitated and added, "Whether I return *you* depends on your cooperation."

Alex remembered loud arguments and raised voices between Ezekiel and their father… his mother's tears… *Mary Celeste's* hurried departure in August… cryptic warnings and assurances from his father along with promises for clear instructions he never received. He nearly despaired in pain and bewilderment, trying to piece together a story line so he could assemble a response. He did not remember his father ever mention anyone called "*T.S.*"

Hoping to avoid another attack Alex improvised. "There was a rigger in Fairhaven. Father used him to adjust the mast rake." A fine-tune to a ship's rig gave Briggs a competitive advantage— fast trips meant high prices if they arrived first into port with perishable cargo. Gant never knew Briggs went to such extreme efforts to best him...

"His name...?"

"Thomas something. Sterling. I think. Thomas Sterling."

"And the last time you saw Thomas Sterling was...?"

"July. Before *Celeste* left Rochester. He adjusted a forestay and two back stays."

"And how well did this Tom Sterling know your ship *below deck*?"

Alex wiped his mouth, his split and bleeding lips, his open cheek. Raca stood grinning and eager.

"He knew it."

"You're lying." Gant concluded. "A rigger doesn't work below deck. Your father would have used a craftsman or a carpenter's mate. Get up!" Alex obeyed, despite the pain. Gant picked up a piece of paper from the table that Pricilla had prepared. "See this list—*Wasp's* company. There's no 'T.S.' here. No carpenters or woodworkers except men I hired. So, if your 'T.S.' does not sail with us, you're the only one who can find what I'm looking for—"

"Why do *you* want my father's strongbox? We hired you to search for my parents and bring *Mary Celeste* home!" Alex protested foolishly divulging his thinking. He immediately regretted opening his mouth.

"Ahhh... Some common ground. So, you *do* know. And you know what's inside the chest I presume?"

"I do not. Most likely a spare chronometer—or an extra pouch of tobacco." Alex said without any attempt to hide the added sarcasm.

"You stinkin' rich-boy, I *own* you, you hear! I decide if you eat, where you sleep. I decide whether you live or die." Gant's ire rose with Alex's cutting tone.

"You'll need me to get on board *Celeste*," Alex said.

The heart of the matter, Gant reminded himself and he calmed. "Mr. Raca, you were right. This boy won't fight to defend himself. But you were wrong about the other. He's not *stupid*." Gant turned to Alex barely able to stand. "Aye, we may need your assistance to get aboard *Celeste*. So, you and I will come to an agreement. Give up your accomplice and tell me where your father hid his strongbox. Do this and you might survive our passage."

"Told you. I don't know anyone who goes by '*T.S.*' Don't know anything about any hiding place or what's inside my father's strongbox." Alex spat out as he silently cursed Ezekiel. Gant looked at him with the dead grey eyes of a shark. Alex returned the look. "Without me, you'll never get near *Mary Celeste*." He knew this might be the only point in his favor.

For a few moments Gant was silent. He recognized Alex was stubborn if nothing else. The boy had a resentful yet determined manner, something between a child's tantrum and a dangerous man. Gant would enjoy changing that.

"Very well. Mr. Raca has prepared new quarters for you. One of our passengers died there recently. Was it the fever, Mr. Raca? From rat bites?" Raca grabbed Alex harshly and tied his torso with a rope. Raca cinched a tight knot and yanked hard. Alex could hardly breathe. "We'll talk each day at five bells in my cabin. Cooperate and we'll feed you."

Finished with Alex, Gant returned to his chicken, tasteless and barely warm despite its well-bronzed skin. Alex's stomach ached in pain and hunger. Gant jerked his head as if to say "*Out of here*'. Raca dragged Alex below to the lowest storage space under the cargo hold and threw him into the wet, cold bilge. His head slammed against slime dripping from *Wasp's* ribs. Raca locked Alex's ankles into old, rusted manacles that cut his skin.

Before he left, Raca turned, smiled, looked down and stomped on Alex's groin. Alex shrieked and jerked his face toward a filthy pool of foul water so Raca could not see his tears.

"Until five bells tomorrow, Master Briggs. Sleep well."

Wasp's officers ate.

Raca, hungry but curious, carefully broached the subject, "So, Captain...?" He watched Gant sitting beside his daughter who was allowed to join the two men only after she had helped prepare and serve the meal. Their new cook had replenished the serving bowls but despite Pricilla's suggestions and spices, their chicken was overcooked and dry, the turnips limp and bland. "...what do *you* think happened to *Celeste*, Captain? The boys down the wharf say pirates. Me, I say mutiny."

"Pirates remain a possibility," replied the captain. But Gant did not wish it. He was not sailing across an ocean to recover a stripped hulk. He knew of a schooner from Eastport boarded last spring near the Azores. Her cargo was stolen, her crew murdered on deck and thrown to the sharks. The ship was stripped of anything of value and scuttled. Pirates ranged free not far from Africa a few leagues south and east of their destination. Yes, pirates might factor and so he was relieved he had his fighting boys on board. With both ships under his command and money from Briggs' strongbox he could buy cannon for both and offer his small fleet as privateers to any nation issuing a letter of marque. Or hunt the seas himself without any pretense of flag or nationalism to cloud his judgement. To Quartus Gant, life was about the taking.

"Or perhaps their crew fell sick Papa?" suggested Pricilla. "Or madness?"

Raca licked his fingers slowly and looked her way. Gant noticed but said nothing. The two men ignored the young woman's suggestion.

Raca offered, "They ate something foul, I wager—foul like these vegetables!" Raca turned in his chair and yelled in the galley's direction. "Cook, we got no salt aboard? We float in salt, but this food tastes like sand!" His wandering attention returned to *Mary Celeste*. "Yes, something foul, Captain. They all took to their cots and died."

"But the English didn't find corpses," Gant answered as he chewed and considered.

Pricilla looked up from her bowl. "Then the crew went over the side. They died and were buried at sea one by one or perhaps in groups. Survivors rowed off to find safe haven." Pricilla minded no one took her seriously but plowed ahead anyway, "If a disease infected her crew quickly like a plague, they'd throw the infected bodies overboard to protect the survivors."

"A plague?" remarked Raca, easily aroused.

"I doubt it, daughter. If Portuguese surgeons found disease, she'd be under sickness quarantine. They would have found evidence—slop pails, records, spent medicines. But there were none..." He thought carefully about what he was saying as he finished, "...as far as we know."

"Then they left of their own accord. If not pirates or theft or sickness, they must have *wanted* to leave the ship," Pricilla argued reasonably. *Aye,* Gant thought to himself. *They wanted to leave. But why would an entire crew want to abandon a seaworthy vessel in the middle of the Atlantic Ocean?*

Pricilla recognized Raca's unease with talk of disease and death. She guessed something else about the mate, payback for the leers he sent her way, increasing by every watch. "Or perhaps it was sorcery or an African shaman. Or the work of Satan. I've heard dark spirits haunt ships who trade the molasses triangle..."

"The Devil you say?" Raca's eyes exploded wide, spittle sitting untended on his cracked lips framing a wide mouth. His expression exposed numerous missing teeth; the ones remaining, were black and broken. His eyes darted toward Gant then to Pricilla and back, thinking of *Wasp's* recent voyages and his duplicitous role.

Pricilla smothered a wily smile and looked down. She knew Raca for all his animal ferocity on deck was a simpleton, uneducated and, not unlike many sailors, prone to wild fantasy particularly when it involved the unknown.

"No spirits! No devil! Daughter—enough! Clear and go!" Gant bellowed. "I don't need your wild talk! I should have married you off before we left. What was wrong with your Fall River cousin? You'll pay him a visit on our return, you hear me?"

"Yes, Papa."

Gant returned to the prior topic: there were many possible explanations for *Celeste's* missing crew. He did not care a whit how they died. He eliminated pirates: they would have taken *Celeste* and stripped her after murdering the crew. But from what he had learned, her hold had been found filled with cargo. Nothing but her people was missing.

Raca forced death and disease from his mind. "Perhaps the British have come to takin' American merchantmen again, Captain, like in the year '12. See, they stole *Celeste's* crew, lied about finding her drifting and abandoned, right? I bet they cut Briggs' throat and threw them dead bodies overboard. They killed'em all!" Raca looked around for encouragement.

Pricilla had gratefully retired to the galley at her fathers' outburst. Gant grunted but took notice of the interesting thought, one of Raca's very few. Gant hated the British and was open to the idea of duplicity in what might be a criminal taking. He had fought them and been their prisoner whereby he suffered great cruelties. He would keep his guard up. Yes, *Mary Celeste's* situation might be due to murder on the open sea. Or Captain Briggs might still be alive, a captive awaiting ransom, or on shore near where the ship was taken. And the fair green-eyed Emma might still be at his side. Gant excised thoughts of her and Briggs together until the end. He finished his ale, wiped his beard from dangling crumbs and determined *Wasp* must reach Sao Miguel as fast as possible. Once there he would use extreme caution before he loosed his fighting boys to steal the ship.

"Mr. Raca—hoist all our canvas. Set all the windward studding sails she can manage. Your watch."

"Aye."

"And Mr. Raca, this ship needs repairs. It's worse because of your inept attention…"

"But Captain, we only had a three-day turnaround. We needed provisions and—"

"The foremast braces have worn. Replace'em. Starboard gate hinges loosened from rot in the upper and lower rails. Install new hinges and replace the rot. We're out for speed not fishing men from the water! And keep your eyes off the girl. She ain't your type."

Seething at the rebuke, Raca slithered away, cowering under the captain's barrage. But after years of subservience to a man he has come to loath he decided the time was fast coming for payback. *If he wants rot repaired, he can repair it himself. I'm only aboard for my cut of the prize. Damn him to hell… And damn his little bitch… my type, my arse. I'll make her my type!"*

Raca climbed on deck and passed Pricilla. He was angry but not a complete fool: she had mocked him.

"Perhaps it was an ugly sea witch come aboard *Mary Celeste*, eh Miss? Her nasty spirit would explain things nice and neat, right?" Her father out of sight, Raca grabbed her waist, but she spun away expertly.

"Go foul yourself," she spat as she retreated to the galley where the new cook stood up and stared at the mate.

"Papa, where is Mister Briggs?" Pricilla asked when she finally dared return with rum and coffee.

"Resting." Gant was deep in thought about England and revenge.

"Oh? Where?" she pressed having found his berth empty.

"Confined. He was… disrespectful."

"I heard he argued as we crossed Pollack."

Gant looked up from his chart. "Aye, he was in my way."

"So he will stay in a seaman's berth?"

"Not your concern. He needs discipline."

"I agree. I tried to be friendly. He was rude."

"He needs discipline, girl, not friends."

"Yes, Papa." She knew Alex had not been fed. She had heard Raca's blows and her father's angry words. She had noticed blood by the door. "Will he be fed?"

"Only water. I'll send Raca."

"So, he's in a berth?" she asked again.

"The bilge. Until he learns. Let me be, girl."

"Of course, Papa."

His daughter left obediently. He turned to look at her emptied space. The girl shared her mother's face, eyes, and spirited demeanor. In earlier days it warmed him to have his daughter near when his wife was not. Pricilla came to understand his trade but kept her own counsel and he trusted her. He wished those days had not ended. His anger rose remembering.

Pricilla knew her father took first watch and slept during the second while Raca navigated and commanded the sailors on deck. Remaining in her day dress, she waited in her wooden berth under quilts, knowing her father would soon be snoring away. Through the thin walls separating their two starboard side berths, behind thick woolen drapery providing her with her only privacy from a ship of peering eyes, she heard her father guzzle a long draught of rum. When she was confident he had fallen asleep, she parted the curtain, stood, careful to rustle nothing. Carrying bread and a small tepid bowl of stew, she tiptoed barefoot down into the darkness and cold of *Wasp's* rat-infested bilge.

Mr. Raca watched her sneak below. He watched her everyplace: as she helped cook and served meals, even as she slept. He watched her door; his eyes stayed on her, waiting for his moment. This voyage would be his chance. He smiled and followed.

"Here, Alexander, drink." *Was the boy sleeping or beaten unconscious?*

Alex thought he was dreaming. He felt a woman's soft hand under his head. He lifted slightly and felt a sweet breath inches from his face. He moaned but drank from the cup she raised to his swollen face.

"You're bleeding," whispered Pricilla.

His wounded mouth and cheeks stung and felt wet and sticky. "Think so," he whispered.

She dabbed blood from his cheek and applied ointment. "Drink more," she urged quietly. "You can't save your family if you're dead."

His mind raced: alone, his legs chained, his life in peril. A crazy mate and master over him. The mate would enjoy beating Alex to death if Gant so ordered. The captain only wanted the strongbox and cared nothing about searching for the missing Briggs family. Alex could barely see Pricilla in the gloom. *And the stench down here, how can she stand it?*

"Let me rest this kid of stew on your lap while I tend your face." Pricilla placed the ship's wooden eating bowl on the uppermost section of his trousers. He groaned. She was surprised such a small weight hurt. She hoped his ribs were not broken. Or perhaps he was not as strong as she had supposed. She peered at his injured cheek and lips. He did not flinch as she tended to the open wounds. "My father has a frightful temper. Do not correct him in front of the crew. You're a strange boy, Alexander. You won't talk to me when I'm trying to be friendly, and you talk too much to the captain when he's angry. I heard you arguing."

"He steered too far north. The channel had filled. I tried to warn him."

"You should have kept quiet. He knows how to sail."

"Right. And he nearly ran the ship onto the shoal... but... never mind... Yes, you're right, I suppose." Alex had no energy to argue. "Why's he beating me?"

"I don't know," she lied. "Just obey him. Here, eat." She fed him stew and he gulped it down without speaking. "I must go. He said you're on a water diet. Don't say I came or he'll—" She stopped short. In the gloom of the hold, Alex heard fear in the girl's voice.

"Your father's like my brother. They enjoy causing pain." He wished he could better see her reaction.

"You must have given him cause," Pricilla offered even though she knew her father did not reserve punishment for fault alone. She suspected he suffers brutal memories he tries to quash. She had often heard his mangled screams in the night: blue, broken faces not letting him rest. He must be suppressing a torrent of pain and loss. She could only guess the cause; he of course, would never confide. He had behaved similarly with her mother. So be it, she left her father alone to his misery and returned to the boy in his. "Be careful what you say and *how* you say it. He doesn't need a reason."

Alex drank the last of the broth and swallowed a piece of soggy biscuit she placed carefully on his tongue. Between the food and her unexpected, soothing presence he regained his footing. "I wasn't polite before... on deck. And now you're kind. Thank you, Miss—"

"Eat. Stop talking. I have to go." Her whisper urgent, she cupped his brow testing for fever. "How badly did they hurt you?"

Alex suppressed a groan, relieved she could not see him squirm like a child. "It hurts a bit. But I'm used to it." He lied as if brutal beatings were part of his life.

She had heard Captain Briggs was a kind man. To hear he beat his sons was unexpected.

"I'm sorry to hear that. I'll bring more food if I can."

"Thank you, Miss. Like you said, 'we should be friends.'"

"That will be difficult now. You're to be kept in chains. And they watch me. You can't trust anybody." She grabbed the empty bowl and like so few before her escaped the bilge reeking of mold, decay, and death. How could she help the boy? His legs were chained to the hull! She began to climb the ladder to the lower deck.

"We don't often have visitors in our special apartments, Miss." Raca sneered.

"You startled me, Mr. Raca. Captain Gant told me to check on our passenger."

"He said nothin' like it, Miss. You and I know it. Now we got a secret 'tween us." He smiled; his greasy skin and rotting teeth revolting her. He swept hair from his eyes and grabbed her arm. "And those who got a secret need to be friendly, right?" His other hand reached around her narrow waist, and he forced her hips into his. She jammed the hard edge of her wooden bowl into his bony sternum. Raca momentarily loosened his grip, and she deftly slid out of his grasp and raced up the ladder without looking back. Raca gritted his teeth and climbed down to the bilge. Pricilla was too far away to hear the rest.

At five bells, in the early morning dark and cold, Raca unlocked the shackles and dragged Alex into Gant's cabin. Two small ports astern let in meager light and a bit of air; Alex wondered if a man's shoulders could fit through.

Gant, studying a chart, said casually without looking up, "Boy, tell me the identity of '*T.S.*'? Where did he hide your father's money?"

Raca hovered, anxious to deliver another blow. He had planned for hours how to deliver maximum pain. He smiled.

"You can beat me... but I can't tell you what I don't know."

"The name," Gant said in a steady low voice, "Where's he hide his money?"

The boy kept silent. Gant nodded. But this time Alex was alert to the mate. He ducked as Raca's heaver-club swept over his head.

The fool! Had it connected, thought Gant, *the boy would be dead!*

Gant noted how deftly Alex sidestepped Raca and then lunged and head-butted the mate into the bulwark. The boy's hands remained tied, so he swung his elbows wildly side to side. Raca hit him hard in his bruised ribs. Alex dropped as the air left his lungs. Raca's boot slammed into his face.

When Alex awoke—was it minutes later? Hours? He was dreaming the same nightmare. He heard Gant's steady voice, "...'*T.S.*' Where did he hide the strongbox?" Alex did not answer. Captain Gant motioned to Raca. "Mr. Raca. Ask cook for a few dollops of molasses." When Raca left, Gant looked at Alex lying in the corner. "Mister Briggs, have you heard of a molasses bath? No? Let me explain. We slap molasses onto a prisoner's skin. Chain him below and wait for the rats. They come from all over the ship. They like molasses. They climb onto the prisoner and eat it. But when they finish with their molasses, they keep going and nibble on what's under. They gnaw on the prisoner's soft skin. They're particular to fingertips, toes, ears, and lips. The prisoner can't move, can't swipe'em away. A molasses bath usually loosens a man's tongue... if he's still got one left." Raca returned with a small kid filled with molasses. He laughed, his foul blackened mouth open, dripping with excitement. "With an uncooperative prisoner," Gant continued,

"Mr. Raca strips him naked, straps him tight with wet leather laces. As the laces dry, they tighten fierce. He spreads a coating of molasses on the prisoner's face and privates. It's pitiful to see a man squirm like that, helpless and lying in his own filth. The rats feast on the molasses and his naked body. Sometimes Raca spreads molasses on his eyes forcing the prisoner to watch the rats as they blind him. When his screams fill the night, sometimes Mr. Raca must use his sharp knife so we can return to sleep." Raca smiled as he enjoyed the description of the torture almost as much as the event itself. "Mr. Raca has the molasses. Thank you. Ears and lips first?" Alex recoiled from Raca's reach and groveled like a terrified cat. "Tell me where he hid his strongbox, boy!" Gant yelled as his mate approached the young man.

Terrified and close to despair, no longer sure about his iron will, Alex remained quiet however deciding truth was not an ally. He thought of his father as Raca gripped his head with two large hands.

Gant suddenly thrust his arm out and stopped the mate. *I may need to present the boy to Portuguese authorities as a rich ship owner's son*, thought Gant, realizing he would need an alternative punishment, one resulting in a less obvious disfigurement. "Mr. Raca, we'll give him until first light tomorrow to gather his bearings. We have a long voyage ahead. Rats're always hungry."

Alex lay awake in cold misery. He had long ago finished a piece of hardtack Raca had begrudged him. A wooden ladle of water was empty. He ached all over and wanted to cry out. He cursed *her*—some friend; she had never reappeared. He had no visitors until dawn two days later when a large seaman approached a few steps behind the first mate.

"Good day," said Raca with a false smile, devoid of even a hint of mirth. "Meet our new cook, Mr. Cooper. He's to help you topside. You're our special guest t'day."

Alex had seen the powerful black man someplace. Before Alex could speak, the cook met his gaze. Isaiah shook his head slowly as if to erase the recollection. Confused but obedient, Alex remained silent as Isaiah guided him to his feet. As they reached the top deck, Alex gratefully inhaled the crisp sea air. The early light blinded him, and he shook from the cold. Dawn was breaking and the air was filled with a soft, uncomfortable mist. It was the kind of morning sailors would rather stay asleep in a warm berth or coiled up in a long woolen coat. He saw *Wasp's* entire company had been assembled as if for a church ceremony... or a punishment...

"Good morning, Mr. Briggs, though it won't be good for you *unless you tell me what I want.*" Gant stood with hands behind his back.

Nervously, Pricilla peeked unseen from the top step of the aft companion ladder. The rest of the ship's company stood on deck and looked uneasy.

"Tell me the name of the man who goes by '*T.S.*'?" Gant spewed. Alex did not answer. Gant looked aloft then at Alex. "Your brother told me you don't fancy climbing to the crosstrees, eh?" He stood inches from Alex's face and pointed up at *Wasp's* mainmast rising 125 feet above deck—150 feet above the waves. "Up there, one slip and you're dead." He paused. "Give me his name!"

Alex shuddered. He could not think, too tired to form a credible lie. "Don't know. Damn you," he said not far enough under his breath. The crew nearby heard and were startled. They knew their captain. How many strokes could the lad endure?

"Prepare punishment," Gant said in haste and anger but immediately reconsidered; Raca might enjoy the spectacle with demonic exuberance and beat to death the only one who could tell him what he wanted. Gant saw the faces of his crew: a mix of fear and morbid curiosity. The spectacle was also for them. The captain had only one loyal man, a dull brute showing early signs of a disaffected subordinate. Only Gant and Raca had weapons. The captain needed to control his violent lot if they were to cut *Celeste* away from armed soldiers and sail past batteries of blasting cannon and fired muskets. To control such hardened men required fear. He nodded toward his mate. Raca grabbed Alex and spread his legs and tied his wrists to halyards, right and left. Raca ripped the shirt from the youth's pale, slender back. To a sailor nearby, Raca motioned to hoist the ropes tight and stretch Alex's arms upwards, his feet barely reaching deck. Terrified, Alex could not breathe. *Wasp's* crew included a mix of hard-living coastal men used to fighting and violence. A few had served in U.S. naval vessels or were impressed by British ships during the last war and had witnessed—and received—the brutal punishment of flogging. They knew what a whip's four separate strands of jagged leather straps with frayed edges would do to a helpless man. Raca seemed comfortable with the weapon; he slapped it from one hand to the other eager to let fly. He flashed his greasy grin dripping with bloodlust.

The men aboard knew that when the first whip-lash strikes a man's back it feels like a heavy, flat wooden club. The leather straps blast air from his lungs and he cannot breathe. He gasps for relief at the same moment a second strike hits the first wound of weakened skin and rips open tender, raw flesh. A man's back has no calluses. Covered most of the cold months, then colored brown by sun in the warmer climes, most sailors' backs have only soft, fleshy skin. After a third lash, blood splatters nearby on-lookers and soaks the victim's pants. Pain sears like a hot knife slicing into bare, delicate skin, cutting again and again. A whipping offers no relief or pause to gather one's senses. Pain fills every moment. A fit able-body seaman can receive 12 lashes punishment for a small misdemeanor or oath directed at an officer; 50 strikes the penalty for disobedience. Any man who strikes a mate or the captain, however, can receive 100 lashes—a near-certain death sentence. After two dozen lashes a man loses consciousness. Soon after his heart stops beating due to blood loss. More than one boatswain has been charged with applying the cat hard against the hanging torso of a dead man. Such is justice at sea. Whipping a crewman on a merchant ship in peacetime, however, was rare, reserved for only the most heinous acts of violence against ship's officers. But *Wasp* was an exception. Raca's whip flew every few days for faults large and innocuous. For a young man unused to hardship, lashes thrown by a large, violent man like Raca was harsh punishment. Gant's crew stood silent, watching the unfolding event. None could imagine what this boy had done to deserve a beating so early in a new voyage.

"Cat's outta the bag," Pierce whispered to Willy pointing to Raca's hand holding the whip's hide, a cat-o-nine-tails.

Gant took in the scene with satisfaction then suddenly reconsidered. Taking Raca aside, he whispered hoarsely, "One hard blow but miss the boy high. Scare the shit out of him. I know you'd like that."

"No flogging? But—"

"You heard me, Mr. Raca. I need him alive and presentable."

"Aye." Raca took the whip from its satchel and approached Alex, pinned spread-eagle. He laid the whip over Alex's shoulders and down his back and leaned into his face. "Feel it warm and smooth, eh lad? When I come down hard on you it won't feel so warm. It'll feel like a hot pike coming fresh outta the fire. It'll sting at first, and then once my blows whip off the first layer of skin from your scrawny back, you'll wish you were never born. Once I'm finished, you won't lay on your back or side for weeks without thinkin' of my cat here. And I gotta'nother cat, with balls at the ends of the straps. They'll crack your ribs in so many places you won't barely be able to take a deep breath without gut-wrenchin' pain, you'll want to jump over the side to escape me—"

"Raca. Enough!" Gant and the entire crew could hear the mate's lewd threats. More than one crewman knew his words to be true. The captain of *Wasp* watched the men's faces as Raca raised the whip and flung it down with a terrifying crack not unlike a topmast snapping in a gale. The leather straps hit the grating inches above Alex's outstretched fingers. The mate turned to Gant hoping the captain might change his mind. "I have no hesitation about using the cat when any man or boy on this ship ducks his duty. This includes answering questions posed to him by his captain. Mr. Briggs is less than forthcoming to my queries, and if he doesn't begin to talk, Mr. Raca will flog him until he passes out or dies. Any man aboard *Wasp* who doesn't obey me, any man who doesn't fear the justice of the cat, makes a grave mistake." Captain Gant's message rang clear; the men cowered. "Raca, cut him down. Send him to the masthead."

Willy Harrison looked at his cousin Pierce; silently, they agreed not to be next and so tucked themselves tight behind the other able-bodies.

Raca motioned to the nearest body. "You. Cook. Get him up. Main crosstrees."

"Captain?" Isaiah looked to Gant for corroboration or perhaps a reprieve.

"Cook, climb with the boy to our mast peak. Retrieve him at sunset. Lash him tight, d'ya hear me?" Gant cried impatiently and said to Alex, "Enjoy the view, Mr. Briggs. Your brother sends his regards."

Isaiah looked back at Gant with blank, deep-set eyes. *Was he hiding fury? Hatred,* Gant thought? Certainly, the freed man had seen worse.

"Aye, Captain," Isaiah said slowly as he guided the limp youth toward the ratlines in order to begin the long climb. "He needs fresh bandages, Captain." Isaiah pointed at Alex's open facial wounds. Gant spat tobacco juice downwind away from his white shirt neatly laundered by Pricilla, then nodded. Willy brought a clean white cloth for bandages from below and gave them to Isaiah. The two men wrapped Alex carefully and Alex nodded his thanks. "...and a coat, Sir, or he'll freeze," Isaiah added. The cook felt Alex's brow. "Your prisoner's on fire, Captain, Sir."

Recognizing Raca may have beaten the boy too hard over the past days, Gant nodded. Willy retrieved his own woolen jacket with a heavy fur lining. Isaiah wrapped the coat around Alex, and together they climbed the mast. Gant watched the large black man gently, powerfully help Alex up one step at a time. *His cooking's worse than revolting,* thought Gant. *And I don't like his look. His eyes tell me nothing.*

Fire. So warm, he touches it, no it burns and peels his skin. A bed with feather blankets, a pillow, no two on both sides of his head. A voice, hers, close by, Mother; but he's so cold, so hot, a wet towel, yes on his forehead, no not so hot, it burns! Ahh, better now she's here, so near as always, thinking of how it will be better. But no, is he dying? Will today be the end and shall he meet the Shepherd? He must search for you Mama, and Paps, too, where out there can he find me, you are out there, but his hands feel bound tight! Tied, yes, wrapped in cords of heavy ropes or seaweed? And he swings with each heave of the ship. Her voice, so near, so kind, no, not you Mama, her, the other one, the girl, a kind voice warm and near, she will save me, or Mama will save me! But no, she does not come to me though I call her name and I am left alone. She must be her father's agent, his accomplice, she deceives, they intend to punish him—her father with his anger, and she with affected pity. The first day he was right: she was false, he doesn't need friends, he has no friends, not on this ship, not in this world where he must fight enemies alone. They mean to kill him, yet he resists for good reason,

right? He doesn't have what they want, does he? He must not forfeit the scraps he knows to be true. But he cannot let them do their worst; they will try, they will kill him. And if his parents survive, good for them, but it will not be he who has saved them. He will die first. The pain... too great... too tired, weak. He cannot breathe. Oh, for a drink of water. Why did he come to this ship? So tired and cold...

Ten hours later and still weak, Isaiah convinced Willy to take his place and carry Alex down from the pitching mast. Their descent from the crosstree took a long time. When they laid Alex gently on coiled ropes on deck the lad did not move.

"Is he alive?" Gant asked Raca as the cook fed him warm broth over cracked, sun-burnt lips.

"I'll kick him, and we'll know, eh?" Raca smirked.

"It was a simple question. Post lookouts and watch for sails."

"Aye. But he deserves another kick—"

"Enough! Get a lookout aloft now or I'll find a mate who can keep his tongue in his miserable mouth!"

Isaiah and Willy moved Alex gently to a warm berth. Though his fever appeared broken, he remained weak. With Pricilla's help, Isaiah changed Alex's bandages and cleaned his cuts.

"The ointment will cool him, prevent gangrene. Boy's resilient. He'll breathe and eat again without too much pain... in a few days," Isaiah said.

Sitting and sleeping comfortably, however, would take weeks due to the kicks to his badly bruised sides and ribs. Isaiah checked on the boy throughout the long day. He told himself Alex was strong and prayed he was right. Later in the afternoon, Alex stirred and found Isaiah by his side.

"Cook?" whispered Alex. "Am I alive?"

Isaiah resisted a smile. "A day aloft in stormy conditions *could* have been a death sentence. You cannot take a seaman's punishment. You've lived a rich and comfortable life with feather beds and hot meals thrice a day. You've never froze in a winter's storm high aloft with leathery skin to protect you. They'll kill you, Alex. Whatever they want, give it up."

"I've done nothing wrong," Alex protested. His answer was automatic and truthful but beside the point. He suspected the cook knew as much. As he regained his wits; he remembered his feverish despair aloft which suddenly, here in the warmth of the berth, seemed cowardly. Still, he could not endure more abuse from Raca.

Isaiah chose not to pursue the obvious: '*Tell them what you know!*' Instead, the cook sent Pricilla to fetch more broth from the galley before he shared with Alex what might save the boy's life.

"Offshore we lead a hard life, Alex. And aboard *Wasp* they persecute you. Your wits cannot beat them while you're chained to the bilge."

"You mean I should fight back?"

"Not yet," Isaiah dropped his voice. "Be ready. You will be forced to make a decision soon."

Alex thought about Raca—older, larger, and stronger, able to hold Alex at arm's length with one hand and beat him with the other. And Captain Gant could crush him. His crew did his bidding and would swear witness to Gant's story of his demise. He saw looks from the crew and none were kind except Willy, a local boy. Alex presumed Willy well understood the realities on this ship.

"My mother taught my brother and me to walk away from violence. And even though my father fought in the West Indies against the British, he told us to listen to her. He never taught us about weapons or how to use our fists—"

"You must learn the difference."

"What do you mean?"

"If *they* bring the fight to *you*." Isaiah thought of the times he also had stood alone. "When they bring it, you must fight back. And you must fight to the end because they will. They see you deflect their attack not intending to deliver a deathblow. And this gives them power. Against cowards and the weak, their violence and hatred makes them bold. A determined adversary smells your fear. He senses it like a deer knows you're near. Even if you hold a gun, a cutlass, or a knife, your eyes mirror your soul. If you don't have the will to deliver a death blow, they will recognize it. They'll win. And you'll die."

"So, I must—?"

"If they bring a fight—finish it. Only one man can walk away. They must know you understand that."

Alex sighed. His wounds screamed. Aboard his father's ships he saw rough conditions and violent men, but he was treated with respect, even diffidence. On *Wasp* the crew despised him. He licked his swollen, bloody lips. He felt energy trickling back and with it some clarity about his situation: impossible, perhaps, but not hopeless. "I don't know anything about weapons. I only have my wits."

Isaiah's face grew stern. The boy was correct but must listen to reality. "You possess inner strength you don't recognize. Use your wits always, of course. But there comes a time when you must fight the evil in this world. If a blade comes at you in the night, no bandage will stanch your blood. Wits alone will not save you."

Wasp carried scores of deadly weapons for ship-to-ship boarding stored in Gant's double-locked compartment. She also carried a crew trained to use them. Gant, however, was not on a hunt for prize as in his privateering past; nor did he want another ship to come upon them until they were anchored safely alongside the *Mary Celeste* in Sao Miguel. He knew unarmed merchant vessels such as *Wasp* were targets for pirates and suspected smugglers by the Navy, so he maintained a steady set of lookouts to scan all horizons from the foremast peak. A man armed with a spyglass, hanging on the narrow strips of parallel oak strips comprising the mast-head crosstree platform, would continually sweep the horizon, identify sails from another ship miles away—'hull down'—before the hull itself appeared above the horizon. Rarely, however, would a man standing on deck pick out another ship before the lookout. Gant worried, knowing Raca had only just replaced the punished boy with a dependable man above.

Standing on his quarterdeck Gant stared nervously toward the east. As if by looking for trouble his premonition spoke—he saw a sail—a *cloud* of sails. There: east by southeast a square-rigged ship coming down fast with a strengthening breeze to intercept them and cut off *Wasp's* path of escape. They had been spotted first. Gant could turn and attempt to run downwind, but he knew he would eventually be overtaken by this large, fully-rigged, three mast ship—a man-of-war possibly. He should never have strung Alex high on the mast for so long. Even here in mid-ocean, over a thousand miles from any continent, *Wasp* had no place to run.

"Sail-ho! A warship!"

Gant did not bother to acknowledge the hail. *Damn right a warship! He'll be on us in an hour.*

Gant turned to Raca. "Is the boy alive?"

Suddenly Gant did not feel so imperial. Although his word was final on board, *Wasp* was an American vessel held to Crown and U.S. laws. Brutal beating as a punishment was a serious crime if a death resulted. The entire ship's company had witnessed it. Would his crew turn on its captain or hide the truth?

"Aye, Captain, he's moving about. Not a pretty sight though…"

"We're having visitors. Tell cook to clean the blood off Briggs' person and change his clothes."

Over the next hour, the cloud of sails grew larger until a dark hull frigate with a white stripe sat menacing off their starboard bow. Her broadside cannon were run out.

"Captain—signals! She's an American frigate. Requests we hove-to," Raca said as he placed the spyglass back at his side.

Gant nodded. He noticed fresh blood on the deck where Alex's wounds had spilled before he had been carried below. *Request my ass.* He spat to leeward and motioned for a crewman to sand the planks quick with a holystone, destroying the last of the day's business.

After Isaiah and Pricilla bandaged Alex's face and wrapped his bruised torso, the youth passed out again. Pricilla took his soiled clothes and bloody bandages into the galley where Isaiah was stowing medicines.

"How did you hurt your neck?" she asked.

"An accident."

"It looks painful."

"I lost blood. I was weak but feel better now. Sea air. Thank you, Miss."

"Were you... set upon?"

"No, not what you think. While working."

"I see."

Isaiah did not want to talk about it but Alex needed allies. "It was a mistake. We used old stands to support a work-boat. They broke. I did not move away in time."

"So how did you get out?"

"I did not see. I heard a strong, young voice. He rigged a hoist. I passed out."

"And they lifted the boat off of your neck?"

"They did."

Pricilla could sense Isaiah wanted to end the conversation, but she needed to know where he stood.

"Alex." She paused. "He can't survive much more of this. Can you help him?" Pricilla asked. She wanted to say, 'help *us*'.

The cook did not answer. Instead, he eyed the bruises on the young woman's arms and neck. She could not shake his gaze.

"Does he hurt you?"

"Who?"

"Your father?"

She thought carefully. "Not really."

"And his mate?"

"Scum!" her eyes flashed. "I can handle him."

"There you're wrong, Miss. You cannot. I watch him watch you. He preys on the weak. Young boys. The injured. Helpless slaves. Women. He intends to hurt you."

She was unaware her situation was so obvious. "What can I do? I can't run away on a ship."

"No, Miss. Get help. Alex."

"Alexander? He's so young. Younger than I in so many ways. And now he's cruelly injured. He cannot win a fight against Raca... Look at him! He's weak—"

"Alex? Weak? You saw my neck." Isaiah came to life. His eyes widened and his heavy presence in the tiny galley grew like a surface-feeding whale. "Could a weak boy rig a hoist in time to lift a two-ton workboat? Miss, the boy saved my life! Could a weak boy survive a man's punishment—beaten time and again and tied to the masthead without food or water for an entire day? Would a weak boy cross an ocean with murderers to rescue his kin? He ain't weak, Miss. He's afraid. He's hurtin' bad, I grant you that. But he ain't weak." Isaiah's eye flickered.

"But he cannot protect me from Raca... or my father."

"Alexander has an intelligent mind. You also, Miss. Think it through. Help each other."

Confused, Pricilla sank onto a stool. Should she depend on Alex or retreat to her berth hidden by a coarse blanket of darkness and sleep? She rubbed her bruised arms. Before this voyage, her father only yelled and threatened. Only six months earlier he would have smiled when she read a story aloud, with her mother spinning cloth nearby. Her father had been quietly proud of her education. Now, anger chased rum. The back of Gant's huge hand followed. And Mr. Raca added to her misery, becoming more dangerous by the day while her father seemed unaware of his menacing taunts and leers. She could see her father's aggrieved distraction encouraged the mate's crude advances. Where could she turn?

"Isaiah." Resolutely she looked to Isaiah, her green eyes steady. "Show me how to use a knife?"

Isaiah smiled knowing damned well what she was asking. "For kindlin', we strip off pieces like this." Isaiah took hold of a knife with serrated edges and a small split log. With five long slashes he split off neat strips of wood used to start the galley fire. Since Pricilla was a young girl, she had started fires with wood she and her mother chopped. To her surprise and with amazing dexterity Isaiah took one strip and whittled it down with chips flying in the air like upside down snow, into the shape of a large smooth stirring spoon with a narrow waist and firm, stiff grip. Without looking up at her, he rounded the edges with the knife blade never leaving the newly formed utensil. He scraped off the rough gouges and smoothed the rounded edges with a coarse file, then a flat file lying nearby in his chest of kitchen tools. He handed the girl the new utensil with a large grin, expecting her admonition.

"I can't defend myself with a spoon, Isaiah." Pricilla said, not unkindly. "I need to know how to use a knife. In a fight."

"It's natural to take the fight to one's enemies. But not always wise. Let them come to you. Otherwise, they'll see your blade and their blood will roil," Isaiah gently pushed back.

"His blood is already roiling. Please show me how to kill a man."

Twenty black larboard-side cannon threatened *Wasp* with deadly intent. After hurried flag signals proclaimed *Wasp* an American merchant ship, the United States Navy frigate with three masts and hundreds of fighting sailors sent over a jolly-boat. Rowed by three men on each side, it also carried four stern-faced marines with muskets. A short officer stood by a coxswain who steered. The young man in a crisp blue uniform boarded *Wasp* through the starboard gate Gant noticed still needed repair.

"Lieutenant Joshua Barker. *USS Bill of Rights*. Papers?" The officer said without a trace of national kinship.

"Quartus Gant. Master of *Wasp*, Rochester, Massachusetts."

"Destination?" Lieutenant Barker thumbed through Gant's leather-wrapped logbook: *Wasp's* positions, charted routes, manifest, and most importantly tariffs paid, were all neatly tabulated in Pricilla's careful script.

"Azores. To return home with the *Mary Celeste*," Gant replied. Without glancing up from the manifest, Lieutenant Barker issued a harsh command to his marines to search below. "We have no cargo, Lieutenant."

Unnoticed, Alex had emerged from his berth below and sat for a time on the deck out of Gant's sightline. "It will not take long. This ship—*Wasp*—has been known to run contraband." The Lieutenant wandered the deck unaccompanied, observing everything, saying nothing. After a few minutes his marines returned on deck and shrugged. The Lieutenant relaxed. "Have you seen any ships, Captain Gant?"

"No, Lieutenant. An unremarkable crossing."

"Your crew—I notice these boys stand apart. They appear jumpy. Look like fighting men to me. I trust they have not deserted. And over there—a few strong, seafaring lads and a negro not looking friendly. A strange mix for a merchantman in *peacetime,* Captain."

"We didn't know what we'd encounter," Gant replied, unapologetic.

"Ahh. You *do* know we have no arguments with Portugal?" He let his words rest. "*Nor any longer* with Britain." Gant did not respond. "*Mary Celeste*? We hear a British merchantman found her drifting without her crew. The Navy thinks a Tripoli raider may have them. There were women on board."

At the Lieutenants' surprising statement Alex rose weakly and called to the Naval officer, "Lieutenant, my mother and sister were aboard *Mary Celeste*. My father owns the ship. Will you continue to go after these raiders?"

Gant turned, alarmed.

The Lieutenant squinted unkindly at Captain Gant and answered Alex politely. "Yes, lad, we *are* searching for pirates. We thought this brig might be a rogue from Tripoli and so came down hard on you." He turned back to Gant. "We must make another pass or two in the trades. We have orders from Boston. Here." He handed a pouch to Gant. "Deliver this to Sao Miguel's port-warden in the likelihood you arrive before us. After two more legs in search of corsairs, a threat weighing heavily on our Commodore, we'll return to Sao Miguel to water" The pouch was sealed.

"Am I allowed to know what it says?" asked Gant.

"No, but since it concerns you, I'll tell you. The United States Government requests the Portuguese authorities ensure *Mary Celeste* remain in quarantine until the court rules.'"

"*Mary Celeste* is the property of Briggs and Sons!" Gant insisted. "This young gentleman here is her owner's son. I have a commission to recover their ship and bring her home."

Stepping closer to examine Alex Lieutenant Barker scoffed, "Are you certain he's a *Briggs*? He looks like a street urchin. What's wrong with him?" The Lieutenant reflexively ran his hand along his clean great coat. His finely creased pants had not a spot of soil or salt. "I shall be clear, Captain Gant. The Navy will not start another war squabbling over a fifth-rate brig. You will deliver this letter." The Lieutenant was not asking. "And you shall not move the *Celeste* until so ordered."

Gant stuffed the letter in his shirt. "Aye." His sullen look to the Naval officer was particularly unfriendly.

Gant had chosen a bad time to antagonize the young Lieutenant who eyed with renewed interest *Wasp's* unsavory crew, an assortment of scabs of all colors and nations.

"The *Bill of Rights* is undermanned. These men appear to be deserters." He motioned at Gant's fighting boys. "We shall take them."

"What!" Gant shrieked. He needed every man aboard to cut-out *Celeste* if necessary, and sail two ships across the ocean.

The Lieutenant waved at 15 surprised sailors who shuffled backwards. Following well practiced form, Pierce slowly led Willy aft out of sight, and the two disappeared below deck. The Lieutenant's armed marines stepped forward.

"You're taking most of my crew! Impressment in peacetime is illegal!"

Gant knew this was technically true but routinely ignored. If a Navy frigate needed 350 men to sail and fight and was below her crew allotment, she could remove sailors from any U.S. merchant ship. A merchantman might argue, but a frigate like *Bill of Rights* had 44 deadly reasons why it was best not to. Worse, as Gant well knew, captured smugglers, or accused pirates could be sunk without trial.

"Corporal Quinn." Lieutenant Barker motioned to a Marine. "Signal the *Bill* to send two boats for our recruits. And Captain Grant..."

"*Gant*," he corrected through clenched teeth.

"Captain Gant, you still have enough men to sail back to Massachusetts or if you must, on to Sao Miguel. This wretch..." he looked at Alex again. "...should be bathed—I notice vermin crawling all over him—even he can trim a sail. Sail your brig like a sloop—spanker with two reefs and a jib. A few able men could manage a small rig in most conditions."

"But I sail with my daughter..."

"Splendid, so you have ample crew!"

Alex seized his chance. "Sir, I'd like to go with you, too. I am held here against my will."

The Lieutenant smiled. "Is this true, Captain?"

"No. His brother hired me to deliver *Mary Celeste*. Young Master Briggs signed on as an able-body, but he's a rich man's son unused to life before the mast. He needs constant encouragement to do his duties. He would not honor *Bill of Rights*."

"Lies!" Alex cried, "They're beating me, Lieutenant!"

Pricilla listened near an open hatch. *No, Alexander, don't leave me here alone!*

With a thin smile, Mr. Raca got behind Alex, discretely grasping him with an iron grip nearly crushing Alex's arm. "I'll return him to duty, Captain."

Lieutenant Barker could use another man. And what if the boy were telling the truth? Would a wealthy ship owner offer recompense for his son's safe return? *Briggs. Vaguely familiar.* He would mention it to the old man when back on board the *Bill* if he caught his captain between bottles. *Then again*, he thought, *no*. He turned his back on the badly-beaten lad. Barker had enough problems. The boy might be a troublemaker or a potential mutineer.

The Lieutenant was last to climb into his waiting launch. The dragooned sailors only had time to grab their duffels and, with muskets prodding them, reluctantly climbed off *Wasp*.

"When I arrive in Sao Miguel, Captain Gant, speak to me in private. Perhaps we can come to another arrangement." The Lieutenant smiled and spoke in a raised voice over the building swells crashing alongside *Wasp*. "And Captain, keep an eye on your glass," he added, "I suspect a blow will descend on us this watch. With your short-handed crew, you'll have to reef with alacrity if a gale surprises you after dark."

Captain Gant watched his carefully-crafted plans row away in three Navy longboats filled with his fighting men. This changed everything. At least Raca hadn't killed the boy. *Eventually young Briggs will give up what he knows.*

"Raca!" roared Gant. "Everyone aloft! Did we lose the Harrisons too? Set every stitch of canvas we got!" He must beat *Bill of Rights* to the Azores. He felt for the Navy letter in his breast pocket and formed another ploy. "Pricilla!" he shouted. "On deck—*now!*" Presently, he would trust his daughter's pen. Deception and speed were now his best chances.

"Captain, we don't got enough men to hoist the spanker gaff. We need—"

"You *need* what we *have*, Mr. Raca—put your three men on the peak halyards at the mast. The rest of us will hoist the gaff and sail. And put the boy to work until he collapses." *Scum,* thought Gant, catching Alex's hateful stare. *Too close...*

Wasp had been left without enough able-body sailors to hoist all her sails, trim her myriad lines, and steer the ship in building swells. They barely had enough hands to fly a set of small storm sails, never mind hoist topgallants and studding sails on the foremast, the powerful rig Gant needed to get to San Miguel before the Navy.

"But Captain, you heard the Lieutenant—a blow's comin'. We'll lose the topmast—"

"You heard my orders, Mr. Raca! No off-watch tonight. Find my daughter. Tell her to mind the glass."

"I can pull lines, Father," offered Pricilla, stepping on deck.

"Aye and in your dress, you'll trip and fall overboard. Your arms and legs are pathetic and weak. Your petticoats will snag. Go below and prepare hot food. Watch the glass and let me know if you feel the ship's motion change. And copy this hand—see if you can resemble it."

Pricilla took the Navy letter. "Father, I—?"

"Do it. Don't use the best vellum until I tell you the words for it. *Go!* Cook—you're promoted to able-body. Climb aloft and help Mr. Raca loose the main tops'l." Isaiah nodded without enthusiasm. Gant thumbed at Alex sitting on the aft deck where Raca had dumped him. "Can he climb?"

"Let me feed him a bit first?" Isaiah suggested.

"Quick then—Raca trim the jib before you go up—I got the helm!"

Below in the galley, Alex gulped a warm broth. Isaiah located ale from Gant's private supply and a piece of yesterday's salted cod. Alex drank and ate for the first time in two days, changed his soiled clothes, and donned his own heavy pea coat.

"Can you climb, Master Briggs? If you're dizzy and fall overboard, he'll not turn back."

"I think I can. Thank you for your help up and down. I've seen you before. Do I know you from… home…?"

"Your father's shipyard." Isaiah extended his hand which Alex gratefully shook. "Isaiah Cooper. But we'll keep this to ourselves for now, eh? We don't want the captain riled up anymore. He and your father are not friends."

"Of course, I remember you. My father thinks highly of you. Thank you, Mr. Cooper."

"I hope we find your parents and sister, son. They need us above, come now. Climb slowly, mindful of the pitch. Slide down the shrouds."

Despite his pain Alex smiled. His father had often advised the same.

Hearing the bustle above him on deck, Captain Stephen Coughlin, U.S.N. commander of the frigate *Bill of Rights*, 44 cannon, awoke from his stupor with a headache and a sour tongue. Many rushing feet had come aboard his ship from what he assumed was another chance meeting with some unfortunate merchantman. He was short of men and if they came upon one of the corsairs from Tripoli harassing American vessels in transit to the Mediterranean Sea, he would need every man, a hundred or more to man the guns, another hundred to sail the ship, and the rest ready to board with steel and shot. But Captain Coughlin knew filling the muster roll was not motivating his prissy first officer; filling his own seachest with purloined specie was what drove the young man. The captain wiped his eyes and washed his face in the water basin by his cot. It would be another long day on patrol, soon to be his last. He was impatient, lonely, angry, and in constant pain. And so, he drank.

A burly man whose Irish-born parents came ashore in Boston from a village near Cork City, he lived in Charlestown, Massachusetts, the town where British regulars lost so many men in May of 1775 in a futile effort to stanch the rebellion before it spread. He had watched the battle from the Chelsea Creek side of the harbor where, as a boy, he had watched a gang cut out and sink a British transport.

After the rebellion and time privateering, Coughlin received a commission in the new Navy, ships built in Boston and Philadelphia. He enjoyed successful years in command of brigs, schooners, and now in command of one of the finest frigates in the small but renowned American fleet. Good years, however, gave way to pain from injuries; horrors of battles marred his body and spirit. He medicated his pain alone in his cabin with bottles stored for long voyages like this. Unlike his prosperous second-in-command, Captain Coughlin was a frugal and honest man, though disengaged with peacetime duty. Lieutenant Barker had not been his choice but, nearing retirement, the captain agreed to take him as his second for this final voyage. He hoped to see the younger man promoted and reassigned. Captain Coughlin was weary of the Lieutenant's ongoing intrigues but chose not to ask what his conscience told him was his duty. Drink softened his determination and draped a veil over his eyes. With regularity, he sat in his cabin and watched his bottle drain, knowing Lieutenant Barker ably commanded on deck; and, although not a fighting man, Lieutenant Barker was a skilled seaman and navigator. But it rankled when the junior officer accepted orders with an air of indifference any observer might consider insubordinate.

"Captain Coughlin? Mr. Barker reporting as you asked."

"Let him wait ten minutes outside before he joins me, thank you, Barnes."

Stephen Coughlin was not a taskmaster or a brute to his stewards and officers as many Navy captains behaved. With European wars settled, the proud frigates of the American Navy were left with little to do but chase the errant pirate or ubiquitous smugglers determined to undermine the tariffs on which the surging nation depended. Still, he was weary of the intrigue; the ships stopped and the sullen men who came aboard in the night were only to be released at some wayward rendezvous with persons unnamed. He knew the game; he ignored it. The ship ran smoothly, his liquor chest not half empty, two more legs between Whydah, or perhaps Freetown and the Azores. His orders would soon head him home to Charlestown to buy a tavern, or a warehouse, or anything not rocking in northeast swells.

"Captain?" Lieutenant Mathew W. Barker stepped into the great cabin of the fine, heavy frigate.

"What is all the commotion?" Captain Coughlin asked brusquely, holding his head in his hands.

"Came upon a brig... Captain." The young lieutenant answered. There it was again. The hesitation between words, an unnecessary inflection telling Coughlin all he needed to know about his subordinate's opinion of him and his many hours below deck in a stupor, or asleep, or staring aft out the transom windows, watching the tail of the wake. Captain Coughlin waited for the rest. "We found deserters, sir, fifteen men."

Of course, you did, the captain told himself. "The brig?"

"Ah, *Wasp.* Rochester, in Massachusetts..."

"I damn well know where Rochester is, Mr. Barker. Her master?"

"An ignorant brute, Grant or something like that."

Captain Coughlin looked up, suddenly interested in the conversation. "Was it *Gant?*"

"Aye, it was. Gant. Sir."

"And he objected, I warrant?"

"He did most vociferously. And he had to deal with an insubordinate crewmember who claimed to be the owner's son of the ship we heard was found adrift. *Mary Celeste.*"

"What do you mean 'insubordinate'?" Coughlin wondered if the word resonated with the younger man or was merely a word Barker had picked up recently in Mr. Webster's new compilation.

"A scrawny lad cried for us to take him aboard the *Bill of Rights* along with the deserters. Said his name was Briggs."

Coughlin straightened, awake now. His memory turned to a time 15 years ago. He recalled a time of war when a few well-built heavy frigates—44 guns were their official armament, but none went into a ship battle with less than 52 cannon primed and ready—fought their weaker, older British frigate counterparts to an uneasy treaty. The British population viewed the most recent American entanglement as an unnecessary, irritating little war, while the United States considered it a chest-thumping manifestation of global and unbridled economic expansion.

During that war, Coughlin had saved a boy and his disreputable Yankee privateering captain from the enemy and had set them free to return with their ship—at the time a brig named *Rattlesnake*. But not long after the treaty signed in Ghent, he had learned the renowned privateering brig had been sold to a man named Gant and renamed *Wasp*. After the peace, Coughlin had encountered this man—turned infamous smuggler and slaver—and his ship in a chase up Martha's Vineyard Sound. But in those foul currents and shifting shoals he had lost *Wasp* in a fog. That he would someday encounter the thief again was a faint hope. A wayward cannon shot from the retreating *Wasp* had split his ship's pinnace stored on deck. The shot sent shards of splinters into his face and head; every night since that day, when the pain became too much, he took to the bottle and hoped for another encounter.

Captain Coughlin's thoughts turned to the immediate. He considered the boy who wanted to escape *Wasp*. The lad bore a familiar name. As a young man in Massachusetts, Coughlin had sailed with an Ebenezer Briggs, Ben as he was known by most, and they had become fast friends. They had remained so until Coughlin's decision carried him into a military career with honor and renown, whereas his friend Ben Briggs was left out of the accolades Coughlin kept for himself alone. It was a hurtful decision but at the time it seemed an innocuous slight, or so he reminded himself when the bourbon's level sank below his fingers' grasp.

"Did I ever mention the action in the year '10 when I was a young master's mate on the *Beaver*?" he asked Lieutenant Barker, still standing, although not as stiffly as minutes earlier. Occasionally the two men had informal discourse, out of necessity on the part of the captain since he had no man aboard whom he could call friend. So, his first mate would have to do in a pinch. As for the lieutenant, he must listen to his captain because he had not been excused. Anything, he felt, was better than a careful inquisition as to the veracity of his account of the most recent impressment. For the mate, this discourse hiding in a veil of implied familiar courtesy was an exercise in patience. He had his way with this captain, his personal accounts grew by every encounter with an unarmed vessel, and soon he could afford a house on the bluff in Magnolia Village near Gloucester where he had been raised. So what if the old man wanted to share dull memories of wars fought and battles joined? Lieutenant Barker was quite happy this new age presented more opportunities for wealth-making than the mortal risks of warmongering. He did not enjoy the sound of gunfire and perfectly hated the sight and smell of spilt blood.

"*Beaver*? I don't recall sir."

"It has to do with what you just told me."

"Aye, Captain?"

"A young man named Ben Briggs and I were officers on *Beaver*. I was first mate, he the sailing master. A good sailor this boy Ben. He had eyes for the shape of a sail like no man I have ever met. We were like brothers for a time. It was during the period when American ships were stopped on the high sea by British naval vessels and our people pressed. *Beaver* was set upon by one of His Majesty's cutters off the coast of Newfoundland, Halifax-bound. Our ship was a sound brig, with nearly 50 able men and boys aboard. We were homebound to Salem and our captain decided to object."

"You fought the British ship?"

"We ran at first but when we came hard up on the lee of Sable Island, we stood to fight. The wind was light, the current kept us off the treacherous coast until the flood began. We had three hours to stand our ground. The cutter fired on us and of all the unimaginable things that could have gone wrong, the worst happened: that first cannon ball hit us on the aft quarter and slammed into our captain knocking him dead on the spot. Not another man was injured or bloodied, only our captain."

"Did you surrender, Sir?"

"Ben Briggs and I decided we would share the helm. We promised each other we'd never call for quarter only to fight Bonaparte and bleed for King George. Instead, we hoisted every stich we carried and sailed into the shallows near the beach where we hoped the cutter could not follow. He sent us a barrage of shot over the next two hours, but we were lighter, faster, and put some distance between us."

"Who commanded?"

"A strange thing. I had the wheel, Ben the lead line and the charts. We were a good team. The men followed our commands as if we were the captain himself, poor soul. After the current turned, we knew we were in for a tough go of it, but then a fog bank appeared, and we disappeared into it."

"You escaped, Sir?"

"Aye, we did. Brought *Beaver* into Salem and the town toasted our triumph. A local newspaper wrote I had commanded while engineering our escape. The article left out any mention of Ben's bravery. I said nothing to correct it. Ben sorely objected, I knew, but kept his silence. Soon after I received a commission for the service. Ben and I have not spoken since."

"That's his boy on *Wasp*?"

"Well maybe. Any chance we'll encounter them again, Mr. Barker?"

"I, ah, can't say, Sir."

"If we do, you'll let me know right away—to receive your *orders*. Am I making myself clear?

"Aye, Sir."

"Dismissed."

As Lieutenant Baker had accurately forecast, the wind strengthened as night came on. Captain Gant steered with increased difficulty trying to hold the bow on a straight line as *Wasp* surged then crashed into the racing waves. Climbing on deck, Alex noticed a slender figure in a knit wool cap heaving a bundle overboard. From behind the wheel Gant bellowed at his daughter.

"What in hell's name are you doing, girl?"

"You said my clothes impede my ability to set sails, Papa." Pricilla turned. "I no longer suffer such a disability. I have trousers and shirts loaned to me from one of our young men. Now I can climb and pull lines with the boys."

Alex smiled from across the deck admiring the young woman's grit until he realized Gant was about to give her the back of his hand. With all his strength Alex leapt to intercept the blow. Instead, Gant yielded, yelling at Alex and Pricilla, "Then aloft both of you! Help the Harrison boys drop the topsail then hoist the flying jib. I want mains'l braces trimmed hard off our starboard quarter. I'll be damned if we don't raise Sao Miguel before the frigate—even without my fightin' boys!"

Pricilla Gant had never climbed aloft before on *Wasp* nor on any sailing ship. Her soft leather shoes were smooth and would slip on wet lines and the loose rope ladders strung between the tarred shrouds. Her feet were tender and not calloused like ship's boys who were used to running aloft barefoot in all but winter gales. Alex watched dumbfounded as she kicked off her shoes, removed her ankle stockings, grabbed the ratlines, and climbed like an unbowed top-man. She slipped more than once, appearing tentative as she pushed up through the lubber's hole on the main top. He followed her and, as sailors do, they loosed the furled sails, mindful of each other's proximity and the danger of hanging on far above a certain death.

Near midnight, Raca, who had taken the wheel from Gant hours before, called out, "Got too much helm, Captain, can't hold 'er!"

Raca, Pierce, and Willy took turns at the wheel while the rest of the crew slept. Even short spells exhausted the three men on deck. The wind had risen to a violent blow, east–southeast. In the race to beat *Bill of Rights* into Sao Miguel, Gant had set every sail his small crew could manage. Despite Lieutenant Barker's warning, he risked the wind would stay down. It had not. And now with only three experienced hands, they could not reef sails fast enough to keep *Wasp* on an even keel—the angle delivering the speed he wanted and until now enjoyed. If he lost his race against *Bill of Rights* into San Miguel, his new plan—armed with the Navy's letter, now entrusted to Pricilla's talents, to get on board *Mary Celeste* and steal the strongbox before the Navy prevented it—would fail. As the wind increased and forced *Wasp's* rudder sideways the ship slowed precipitously. She heeled hard as her bow crashed into building waves. If they did not reduce sail soon, a support shroud might break causing the topmast to collapse taking strained sails and yardarms with it. Losing any part of the rig here would stop them dead against a foul westerly current which pushed hard against the hull as they steered east toward the Azores Islands. Raca and Willy with all their combined skill and muscle struggled to keep the wheel straight.

Raca yelled over the crashing swells, "We need to douse the main course, Captain!"

Gant surveyed his options. "You and you." He pointed to Willy and Pierce. "Aloft and reef the course."

The sailors obeyed but looked at each other with wide eyes. Gant realized as they started climbing that he would need the brig's fore topsail reefed as well. The seas were rising, the howling wind on their starboard quarter. He needed more men.

A gust stretched the fore topgallant sail clew to clew, and the topmast swayed and creaked, straining near its breaking point. If it let go and the ship turned on her beam into these cresting waves, he risked a broach. *Damn the Navy to hell!*

Alex felt the ship's gyrating motion from his hammock below and recognized *Wasp* thrashed about nearly out of control. The lives of his family and crew of the *Mary Celeste* depended on *Wasp* reaching *Celeste*. If they lost a topmast here the search was over. Alex forced himself to ignore his pain and climbed onto the deck, saw the Harrisons on the mains'l yard, and decided without any forethought to handle the topsail by himself.

"Boy, where you going?" Gant cried from the helm as Alex climbed up the bulwarks for the shrouds.

"Someone's gotta go. Before we lose the topmast."

Alex clambered onto the rail holding the ratlines tight with both arms. His chin rested briefly on the wet ropes. Slowly, he ascended to the foretop platform where he stopped. Breathing hard, he glanced up and shook his dizziness away. Ignoring his aching ribs and limbs he climbed expertly up and over onto a second ratline to the fore topmast creaking side to side. There he grabbed hold of the highest wooden yardarm, hanging ninety feet over the waves. With bare feet he slid sideways along a thin support rope. His hands stung from wet and cold, his fingertips numb. His foot slipped; he caught himself, all his weight on the other leg. Six inches at a time, Alex continued to slide sideways on the yard over the waves, as wind raced through his ears and *Wasp* lurched side to side. His stomach, from pain and sea motion, ejected his recent, hurried meal. But he hung on and pulled in the sail—it *had* to come in. He saw the shroud tight as an iron rod and the mast top arcing in a crescent about to give way. *I'm a fool to be up here!*

Willy and Pierce reefed their sail on the mainmast and retreated with difficulty to the deck. Not anxious to climb again they were relieved to see Alex working high above on the foremast. Because of their reef, pressure on Alex's still-loaded sail had increased. He grabbed the stiff canvas and pulled with all his strength. Willy and Pierce loosened the sheets and halyards on deck and the canvas came up a few inches at a time. Typically, three or more sailors clung on each side of the yardarm pulling sails, tying bunt lines under and over as other men gathered in the loose canvas. Alex, however, had to furl by himself—gathering and tying—while hanging onto the yard with his arms and chest, his only support a thin line strung below the yard on which his feet tentatively rested. He gathered, first half and finally, all the topsail. He tied the gaskets twice and slid his bare feet sideways further over the ocean to gather the last loose section of sail when, without warning, a rogue wave crashed into *Wasp* like an unexpected clap of summer thunder.

The wave had come from behind the ship unseen in the black night rising larger by double than the waves preceding it. More critical than its size, however, its force broke *Wasp's* steady, predictable motion. Under normal conditions, Alex above and deckhands below could sense this synchronous wave motion. It told them when they could risk moving and when to hold on. But when this massive wave hit *Wasp's* quarter, she lurched awkwardly. The ship fell off the backside of the rogue into a deep trough and landed with a crash into hard ocean water. Every line not secured tight cracked wildly in the wind. Every soul not holding on with every muscle was thrown about the heaving deck, swamped by sea water.

Frantically tying the last reef line, Alex never saw the wave. It heaved the ship, and the motion pitched him backwards off the yardarm into the night without a chance to cry out for God's mercy. His hands grabbed a loose brace leading below and he swung sideways over the deck. His flying foot caught between a yardarm and the buntline below it where the line used to furl the sail caught his ankle and held tight. The ship lurched to weather and his twisting motion wrapped the line twice around his leg, cutting his skin, choking all circulation. His grip on the brace slipped, he lost hold of it and fell helplessly headfirst. He expected a quick death: his skull crashing into the deck or perhaps striking the frigid ocean. Instead, his wrapped ankle yanked his torso upwards, suspending him in the air. His hands dangled below his head, helpless, but his captive foot held firm. Alex hung upside down, swinging 70 feet above the deck of the ship pitching to and fro in the storm. He could not right himself or reach any lines. Nor could he reach his trapped foot. He was beyond panic and prayed for help from the Good Shepherd as his mother had taught.

On deck, Willy and Pierce watched Alex dangle but dared not stir. Hearing Alex's screams, Isaiah rushed to the deck followed by Pricilla. They looked up expecting Alex to fall. Gant at the wheel glanced up and then back at their wake flowing straight and true. The boy had saved *Wasp*, the ship now on a level trim sailing in control.

"Harrison boys! You two—get him down!" A week earlier, Gant might have let a man dangle as punishment for his carelessness. Now he needed every hand. He also admired the boy's fast action. *Young Mr. Briggs may become a casualty of the voyage but not like this, not today*, thought Gant. Willy and his cousin remained frozen. Again, Gant cried, "Get aloft, now!"

"We were lucky to get *down*, Captain! The wind—it's howl'n fierce!" Pierce squealed looking at Raca who nodded as he too backed away into the gloom of the quarterdeck.

Pierce spoke the truth. The seas had grown from frustrated and angry to ferocious and deadly. The wind blew a gale and whistled through the rigging. *Wasp* pitched from one side to the other, her lower spars touching waves on each yaw. To climb the mast, a man must hang nearly upside down as *Wasp* lurched on a wave crest. He must hold the wet ratline straps with wrists and fingers in cold saltwater spray, fighting gravity and the ship's rocking and unpredictable motions. Willy looked at Pierce and his eyes pleaded to help him save the lad. But Pierce would not sacrifice his skin for the boy. Raca stood silent and absent.

Without a word the smuggler's daughter darted from behind the seamen. Before Gant could object, Pricilla hopped onto the bulwark and clambered nimbly upward. Steady at first, as she rose higher, she grew tentative. *Wasp* came up hard on a roller and the yardarms dipped; Pricilla stopped and clung tight. Daring not to look down, nor could she look up. Her feet reddened as she reached the first platform.

"Daughter, mind the rogue waves!" Gant roared.

Pricilla rested, then pulled herself further upward. With but 30 feet higher to go she climbed tentatively. *But after?* Gant wondered. *Has she a plan? Will she remember what I taught her?* Captain Gant wanted to flog his sailors who would let a girl do their job. Instead, he watched the ocean's rhythms and tried to keep the ship on a straight course steering up when it surfed down a wave, steering down when a roller caught them from behind.

Gant watched as Pricilla reached the yardarm where Alex hung upside down. *Leg must be broken*, he thought, recalling a sailor trapped thus; his leg snapped and ripped from his hipbone as he fell dead to the deck, the leg remaining hideously above. Gant had no great hope for this boy. Glancing aft he felt a slight lull in pressure.

"Ease sheets. We shall go down!" This order his crewmen obeyed. And as *Wasp* fell away the ship stabilized momentarily. Pricilla recognized the maneuver. Her father could backwind the sails and stop a ship in its length if he chose. She had her chance and waited as *Wasp's* sideways rocking motion eased. She took cook's knife and cut a line. It swung into Alex's face. He missed it. "Alexander, grab the line, pull up! Take pressure off your ankle." She shouted above the wind. She tried again. On the fourth try he caught it. "I'll cut you free, hang on!"

The knife was sharp and heavy, its ragged serrated blade meant for butchering a carcass. She had watched Isaiah use it to whittle a whale bone into a small dagger. Only one of her hands was free to cut as the other wrapped around the wet yardarm. She leaned over and began to saw away at the line wrapped tight around the boy's leg. Alex struggled and gradually pulled himself up into a half-sitting position. Pricilla hung over him, chafing at the sturdy line. If it freed, Alex's ankle would spring loose. And so loosened he would fly outboard, wildly swinging in the black night.

"I can't hang on. I'm going to fall!" cried Alex.

"Stop talking! Try and pull yourself up higher!" Once, twice, three times she cut with the heavy blade's edge. "Hang on! Hang on tight! Once it breaks, you'll swing out!"

"My leg's breaking!"

Pricilla looked at his face and recognized the same desperate fear she felt the night her mother lost her battle and Pricilla's world had fallen apart. She must not fail again.

Alex recognized once cut free, *Wasp's* violent rocking would swing him out over the ocean and on the ensuing roll slam him back into the mast. At either extension he could lose his grip, slip off the rope's loose bitter end, and fall to a certain death.

"This will work!" Pricilla yelled over the roiling ocean and whistling wind as she worked with as much strength as her single hand and arm could bring. "Hold on tight!" She looked directly into his upturned face.

After two more deliberate cuts with the serrated blade the line suddenly snapped loose and without warning released Alex's leg. He swung free like a stone shot from a slingshot and flew 20, 30, 40 feet over the ocean. He held on tight with his cramped, cold hands but immediately began to slide down the wet, swinging line. Beneath him its tail whipped about. Flailing, he could not snare it to wrap his feet and slow the slide. With one more swing he would reach the tail end and fall either onto the deck or into the sea. Pricilla expected this wild swing and knew her father would have his eyes on two things: her and the approaching waves. She waited until Alex was at the apex of his swing. Just astern, she could see a lull in the waves. She waved at her father and pointed in the direction for him to steer. Gant read her signal. He spun the wheel hard to larboard and watched as Alex swung back toward the *Wasp's* upper foremast. As Alex was about to crash into it, Gant spun his helm again but this time to starboard and immediately back again. The ship shuddered and stood upright; the wild rocking motion stopped for the briefest of moments. Alex got what he needed: his arcing swing stopped as *Wasp* lurched upright. He let go his rope and lunged for the foremast. On contact, he wrapped his arms and legs around it and clung onto it for life. He slid down 15 feet, crashing hard onto the foretop platform. There, he dug in his fingers and pressed his nose into the wet slats. His first thought, *I am alive...* was followed by, *because of her*.

From above Pricilla watched. Her father had rescued Alex as much as she. Together the two youths slowly descended on the windward side of the ship. Alex slid down a shroud while Pricilla picked her steps gingerly on the ratlines. On deck, Alex shook, barely able to walk or speak. Swollen black, his ankle held his weight; he was relieved it was not broken. The two young people looked at each other amazed. He was grateful to be alive but was embarrassed she heard him wailing from the deathly trapeze. Clearly Pricilla was the braver; he must remember that. He collapsed at her side onto the deck. Shivering, her legs crumbled as well. Pricilla slumped down beside him. Instinctively they reached out and held each other tight. Gant gave up a brief nod to his daughter. She nodded back yet could not bring herself to smile. Each day on this voyage they had fallen further apart like a wave leaving a ship behind forever in its wake.

The two sailors who had shrunk from their duty stood to the side, hands ostensibly tending some wayward line, Willy mortified by his lack of courage. Raca withdrew further into the shadows aft.

Only Isaiah found the courage to speak what the entire crew knew to be the truth. "The Lord was with us tonight, Captain. The boy saved your ship. Your daughter saved him." The cook slid his kerchief higher on his neck, self-conscious of the scar, ignoring the pain, weak still. He doubted he would have had the strength to climb like the girl. Isaiah turned to go below. Gant grabbed his arm.

"You're no cook. How did you come to this ship?"

After a few hours of fitful sleep, Alex rested below deck in a forward hammock. Pricilla approached with a serving bowl and ladle. He slid down stiffly and sat on a worn wooden seachest he had not noticed before—a chest one man could carry without help from a mate, two-feet long and about 18 inches deep, likely hastily abandoned by one of the conscripted crewmen. He studied it and pictured the open ports in Gant's cabin. *Might it fit through?*

"Cook and I made you something better than usual," Pricilla announced, having changed into a set of dry cotton clothes Willy had kindly given her. She wished she had kept her blue day dress with the long sleeves; it was more comfortable than the constricting trousers. "How do you feel, Alex?"

"Better. Thank you, Miss."

"Please call me Pricilla."

"Thank you... Pricilla. You can call me whatever you want." He smiled. "I'd be dead if you hadn't climbed. Was no one else willing?"

"We were rolling hard. I thought it best if I tried first. Cook wanted to help but he's old and a bit weak."

"You know how to climb and use a knife. You waited for a roll to cut me free..."

"This isn't my first voyage. My father taught me about the ship." Pricilla thought of those earlier voyages in between classroom sessions. "He never had a formal education. He thought I should. For a time."

Cook's chowder and the sight of her bright eyes warmed him like a campfire. He smiled though his ankle throbbed. With each gulp of the thick soup his rib cage pounded painfully and the open cuts on his lips and cheeks stung. He stopped eating and gazed into Pricilla's green eyes and freckled face for a long, lazy look. And this time he did not turn away when she eagerly looked back.

As she reached over to ladle another serving, he stared at her bare arms: black and purple bruises. She quickly pushed her sleeves down.

"Does he hit you, too?" Alex asked thinking of Raca.

"Only when no one can see. Alone in our cabin."

Her father? Appalled, Alex changed direction. "How old are you?"

"A bit older than you, I expect." Then she smirked. "Old enough to marry as soon as *Wasp* returns—or so my father threatens." Gant's words hung over her like a cold fog. For weeks she had slept poorly, hoping at sea she might earn back the affection he had sometimes shown her while her mother was alive, when he impatiently but diligently explained the methods of his trade—the commerce of smuggling and theft. Her only hope was if she obeyed, she might gain her freedom when this miserable voyage ended: freedom to continue her studies in Cambridge or New Haven; freedom to find a partner to love and respect; freedom to live a life without her father's disdain and constant, overpowering, and oppressive rages barricading her from her future.

As the ship sailed east however, instead of freedom, her father's temper rose by the day. He treated her cruelly no matter what she did or said. Early in the voyage he had only yelled and threatened. But once the Briggs boy refused to cooperate, Captain Gant started to slap *her*. And after the Navy stole *Wasp's* crew, Gant gave his daughter the back of his powerful hand at every perceived fault. Her body ached and she cried each night hoping to wake to a different dawn. She learned to stare back with wet eyes and tried to understand the reasons for his angry behavior.

But she knew: he blamed her for his beloved wife's death. Tears only brought on another beating. Silence was best though cowardly. She could not fight back.

"Why does he treat you so? You don't cross him... like I do." Alex smiled hoping to help.

She answered thoughtfully, "My father has always been an angry man. And now he's lonely since my mother died last spring." She rationalized his cruelty in simple terms but suspected his demons ran far deeper than the loss of her mother. "I clean his clothes and prepare his meals. On board I help cook and serve. Mostly I stay to myself. I read a lot. He doesn't listen to me. We don't talk much anymore." Her eyes moistened unintentionally. "He hits me for no reason... something he never did before. But enough. You're the one in danger, Alexander, not I. They talk about you. They need you desperately. But once they get what they want, they won't. Alexander—" She glanced around *Wasp's* lower deck and whispered softer, "They're planning to leave you behind."

"Behind? Where?"

"On an island."

The news was not entirely surprising. "Will I be alone on this island?"

She looked down and probed softly, "Are you asking if my father would leave you stranded?" Alex feared the answer. Pricilla said nothing and looked around.

"I will escape. We both will." He changed his mind about divulging all he knew to end the misery. He could not let her down. At least his beatings had been in the open. Pricilla suffered in darkness. "And Raca? Does he always watch you?"

"Yes. I have no privacy."

"We need someone to watch him."

"Who?"

"Perhaps Willy. He has eyes for you. He looks your way when you don't see it. He could help you. Help *us*. Be kind to him. But don't let Pierce see. He's a scoundrel."

Pricilla didn't like the sound of that. "What about the cook?"

"Perhaps. Have you seen how strong he is? He practically carried me up the mast."

"Isaiah is kind," Pricilla murmured.

"Then ask him to protect you. Ask him to help us."

"I believe he's your friend, Alex. But my father has a nose for mutiny. He shows no mercy to disloyal hands. Especially foreigners… never mind a black man. We must be careful who we talk to and what we say."

Isaiah was a curious fellow Alex reasoned in silence, agreeing with her caution. He seemed to stand between low and high tide, watching and waiting, following Gant's and Raca's orders without defiance but without enthusiasm either. Alex could endure the beatings and the pain but must tread with caution or find himself in chains again, his family doomed, the end of everything. But he regarded the meal prepared by Isaiah: large pieces of bacon spicing the chowder, firm new potatoes, and a wad of precious sweet butter. A healthy, generous serving any captain would admire.

Willy re-dressed his bandana tight around his wounded neck. Despite a daily change of bandages and washing with fresh water from the scuttlebutt, his raw wound was not healing by itself. He knew from previous fights that the neck was among the worst places to take a nick. But, happily for him, the neck was the ideal target for a thrust to kill.

"Yer not explainin' how you come at that."

"Aye, I am not." Willy avoided another of Pierce's queries as they sat together in a lonely mess, downing the worst dinner either cousin could remember. For Pierce it was a new low. Of late, hearty meals with fresh ale or a tot of whiskey were doled out only to the captain and his lackey Raca.

"You'd better run it by the cook. He'll close it up or you'll stink rank before we run ashore."

Willy knew Pierce was right; he nodded, wincing as he tied a tighter knot but sensed there was more behind his cousin's pestering. Even slowly, as it usually leaked out, Pierce kept his primary thinking to himself. It might take an hour or two or even days before he made his point clear, enough time to determine if it deserved a response.

"I see what you doin' with the girl." Pierce offered, hoping for a confession.

"She lights the darkness... any man would see the same."

"Aye, but any man don't take her into the shadows."

Willy stared at Pierce, a cousin yes, but an obtuse coward unless bolstered by scores of mates behind him. "You been following me?"

"It's a small ship, cousin. You're not making friends with the first mate. Everyone knows, except for the boy. He's daft as a pigeon." Pierce looked away hoping to direct his father's favorite nephew to his way of thinking. "She's leadin' him on, too. To help her if she comes to blows with the mate. Doin' the same with you."

"I can handle myself. Raca don't scare me... like he does you." Willy Harrison was not going to let family ties slow his growing passion or bend his backbone. He would soon confront the mate. He knew it. The girl deserved it.

"Aye, I know you can. I seen the blood on your pants when you stumble into the shed after a night in the *Cock 'n Bull*. I know you're handy and quick. And your knuckles find their way fast to the chin or the throat when the other bastard's lookin' to run. But we're kin." Pierce let the words drift in the silence only interrupted by the leeward side slush of passing water, creaking the knees above their head and the stays out of sight binding the entire enterprise like a spider to its web. "But unlike you, I been watching the mate dearly these past days. He's always been brutal, I'll give you. But something's changed. He looks at me the way a hound looks at a cat before he rips it apart. He'll murder someone before the end of this next leg, mark my words."

Willy did not respond. Pierce made sense. The mate seemed... rabid. Willy could see it—an explosion about to erupt like a waiting 18-pounder with a slow match. But Pierce was not finished.

"I'm guessin' you got some plans. With *her,* eh? Don't deny it cousin. You two'll slip the ship the moment we find the bottom in San Miguel. Captain'll curse and him and Raca will take it out on us who's left." Neither said a word for a long moment. Willy could not ignore the scenario. He had no wish to antagonize his cousin. "She may be the reason many leagues will come between us, Cousin. I can't lie to you."

"And leave your kin to suffer Raca's worst abuse?" They ate for a few minutes in silence. Willy, thinking of how much more he had to prepare for an escape for two missed Pierce setting a hook—barbed, sharpened, and taut.

"If your neck took the bastard's blade and looks as ugly as it does, I'm supposing he got it the worse, eh, Caesar?" Pierce feigned a smile.

Willy relaxed. "Aye, he got it worse."

"That bastard won't be seen at the *Cock'n Bull* any time again, I wager?"

"Aye, he won't." Willy smirked.

"You done killed the bugger?"

"I finished what he started."

Pierce leaned in, his breath hot with stolen rum. "Then we got a secret, don't we?" Willy stared into the air avoiding Pierce's face. Pierce pushed. "If it leaked out, a murder on the same night *Wasp* left Rochester. There'll be questions when we return."

"You wouldn't say anything."

"Raca's raging outta control, Willy boy! I need the protection of your knife to make sure he don't take it out on me. We're kin. If you leave this ship with the trollop—"

"Mind your bloody mouth!" Willy stood ready for an encounter. It would not be the first time between the two, but the first time he was so furiously motivated.

Pierce finished his piece, "...then I canna say what I'll tell them back home. But if you stay... We're kin, Willy boy. Leave her be. We'll make our way home, Raca or no Raca. We'll help the captain find his gold and get our squeeze. Forget her, Willy. She's gonna forget you."

At Pierce's urging, Willy finally asked Isaiah to tend his injury still open and painful weeks later. "Coop, why'd you tell them you're a cook?" Willy asked as Isaiah applied a mixture of herbs and oils to the thin red, puffy slice below his ear.

Choosing not to answer, Isaiah said, "This was close to your artery, Will. It might have cut through."

"Any rot?"

"I think not. Whatever caused this was sharp—and clean. You've been to the taverns again."

"Aye." Willy wondered if he should confide how it happened. He and Isaiah Cooper were not friends but had both worked in the Briggs' shipyard readying *Mary Celeste* for her last voyage. He suspected Coop was closer to Captain Briggs than most workers; rumors had him voyaging with the captain in his youth. Coop lived as a free man, a reward for some honorable action, he presumed. Willy liked the man, but on this ship, he dared not trust anyone. He wanted to know more about the owner's son and if three could escape with a future recompense. He knew Alex was brazen and obdurate, yet skilled in the kind of seamanship sailors admired. The older Briggs brother, however, was known far and wide for incompetence and disrepute. Yard workers said he was as foul as rat-infested bilge water.

"How well do you know Ezekiel Briggs?" Willy asked.

Isaiah looked at him carefully as he finished a clean cotton wrap. "He has a mean-spirit, Will. Not his father's son. Rochester's different now."

As Isaiah leaned close, Willy noticed Isaiah's own bandage. "You too have been injured recently, and you hid it, like I. I've never seen you in the taverns at night. Who did this to you?"

Isaiah rubbed his neck where the splinter had made a small incision, nicking a vital vessel. His wife's needle and thread had closed the wound, healing fast now as he changed bandages every watch. He pushed his bandage higher and did not answer Willy at first. Instead, he thought of the deadly men aboard: Raca, a killer. Willy who could likely counter Raca's violence. His own deadly capabilities Isaiah would keep to himself. And so it must remain.

"An accident, that's all. Nothing more to it. Will..." Isaiah lowered his voice. "...this is a dangerous ship. We're all in peril unless we find Captain Briggs alive. There's more in play than a rescue. Keep your knife by your side and don't let Raca get the better of your patience." He looked severely at the young man whose massive arms could break a man's neck. "It is known you got a mighty temper. Raca will use it to his advantage."

On a small unhappy ship, the mid-Atlantic Ocean is a forlorn place. For two days after the gale *Wasp* sailed smoothly, though slower than Gant would have liked, through warm skies of spongy clouds under endless stars. Life aboard the small ship returned to a stiff normality: six shifts of four hours each day and *Wasp's* small crew spent their hours trimming sails, making repairs, eating, and afterwards falling into exhausted sleep. Normal, except for Alex Briggs.

He woke abruptly each time Raca kicked him to stand watch. Gant did not trust Alex to steer and with his ankle injury he was unable to climb. He walked with a pained limp dragging his leg, and only with difficulty could he climb the companionway ladder. Leaving the dreary dampness below, on deck the clean sea air cheered him. As Alex pulled lines and set sails from deck, he noticed the seas had calmed overnight. *Wasp* ran comfortably but with a determined haste steadied by a strong westerly breeze. When he saw Pricilla standing alone amidships, he smiled; they enjoyed another long, private look. Rochester seemed so long ago. *Had it been only two weeks?* When *Wasp's* voyage began, Pricilla had kept quiet and stayed mostly below deck. With the skeleton crew, however, she stood a full watch, climbed masts, and set sails shouting answers from deck commands. She had quickly learned the fine points of the jobs high above and both he, and increasingly Willy, eagerly helped her. When they left Rochester, she had worn plain skirts with billowing blouses and a tight bonnet to contain her lustrous auburn hair. Now many leagues offshore her blond stresses shone sun-bleached and flew wild and loose pointing back at the ship's recently traveled course. Aloft she resembled a young sailor skipping from yard to mast, but close-up on deck her far better skin and sunset lips revealed a bright young woman, her fine feminine shape unmistakable even in a sailor's baggy clothes. Her creamy-white skin became accented with freckles and sunburn from the day's work, and her lips glowed like a ruby on white sand. Yet her eyes did not stay long on a person. They darted from deck to sky and back again, unsure. Despite her brave words it was clear she was terrified, afraid of talking out of turn or being overheard. The painful consequences of speaking her mind were evident in her constant, wary reticence, fleeting eyes, clasped hands, and always-nervous fingers.

The previous day while drinking water at the barrel set up on deck known to sailors as the scuttlebutt, Willy told Alex Raca's obsession with Pricilla was not new. The entire crew saw how

Raca lusted after her. Her father appeared dismissive, which every crewman thought unnatural. Cruel assumptions spread among lonely men far out at sea. The crew understood Pricilla was nothing like a port wench but still they fantasized. She had earned an education and read better than most of the learned men in Rochester. The captain's daughter was kind, fed the crewmen, and tended to them when they were sick or injured. But not one man dared cross the brute mate nor inform their captain how Raca bragged below deck how he intended to *have* her— and not by winning her heart; his intentions were vile even to men accustomed to such talk. Even Willy, tough and able, chose not to interfere. Though his ability with a knife equaled Raca's, he did not relish the idea of a fight to defend the girl's honor; besides, he was betrothed to a waiting south coast girl. He intended to return to her in one piece.

And so burdened, caught between two violent men, Pricilla Gant suffered in silence. Confined on a small ship on an endless sea, she had no place to hide. One man seemed intent to kill her. The other seemed indifferent, unless his drunken back-hand killed her first. As Alex pieced together the extent of her torment, he had no illusions about life's fairness. On board *Wasp*, this young woman existed in darkness and constant fear. He alone among her admirers, the least empowered and most susceptible to painful reprisal, vowed to act.

Despite his own injuries, Alex Briggs felt a breath of energy these past days. Pricilla had a great deal to do with it—he began to wonder if she was hope for a better life. He looked forward to every watch they shared, the private looks between them, and their small conversations. Each interaction with her renewed him.

His purpose for the voyage, however, remained determined. He must let nothing distract him: not the recovery of *Celeste*, not locating his father's fortune, not overcoming his fear of murderous sadists, not saving Pricilla Gant—a brave, terrified young woman whom he yearned to know better, to reach her soul and free her spirit—*nothing* must stop him. He started this voyage with one directive, and he must not fail to find his family before they perished. He felt guilty and a bit ashamed therefore when Pricilla earnestly asked after *his* well-being on account of his beatings and injuries. She asked every day and every night, on every watch, at meals, in passing. Alex looked forward to her quiet greetings.

"How do you do on this fine morning, Mr. Briggs?" she asked with a smile as he hobbled awkwardly toward her. Her eyes welcomed him to a bright morning of promise. He shrugged intending to dishonestly win even a bit more sympathy than he deserved.

"Uneasy," he answered, thinking ahead. "I wonder if I'll find my parents... I wonder if there's anyone besides you I can count on."

Pricilla looked at him carefully. She took his arm. She wondered about many things too: Would some young man take her away from here? Would she meet her death before she next saw land? Would her father ever come to forgive her, to love her again? These past few days she felt different in her sailor's clothes. She felt a freedom like never before. After climbing the mast and saving Alex in the storm, everyone—even Raca, Willy, and her father—looked at her differently. When she climbed now to furl or release a sail, she felt alive. In the wind, moving free high on the masts, she reveled in the serenity and safety up high, away from the dangers below. Sometimes she sat on the maintop platform and rested for an hour or more. She brought her knees to her chin, her arm hanging around a tensioned rope and looked at the stars, sunsets, or sunrises and smiled, remembering her mother and a happier life when the promise of a new baby portended renewed joy for the family. She also thought about the two handsome young men always watching her from the deck. Alex's life dangled on an edge as thin as the ropes she held in her blistered hands. The dangers he faced kept her awake every night. The way he looked at her, however, coupled with her heightened eagerness to see him every watch, made her wonder if their future was linked. But then she'd see Willy wave from below, tip his cap, and she felt a different kind of thrill. Life was indeed confusing.

It was clear her father was annoyed she wore a sailor's garb, but he had no option until they reached shore for her to dress otherwise. Perhaps he privately admired how she handled her duties aloft. But her painful bruises and scrapes reminded her of his ritual cruelty when launched cabin china broke and tears flowed. And she sensed Raca would do her deadly harm if he caught her alone again. The more she complained about the first mate's unwanted attention, the more it angered her father. One night, Gant threw her to the cabin floor telling her she was encouraging the mate. Pricilla's head crashed hard against the bulkhead. Her father's next well-aimed blow during a rum-soaked night might be her last memory. And so, she befriended Alex and spent all her quiet time close to him. She stayed apart from her father except in their cabin where they each had their own sleeping berth with thin pine panels separating the two, barely masking his digestive eruptions, though effectively smothering her quiet tears. They ate together in a silent temporary truce, her father a fulminating volcano of confusion and anger, frustrated ambition, and obsessed drive. What drove him so, what lay behind his force and fury, she could only surmise. She prayed he might talk to her and explain. He refused.

Pricilla remembered a kinder man who had carefully shown her the ropes, the sails, and the charts. She fondly recalled nights sitting with her mother reading quietly by the hearth, her father smoking a scrimshaw pipe, complaining about some crewman or business partner. It was not long ago, his eyes clear and steady not clouded by drink, when he was as eager as her mother for the new baby—they all were.

Her father's most recent orders resonated harshly: Raca and his boots had failed so her father told her it was up to her now to learn from the boy what the beatings had not. She had neither agreed nor refused but took the course most likely to avoid his hand; on this bright morning, he was sure to be watching from somewhere.

Pricilla looked over her shoulder and smiled tentatively. "Did you ever hear from your father after he sailed from Rochester?" she asked smoothly.

"He said he'd write from New York and tell me more about his voyage. I believe he had plans in motion concerning our company." Alex admitted more to Pricilla's simple smile than he had to Raca who almost beat him to death.

"Nothing else? Not a message or a messenger?"

Alex stopped short and looked at her. She did not blink or look away. Was she her father's agent? He wanted to trust her. Without help his family would surely die.

"No."

She looked around the deck a second and a third time. She took a deep breath. Perhaps, she told herself, she could have it both ways. "Alex, I have something to tell you. Your father did write to you. He sent you a letter. He was—" Pricilla paused for a moment before continuing, "...*is* proud of you. He also asked someone to watch out for you while he was away."

"Watch out for *me*—who? How do you know this?" He squeezed her arm where she was newly bruised, and she pulled back angrily, almost changing her mind.

"Please, let me go." She rubbed her injured arm. To continue talking this way with Alex might result in far worse. She then said slowly, "...*my* father stole a letter *your* father wrote to you. He took it from the county post office before it got to your house. He does this all the time. He knows *everything* about your father's business." Her eyes flashed with anger. Alex said nothing. She sighed.

"You know more about my parents' disappearance than I," he replied.

"I read stolen letters to him. Sometimes I make copies. Send the originals along. No one knows about this. My father poached a letter your father wrote weeks ago. I read it to him, resealed it carefully, and then sent it to your house on Water Street. My father assumes you read it. He assumes you understand his questions."

"I never got a letter from my father…" His voice trailed off. He knew Ezekiel habitually scoured their incoming posts. "…my brother must have it. I never heard from my father after he left. *You* read it? What did it say? *You* know what's going on? *Everyone but me* knows what's going on!"

"Shhh!" She looked around to be sure no one was watching or listening. "I can explain." Alex was astounded as she whispered, "His message was: 'Don't trust Ezekiel.'"

"My *father* wrote this—?"

"Be civil. Listen! 'Avoid his new associates…'" Alex had been nervous when Manny G. skulked about their boat yard—hands in pockets, looking over his shoulder with dull grey eyes. "Someone called '*T.S.*' will help you… help you find something quite valuable."

"My father keeps a chest on board with papers, receipts and stuff, but nothing valuable. All our gold sits in Boston banks, some working cash in New Bedford. He might have taken a few letters of credit on foreign banks, but that's all."

Pricilla looked at him amazed. *He doesn't know.* "Is that what Ezekiel told you?" Alex nodded. He tried to remember Ezekiel's exact words but had paid so little attention to anything his brother ever said. He regretted it now. "Your father wrote he stored *gold* in his seachest. A *great deal* of gold. And he hid the chest in a secret compartment deep in *Mary Celeste* where no one could ever find it. However, this '*T.S.*' whoever he is, could lead you to it."

Alex recalled bits of his last fraternal evening meal. "My brother told me father's chest contained papers, correspondence, bills… petty cash—but he never mentioned gold." *Ezekiel had lied. This entire voyage is based on lies!* It gave Alex confidence to learn at least his father tried to share his plans and warn him.

He had not been abandoned. He had been left at home to ensure a future for the family despite his brother's insidious plans. But why could his father not convey this before he sailed away? Why keep Alex in darkness for weeks? *I'm in worse danger now than anything Ezekiel might have done!*

"My father thinks you know where the gold is hidden on board *Mary Celeste*."

"I don't." Alex fumed. Gant had played Ezekiel, Alex, *and* his father for fools!

Pricilla's eyes shot from the foredeck to taffrail. Raca could hide in plain sight. Her father could hear a cat purr through a hurricane's wail. Cook had been strangely distant of late. And except for Pierce steering and Willy forward watching the jib's trim, she and Alex were alone. The only sounds were waves slapping dully against the wooden hull squeaking as it rose in the swells. They had otherwise enjoyed the quiet morning at sea. Pricilla sensed Alex Briggs' anger at learning the truth of the voyage; her voice dropped lower. She placed a single long slender finger on the top of his hand.

"Alexander, I believe you. But my father thinks you're lying."

Alex ignored her hand. He should have realized this was no rescue mission the minute Gant did not welcome him on board. Gant had no intention of searching for the lost crew of *Mary Celeste*. With his father's strongbox, *Wasp* and *Mary Celeste* as a fleet of fast smugglers, Gant would never return to Rochester. This rescue voyage was nothing but a greedy hunt on a miserable little ship to steal money. Alex had been outwitted by a jealous brother and a petty smuggler while his parents and sister were possibly still alive, scanning an empty horizon hoping and waiting for rescue. The Briggs' second son remained their only hope.

"I never got a letter from my father... Ezekiel must have taken it. This explains why he agreed to charter *Wasp* without much of an argument. Ezekiel wants the strongbox, too." Alex realized suddenly that her hand remained resting on his. He looked at her eyes and tried to read her. "I want your father to find my family! Nothing else matters."

"Then I shall tell him so," said Pricilla.

What happens to me then? Alex wondered. The truth was dangerous, conceding it unnecessary. He was alive and needed above deck, better than chained in the bilge.

"No, Pricilla. Don't say anything. He'll need me to sail *Wasp* home to Rochester. He needs me to get on board *Mary Celeste*. Better that he believes I can find the strongbox. I do know the ship. I've sailed her many times with my father. Perhaps once I am on board again and see—" He decided to tell her nothing more. Alex knew he could not counter Raca's strength or Gant's brutal determination. But perhaps with a plan of action and with a little help he might save his family. He regarded Pricilla's intense beauty so close beside him. Was she also keeping her thoughts private? Despite the risk she took—having told Alex her father's secret—he wondered on which shore she stood. *No matter*, he reminded himself—*my father trusted me with the future of our family. I must not fail. I must find them. Pricilla must choose her own shore.* "Let your father continue to assume I read my father's letter. At least until we find my family. Will you do this for me?"

He was asking her to lie although he knew she would suffer. She did not answer. Alex placed his hand gently on top of hers. She turned her palm upwards and embraced his fingers. Like floating strands of silky kelp, intertwined, she felt his warmth and looked at his injured, intent face. *It must be now*, Alex thought. He had to make Pricilla believe in him and turn away from her father and help find the lost crew, perhaps to save their own lives. She nodded and trembled, whether in fear or relief he could not discern. His eyes never strayed from hers. He knew his future was as unsure as a single drop of salt spray flying through morning air, landing wherever the breeze chose.

A random wave hit the windward hull. *Wasp's* deck suddenly rose and dropped. Pricilla looked about, alarmed. The moment had passed. She reclaimed her hand. "But my father is *so* angry with this voyage, with your father—with me. But most of all, he's angry with *you*." She looked at him intently. "And Raca! He's rabid. Even Willy says so, Alexander! He could crush you like a rat under his boot. He hates you. He breaks other young men, but you don't cower."

"I'll watch Raca, don't worry." Alex was not thinking about Raca. His mind raced ahead. Momentum was churning his path like an incoming tide.

Pricilla nodded slowly, for the first time feeling a bit reassured. This young man was smart, balanced, and heading on a straight course, no longer just a rich boy from their village. She knew she would follow him but was afraid where it led. She took his arm in hers and rested her head on his shoulder. Perhaps touching him would give her the strength she needed. She did not care who was watching.

Alex winced from his wounds and aching ribs. But despite the pain he was happy Pricilla's head rested on him. He felt her hair brush his bare neck and lacerated cheek. He thought about what she had admitted: *She reads all her father's correspondence. Clearly the captain enjoys excellent vision. So, this means...* Alex needed to think like his father and fill his quiver with the honed shafts of deception. Alexander Briggs and Pricilla Gant stood close together, watching the waves roll east. Not another word passed between them for the rest of the watch. They did not need words to tell them what must happen.

Below deck under a candle dripping cheap and musty tallow, a well-used knife was carefully sharpened. It bragged a steel blade able to cut through a man's muscles and a razor edge sharp enough to split a single strand of human hair.

For three days, *Wasp* enjoyed fair, dependable winds and a gentle rolling sea. Gant steered as they approached the archipelago of the Azores Islands 950 miles off the Portugal coast. Long before becoming a captain, he had visited when Sao Miguel had been a busy port provisioning southern ocean whalers. Because the largest of these islands were spread many miles from each other, separated by deep ocean water and violent currents, transit in small crafts between the islands was dangerous. The captain steered to the largest of nine islands, Sao Miguel, passing Pico with its high, snow-shrouded peak, and Sao Jorge with its busy commercial center. Ezekiel had sent a note to Gant informing him *Mary Celeste* would be found anchored among the whalers waiting for water and food in Sao Miguel's modest harbor. Hoping he had bested the Navy frigate in his race to the Azores, Gant nevertheless remained anxious, furious with the sea, the winds, and the gods. He itched impatiently to sail faster but had not the crew to hoist all *Wasp's* sails. He could barely find enough arms and legs to jibe, come about, or trim. And without his fighting boys, his only remaining hope was to get aboard *Celeste* before the U.S. Navy arrived to enforce a suffocating political policy. His daughter had obediently worked the letter entrusted to him by Lieutenant Barker. He hoped to be away with the *Celeste* before their deception was discovered. He charted escape routes north and east—but not west. With luck, there would be no reason to sail west ever again. But if this gambit failed, his only remaining option was to get the willing cooperation of young Alexander Briggs. *He knows the game*, Gant told himself, *but like his father he lies to my face!*

During the day Alex avoided Raca, increasingly drunk and unsteady. But at night, Raca found him and demanded the same answers to the same questions. He kicked Alex's raw and opens wounds and slugged him in his unhealed, bruised ribs. In pain, Alex retreated to his hammock after each watch. He thought of asking Isaiah to sleep next to him for protection. He thought of asking Pricilla to help as well but feared she would give away the truth in order to stanch her own beatings. As the voyage dragged easterly, she rarely showed herself after darkness fell unless on watch. She smiled and spoke briefly to Alex when they met on deck, but he did not tell her or anyone about Raca's ongoing, increasingly vicious attacks. He wondered if Raca was now beating him for his own amusement or if Gant had settled on a deliberate strategy of relentless, mindless torture to weaken Alex's resolve.

Without a weapon, Alex could not overpower Raca's muscles *and* weapons—a knife proudly displayed in his belt. And so, Alex carried on, marking their last miles to the islands wondering what would happen after *Wasp* dropped anchor. Would he be allowed to board his father's ship? Could he read *Celeste's* logbook and search for clues? Sometimes Pricilla joined him as he stood by the rail in the early morning. They talked about Rochester, people they knew, stories of town. They did not talk about the harsh life aboard *Wasp*. No one discouraged Alex and Pricilla from speaking daily—freely—these last days before landfall. Alex was aware Gant watched as they stood by a rail or shared a meal in the shade of the main course. Alex considered the captain might expect his daughter to learn more with charm than Raca had with bloody force—a likely tactic. Alex Briggs decided to play his game.

"You never told me what you think happened, Alexander?"

She and Alex stood alone watching clouds change to orange and red. The scorching sky meant a familiar westerly wind would push them comfortably for at least another day.

"As soon as I see her ship's longboats, I'll know," replied Alex. "If they're missing, the crew might be still alive. If the boats remain secured, I'll look to her spars. If she has damage to her rigging—broken lines and snapped studding sail booms—I'll know another ship came alongside, perhaps pirates. I'll look for evidence of an armed boarding on her hull: I helped paint *Celeste's* topsides last spring. If she has scratches, damaged rails, splinters, or broken planks—it'll mean the ship had been taken. And we'll receive a ransom letter. It's widely reported we're wealthy."

"But why would pirates abandon a perfectly good ship?"

"Perhaps my father said the crew was diseased. Maybe it was true." Neither scenario seemed likely though. His father would have found a way to stay alive and save his crew. Nor would he have surrendered the ship without a fight. "I'll look to see if her cannon fired. An approaching threat would have received a warning shot." Except if a ship attacked in the dark of night. Or was a man-of-war like *Bill of Rights*. "My father's clever," Alex continued. "When I was young, he'd tell me stories of famous battles between sail-of-the-line ships blasting their cannon at enemy ships only fifty feet apart. He described how sailors steered these massive sea fortresses blindly through smoke and musket shot, how cannonballs ripped through torn sails, each ship trying to find a weather advantage so gun crews could find a target. He told me stories straight from his imagination—of myths and magic, of sea witches and narwhales, of giant squid crushing whaleboats in its beak, stories about hurricanes sucking ships from the sea casting them miles inshore, stories of slavers and ghost ships."

"Quite the imagination," Pricilla murmured.

Breathless, Alex continued, "Yes. He told fabulous stories, Pricilla. And I never grew tired of them. He never told the same story twice. New adventures came out of his head like bees from a hive." Alexander Briggs looked out at an empty sea and closed his eyes. "I remember how he smelled. His clean shirts were immersed with sweet pipe smoke. And his eyes flickered like a candle atop a lighthouse." Alex turned away from the waves and looked into her eyes, fixed on his, fascinated. His face opened wide, and his tone softened. "I wager my father invented a clever story to save their lives. Pricilla, I'll bet he tricked them."

Twenty days sailing from Rochester, a few minutes after eight o'clock on a humid morning, low hanging clouds on a near horizon foretold land was near.

"Ten degrees to larboard. Land under!" Alex bellowed.

Word spread fast below deck. Willy at the wheel hooted his excitement. The cries of joy brought Gant from below with Raca and Pierce close behind. Cook and Pricilla followed.

"Did you say 'larboard' or 'starboard' boy?" Gant had his glass in his hand furiously looking to his right doubting his navigation.

"Larboard, Captain—look!"

Gant looked north and went below to check his charts. He returned quickly shouting to Willy. "Down fifteen degrees! They're inhabited out-islands. We shall stay south." His meaning was clear: as *Wasp* approached Sao Miguel, they would not sail close enough to see any sign of *Mary Celeste's* castaway crew on this secluded shore.

"But we have plenty of depth—sailing closer won't cost you *any* time! Off fifteen degrees out here we can't see anything!" Alex yelled as he strode up to the captain, then wishing he had another 50 pounds.

"I will not search *until* I have the strongbox," Gant's eyes narrowed.

"But these islands sit down-current. *Celeste's* boats might have washed up here…!"

Gant meant what he said. "Clean yourself. We'll meet with Portuguese authorities as soon as we anchor… *then* we'll search. Put on rich-man clothes, shoes and stockings, too. I want your face and hair presentable. Cook, change his bandages and feed him." *Master Alexander Briggs has motivation to make this voyage a success,* thought Captain Gant. *Let us assist him.*

As Alex climbed down the companionway ladder, Raca kneed him hard in his lower back. He carefully chose the location where he had brutally jammed a belaying pin between his ribs the night before. Alex cried out, crumpled and nearly fell.

"Stop it! If you hurt him again, I swear…!" Pricilla raged.

"Eh? You'll swear? Aye, you'll swear! I'll hear your sweet swearin' when your mouth's breathin' close to my ear, eh?"

Alex regained his balance and turned to his attacker. "Once we find my family, I'm going to kill you." Whether it was Pricilla's angry voice coming to his defense or the searing pain, something finally snapped.

Isaiah was correct. A fight to the death was coming. But Alex decided he would select the time and place. *I will have the advantage. Not here, not now.* Not with the light and freedom the day gave his oppressor.

Gant followed, having missed seeing Raca's assault but he did hear his daughter's angry cry. Even so, the captain spoke only to Alex, "You've threatened a ship's officer, Mr. Briggs. Your words will be recorded in the log. If any misfortune should happen to Mr. Raca, we'll know who to hang."

Raca smirked and was about to punch Alex again in retaliation, but Gant's stern look indicated '*enough*'. The mate leered at Alex and saw abject hatred in the boy's face. Raca's smile disappeared.

Two hours later on a dying breeze, *Wasp* entered Sao Miguel's small, shallow harbor. The protected bay was surrounded on three sides with bold, rocky cliffs, a rocky beach, and mountains of green firs. Slopes slid abruptly into a small town filled with tight rows of brightly colored, single-story homes, storehouses and fish shacks leading to a central wharf jutting out 100 feet from a stone building on stilts where a Portuguese flag fluttered in the languid air. The crew could not discern any forts with protruding cannon protecting the anchorage from seaward. A small battery inside the anchorage remained a possibility, however. On the far shore near the rocky beach two whaling ships anchored. Their canvas sails hung limp drying in morning's gentle breeze. In the middle of the harbor sat two merchant ships moored near one another, swinging according to the incoming tide. Alex instantly recognized *Mary Celeste* and a nearby packet he assumed was *Halifax*. He held the spyglass tight as they sailed around the bight. Straining to see *Celeste* through the glare on the glassy harbor waters, he finally got an unhindered view: *Mary Celeste* sat quiet at anchor floating high above her waterline. Her two tall masts rose securely in place and all her spars appeared undamaged. Her rigging, however, fell slack. Sails were loosely and carelessly reefed. Most appeared torn. Secured carelessly, *Mary Celeste*, a smart vessel and well-built, looked disheveled and sad. For such a beloved ship, she floated in desperate need of repair.

Despite her deplorable condition, Alex's heart soared: her three longboats were missing.

*W*asp dropped her day anchor conspicuously close to *Mary Celeste* as if to claim her in view of the world. Gant watched armed Portuguese guards on board the quarantined ship waiting with muskets in hand as *Wasp* approached swiftly from windward. He counted six uniforms on *Celeste's* deck and then trained his spyglass on the nearest shore where he saw two small cannon with crews at the ready on a seawall above the beach. This was no day for a fight. The Portuguese were prepared. Captain Gant was not.

Gant considered his pathetic crew: Raca, an obtuse moron yet a weapon unto himself; Willy with only a poorly concealed long knife; Pierce dully chewing a stick to clean his teeth; Alex limping, his spanking fresh clothes barely disguising seeping, bloodstained bandages; a quiet, middle-age cook with an unsettling strength that the voyage had seemed to restore. And his increasingly reclusive daughter with her accusing glances. *Damn her insolence and her newly affected limp.* He was sure he had not kicked her that hard.

"Willy and Pierce, stay aboard *Wasp*. Clean her tidy and put a tight furl where you can. Liberty when we return but not a drop out of my cabin or, by God, I'll string you up." He turned to the others. "Briggs, Raca, with me. Daughter, you and Cook buy fresh provisions, port and claret for me, rum for the boys. You might buy a dress."

Willy and Pierce, along with a wounded Alex, struggled to hoist the heavy longboat by the davits. They swung it over the side and released its supporting lines carefully, lowering the boat foot by foot into the placid harbor.

Gant leaned over to Raca. "Prime and load both pistols. Hide one in your shirt and give me the other. If he says even one wrong word..."

Raca smiled obscenely, his mangled teeth—part rotted, others ripped out after one drunken brawl or another—broadly displaying his anticipated pleasure like a lonely sailor eyeing a seedy brothel. "Aye, Captain."

Preparing to climb through the gate from the deck, Gant grabbed Alex's arm harshly. "You know what I want, boy. In Rochester they say you've got smarts, though I've seen little sign of it. I need to get onto *Mary Celeste* without guards. You're the owner—tell them."

"My brother gave me instructions," Alex retorted planning to ignore everything Ezekiel had commanded.

"Mr. Raca will plunge his knife into your gut if you turn against me. You'll never get back on board *Wasp* alive." For the first time, Gant threatened to separate Alex and Pricilla forever.

It worked. Gant, Alex, and Raca rowed to shore without speaking. They walked in file up the short pier, Alex looking for possible escape routes to the hills, Raca watching his every move. They entered a small tidy office of Sao Miguel's port-warden who had been expecting a ship from America to reclaim the recovered brig. He was not happy to see them; he did not offer chairs.

Earlier that morning, portly, white-bearded Captain James Breton had also watched *Wasp* approach the anchorage. With an air of condescending authority, the sturdy professional mariner was determined to keep the Yankee ship he had salvaged. As a Lieutenant and finally a post-captain in His Majesty's service, Breton's career languished largely because of a lack of enemy action. Thrown ashore without a command, he offered his services to the East India Company and began to ply the West Indies packet trade. Captain Breton's hips ached with a constant reminder of the wasted war against these people in the year '14 when a Yankee privateer, *Rattlesnake*, made a smart move around a ledge and put a broadside of six 18-pounders into the undefended stern of Breton's frigate blasting shards of the taffrail through his thigh. In '82, Yankee militiamen had also killed his two brothers in the Carolinas. Breton had good reason in bulk for his antipathy toward these people. Studying the newly arrived brig through his glass he saw an eerie resemblance to that treacherous privateer.

Instead of sailing to London with his soon-to-spoil cargo, he had waited patiently in the Azores to learn the fate of *Mary Celeste*. Captain Breton determined no Yankee scab would cheat him out of his prize. With taught naval discipline he prepared the two ships for sea, his crew readied for a violent confrontation with the Americans. And although cannon shot has its place, today he must follow Nelson's balance of strategy and diplomacy tinged with stealth and topped off with brutal ruthlessness. Today's encounter must serve as recompense for his lost years. As soon as this new ship anchored leaving her sails only roughly furled, Breton had raced ashore. Stranded in Sao Miguel for weeks as *Halifax's* claim went to London, Breton was desperate for a decision. The port-warden commanded *Halifax* to sit tight, but Captain Breton's patience with corrupt port authorities was spent. He had gold—payment for a successful voyage to the West Indies—and he calculated carefully the going rate for a blind eye. The port officer had not yet accepted his offer.

Breton watched the American brig anchor and her longboat lowered. He hurried to beat them to the Portuguese official's office to ensure his proffered gold had its intended effect. From the far-left side of the room, he sneered as the Yankees strode proudly into the low-ceilinged office.

He did not shake hands with the Americans. Instead, he stared at the master who towered over the assembled, a man larger than him by weight and height. But no match, Breton was confident, to his own familiarity with European custom. Yankees were heathens and uncultured fools; this one likely no different.

Captain Gant spoke first to the room: Port-Warden Evaristo Gabriel, Captain James Breton and his mate, Stephen Levy. Raca, with a loaded pistol and knife hidden in his trousers, slouched behind Gant who kept his arm heavy upon Alex's shoulder.

"My name's Quartus Gant, Captain of *Wasp*. The lad here is Alexander Briggs of Briggs and Sons who owns *Mary Celeste* anchored yonder. We're bringing her home to the United States," Gant said his last words slowly, confidently. *Wasp* had won her race against Lieutenant Barker's *USS Bill of Rights*. Gant would gamble everything on an implied threat.

Captain Breton of *Halifax* responded with thinly veiled condescension, "Gentlemen, gentlemen. Great Britain and the United States are friends again. We each are our most important partners for trade and commerce. What we have here is not a dispute between our countries, only a disagreement about salvage procedures. *Halifax* found *Mary Celeste* adrift and in disrepair. Abandoned in mid-ocean. We took possession and, at great cost to our voyage and risk to our safety, brought her into Sao Miguel. We pumped and kept her afloat. We have taken nothing, disturbed nothing. By rule of maritime law, a shipwrecked vessel becomes the property of whomever salvages her. This would be *Halifax*. Gentlemen, these facts are beyond dispute."

Without turning to acknowledge Captain Breton, Captain Gant responded to the air over the head of the Portuguese authority with a declaration as blunt as the force Raca had dealt Alex's ribcage, "*Mary Celeste* is a private vessel and flies a United States flag. We're taking her home." Gant then turned and threatened Breton, "The U.S. Navy could charge you with piracy." Gant reached into his pocket and waved the sealed Navy letter. *Was the seal tampered with?* Alex wondered. He had come across Pricilla intent and head down on a document the day before. She scooped up the paper and did not show it to him. He knew she was skilled at her father's correspondences. *Had she other hidden spurious talents?* "I carry orders from Captain Stephen Coughlin of *USS Bill of Rights*, forty-four guns out of New York. She'll arrive here in the next day or two and will confirm we're authorized to repossess *Mary Celeste*." Raca edged closer to Alex and pressed his injured back. "Our Navy will protect American merchantmen and enforce international maritime law."

Port-Warden Gabriel refused Gant's offered letter. Instead, he spoke with authority familiar with merchant seamen and their bluster. "No one is charging anyone with piracy. My instructions come from Lisbon not the United States, Señor. I will comply with the salvage court's order when we get it. And if anyone threatens violence, I shall impound *all* American vessels moored in Sao Miguel!"

Gant's bluff had failed.

Alex grasped the opportunity. "Captain Breton, Sir. When you first encountered *Mary Celeste,* was she underway?"

Suspicious, Captain Breton looked at the young gentleman with the wounded face.

"She was drifting in a gale."

"Sails hoisted?"

"All sails, aye, torn and loose. *Drifting*," he said slowly and sarcastically. "And this damned *drifting* ship nearly sank us."

"And you could determine from your deck in a storm *Mary Celeste* was 'abandoned'?

"Aye. Anyone could see it."

"You could tell from hundreds of yards away—in a gale—no crew was on board?"

"I knew she was not manned."

"But how did you know she was abandoned?"

The British Captain turned from Alex. "I don't understand…" he said to Port-Warden Gabriel "…why a Captain of His Majesty's merchant services must submit to questions from this young—"

"Because I am the owner of Briggs and Sons, and you have stolen one of my father's ships!" Alex shouted as if to an equal.

"I'll oblige you though everyone here knows I am within my rights as salvager of a shipwrecked vessel—"

"To my point, Sir!" The British captain had made a critical error in the term he selected. Alex pounced. "A 'shipwreck' defines a ship helpless, hard aground or stuck on a reef. Or high and dry on a beach with a hole in her hull and her masts down. But when you found *Mary Celeste*, she was *sailing*—not shipwrecked. She was not *wrecked* at all." Alex turned to Stephen Levy, *Halifax's* flaccid mate standing next to Breton. Levy shrank. "Was she 'wrecked' or 'sailing' when you found her, sir?"

The mate looked terrified and turned to Captain Breton, but Port-Warden Gabriel spoke first, "Yes, I wondered myself. Describe for me her exact condition when you first came upon her?"

"Ship-shape, sir," The mate answered, hat in hand, hair in eyes. "Everything in order."

"So *not* wrecked," stated Alex.

"Wrecked?" Levy looked at his angry skipper and backed off. "No, not exactly wrecked, but not Bristol-like tidy either. Not tidy at all, sir. Lines all about and sails ripped and flapping, stays were limp, and her wheel was spinning loose. She had three feet in her bilge…"

"But her hull and rig were in-tact. Correct?" Alex stared at the nervous mate who looked again to his Captain. When he did not hear an answer Alex completed his own question, "She was in-tact, sir, and able to sail. Sailing *on her own* was she not? Not wrecked in any way. Correct?"

The port-warden looked at Captain Breton for clarification. The story took a different twist. Marveling at Alex's hubris, Gant added nothing to the inquisition.

"*Mary Celeste* has become the property of His Majesty's merchant services," came Captain Breton's retort with a haughty tone meant to end the heated argument as if he were the master of the house addressing the downstairs servants.

The port-warden did not like the angry looks in his crowded office and suspected his guards outside were not the only armed men nearby. He opened a window. He wished he had asked Corporal Soars to step inside. He spoke quickly, "A claim by *Halifax* was sent by packet to London last week. In another week we'll get a ruling, after which, I will allow ships to weigh anchor with their respective owners—new or otherwise."

"I have more questions, Sir, if you please," said Alexander Briggs. "Captain Breton, when you rowed across to *Celeste*, was there nobody on board?"

"Aye."

"Not my father, not my mother, not my nine-year-old sister? No sailors? No one at all? Not a dog or a cat?"

"There were cats," Breton sneered.

"Why should we blindly accept your story?" Alex challenged Captain Breton and Levy. "Perhaps events did not happen the way you claim. Perhaps there *was* a crew aboard *Mary Celeste* when you found her. Maybe they were sick or injured. Perhaps something worse happened to them *after* you discovered them? Perhaps there's blood on your hands, Captain!"

Gant had not anticipated such a ferocious verbal assault. His young prisoner surprised him. The tension heightened.

"Son, do you accuse an officer commanding one of His Majesty's vessels of *murder*?" Breton cried.

"What do you want us to believe, Captain?" Relentless, Alex bit off his words sharply. "That you found a sound new-built ship with valuable cargo containing sugars, oils, beaver, and corn sitting there in the middle of the ocean?" It was clear to Breton that Alex also knew the contents of her manifest. "Did you believe she was waiting for a lucky captain like you to scoop her up? Who'll believe this fiction? London? The United States Navy won't!"

Captain Breton's tone shifted. It took every ounce of his control to speak slowly, "We came upon *Mary Celeste* drifting. There was no violence done to her people on our account. You have my oath." Captain Breton looked soberly at Gant and the port-warden. Piracy and murder on the high seas was a capital offense in Great Britain, the United States *and* Portugal. Breton faced Alex directly, and added, his tone forbearing, "I am sorry about your family, son. We did not harm them. We did not find them."

Alex stood his ground. "So you say." He looked to Gant as if they were confederates. Then he looked darkly at Breton and turned less confrontationally to Port-Warden Gabriel. He almost lost his nerve to ask the next. Up to this point anger had driven his words. He must think like the port-warden, not a rich man's belligerent son. "What say you, Sir? *Celeste* obviously is not a salvage situation, so you need not wait for a court ruling. My family is missing. Will you release our ship so we can search for them? We must try to save the lives of twenty people, among them my father, mother, and young sister. Two ships can cover more leagues than one. Won't you help us, Senõr?"

The port master squirmed facing a delicate situation. He had handled other salvage cases most often favoring the salvagers. But he understood the lad's point and even a legal man could conclude *Mary Celeste* was not a *wreck*. This might not be a matter of salvage at all, but of theft—and possibly murder. If he ruled wrong, he risked censure and recall to Lisbon. He enjoyed Sao Miguel's climate. He weighed the boy's plea against the Englishman's generous offer.

Gabriel listened with keen attention as Breton responded, "Sir, *of course* we're dealing with salvage—we found her with not a living soul on board! She'd be on the bottom if we hadn't manned her damned pumps!" Captain Breton was losing composure he swore he would control.

"*When* Captain Gant and I find my father, this becomes a situation of *temporarily* displaced crew—*not* a wrecked or

170

abandoned ship. She is neither lost nor abandoned when her captain reappears. Perhaps the crew was stranded on an island after they went ashore to hunt or enjoy a picnic."

"She ain't got no longboats," interjected Raca, speaking out of rank.

For a long uncomfortable moment, the men stared at Raca.

"Are you saying, lad, your father let his ship sail away without him while he was engrossed in a *picnic*?" Captain Breton sneered.

"No, but everyone here understands my meaning. *Mary Celeste* was not wrecked *or* abandoned. A ship cannot be abandoned if her owner rejoins her. I am her lawful owner. Even if my father finds himself presently indisposed—*I* am here. And I intend to rejoin her!"

Gant grunted. *Well played.*

Captain Breton appealed directly to Port-Warden Gabriel, "*Halifax* carries citrus fruits from the West Indies. They will soon spoil. We must weigh anchor. We need an answer, or we won't make our market!"

"You could make *mar-malade* with your stinkin' fruit, mate." Raca spoke out inappropriately once again as Gant stared him into the floor.

Port-Warden Gabriel ignored the interruption but had little choice. A new claim appeal from Alexander Briggs and his brother would go out on a packet to London on the morning's tide returning in due time. *Celeste* was not going anywhere until the administrator had a safe answer covering whatever decision he might make. "It may be weeks before we get a ruling," Gabriel said, "and you people of *Wasp* stay away from *Mary Celeste*." To *Halifax*'s Captain, Gabriel added, "You can leave now or wait. Either way *Mary Celeste* remains in quarantine. Good day."

Captain Gant led the way out of the port-warden's office with huffs and *humpfs* echoing from Raca. Gant thought he knew this man Breton who stood between him and a fortune. In some decrepit watering hole on a forlorn shore, he and the Englishman must have once crossed paths—or swords. The bottle in his cabin would help him remember.

"We can start the search now." Alex said to Gant as they rowed back to *Wasp*. He chose with care not to frame it as a question never mind a request. He would not relinquish his role as charter-master.

"The strongbox remains on *Celeste*. We'll stay close to her until I get it," Gant retorted.

"But waiting on a ruling will take too long! If my family is alive, they might be dead by then…"

"Boy, your parents are dead *already*! We both know it. No one survives in small craft for weeks. It don't happen. If we see longboats run up someplace on our return, I'll investigate."

'…*perhaps*…' Alex thought he heard. Were his leather-wrapped oar not shipped tight into his oarlock, he would put this bastard overboard with a blow heard in Greenland.

Raca smirked from his seat next to Alex as they pulled in unison. Alex kept silent. Raca did not. His greasy sneer implied all the foul intentions on a helpless victim his morbid imagination could conjure.

"Aye, Captain, and when we get aboard *Celeste*, we'll tear her apart, right? We'll leave her bilge to last, in case he hid his strongbox in Master Briggs' quarters. Don't forget the molasses boy!"

Alex needed a plan. Once Gant found his father's strongbox, he would have no reason to search for its rightful owner. The captain and his ignorant lackey would sail to a foreign shore and live the life of smuggler princes. If, however, he got onto *Celeste* but *did not* find a chest—if Gant thought Alex was lying and hiding what he knew—Gant would stay closer to *Celeste* than a barnacle on a ship's rudder. Gant would wait for his chance, hire another crew, and steal the ship. Like Raca said, he would rip her apart until he found the strongbox. Alex needed to find reason why Gant might agree to search for his parents while they waited for a ruling. He looked carefully at Gant sitting and smoking a pipe watching *Mary Celeste's* stern as they rowed past. Captain Gant's dress, his hair, and his entire person were meticulous and clean. He was fastidious about his personal attire. But his ship? *Wasp* was ill-kept with dirty decks and spars and sails in disrepair falling apart from neglect. Gant spent less time and money on maintenance than any captain in Rochester. *What kind of captain would do that? A captain whose greed for gold overwhelmed everything he did; greed blinding his otherwise careful plans.* That random thought triggered another in quick order. An idea blossomed. Alex slowed his rowing. Fearing his parents were marooned without provisions, likely dying, he prayed he had not run out of time.

"Keep pace, boy!" shouted Raca.

Alex's new idea had great risk in equal measure to its chance for success. But he would need help from someone Gant trusted implicitly.

Back on *Wasp,* Gant and Raca disappeared below. Once they were out of sight, Alex rushed to find Pricilla. In the tiny galley she and Isaiah were offloading fresh mutton, potatoes, and cod they would salt. Nearby barrels indicated ale and rum were in ample supply. Alex motioned and she followed him up the companionway ladder and joined him on the forward deck. Pierce and Willy Harrison sat on coiled ropes to starboard with knives in hand, wood shivers at their feet. Willy watched the two walk to the bow. He kept his silence and his distance. Pierce nodded but did not look up.

"Is *Celeste* ours?" Pricilla asked assuming the answer, seeing his eyes.

"No. Quarantined. And worse. Your father will not search until *Celeste* has been released to us... which will take weeks if it happens at all."

Celeste's crew will certainly have perished by then... Pricilla understood. "I see," she said sadly.

"But does your father want the *ship* or does he only want to steal the strongbox?" Alex pressed her to give up secrets of the officers' cabin.

"They only speak of money," she said carefully.

"What would he do if he *had* the strongbox?"

"Sail home I suppose. *Wasp* isn't quarantined. Only *Mary Celeste.*"

"And on our way..."

"He might agree to search. I suppose." Pricilla was tired, worried, and distracted. She rubbed a new painful bruise on her thigh. Hours earlier, she had again fought Raca off. In doing so, she had fallen down three steps. Before hitting the floor at the bottom, Willy had caught her, and reached for his knife. But her hand stayed his intention to go after Raca. Events were fast devolving into anarchy.

"I have a plan." Alex studied her eyes intently. "But I need your help, Pricilla."

"What kind of help?"

"You manage your father's accounts and ledgers. His logbook appears to be in your hand. Why?" Alex suspected this was a well-kept secret.

"Do not tell anyone."

"Why?" Alex insisted, "Captains manage their own accounts."

"He trusts me... and I read and write well."

"And he does not?"

Pricilla knew her father's agent in Rochester suspected but no one else. "Yes." Pricilla had crossed the line.

She thought of recent voyages with her father when she sat below deck, counting goods as they came illegally off another ship late at night. Avoiding duties, taxes, and tariffs she well understood her father's profitable trade in contraband. A smuggler's daughter found no moral dilemma in rich merchants taking from their own kind. Her mother had enjoyed the finery it bought and asked few questions. Nor did Pricilla object to her own education. She remembered earlier voyages when her father's commands were neither directed harshly at her supposed incompetence and abject stupidity nor followed by a quick blow. Her father had once shown her a generous heart; now she suffered in silence. It must end.

"You also track *Wasp's* cargo manifest—usually a first mate's job."

"Raca is as dumb as a cockroach," she said her eyes flared with loathing.

"Then listen, Pricilla—"

"Daughter!" Alex was suddenly interrupted by Gant yelling from below decks, "Have cook prepare a hot meal with the fresh pork you bought. And send down ale."

No, not now. Not yet! Alex cursed her father but caught Pricilla's thoughtful look as she scurried away. She did not seem as afraid as in recent days. Had something changed? He hoped she understood the direction of his thinking. But on which shore did she stand? He remained unsure. There was not enough time to row her to his side. She must come over herself.

Minutes later, Alex entered Gant's cabin. Gant and Raca sat with pipes and a strong smell of rum filled the cramped, dank space.

"You're early for your afternoon beating, eh, Master Briggs?" Raca wheezed through an exhale.

Alex ignored him. "If we were to find the strongbox before London rules… what will you do?"

Gant stared. "So, you *do* know where he hid it? You've been lying."

"No, I do not and no, I have not. Only—" Alex answered firmly intending to make an offer. Gant offered first.

"*Only if I* get what I want will I give you what *you* want?"

Matter of fact, yes, thought Alex.

They both remained silent.

"Captain, lemme beat it outta him..."

"We may go there yet, Mr. Raca. Continue, Mister Briggs." Gant appeared calm though Alex suspected he was not.

"Say you will search," Alex said. "Agree to it."

"If I have the strongbox aboard *Wasp* on our voyage back to Rochester—yes—I will search."

"For one *full* week. As you agreed with my brother."

"Aye."

Alex did not believe him but what choice did he have? What chance would his family have if they were not found soon?

"I will speak to the port-warden again. My father left personal items on board and so did my mother and sister. I will ask to retrieve them. You come with me. No one else."

"And you'll find the strongbox?"

"I wager I can guess where to look. My father designed clever compartments—protection against thieves." His meaning was clear. Gant ignored the taunt. "*You're* not clever enough to find it." he said contemptuously as he turned to Raca. The first mate pushed his chair back and lunged. He struck Alex hard in his gut. Briggs fell onto the bulkhead. Ignoring Raca, Alex glared at Gant. *This better work,* he reminded himself, *or I'm dead.* "If you kill me, you'll never find it. You'll never get on board."

Raca seethed, "We'll get on board, boy, when they give'er back to us! We'll rip'er apart just like we'll rip you apart!"

"And if we lose the claim? You don't have enough men to steal her now, do you Captain? You saw the soldiers and cannon. Do you expect Raca and Willy to row in and stab them *all*?" Gant gave no hint of anger, so Alex knew he had the captain's full attention. "If the courts learn the crew died then *Celeste* isn't *lost*. Courts won't care how her crew lost their lives. They died at sea. And if we can prove an accident happened, if we prove she was *not* abandoned—*Celeste* was drifting in perfect condition, not wrecked remember Captain Breton and his mate already conceded that—then we have a valid claim. All we need to do is find out what happened to the crew. Captain Breton will have no legal right to take *Celeste* from... *me*..." Alex let his logic hang in the air before he continued, "If however, the crew's whereabouts remains a mystery—or if I disappeared too..." He glanced at Raca. "...it will appear *Celeste was* abandoned. The court will award her to *Halifax* faster than a bass inhales a herring." Gant again made no response but puffed and exhaled. "And Captain, I can make this case to the port-warden today. I'll ask him to give us time to search for my parents before he releases *Celeste*."

Gant grunted but said nothing.

Alex reiterated the parts of the plan most important to Gant, "And I'll ask him to allow us to board her *today* to collect my parents' personal belongings. I'll search in a few places where my father might have hidden his strongbox." Alex added, "If we find it, we'll have trouble getting it off the ship, though. His chest is large and heavy." Alex paused. "And after I find the strongbox for you, we'll leave and search for the crew."

Gant seemed lost for a minute. Abruptly he stood. "Agreed. We'll return to the office. Raca, find cook. Tell him to bring the large tarpaulin satchel. A strong one."

"No. Only you and me." Alex looked at Raca's gun wondering if he would dare use it in port.

"Listen, boy, I got hungry rats below. Mr. Raca's whip aches for a work-out. One word from me and you'll never see daylight again!"

Raca struck Alex in his face to remind him he was there.

"Enough, you fool!" Gant yelled as Raca backed out of the captain's quarters.

177

"After… we will search. Say it, Captain." Though Alex's mouth and nose bled he ignored the pain. His eyes never flinched or left Gant's. He must demonstrate he could withstand extreme physical punishment and would never give up. It was important Gant understood this.

Gant smiled reluctantly at the boy with blood dripping from his face and his hands holding his ribs. "You keep coming at me, eh, boy? You'll never let it be. Aye. You have a bargain. We'll search." Isaiah's large head appeared in the doorway with Raca standing menacingly behind him. "We'll need my daughter as well cook."

As Isaiah left the captain's quarters with Alex in tow, Gant detained Raca until the others were out of earshot. Then the captain confided, "Mr. Raca, we'll need Pricilla if we find anything other than gold."

"Aye, she reads good. I been watching her."

"I know you watch her," Gant said barely hiding his venom. "It better not go further than *watchin'* or I'll hang your manhood from the ensign halyard."

Isaiah gathered the satchel and looked carefully at Alex's latest injury. "An inch closer, Master Briggs, and you'd'a been a blind man. You sure you don't encourage the mate?"

Alex did not answer. He appreciated the cold, wet cloth Isaiah held up to his bloodied face. He did not want to admit he deliberately solicited the reaction he wanted and expected.

"Gant understands hardship and blood, Isaiah…" Alex paused while Isaiah secured a bandage around the boy's ribs. "…but mostly he understands fear. If he's to follow my improbable search for twenty half-dead souls who could be stranded on any one of hundreds of islets and sandbars, he needed to know something real about me."

"That you have no fear, and you'd never admit to feeling pain?" Isaiah said, but thought, *Is that the best you could come up with?* Nodding and wincing as the cook secured the bandages

Alex hoped and prayed resilience might be something Gant respected. *With respect he might follow.* Isaiah continued to apply ointment to his broken face and whispered, "Captain Gant does not take suggestions. I remember a few weeks back... we were near aground on Pollock..."

"That was different," said Alex. "I offered him information he didn't have. But out here no one knows what's real."

Isaiah looked at the young man with his injuries, bandages, scars, and limp. "Master Briggs, you look more like a young midshipman in battles when shrapnel and exploding shells didn't discriminate between high-born or enlisted men looking for adventure or workers stolen from the street by impress gangs."

Alex smiled slightly at the comparison. But he did not fight for flag and glory, king and country. "I'm fighting for my family," he said simply. Alexander Briggs knew he would have a long and difficult fight to find the lost people of *Mary Celeste.* They were nearly out of time.

"Do you think this will serve?" Isaiah asked Alex, showing him a large tarpaulin satchel Gant had told him to bring.

"It should do, thank you. I meant it when I said I wasn't sure what I'm looking for. If something happens to me..."

"Rochester men don't think like that."

"I know, but Pricilla will have no one else..."

"You make a fine pair. And I hate to say it, Master Briggs, but she's a better navigator than you." Alex smiled. "Your mathematics studies must have been scheduled during the autumn bass run off Squibnocket Point. Your education's missin' important chapters."

"Perhaps Pricilla will fill them in for me. What do you think?"

"Aye, Master Briggs, but you must think of her as a woman. Do not mislead her, Alex."

"But I must be sure I can trust her with my life. Everyone's life."

"You can trust her. She is conflicted but not dishonest."

"You sure?"

"Yes, but do not assume her intentions or take advantage of her heart. She hurts as bad as you."

"She's brave and smart." *...and sweet and pretty, unlike any girl I've known,* Alex thought, half listening to Isaiah's counsel. But the cook's next words brought him back to the reality of *Wasp.*

"Aye, she is. But I fear for her life. You must get away from this ship. Together."

The tired port-warden longed to return to his siesta and a tipple of *porto.* His stuffy office appeared smaller for this second gathering of the *Wasps* even without British company.

"Captain Gant, I thought my instructions this morning were clear. What do you want?" The administrator had been nearly asleep when his guard told him of another intrusion, his patience at its end softened a bit as he saw the boy's respectful countenance. Young Briggs had come with the captain and his enforcer of course, but also a West Indies man of prodigious size and a young girl strangely dressed as a poor seaman.

As planned Alex Briggs stepped forward and spoke respectfully. "Senõr Gabriel, I thank you as would my father, Captain Ebenezer Briggs, were he here." Alex paused a moment as a sharp pain shot through his ribcage. The lag, however, served only to pique the interest of the port-warden. "If we find my family—alive or dead—the courts would conclude they did not abandon ship. They had an accident, or an unexpected event took place aboard *Mary Celeste.* The ship was lost—not abandoned. The distinction makes a great deal of difference. Were you to support this supposition, once we provide you with proof, the courts would likely agree. And we would be grateful."

Gabriel was moved that the scrawny lad with a bandaged face and a limp was the only one who had spoken; and he spoke beyond his years. The boy made sense, though his promise of gratitude did not have the same luster as a heavy bag of English sterling. On his meager salary, Port-Warden Gabriel supported four children and two grandchildren from a deceased daughter. Beleaguered, Gabriel looked at this sorry lot before him: a crusty, well-dressed captain in middle age. Standing behind him towered a large black man with scarred knuckles beside a striking young woman staring at her feet but occasionally glancing up at him, her eyes asking for something. Behind them stood a brute, all hate and ignorance spewing from his crooked face and rotted teeth. The port-warden concluded it was prudent to appear cooperative.

"If you solve the mystery of *Mary Celeste's* missing crew, I will send another letter to detail your findings. The court would likely favor your claim. But *only* if you find evidence of what happened. Bring me a log or bodies or a wrecked longboat… something."

Alex got what he wanted. Not so Gant.

"Sir, Mr. Briggs' parents left personal belongings on *Celeste.* May we board and retrieve the personal effects in the event we do not find survivors?"

The port-warden looked at Alex.

"Books, Sir. My father also kept a private journal in his seachest. A handkerchief my mother kept with her always, a gift I gave her when I was ten. A comb, a locket, and a few trinkets of my sisters… Father's spyglass… worthless to anyone else but cherished by me and my brother…"

Port-Warden Gabriel hesitated. He did not trust the captain. But he thought about the American warship soon to anchor and looked at the young man with the injuries. *I must appear impartial*, he thought.

"Agreed, Señor Briggs," conceded Gabriel. "But my soldiers will inspect anything you remove. Take nothing of value and bring no weapons on board. Understood?"

"Aye," Gant replied. Gabriel's fatigued eyes shifted to Gant whom he had disliked from their first encounter.

"Trouble me, Captain Gant, and I will quarantine *Wasp* alongside *Celeste*."

"Thank you, Sir," said Alex, bowing slightly though it hurt his torso to bend.

Port-Warden Gabriel dismissed the Americans with two sweeping hands. They clustered through the small doorway, and he called after them, "I want you off *Mary Celeste* in one hour!" He watched Alex and Pricilla limp away. "And Captain..." Gant turned to the port-warden with feigned respect. "...while you are a guest of the Kingdom of Portugal, you will not beat your crew!"

Gant nodded. *Fool Raca—the face—never the face.* He watched his daughter as she walked stiffly down the dock. Until now, Gant had not concerned himself with her limps and assorted bruises. However, he had not laid a hand on her since two days prior. *Raca!*

Alex scrambled up the side of his father's brig. Captain Gant, first mate Raca, Pricilla, and Isaiah followed. Each of the weary travelers felt nervous and constrained knowing they only had precious few minutes to search a ship 120 feet long. The port-warden's corporal came up another side armed with a pistol and a sword. His boat was rowed by two uniformed soldiers who carried muskets. In silence, the corporal stood and watched the Americans.

Loud enough only for *Wasp's* crew, Raca said to Gant, "He'd hide his gold in his cabin, right?"

Gant looked to Alex.

Alex nodded and they walked aft. All the while, Alex looked for clues; though the ship was in disarray, nothing was damaged, broken, or out of place. He could discern no signs of violence, only lack of attention. Looking up, her rig showed no snapped yardarms or stun'sail booms; looking down, her rails, bulwarks, and paint were smooth and undamaged. The brig was tired and dirty but had not been violently boarded by another ship and taken by force. Alex was fast running out of ideas.

"My father built more than one hidden compartment. We'll start in his cabin."

"Go," Gant said. He looked around, planning a path back onto *Celeste* as soon as darkness fell.

Alex entered the cabin where his parents ate their last meal aboard. As *Halifax's* Captain Breton promised, nothing had been moved. His mother had set a proper and comfortable table at sea and here was her touch: flowers. In Rochester she dressed their family table on Water Street with fresh blooms each day—purple hydrangeas for this time of year. On *Mary Celeste* however, the flowers set out weeks ago had withered. Alex picked at a dead petal; it crumbled in his fingers and fluttered to the cabin floor. He looked away.

"Quick now!" commanded Gant.

Alex went to his knees and tried to pry open a loose sideboard. Nothing moved. He changed positions and told everyone to step back. They obeyed and he tried another panel. It gave way, sliding out sideways, and he reached under and found a wooden bar. He rotated it counterclockwise, thereby releasing a hidden shelf. To the cabin's visitors, the shelf was invisible, but opened to a space behind.

"Here's his secret compartment. Enough room for even a large chest." He looked up at Gant. "See?" Gant dropped to his knees, stuck his head in, and looked up. He felt the open space with his hands and searched a good bit before he understood the shelf was devoid of anything of value, only a few hidden bottles of Madeira, dusty and forgotten. Alex was prepared. "I told you my father has more than one hiding place. And he may have brought more than one seachest on board. He often keeps bullion and currency in one chest and another with ship's papers—invoices, itemized cargo logs, bills of lading, manifests, and the like…" Alex looked at Pricilla. She returned a blank look, not assuring him she understood. He could do nothing else but stare at her, his last hope. "…mostly worthless papers and company correspondence."

"But he'd keep his gold and currency near him, right?" insisted Raca.

"If we only find ship's papers but no gold… yeah, you're right. Since there's no chest here in his cabin, he most likely took it with him into the longboats."

"Where else do we look?" Gant asked, increasingly concerned but not buying into Alex's conclusion without more evidence.

Pricilla watched Alex draw her father into a trap like a spider. She was not sure what she hoped for. They searched but found nothing in the other officers' bunks or the galley and so walked forward. As they passed an open deck where hammocks swung with night-blankets they saw personal items strewn about. Far forward they came into *Celeste's* forecastle where the crew ate. There, Alex looked up at the small hatch admitting harbor air and light. Compared to the port window on *Wasp*, *Celeste's* forward hatch was larger by half, as wide as a man's shoulders.

Their allotted time was almost spent. Alex walked directly to a starboard side bulkhead panel. After trying a few loose timbers, one gave way to his determined push. As in the cabin, this opening led to a latch concealed inside. But this latch opened an even larger shelf that folded cleverly out of the way. This shelf was not empty. On it sat a small wooden chest, sturdy-built of heavy oak. The chest was 15 inches wide and 12 inches deep with worn edges, plain leather hinges, and thick rope handles bound by twine connected to a heavy fitting on each side. Its wood surfaces were rough and split, damaged after years carried by sailors on and off ships. The chest was neither large, impressive, nor anything like what Gant expected.

"The strongbox!" cried Raca rushing toward the opening. Gant held him back. The chest had no lock—strange for a box supposedly full of gold. And why was it hidden in the crew quarters? He approached suspiciously and flipped it open. It was filled with papers. "What's this?" Gant demanded as he backed away.

"I'll tell you," said Alex with disinterest. He knew Gant watched every muscle in his hands and arms, studying every nuance of his expression. The chest didn't appear large enough to carry gold. He must convince them they were right.

Gant reluctantly stepped back. Pricilla squinted to see. Alex leaned over, reached in, and picked up the chest by the rope handles as if it weighed no more than bluefish bait. He set it down with a light touch on a larger seachest in the middle of the cabin. Rifling through the top, he selected a few papers and read them, opened envelopes, and said nothing sensing Gant's questions about to explode. Page after page he read quickly. As he suspected... the parchments explained so much. He remained calm and appeared bored as he flipped through.

"Well? Tell me!" Gant finally cried.

Alex shrugged. "Ship's papers. Invoices. Letters. Money we *owe...*" Pricilla listened carefully. "Seems we owe a *great deal* of money to a number of people. Mostly banks."

Gant, the 40 percent owner of Briggs and Sons, angrily shoved Alex aside. He stuck his hands in the chest and dug deep: nothing but papers. No coins. No gold. No currency. He stared at the documents and froze. He looked at Pricilla who reached over and grabbed the top of the stacked papers. Alex kept a blank face as Gant looked first to Pricilla then Alex then back at Pricilla.

Aching to glance up for Alex's guidance, she read out loud, knowing her father's eyes were trained on hers, expecting her to do her duty. Alex's eyes never left Gant. Pricilla was on her own. She read in an even voice:

"*For Payment: MP Makepeace and Co. Thirty dollars for crops received 18 June...*"

"*For Payment: Suffolk and Co. master builders. For lumber received 16 May...*"

"*For Payment: Newton Ice and Coal. For five tons heating coal...*"

"Father, these are only bills. Here... this one is a lien. Oh, a large one. On the entire shipyard. It appears Briggs and Sons may soon be declared insolvent unless they have gold and silver squirreled away someplace else. Mr. Raca, see? *You* want to tell him the bad news?" Her voice started to rise.

Gant suddenly realized his folly and his worthless arrangement with Ezekiel Briggs. *The dog—he knew. Damn him!* Raca looked at a page she waved in his face. She had presented it to him upside down.

"Yes, sir. She tells it right. These papers ain't worth shit."

"Father, we sailed across the ocean for *this*? There's nothing here worth stealing!" She stuffed the papers back into the chest. *"Nothing!"* As she stormed up to the deck, Isaiah, holding his empty sealskin-lined sack, quietly closed the lid of the wooden chest.

In a fury Captain Gant raced topside. Raca followed and as soon as the forecastle was clear Alex whispered to Isaiah, "Will you place the chest back into the compartment and close the shelf?" Isaiah nodded and remained. On his way out, Alex carefully sized up the hatch once again then rushed up the ladder after Gant and Raca.

On the main deck, Raca took Gant aside. "What do y'think, Captain? Y'a think he kept the gold with him when they went over the side?"

Alex heard his question and thought, *Yes, let greed be your guide.*

"What would *you* do, Captain?" Alex posited, approaching Gant and Raca on the main deck. "You bring your entire crew, your wife, and your daughter into the ship's longboats. Would *you* leave your *fortune* behind?"

Gant was considering where else on the ship to search, but the Portuguese Corporal marched up with two armed soldiers. "Two o'clock, Señor! I order you off this ship!"

Gant had no choice but to follow the boy's logic.

"Where is cook? Pricilla, Briggs! With me, now! Cook, what in damnation is keeping you?"

"Coming, Sir," Isaiah said as he appeared with the canvas satchel in hand.

"What's in there?" accused Gant noticing the sack for the first time during their search of the brig. Alex stared at Isaiah. As ordered, the port-warden's soldiers approached as well to inspect. Isaiah set the canvas bag down on the deck and opened it casually. "Books, sundries, Captain Briggs' spyglass, and shawls from the seachests of Mrs. Briggs and the boy's sister…"

Gant looked in. Satisfied, he grabbed the heavy brass spyglass far superior to his own and glared at the soldiers. "I'll be keeping this," said the angry Captain Gant and they stood back. To Raca and Alex: "We're off on tomorrow's tide."

Early the next morning, Pricilla found Alex on *Wasp's* lower deck huddled over a chart he had spread out on a seaman's abandoned chest.

"Alex, look." Pricilla placed another rolled chart on top of the seachest.

First light was two hours past. But they had an hour before the ebb tide when they would haul *Wasp's* anchor and begin the search for *Mary Celeste's* missing crew.

"Where'd you get this?" Alex smiled.

"I returned to the port-warden after we left *Celeste*. I had to buy provisions. I asked for his help. He said we could depend on these. They're quite detailed. Note the narrows here… and here… like Robinson's." She leaned over his shoulder and tried to get him to focus on the new chart. He was looking at her instead. She did not object.

Alex finally looked down at the new chart. Markings for rocks, rips, and reefs were clearly depicted—unlike *Wasp's* charts. "Currents here run in one direction while tides, at times, run opposite simultaneously. Roiled seas between many of these outer-islands would be treacherous for a small boat," Alex said partly for the girl, partly for himself.

"When do the currents change?" she asked. "Slack is calm enough for a small boat."

Alex studied Sao Miguel's current tables. "I estimate ten hours difference to the west past these small out-islands and sandbars." Along with reefs and rips, the port-warden's new charts also depicted shifting sands below the water's surface. "Without accurate timetables for the out islands we can only guess where to look."

"The port-warden said we'll not find anchorages to the southwest. There's one small cove fishermen use for refuge during storms. He's not sure where to find it though. He didn't have a log for currents west of San Miguel but suggested you might add six hours."

"Six hours? Not ten. Hmmm." He needed an accurate local current table if he was to track the castaways' last course. At least he had a rough set of current tables from the Portuguese whaler. It seemed like years ago when he traveled to New Bedford returning with calculations hand drawn from an old timer's memory and a half-formed plan to rescue his family. It had only been two weeks. Alex touched Pricilla's hand. "Thank you. Your chart helps a great deal. See this rock? We might have tried to squeeze between these two sandbars. The rocks would have sunk us."

"The port-warden expects these charts returned, Alex. I reminded him we only have a week."

Pricilla glanced along *Wasp's* lower deck mindful of unwelcome company. Alex's eyes caught hers. One week was not much time to search but an eternity for castaways. *Wasp*, with her shorthanded crew of only two able-body sailors, Pierce and Willy, officers Raca and Gant, Isaiah, Pricilla, and Alex—who could barely walk never mind climb the ratlines—would need to search scores of unfamiliar islands. He must choose with precision where to begin.

With *Wasp*'s charts and those borrowed sitting next to each other, Alex plotted longitude and latitude where *Halifax* first saw *Celeste* drifting south and west of Sao Miguel:

40' 71'' 40 W
79' 53" 30 N

"I suspect Captain Breton has motivation to mislead us. But we've got to start someplace." He worked both charts, made notations, took a ruler and backtracked their possible drift. *"Two hours after a morning flood current begins, water runs at two and a half knots against a boat rowing northeast,"* Alex read, hesitated, then continued remembering his father's lessons. *"After two more hours, currents run at peak, and in another two hours turn slack when water does not move at all."*

"And the moon's gravity," Pricilla chimed in, "rises and lowers tides but the earths' spinning motion powers the currents."

"They do. But tides and currents can run in together or fight in opposite directions."

"And a fierce wind can complicate everything…"

"Damn," said Alex.

"We need more than charts!" They said together.

They also needed more than current and tide tables drawn from memory and scraps of journals from an old whaler. Then a solution occurred to him: if he could estimate for how long *Mary Celeste* had sailed by herself, he could backtrack to where her crew must have left the ship.

"Pricilla, do you remember the leftover food in the cabin? Dried hard in the heat."

"Yes."

"It reminded me of scraps left by workers in our work-sheds. Meat shrinks after about two days before it hardens. In this heat perhaps another day passed before it turned solid." Alex's mind raced. "I'm guessing *Celeste* drifted for three days after my father left the ship."

"But wasn't there a storm when *Halifax* came upon *Celeste*?" Pricilla remembered.

"Yes, but it must have blown through fast—more a narrow front than a full-on gale. Otherwise, there'd be more damage to her rigging and spars. I suspect the weather pushed *Celeste* at six or seven knots for only about two hours then she would have eventually turned upwind and stalled. Taking her east-northeast... to... *here*." Pricilla leaned close to him as he pointed to *Mary Celeste's* rendezvous with *Halifax*. He traced a line back west-southwest, well below the major habited Azores' islands. "The *Celeste* was likely on a straight course to Sao Miguel to provision. But if she sailed by herself for a few days and ended up here where *Halifax* found her... the crew must have left her..." He looked at his original chart and compared it to the one Pricilla was holding flat. "...there!" He marked the location.

"Let me." Pricilla took out a navigator's ruler and made measurements and a few calculations. She counted and double checked his math. "No, Alex. Not *one-point-two degrees. One-two, point zero*." A wrong decimal point would place *Wasp* 10 miles off the desired course. They smiled at each other.

"Right," Alex said. He forced himself back to his task, but it was hard not to look at her. She was so *near*. "They were only thirty miles to here..." A set of islands showed clearly on the port-warden's chart 100 miles down-current from Sao Miguel. "My father would have headed for the nearest settlement. But they'd have been sailing against the prevailing winds from the northeast..." He stopped and looked away.

"How well do her longboats sail against the wind?" Pricilla asked herself out loud. But it wasn't really a question. She knew the answer.

"Poorly. Not much of a keel. Their shallow rudders lift in a breeze and force the boat into the wind where it will stall. Their sails were designed for the trades with the wind behind or on a reach. If *Celeste's* longboats were already west of the settled islands, it would have been near impossible to sail back."

"…and against strong currents," she added, suddenly realizing the impossible conditions Captain Briggs likely encountered. Only a desperate crew could succeed against both wind and current. And though Captain Briggs and his crew were certainly desperate, had they tried, they would have failed.

"If they had to fight currents while tacking upwind…" Alex hesitated as the picture became clear. He realized for the first time Captain Briggs probably never got within hailing distance of habitable land. But rather than dwell on his father's hopeless situation, he thought like his father would have. "…Father would not waste his men's strength if he could sail downwind" Alex's finger retraced a course starting from where Captain Briggs likely abandoned *Mary Celeste.* With a ruler he drew a line due west. Less than 10 miles away were small islands, bars, and reefs. A few islands appeared to have anchorages. Perhaps fishing shacks or villages awaited *Mary Celeste's* castaways. "We'll start where they left *Celeste.* We'll drift and see what direction this current takes us. I'll mark when it turns. I suspect we'll not drift north but west." He quickly referred back to the whaler's current tables—they filled in the missing pieces: *It fits!* "We'll start our search…" He pointed confidently to the small group of islands. "…here."

Captain Gant stomped down the ladder. He'd been ashore. "What's this?"

"Papa, Alex has a notion where *Celeste's* crew might have drifted. A few islets not too far—"

"We'll search where I say," he interrupted.

Alex jumped up. "We'll waste days if we look in the wrong place! Look—!"

"I *have* looked. And I *also* spoke with the port-warden…" he looked sternly at his daughter. "He gave me suggestions. And I spoke to *Halifax's* master. He's an arrogant bugger, but he confirmed the same longitude and latitude he gave you where he came across *Celeste.* I believe him. He's playing nice because there's talk ashore about piracy…"

192

In 20 years of trade and thieving Gant had come across many a British master. Some were amiable to the conditions Gant set forth; others argued or fought him and his boys. One of these Englishmen in his life's path was this bastard on *Halifax*. To trust his word was a risk he feared. For hours he had searched his memory of voyages and violent encounters. *Where had he known this Breton?*

Gant eyed Alex. On shore he had learned Port-Warden Gabriel and Captain Breton shared a concern about Alex's accusations of conspiracy, murder, and piracy. And with a United States Navy frigate about to arrive, they hoped *Wasp* would solve why *Mary Celeste* had drifted without a crew before the situation turned from a rescue to a battle. Gant stopped short of a compliment. Instead, he scowled, "We start here." On Alex's chart, Gant pointed to the exact spot Alex had chosen. "And go west. Strong currents block east or north. They had one chance for landfall. Here…" Gant leaned over Pricilla and Alex and pointed his long finger at a group of islets. Alex mumbled his meek acquiescence; Gant had independently selected the same likely landfall. Gant had expected an argument. He calmed and became less obstinate. "But if currents took them more to the southwest, they would have missed land entirely. Beyond these islets there's nothing but ocean for two thousand miles." Gant looked stern but his energy rose. "We need all hands to raise our anchor. Six can do it, but we'll need a double wrap on our capstan. Has your strength returned, Mr. Briggs?"

"A bit. As long as Raca stops…" Alex's voice trailed off. He did not want to anger Gant with the search about to begin.

"I called him off. Unless we don't find the strongbox," muttered Gant.

Alex was grateful to get a temporary reprieve. He glanced at Pricilla. Had she spoken on his behalf? The girl had been watching her father and Alex come to a peaceful agreement for the first time. She tapped her fingers on the wooden chest displaying the charts. She sometimes did that when her nerves got ahead of her, and she forgot the New Bedford Sisters' admonitions to control these ungodly habits. She stopped suddenly when she realized her father was staring at her hands. Gant was annoyed his own nervous affliction carried down through his bloodline, shaming them both, an obvious weakness visible to the world. Alex, however, remained calm, quietly relieved Gant was committed to search even though his motivation was pure greed. Alex's relief, however, was tempered when back on the main deck he saw both Gant and Raca had pistols and long knives openly displayed in their belts.

Alex wondered if his father and any survivors might still have the strength to defend themselves against people so intent on stealing gold, so devoid of humanity. There had been no talk of bringing survivors back to Rochester. This might be a rescue voyage, but it was an armed one.

Wasp drifted uneasily in the early morning swells. The wind died to a murmur and her aft gaff rigged spanker and one jib forward were set but not tensioned. These two sails were all their short-handed crew could manage if the wind increased. Whalers in San Miguel had raised anchors and taken the few unemployed sailors looking for a berth, so *Wasp* remained short-handed. Her sails slapped against their sheets while yardarms listed with each roll of the deep ocean rollers. The ship did not like the hove-to position any more than her waiting crew who awkwardly roamed the deck. Willy dropped his lead overboard on a long line and measured their drift.

"One knot west, Captain." It was oppressively hot in the mid-Atlantic sun. The skies were clear and clouds thin and disbursed. One hour later: "Now two." A few more readings charted below by Pricilla and searchers would know which direction to sail.

"Papa." She came on deck with a rolled chart. "I've charted three positions. See?" She unrolled her chart so Gant could look down from his seat by a rail near the wheel.

He did see. They had drifted north and west, as good an indicator as they were likely to get. A ship *Wasp's* size would drift faster than three small longboats; but a current moves in the same direction for ships, small boats, driftwood, or seaweed.

Gant spun his wheel to starboard and yelled, "Mr. Raca, I want her jib trimmed and our spanker-sheeted tight. We'll sail thirty points off our wind to the north."

Alex ran as well as his injuries allowed and with Willy's help trimmed their smallest jib. *Wasp's* hull noticed the adjustment and came out of her lazy sleep. The ship underway felt the current push her along at an extra knot. Alex had marked when the ebb turned and was greatly relieved that he had likely discovered the course *Mary Celeste's* longboats may have chosen. He felt wind in his hair and stood by *Wasp's* rail looking out to an empty horizon. For the first time in many weeks his stomach did not churn. Hopeful as the rising breeze, he felt sure they were sailing in the right direction.

Three days later, *Wasp* had searched six islands yet found no wreckage, no longboats, no tents or lean-tos, and no sign of *Mary Celeste's* missing people. There were hours of idle time for crewmen not in a landing party. Gant did not like the looks of his weary seasoned men—the sailors barely hid their looks of impatience, boredom, and muffled anger. He kept his pistol loaded by his sleeping berth.

"Mr. Raca!" Gant shouted as a boat was lowered to search a small island.

"We shall use this idle time for repairs. I see you have not attended to the rot or secured the starboard gate. See to it. And when you finish, I want you, Willy, and Pierce to replace the foretopgallant larboard brace. Did I not tell you weeks ago?" Gant spoke harshly.

Since beating the boy to extract his knowledge no longer fit into Gant's thinking, Raca's vile techniques were no longer critical. The ship, however, desperately needed work. Raca could saw, climb, and sweat like any forecastle jack.

"Aye..." Raca did not hide his insolence. He turned and mumbled something sounding like 'Captain' but it might just as easily have been an oath.

Willy and Pierce looked over their shoulders curious about the heated exchange and shared raised eyebrows. They faced a delicate dilemma: if Raca exploded and killed the captain, they might be seen by the murderous mate as sympathetic to the captain. However, they both knew what the captain was capable of. The cousins dared not take sides despite duplicitous loyalty being a sure sign of cowardice. Whereas Pierce reveled in the anonymity of shadows, Willy had never before run from a fight. Forced to choose between the murderous mate and his vicious master would not be an easy decision; they deserved each other.

Raca decided he'd make Gant's damned repairs—but without care and incomplete. This captain had spoken to him with disrespect for the last time. The only thing holding him back was the girl. He stumbled amidst the refuse cluttering his jumbled brains; confused about what he imagined had been promised. He decided the time was right to take what was his. Pierce snapped to his call—the cur knew his place and feared Raca as he should. The first mate could count with his fingers: two guns and two knives could kill the old man, the urchin, and the girl. Pierce assured him Willy would go along. Isaiah, Raca told Pierce, was an 'ignorant negro' and would cower from any white man holding a whip. Gant would bleed under his knife. *The girl will watch my butchery before I drag her below.* But before relishing the pleasure he so craved they had to find the strongbox.

Contemplating the dangerous gang of disaffected men, Gant stared back at the increasingly mutinous faces—a hazard captains feared worse than fire.

"Harrison boys. Mr. Raca." The three men assembled obediently in a semi-circle around the captain. "We got a bloody business here. But I've seen worse and so has Mr. Raca. Do you remember the middle passage a year ago spring?" Raca nodded wondering where Gant was headed. That murderous but profitable voyage had been one of the Captain's many voyages in the triangular trade, though Raca's first. He looked forward to more such rewarding voyages where his natural inclinations could flow unchecked. Unfortunately for Raca, once Gant started dragging the girl along, the African voyages stopped. "We had a guest on this voyage—Mr. Malaki they called him. A king of some sort in his own country who ended up on the wrong side of a war." Gant looked at his three crewmen—two rapt at his words, his first mate looked down avoiding the captain's eyes in a failed attempt at objecting to the memory when in fact he savored it. "Mr. Malaki objected to his treatment aboard *Wasp*. He could speak some English, right, Mr. Raca?"

Raca finally looked up with unrestrained pleasure. "Aye. We got some nice'n rusty chains tight around his legs. And no water for three days…"

"And so, Mr. Malaki created a great deal of noise below. He encouraged others to take up his cause and they formed a mad rabble. I brought the king to the top deck. I assembled our crew and officers. His family too and some of his servants attended him. Do you recall the gathering, Mr. Raca?"

"Aye…"

"The king was dressed in full chains—manacles on his feet and hands, shoulders, and arms. Near seventy pounds of iron. But quite unclothed otherwise. I asked him to stand to the side, downwind so we didn't have to breathe his stink. I told him to make his case. We would listen and then act upon it according to law and mercy. He spoke eloquently about food, water, life, sanitation, and freedom. When he finished, I walked over and with my boot sent him flying backwards off the deck. He sank in seconds. We never had another complaint from our passengers, did we Mr. Raca?"

First mate Gregor Raca enjoyed watching the fine lass, long and luscious. Lean where he liked, balanced with curves and gentle waves. He knew he had to tread carefully, however; he had seen the vicious punishment the old man could still dole out to any crewman who defied him or did not jump to his duty with the speed demanded. But the old man's eyes were not always on his mate, his trusted mate whom he needed the more as every league led east to their reward. The old man's eyes paid little attention to his comely daughter—*the bitch* would never admit to her flirtations below decks. He was onto her. She shared secret looks and smiles with the boy, but more, *much* more, with the new crewman with the knife. Raca knew about the knife. He had seen it cleaned, sharpened, admired, and fondled; a threat more real to him than the old man's ire. The wicked girl deserved a cruel fate. Her smiles favored only the young and fairest among the crew, not a word of kindness toward him. *I will have her.* Not tonight, but soon, in the galley or the forecastle between watches of this threadbare crew searching for corpses in the hope of finding a strongbox. He smiled as he remembered the old man's orders about the shore parties: any discovered castaways need not be returned to the ship—with or without the strongbox. One order he did not object to.

At the end of tonight's watch, Raca accosted the youth in his berth. To rouse him for his turn on deck, Raca had delivered a swift kick to his side, in the same spot Raca suspected his ribs were cracked from his daily, carefully aimed attacks. The boy screamed a muffled cry from his sleep and crawled off. Leaving the boy and his groans, he met the girl unexpectedly at the bottom of the companionway ladder. She glared at him, lathered up in spite—just the way he liked'em.

"You despicable coward! Leave Alexander alone!" Pricilla Gant spat out having failed to comfort Alex as he brushed past her in silence and shame. There had not been combat, but she knew, the entire ship knew, it must come to that. And she knew the inevitable outcome if it did.

"Aye, but who's the coward, Miss? You pretend to be a blushing maid, yet I seen you sneak into the corners. Right? And you're leadin' the boy along, so's he helps you set us against each other. I seen it all." Raca stared, breathing close to her face.

"You're the one who's pitting us against each other! Yes, that's the word—a pit, you deserve to be thrown in a pit... you only understand brutality."

He grabbed her arm stronger than he had dared on their encounters these past weeks when a brush-back became a shove, a glance became a prelude to an attack. Gregor Raca startled himself with his uninhibited embrace: an iron vice-grip from which the girl had no escape. Only screams might release her as his spittle dripped onto her face and his misery poured into the darkness.

"A pit, you say? You don't know nothin'bout nothin'. A young'un only becomes a man if he can take the man's punishment. A young'un don't know shit. He steals and wanders and lies and cheats but the punishment makes him strong, strong enough to be a man. But the man don't let him off from his stealin' and cheatin'. A pit, you say? Well, you ain't got no understandin' of a pit. The man makes you dig a hole down three, four feet and strips you naked. He throws you in the pit and fills it with mud and stones to squeeze your breathin' up to yer nose so you have to raise your head and stretch to find some air. But the man aims to make sure you don't breathe no nice, clean air, no, Miss. The man fills the last two feet of the pit with dung from the barn and the wet stinkin' pile from under the outhouse. No food, no water all day with the sun or all night with the rain or the snow. And the man leaves you there until the critters snoop around and take a snip outta your face. Seen these ears? I lost parts of'em once—a coon it was. After he's made you straight and honest, he digs you out and you fall numb into the mud. After a few days you can walk again. Until the next time. Until the next whipping, the next pit. Until you escape to any ship sailing away from hell. Aye, I know about pits. It made me strong. Something the boy'll never understand. You neither. But I'll teach you what the man taught me. You wait."

He turned, realizing he had said too much, his tongue running wild like a loose sheet in a gale. She heard secrets he had buried deep. He could not let it stand. He felt new urges no longer simply carnal. As she rushed away, he thought of mud and creatures of the night and waited for the screaming in his head to stop.

Pricilla kept to herself during the landings. If Raca remained onboard, she came with Alex and others to search the shore. If Raca went ashore, she stayed on board, but far away from her father. Gant never left the deck. More than once, Alex watched *Wasp* at anchor or drifting near a lazy lee shore and wondered if he would see the ship sail away without him. But then he saw Isaiah or Willy scramble over rocks seeking signs of castaways and he relaxed. He gambled Gant's greed would overpower his hatred from bygone disputes. He hoped he was right. Alex felt better whenever Pricilla joined him on a shore party—she guaranteed his safety.

On one beach he said what he had been thinking, "I am happy you're here with me."

"I'm happy to be with you, too," she replied. Alex did not see her warm smile.

"Yeah, I'm safer when you're ashore with me," he said foolishly.

"Oh?" She turned and cried, "So, as long as I'm walking on a beach with you, my father won't maroon you? Is that what you're saying?" Hurt and angry, Pricilla walked away.

Alex realized his blunder a moment too late.

"Wait! Pricilla!" He ran after her. "I didn't mean what I said, I'm sorry. *Neither* of us is safe. Our situation is getting more dangerous with every empty beach."

In silence Pricilla heard him out but walked away without comment.

Their search had turned up nothing but sand. Her father would soon lose his paltry supply of patience. No part of the rescue was going as Alex had hoped. Her father was angrier and more frustrated than she had ever seen him. And Mr. Raca would not leave her alone. He walked close to her whenever he could: pressed his body against hers. His hands grabbed at her as she passed in a companionway or along the deck. She had to escape Raca, escape her father, and escape this ship. But if she begged Alex for protection, what could he do? Raca could kill him with a swift swipe of his blade. And once they found the strongbox, she was sure her father would unleash the mate. No authority in Rochester would hold her father or Raca accountable, given his connections and those whom he paid for silent cooperation. *"Overboard... an accident... careless boy... a pity,"* her father would have her write in his captain's log. No one back home would believe her account of the murderous men on this ship from hell. Pierce Harrison surely would have practiced his account of how the careless boy fell over the side. She peered down the beach to find Willy. In his special way he knew how to comfort her.

It was morning on the fourth day of the search. They had sailed into islets, rowed ashore, scouted promising beaches and rocky cliffs looking for flotsam, debris, or any signs of habitation. Alex had come off watch where he had helped drop *Wasp's* day-anchor, a lighter anchor than her primary, able to be raised with only three men at the capstan. He went below and came around a corner near the galley and an empty, cramped officer's cabin from which Pricilla suddenly appeared. She looked abashed, but quickly smiled and fidgeted with her hair, fixing her loose curls with a string, her custom during her watch. Clearly, she was surprised to see Alex and her cheeks turned a sudden blush. As he was about to complement her looks Willy followed her close behind.

"Hey ho, young man. Any news from deck?" Willy smiled a smile men share and gave Alex a good-natured slap on his uninjured butt as he pressed by and climbed onto deck. Pricilla said nothing but smoothed her shirt and rearranged her belt. She smiled at Alex, surprised he did not return it. She did not expect to see his stern reaction.

"What?" she said as she dipped into the galley.

An hour later, Gant assembled the crew and announced this was to be their last leg. Isaiah set down coffee and hardtack. They ate at the communal table while Gant laid out the plan for their final attempt.

"We got no more time." Gant was mindful *Mary Celeste* could be released to the British any day. *If the gold wasn't out here… then where the hell did they hide it?* As much as he had hoped to find the lost crew with the strongbox nearby, he was equally frantic to secure his prize moored in San Miguel. He had gambled he had enough time for a rapid search before any ruling released *Mary Celeste*. "We'll set two jibs and a spanker; if our wind stays down, our main'sl, too." He spread his chart on a table in front of his daughter, Raca, and Alex. "Only one island left has a possible anchorage. It's tucked inside a reef. I will not risk *Wasp*, so everyone stays on watch. We'll search there then return to Sao Miguel." Alex squealed a protest. This would shorten their search by one day. "You'll get your week boy, but we only got three islands left. Pick any one and I'll anchor. *One!*" Gant sounded angry but hoped Alex's navigation remained accurate.

The captain had noted the boy's skill at reading charts, factoring current tables, and steering by the wind and tide. If the young man survived the voyage, he would make a good mate. Gant then looked at Raca who, like many a seaman, was consumed by loneliness, demons, and drink. Finally: Pricilla. He considered a different future for her with a family near a warm hearth and large feather beds like the one he and Claire had enjoyed for the better part of 20 years. His daughter once had a chance for a meaningful, rewarding life. Was it forsaken? Had he stripped all the kindness from her? Like he had abandoned the shore life, had he dragged her from the world she wanted, accommodating him in order to receive an education?

His thoughts turned on his own fate and rued yet again his decision to fit in one last run to Maine before the spring. He had stayed true to the sea and to its limitless horizon. It cost him his woman and their boy.

Gant climbed on deck and standing at the rail in an Atlantic breeze he admitted he would never enjoy a peaceful life ashore. What succor other men in their later years enjoyed did not resonate with him: family, women, worthy offspring—none fit into his existence; what remained now was only loneliness and anger. And the taking. Always the taking.

After hours of hard sailing, darkness began to fall. Early evening winds increased without warning—perhaps generated by rising heat from the approaching island. As before, *Wasp* flew too many sails. Alex, watching the ocean's telling signs like a sea hawk, dropped their flying jib right before *Wasp* became difficult to steer. The brig was well balanced once more with two sails—one fore and one aft. Gant noted Alex's quick action as he told Pricilla to read their chart and call out their position every few minutes from her seat just inside the aft companionway below on the lower deck and out of the weather. He was wary of the reef he could not see and needed her to chart every hundred feet of *Wasp's* movement. Their target island was one mile long and one half-mile wide protected by a reef 200 hundred yards offshore. To reach the anchorage they must sail past this reef, round it sharply, and dip into a lagoon tucked close behind. As they approached, currents began to force *Wasp* toward the reef harder than Gant had expected. He was sailing into unfamiliar narrows and night was near. He suddenly had doubts.

"Rocks to starboard one-half mile ahead, Papa!" Pricilla raised her head from below. She was anxious and thought they should turn away now. Approaching from the north might be a safer approach. She dared not offer advice but hoped her father would come to the same conclusion.

He did.

"We shall come about!" Gant cried.

He did not like how the current pulled the ship nor did he know for how long the reef extended. He would go around the reef instead. His crew—Alex, Willy, Pierce, Raca, and Isaiah— all sprang into action without need for further instruction. Pricilla, too, came on deck to release jib sheets from belaying pins on the rail. Gant watched his aft spanker. This was a lot of movement for a short-handed crew, but they had trimmed sails many times already this long week. There was no talking at first.

"Captain!" Alex suddenly called out. "We're losing the breeze! There's not enough pressure on the sails to bring her through a tack."

Earlier in this voyage, Gant would have ignored him and flung the wheel over. But earlier he had 20 boys to set sails, move the backstays, steer, and tack. He looked up at his near-flaccid sails.

"Belay that!" Gant yelled.

Everyone had heard Alex. The crew stopped and wrapped lines back onto belaying pins and waited. Gant felt his helm. The current pulled *Wasp* sideways toward the reef. If he turned his wheel and the ship tacked away, they would sail for open sea and the safety of deeper water. But if the bow did not come all the way around to the new direction, if current and lack of wind held her back, *Wasp* would stop moving forward. The ship would fall back to her original course but without enough speed to squeeze between the reef to the left and rocks to the right. If *Wasp* changed direction in this dying breeze, she would need one-quarter mile to regain her previous speed and forward progress. *Wasp* did not have one-quarter mile. Gant knew his ship. He never asked advice. However, with only three experienced sailors and a lad to help him coax her through her turns, his options were limited.

"What do you say?" He glowered at Alex thinking, *You'd better be right!*

"She'll not come over. Not enough breeze. But we can hoist another jib, gain speed, sail her high, and perhaps squeeze by. You know her trim best. Slide past and bounce her along the reef." Alex tried to sound confident; he had done this on *Sea Smoke* but never in a ship the size of *Wasp*.

"Raca?" Gant bellowed for confirmation.

Raca was unsure how to answer. He was also painfully resentful Alex and Pricilla had absconded with a first mate's navigation duties. He looked at *Wasp's* luffing sails. The outcome was certain given the invisible reef.

"Aye."

"Aye *what*? Damn you! What do you say?" Gant bellowed.

Raca swallowed. "Boy's right. Ship won't come around. We're near dead-stopped."

Captain Gant had not noticed the fluctuating winds early enough. *Fool!* His light was gone and in this dying breeze they could not afford to lose any more forward motion. His hands gripped his wheel which confirmed Alex was right.

"Hoist the jib! Now! Cook, get on the spanker. You and the girl—trim it tight! Tighten my back stays. I must have steerage!"

The crew of *Wasp* worked the deck with deadly intent. Pricilla lunged at a sheet and almost lost her grip, but Isaiah held it tight. Raca and Willy trimmed jibs. Pricilla saw her father struggle: currents were pushing *Wasp's* rudder left while her hull tried to go right. They caught a puff of wind and *Wasp* momentarily sailed away from the reef. *Saved?* Pricilla looked astern and saw their wake told a different story: *No! Wasp* had slipped sideways. Pricilla eyed the obscured island, looked opposite, and squinted in day's last light.

"Alex, can you see breakers off our starboard bow?"

"No!"

"Call out as soon as you do! They're close!" She turned to her father. "I'll go below and mark our progress as best as I can dead-reckon. Keep her high. I'll tell you when we're clear."

It was strange for Gant to listen to his daughter. Even stranger he replied, "Aye." He had all he could do to keep *Wasp* balanced and moving away from the reef to his left yet clear the rocks to his right. The channel was narrow, and the current ran hard. He was losing; *Wasp* slipped to larboard and there was little he could do. For a few tense minutes no one spoke. The only sounds originated from waves crashing on a nearby invisible shore.

Alex broke the eerie silence, shouting, "Breakers and rocks to starboard! But we're below them—*far* below!" Alex's cry told Gant they were too close to the reef. If *Wasp* hit, current and wind would push her hull hard aground. *Wasp* would founder and break up.

Pricilla leaned out. "I heard *breakers!*"

"We're too far below 'em!" Gant called. "How far to the end of the reef?"

A moment later she shrieked what he dreaded, "Papa, we're on top of it *now*! We'd need another two- or three-hundred feet to clear…"

Wasp slammed onto the reef. Her masts and sails swayed. The wheel lurched in Gant's hands as he fought to control his rudder. Alex fell to his knees. The others clutched the nearest shroud. But *Wasp* did not run up onto the reef and die; she slid off and continued alongside. The instant the ship hit, Gant adjusted the wheel—not hard over as if to miss an object straight ahead—but a delicate shift up and away and he gained a bit of sea room. He immediately steered back preserving his forward speed. This smart move avoided the reef for another 100 feet. But a minute later the sound of rocks scraping the hull again ricocheted along the deck. Everyone heard the awful, gnarled sounds of coral and rock scraping *Wasp's* old wooden planks. Unlike warships, *Wasp* did not have a copper-plated bottom to prevent growth of barnacles and seagrass but was built with hardwood, weakened over time in saltwater; a sharp rocky reef could rip out a hole in the bottom within minutes. Once more Gant steered up and away and gained precious room. But *Wasp's* forward speed had dropped precipitously. The next time *Wasp* hit the shoal she would lose all headway, drift to a stop, her sails useless.

"How far? Can you guess?" Gant yelled at Pricilla.

Her hair swirling, she clambered onto the deck peering in the diminishing light for breakers to larboard, then scanning the shore to starboard. She leapt back down the ladder to inspect her charts. From below she cried out, "One hundred feet—the reef's far end sits directly abeam the breakers to starboard!"

That was hard information he could use. He glanced at the waves suddenly visible off their starboard bow. He felt *Wasp's* aft hull begin to scrape the reef. She was about to be thrown sideways. But he had one priceless bit of boat speed remaining. He would attempt a final frantic maneuver.

"Blow the spanker sheets. Fast, now! But keep jibs trimmed tight!"

Alex, Willy, Isaiah, Raca, and Pierce jumped. They expertly laid out the sheets. The large spanker quickly lost its wind and power. As a result, *Wasp's* bow, driven by two jibs, headed to larboard and toward the reef. Alex watched, saying nothing. He recognized the captain's ploy: to miss the reef he would drive straight over its outer edge where the water might be deeper. Gant waited and counted: *One. Two. Three.* He regarded the breakers and glanced down. Pricilla caught his eye. She had been counting as well.

"Now!" she shouted.

He threw his wheel over. "Trim the spanker! Ease jibs slow now and catch the wind. We need boat speed!"

Currents swept them hard toward the reef and *Wasp* gained speed, her sails propelling her with renewed spirit. Like a child's slingshot flinging a stone against an angled wall, *Wasp* changed direction and slipped around the reef's far end. The ship scraped a top edge of the reef and without more momentum would become stuck there; but her increased speed from Gant's aggressive maneuver powered the hull up and over the last hidden rocks forming the reef's outer edge. The crew could hear the sound of rock meeting wood—a portent of certain sinking if it continued. Gant turned deep down-wind toward the reef and the ship gained a final burst of power. Everyone heard a loud collision as the ship lurched upwards but then splashed low in the water. Suddenly everything became freakishly quiet.

In a flash *Wasp* had broken free. The water in the cove protected by the reef was still. *Wasp* had powered over the far edge of the sunken rocks and sandbars of the reef and rested in calm water of an empty lagoon. *Wasp's* crew heard the waves breaking behind the ship cursing their improbable escape.

"Ease!" Gant cried and all the sails fell loose.

"Where are we?" Alex cried as he rushed aft.

Pricilla looked at him bewildered: *Wasp,* she thought, *had no right to be floating high and free.* "I saw a lagoon on our chart. It's deep here: thirty-five feet, Papa."

"Drop the sails, let go the anchor! This current swept every damn thing from the channel into the lagoon. I didn't expect such velocity..." Gant leaned over onto his knees exhausted and recalled another night of terror in his days as a privateer, running from a ship trying to sink him, a reef and 50 dead men.

Alex looked out beyond the reef. Then he stared into the lagoon and asked respectfully, "Captain, you said currents sucked everything from out there into here?" Gant nodded immediately following the implication.

The crew looked at Alex pointing to a horseshoe shaped beach barely visible in the day's last light. Alex, eyes wide with excitement stared first at Pricilla and then her father.

"They'll be in there."

The western sky had turned black by the time their anchor cable found secure holding ground. *Wasp* rested comfortably unlike her crew.

"I don't see any fires. Any boats? Or tents?" Pricilla asked as she stood beside Alex holding his arm.

He scanned the shore with his father's spyglass. Sweeping back and forth from the beach to a rocky ledge rising above, he did not answer at first. "We've lost the light, Captain—we must go ashore."

Gant watched the shore as well. Well accustomed to nighttime landings on forlorn beaches waiting for men to come out of the shadows, he knew what to look for. This beach was barren. "We'll not risk landing in darkness. I don't see any fire. We'll go ashore at first light. We need food and rest. Cook? Something hot. Mr. Raca check the bilge for leakage. We hit the reef pretty damned hard."

Pricilla waited to be sure her voice was out of her father's hearing. "Alexander how many weeks has it been?"

"Five maybe six. With water and fish, they could have survived."

"Do you think there's any fresh water in there? It looks rocky…"

"If there's water, he'd find it." Alex also noticed they seemed alone. "Where'd they go?"

"My father's hanging by the taffrail, smoking with Pierce and Isaiah. Alexander, we must talk fast… I want to go ashore. But if Raca comes, too—"

"He will."

"I'm afraid of what—" She seemed calmer than her words, deathly concerned, enough for two. "I won't leave you alone with him."

"Or you can stay on board with your father."

"But if I stay on *Wasp* and you go ashore with Raca and he finds the strongbox, Alex he might..."

"…leave me here?" Alex finished her thought. "No. I'm sure they won't." His certainty surprised her. Pricilla had trusted him, helped him, *lied* for him; was he keeping something from her? She let his comment pass but thought hard about it. Alex continued. "I'll go ashore with Isaiah. Raca will come. You should stay here."

"No. I won't leave you. And please don't leave me."

He did not argue. "Stay close then."

"Alexander, I'm scared."

"Me too," he admitted. Alex Briggs did not know if they would discover his family dead or alive. He knew, however, what they would *not* find.

Raca ran below and peered into the bilge. He avoided the dark, foul lower deck unless to inflict pain on some miserable captive; tonight, it was necessary. Rushing water sounded where only rats should be. He climbed down and crept forward hunched over in the gloom like the forest creatures he despised. A weak whale-oil lamp showed the way without surrendering evidence of damage to the hull. His boot soles felt seeping seawater. Then his ankles disappeared in the gloom and the cold. He sloshed alone along the larboard side and felt the supporting knees overhead for cracks, planks for stove-in condition. Suddenly the water rose to his shins, a rate capable of sinking the ship and marooning them in this desolate strip of sand and rocks. He neared the bow, but still saw no visible evidence of any hull fracture. Even so, the water continued to rise steadily—six inches or more. He knew the pumps could handle a foot every hour, not more. Nor did *Wasp* have enough crewmen to man the pumps but for a short time before exhaustion would overcome them all.

The fear of imminent drowning gnawed at his resolve, and he felt dizzy. He tripped over something cold and hard below the rising water. An old, rusty set of chains with heavy manacles lying on the floorboards sent him crashing face-first into the cold water. Though the leaking water was only inches deep, the mate panicked. He screamed like a child. Having never learned to swim, he feared any water level higher than a teacup. He tried to jump up before securing a hand-hold, and the jerky motion caused his left foot to slip between two pieces of old metal. And there it stuck, past his ankle bone. His foot was jammed painfully in between the rusted heavy manacle and its sturdy iron fastening, hard into the larboard hull. He could not move his leg, only stand in place. The pain increased tenfold as he tried to free himself. He could not.

"Captain! Help!" Raca cried. After no response, he cried again, "Willy, Pierce! I'm trapped below! For God's sake, come get me!"

The water continued to rise.

No one on deck missed Gregor Raca. Nor did they hear his cries from the bilge far below as they all lay far forward, exhausted on the quarterdeck. After a time, Gant remembered he had not gotten an answer from Raca to his prior command.

"Where's Raca?" he asked no one in particular. The crew all shrugged, not caring. "Pierce, go below. Find out what's keeping him."

"Aye, sir," said Pierce and looked to his cousin who rose without enthusiasm.

"He don't need you both. Willy, secure the loose sheets and braces. We'll all eat and get some rest."

"Captain!" Pierce shouted a few moments later. "Mr. Raca's trapped. Can't move. Water's comin'in at a good clip, sir!"

Gant cursed. He struggled to the main companionway motioning for both Harrisons and Isaiah to follow. "Boy!" he yelled at Alex. "You and the girl man the pumps 'til I relieve you—quick now!"

Alex stumbled over to the ladder, climbed below, and took a grip of the long handle to the pump typically manned by three or more hearty sailors. Pricilla followed and grasped the other side. Together they began the arduous task. Slowly they felt suction take hold and heard water rising through the hose to drain overboard. The two barely made a dent in the volume of water rushing in from below. *If Raca was trapped, how much rising water would it take…?* Alex wondered and considered slowing just enough.

Below in the bilge the water had risen to Raca's waist. He met the captain and crew screaming, "Outtahere! Cut me loose!! Now, damn you, now!"

The ship suddenly listed to larboard, and in doing so the water rose even higher up to Raca's chest.

"Shut up Mr. Raca, you aint' helpin'!" shouted Gant as he pointed. Willy leaned into the frigid water and yanked Raca's trapped leg with his powerful grip. It would not budge: the rusted manacles were seared tight to the iron fitting and indicated no interest in releasing the mate's leg. "Boys, we gotta stanch this inflow or we'll lose the ship. Willy, dive under, find the leak!"

"No, damn you, Captain, help me get out first! I'll drown!" Raca screamed, spit flying, eyes wild.

"Aye, we'll all drown if we don't find the leak. Willy and Pierce, crawl under the water, feel for a break with your hands and arms."

"We neither of us can swim, Captain!" Pierce squeaked like a child.

"Dammit, water's only three feet deep, no one's gonna drown!" *Except for Raca, it appears*, thought Gant regarding his trapped beast.

In the darkness of the filling hull, Willy and Pierce took turns dipping under the water. Out of breath after mere seconds, they rushed to the surface, suffering mightily from the cold.

"Nothin', Captain."

"We need more men on the pumps," Gant realized watching the level rise. "Cook, you and Pierce, to the pump. Willy, this ain't doing us no good. Raca, you stand fast and keep your whimpering down or so help me, I'll stick a sock in your mouth!"

The mate thrashed around in the water now chest-high. Gant followed the others up the companionway ladder where Alex and Pricilla were near to exhaustion.

"Willy, you and Pierce take over. Cook, you, too." Gant gestured to Alex to follow him. "You swim, right, boy? And, daughter, you too, as I recall."

As Gant descended the stairs, he explained what needed to happen. First, save the ship. If done in time, if the pumps could keep up with the leak, then save the life of the mate whom none would mourn—least of all Alex Briggs and Pricilla Gant.

Below, rats from all over the ship were swimming for their lives. They surrounded Raca as he screamed. Two rodents climbed on his shoulders and head, desperate to find dry land. He swatted them away with his hands, but they found his neck and shoulders. A numbing cold slowed his reflexes, but he thought of his knife strapped still to his leg. If he could not release his foot, might he free it in another ghastly manner? He yanked his leg again as the water rose to his neck. It lapped his chin.

On the top deck the two appointed swimmers with lines in their hands laid out a spare topsail flat fore and aft. Alex had listened with unusual care as Gant explained the drill: years before this same ship, then a privateer, had sprung a forward plank yet was saved. But 20 years before Quartus Gant had 50 able crewmen to drop the sail over the side, drag it under the hull, and haul it back up again on the other side where it would be hard-pressed against the leak. Tonight however, on this far-away shore he had only a girl and a boy to do the same maneuver, two youngsters who would just as soon see *Wasp* sink with him aboard as they stole off in a ship's boat. He did not trust them. He commanded and they obeyed. Without *Wasp*, the boy had no chance to find his family. And she, even her father could see, rose each morning only to ensure the boy's success.

Pricilla understood the drill. While the men pumped with vigor, she and Alex ran lines fore and aft to hold the clews when they dropped the sail weighted down with lead over the larboard side. With lines run around bow and stern, they drew the sail under the hull and back up tied tight on the starboard side. Pulled taut, the new tarp should slow the leak. Despite lingering injuries to his ribs and ankles, Alex remained limber enough to climb over the bulwarks with a line and thread it around the cathead securing their second stowed anchor. But in order to bring it up the other side, outboard the jib sprit, he must go into water as black as night.

He dove with the line tied to his waist, dragged it around the bow and then up the other side to starboard. He and Pricilla worked as a team to do the same around the stern; she climbed out on the long spanker boom extending 10 feet past the stern rail, ran the line under it, and then around again to the starboard side. In the water, Alex made sure the line did not snag on the rudder.

The lines in place, Alex climbed back aboard, and he and Pricilla dropped the sail over the forward larboard side into the water and secured it tight with lines and belaying pins. They rushed to the other side and began to pull both overboard lines in unison. Hand over fist, they gathered the wet line for 30, then 40 feet of free line before it became taut.

Below them, in the pitch-black of the bilge Raca continued to scream. He cursed the devil who had ruined his life, alternating between cries and shouts, begging, pleading for help. In minutes or even less the water would cover his upturned head and silence his rants. The cloying rats swarmed around his shoulders and head. He swatted them away with the last of his strength. The cold debilitating his body and brain, it had numbed his toes and hands he could no longer feel. His vision grew cloudy, and he knew he would soon pass out, slip underwater, and end the misery. Worse than the rats clamoring for a hold on his skull and cheeks, however, was anticipating the nightmare of sea water rushing down his throat where air should flow. *What happens to a man who inhales seawater*, he wondered? Does he gag for interminable, agonizing minutes or simply stop breathing after a single, fatal gulp? Will the horror of his final conscious minutes be worse than the terror leading to it? Raca recalled a few of his most despicable deeds. Were stories of the never-ending fire true?

"Damn all of you bastards! Free me—now!" he cried. But all of those *bastards* were too busy saving their own lives.

Willy and Pierce did the jobs of four men on one side of the pump, Gant and Isaiah the same on the other. After the men had been on the pumps two hours, as the sail-tarp was readied, Gant rushed below to measure the flood against his first mate's torso. What he saw was pathetic, but reassuring: the water was stabilizing, perhaps even lowering a bit. The mate remained crazed, but strangely, still conscious, upright, and alive.

"Willy, Pierce, avast your pumping. Alex and Pricilla, take their places. Willy and Pierce, take a hold of the starboard lines to the tarp and secure it as tight as a sea nymph's teat then run below and find the damned leak. And shut that bastard's mouth!"

The Harrison cousins ran to their task. They tightened the sail, tightened the forward hull, and although not water-proof, it worked; the water level rise slowed as long as the pumping continued. Willy climbed below to find the leak. As ordered, he ignored Raca's rants and dove in a spot where he had not searched before. Nothing. He dove again and crawled further forward. His frozen hands felt a stream of water coming toward him; a rivulet of ocean water, with some force as through a faucet or a brook. He crashed to the surface and yelled.

"Found it!" Hearing this, Gant rushed below. "Captain, ten feet forward of Mr. Raca, larboard about two feet from the keelson."

"How bad?"

"If we pump, we can jack it back together and re-caulk the seam. I didn't feel a break, just a seam let go. But I can't swim. Can't reach it!"

If we can pump... Gant reconciled. They had been at it most of the long night, his crew half dead. He needed his strongest arms on the pump. Another would have to close the sprung plank. He glanced around the flooded bilge; pumping it dry would take hours. The mate was fast losing the ugly color from his face. It wouldn't be long before Raca's legs would collapse and his head slip beneath the water. Gant had seen what cold ocean water does to a man. First, he starts to shiver beyond his control. Whether the air around is muggy or freezing, his body has lost its natural warmth. He begins to feel as faint as young miss watching her first cockfight. His head falls to his shoulder, he collapses, and then his chest stops beating. His skin turns a pasty grey and he is gone. Gant needed Raca—at least until they found what they came for. There remained one last option. "Get the boy down here!"

When Alex ducked his head below the low beams of the hated bilge he listened to Gant's instructions. Raca stared at them, his frothing mouth quiet. Alex shook his head and said, as if the mate were not only a few feet away, "I won't do anything to help him."

"You ain't doin' it for the mate," barked Captain Gant. "He's close to dead already. But if we have to pump all this next day because we can't keep up with the leak, when we get it dry enough to raise sail, we're out of here forever, back to San Miguel for repairs. And we ain't never coming back."

It was not a threat. Any reasonable captain would do the same. Alex could not fight the logic: if they were to search this last, desolate cove, the leak must be stabilized quickly. Raca looked out with cold, evil eyes at Alex who returned the hatred but bent to his duty. He could not let Pricilla see him falter.

The first mate was nearly unconscious from the cold water as Cook tied a sturdy three-quarter inch line around Alex's waist. He led the line aft to where Gant and he, in shallower water on the starboard side, could pull Alex back if needed. Willy slid two heavy wool jackets over Alex's shoulders; they might sink him or inhibit his swimming but would keep his blood moving. Gant placed a heavy hammer and six long, sharp spikes in Alex's grip. Pricilla stood by the ladder shining a lamp into the water-filled bow. With only one man on the pumps, the water again began to rise. Through delirium, Raca panicked—screaming something about forest animals. Willy swatted away a pack of three rats intruding on the space under Raca's nose.

Alex dove into the dark water. A strong swimmer, he was surprised how hard it was to dive the few feet below the surface and reach the spot Willy had identified. His arms and legs made powerful strokes, his ability to swim was not hampered by his injuries as much as walking or climbing would have been. On this Gant had also factored. Alex knew he could hold his breath for 30, perhaps 40 seconds. He had done it many times back home, scraping off barnacles from boat bottoms. Within those seconds he felt for the sprung plank: there—stove in from outboard, bent but not split.

He burst to the surface for air. "Got it," he gasped and disappeared again.

Underwater he could not see a thing. He felt where the plank opened to sea water. The rib supporting it was nearby. He hammered a spike with enough initial force to keep it in place. But his lungs gave out before he could hit it again. He resurfaced nearly beyond his limit. But if he stopped now there might not be any going back. He dove. He struck the spike harder. The effectiveness of a hammer's blow underwater was far less than normal, and the spike made little progress. But followed by another two strikes, it was nearly through to the rib. After two more surfaces and three more strikes, he felt the two-inch-thick plank: it had closed in on the rib—it was working. He dove five more times and hammered two more spikes before he felt his eyes closing shut. Alex surfaced and Gant saw the boy's pupils disappear into his head and pulled him out fast to the high side of the listing hull. Alex gasped for air and choked.

"And so?" Gant said without his usual spite.

"Got three in. Need to pump. To get the rest."

"All hands to the pump! Briggs, stay with Raca. Keep his head above water until we get the water level down."

Raca and Alex traded glances. Raca feared the boy would do no such thing; Alex thought of ways to encourage an accident. Gant saw the looks and the hate; he recognized his own world.

"Daughter! Help Mr. Briggs keep our mate upright." Gant turned to Alex. "I will consider it a deliberate criminal action on your part if Mr. Raca does not survive this night."

The two took turns holding the inert mate erect as the water slowly receded—which it did gradually over the next few hours. The sail wrap held the plank tight. Once the water receded enough to reveal Raca's trapped foot, Isaiah and Gant took turns with a saw and an ax on the rusted manacle and by four o'clock in the morning, Mr. Raca was freed and staggering, and helped to his berth. There he ate and drank what the cook quickly heated. He lay on his berth with hot plates from the galley fire warming from below. He mumbled the briefest of thanks to the cook, but for the most part remained quiet, deep in a mindset of retribution.

In the bilge, the Harrisons finished hammering spikes and filled the plank seams with cotton and hemp. The ship lived.

Alex shed his soaked clothes and Pricilla wrapped him in blankets. Gant approached holding two mugs of steaming coffee. He handed one to Alex.

"We'll go ashore at first light. You got two hours to rest," said Gant, noting Alex's blue lips. *Aye*, Gant thought to himself, *the boy's walking into a hornets' nest tomorrow. Raca will go ashore if he can stand and stick to Briggs like a tick. Boy had his chance. Raca knows his mind. But I need 'em both, for now.* "Stay close to Isaiah, boy. And keep your mouth shut. Mr. Raca doesn't need another excuse."

One half hour before sunrise, Isaiah and Alex clutched the oars in the middle seat of their longboat and rowed as fast as their arms could move. Raca, grim and only beginning to recover from his ordeal, sat quietly in the stern with the spyglass. Pricilla crouched in the bow anxiously looking forward. Her father ordered she remain on board, but she defied him; she was determined to stay close to Alex. Although she could not defend Alex against a pistol shot, Pricilla did not believe her father would let Raca murder the boy before her eyes. Willy and Pierce remained on deck out of the line of battle. Pierce's hold on Willy remained strong but loosened day by day as Pricilla's eyes pleaded for Willy to make a stand for her. Or just to stand *against* the mate. *Do something, damn it,* she privately scolded his imagined presence. Before departing *Wasp*, Alex noted Willy and Isaiah talking in hushed voices as the eastern sky momentarily brightened, only to be followed by the gloom of a continued night—a false dawn when suddenly the sun's reflection on the clouds promised more hope for daylight than the hour delivered. And as he helped lower their longboat Willy glanced at Alex and smiled as if to offer a kind of reassurance. Or was it sympathy? Willy's rumored lethal knife, strapped to his hip well-hidden, appeared natural yet ready. *For what purpose,* Alex wondered?

The lagoon's flat water lapped the shore. A rocky beach curved by water and wind into the shape of a crescent moon presented a safe landing for a small ship's boat. At first light, Alex had scanned the beach but the nearest end—which offered maximum protection from ocean winds—remained hidden by the bluff. He glanced over his shoulder to the right hoping to see indications of human life. As they rowed and cleared a last set of boulders near shore what he hoped for came into view.

"A boat!" Pricilla cried.

Raca focused a spyglass on the boat and on gear strewn nearby. It appeared about 26 feet long with a white hull. Dragged above high-water marks, it left streaks in the rocky sand where it had apparently been launched and retrieved many times. It bore no visible damage. Tracks nearest the water, however, were dry. And at water's edge there were no tracks at all.

"See anyone?" Alex cried.

Raca was not looking for people. In a cracked voice from his incessant screaming all night, he replied truthfully, "No one's about. Maybe they gone a-huntin'."

Inland higher up the beach near large sterile boulders showed no sign of people either. The island had no tents, fish shacks—no buildings of any kind, no trees. Nothing rose above the silent beach but naked scrub bushes and wind-blown dunes. Close to the shore, Alex dropped his oars and jumped out.

"Boy—secure the damned boat!" barked Raca.

The launch turned sideways against gentle waves lapping onto shore. Isaiah brought her bow back in line. Pricilla climbed out and ran after Alex and grabbed his arm.

"*Stay* near me," she commanded. "Raca has a pistol. But I have a knife, Alexander. So does Isaiah. He showed me how to use it."

"There won't be any fighting here," whispered Alex as they walked toward a small campsite.

A few rocks had been placed in a circle forming a fire pit. The remnants of scarred embers lay scattered but there were no burnt logs, cooking utensils, or fish bones. Only a few discarded clamshells littered the ring. *How many had landed here he wondered? Where did they go?*

"Hello! Captain Briggs? Father, Mother? Anyone?" he yelled as loud as he could to an empty shore. "Lizzy—?" Alex's voice broke as no familiar voices answered.

Holding back tears, he ran to the longboat: cut into her aft transom was a script he knew well—*Mary Celeste, Rochester*—in clean, simple letters. He rubbed his fingers over the words. He looked around. No trees. No streams ran into the lagoon. *No fresh water.* The lagoon's bottom dropped deep close to shore. Perhaps fish swam near; but he saw no mudflats or marshes where one could dig for shellfish. Without tackle, catching enough fish to survive would have been difficult even for his father. Alex and Pricilla looked behind a few large rocks. One hundred feet away, Raca scornfully kicked at sundries—oars, loose ropes, bailing buckets—left near *Celeste's* longboat. Slowly, Isaiah climbed alone to higher ground; a few minutes later he returned.

"Come here you two," Isaiah called softly to Alex and Pricilla. Alex scrambled across the rocks and ragged boulders. Pricilla followed fast behind.

Graves.

Rocky and without adornment, they were graves without doubt. Carefully laid, two were close by each other. One was smaller. Three others were not far away. Five were buried within view of the ocean that had forsaken them. Isaiah searched around another boulder and returned. "Six more. No markings," Isaiah said soberly. Alex felt weak and fell to his knees. The smuggler's daughter instinctively knelt beside him. He held onto Pricilla and looked at the graves. *Did his mother lie here? Lizzy? Where's Father?* "Stay here, son. Someone lived to bury the others. A sight you should never have to see. I'll return shortly." With sad eyes Isaiah walked toward his task and saw Raca roughly examining what was left of the longboat's supplies, kicking debris, yelling oaths. The cook felt for his knife and went around other rocks and returned. "They made a camp of sorts over there.

Two outlived your father. None of the last were buried. The birds had at them…" Pricilla rested her head into Alex's chest. He held her tight. "Do not go back there. I will bury them. You can join me in prayer after," said Isaiah.

Alex sat on a rock staring at his family's graves. He had not noticed at first: a small piece of wood placed under a few rocks on the grave protecting it from harsh North Atlantic Ocean winds.

Carved with care was a single word: *Emma.*

After a brief prayer over the rocky graves, Isaiah waited for Raca to wander away—still looking for the strongbox. "I found your father's log." Isaiah said. "He wrote until the end. Here."

Alex took his father's leather-bound book. Never far from his side, Captain Briggs kept his log in a sea bag ready to go ashore or into a launch. Would it reveal why they died?

"Do you know how they… met their end?" With tears in his eyes Alex looked at Isaiah.

"I see no signs of fresh water. No fish. No shade. Nothing out here but rocks and sand. They landed on a barren, inhospitable shore. Without water in this heat, they only had days. They did not suffer for long."

"Why'd they stay here?" But Alex knew. Like the castaways, *Wasp* had been sucked into the lagoon by a strong unseen current. To row against it while sailing into a stealthy northerly wind looking for some distant habited island would have been impossible for a starving crew. And which direction would they steer? There was no visible land east where they knew the Azores lay and to the west where currents ran hard, they would only find an empty ocean. *Mary Celeste's* survivors had become trapped in a lonely lagoon with no way out.

"Please, Pricilla…" Alex handed his father's logbook to Pricilla. His eyes were filled with grief, but he had to know.

Pricilla opened and read in a soft voice:

"*October 18, in the year of Our Lord, 1832*

224

"*Herein find the final words and testament of Captain Ebenezer Briggs of Rochester Village, Massachusetts, master of the brig* Mary Celeste.

"*Today I buried my dearest wife, and have only two living crew left of those who landed here on this rock one month ago. Our sweet child Lizzy succumbed to hunger and thirst and died Saturday past, and we buried my wife alongside her. Whether my wife died of the same or a broken spirit, I cannot say.*

"*I too am falling into despair. My lads still alive have no longer enough strength to launch our ship's boat in search of fish which—though hard to come by—sustained us for our first weeks. I do not expect to outlive the next few tides and will join my wife and daughter.*

"*Our two strong lads have served our family well. Peter Dexter of Wareham and Thomas Gauvin of Plymouth remain alive, brave and loyal to the end and should be well-remembered as honest and true souls. I pray for their deliverance from this place as they have been kind and brave. They are strong God-fearing men. I shall miss them.*

"*To anyone who finds our graves and who reads this log may wonder how this calamity came to happen. If the* Celeste *was found, I know not. She could steer true on her own, but after the gale she must eventually turn up and hove-to. Or else run up on rocks and sunk. But I trust our disappearance has been noted. I pray each day for my living sons, and may God protect them as I can no longer.*

"*To anyone who learns of our story should know* Mary Celeste's *people died in peace and love with no ill will disposed to any man. Our fate was determined by unknown powers and my own folly.*

"*On Thursday the seventeenth of last month all was normal. My second watch was on deck and had trimmed sails at my command. The rig was full of canvas—topgallants hung over mainsails, and I flew our flying jib trying to eke out final breaths of a generous westerly—our kind companion these past weeks. Our voyage east had been steady.*

"I had look-outs aloft each day scanning for friendly sails and raiders alike which I had cautioned all about since we neared shores where corsairs from Africa pounced on unwary merchantmen.

"But I had Celeste *prepared: we had loaded in New York a sturdy twelve pounder, more for effect than hull-damage, but she roared with a double-shot to a lasting impression. We had our long rifles, newly cast in Springfield, a sample of our future cargoes for British armies. We had cutlasses to repel boarders. I had my strongbox and gold recently moved and safely hidden.*

"As I left my quarterdeck and joined my family for our midday meal, I noticed a peculiar odor from below deck. At first, I thought of rotting foodstuffs or dead vermin wafting from our bilge. But I recalled our cargo: casks of sugars, molasses, oils, alcohol, and vinegars—was fermentation from sugar to alcohol taking place from unseen leakage? Even on deck I could note the odd acrid smell. I thought on this as I sat to my meal and tried to enjoy the fine table Mrs. Briggs had set. We were soon interrupted by my first mate who had noticed the same foul smell from below-deck. He and the others in the crew were worried for the ship. Their fears: an escaped vapor might ignite.

"All men who go to sea in ships of wood and tar share a mortal fear of fire. With no means to quickly douse a fire, flames can spread fast to sails and spars. Once afire and sails are ablaze, unless a torrent of rain appears, the ship will burn and sink. I shared their fear.

"I knew my men were anxious but decided to show resolve and calm, and for my ladies too (my dear Lizzy, her first time at sea). I responded I would join them presently. Mrs. Briggs said little so our hearty meal would pass swiftly, which to her credit it did.

"On deck our men circled. My sailing master Louden Creighton retold the story of the SV Charles of Camden a disaster

in '22. Sugars and molasses fermented somehow and leaked into the air and a spark—from where no one ever learned—ignited alcohol contained in the cloud. The Charles *was engulfed in a fireball to her waterline and only a few badly burned souls survived.*

"I too had heard this episode: forty-two men died. Twenty thousand dollars of cargo rested on Stellwagon Bank. If we faced the same, I had only minutes to save my crew. The Celeste *herself, I realized, may already be lost.*

"I called for my family to quickly appear on deck and gather a few things for comfort. I launched our three longboats and loaded all hands. I grabbed my spare sextant and the log and noted our emergency bags were aboard each boat as was our custom at sea with enough water and hardtack for a few days.

"In a dying westerly with a stale air all around us, fate played her hand. The air was more putrid than a minute before and suddenly came a bright flash. Not a boom like a thundercloud erupting but a crack as when lightning finds a target and lands near. Hairs on my arms stood and my eyes, which I shielded with my arms, saw a bright light.

"'To the boats!' I cried and our crew needed no further encouragement. Mary Celeste's *deck erupted in a fireball of exploding gases.*

"I had instructed my lads to attach long painters to each boat secured firmly to Celeste's *stern. A few boys to escape had leapt into the sea by their feet, others head and arms first. We retrieved them from the cold water, and I had all three boats drift back one hundred feet to stay clear of the impending conflagration.*

"But a strange and blessed event took place: the fireball, erupted from leaked gasses expanded but did not quite reach our dry sails when it suddenly expired. The fire had exhausted its explosive fuel source and was done. 'Done for a time,' I told myself. A new cloud could reform at any moment. Would another fire ignite? Since we did not know, I had our boats remain safely astern watching and waiting.

"I hailed my other two boats: 'Stay in tow for a full watch. We shall monitor this smell and leakage before we re-board.' I had already set my mind upon re-boarding all flasks and barrels would be summarily chucked overboard. Our cargo lost, but our lives, my strongbox, and our ship would be safe.

"At the moment when I felt hope for the first time, I felt a drop of water on my neck. I put my hand there as another drop fell. I turned to see an angry black sky approaching fast from southwest. In our desperation to escape we forgot to keep our weather-eye out and now faced a fierce blow. Alarmed, I turned back to look at Celeste. *She sat calmly with full and still-limp sails on each mast, luffing and rippling. Bloated like fresh laundry on a washerwoman's line, once this violent front hit, her sails would capture the wind and propel her out of control without us. With no crew on board, she would eventually sail up and hove-to stopping allowing us to re-board. If we could re-board her. The storm hit us before I could even announce an alarm, but of course my crew saw what I could see. A cold squall hit us, and* Celeste *sailed off.*

"At first, she took our boats on a gentle tow. My longboat rode high as I moved crew aft and put two hearty souls on the tiller to keep her straight. When Celeste *rounded up, we would be saved. But* Celeste *proved a good and steady sailor—too good. She did not round up, but instead purposefully held her own course as the winds rose. We would never regain her now. We surfed behind on waves, hanging by balance and muscle. As the wind reached a fury,* Celeste *sailed fast through steepening waves. I knew we could not stay in tow. If we foundered, we were dead. My wife and daughter, though sea-faring ladies, in their great petticoats and skirts would sink fast if our longboat overturned. And the cold water would kill us all. I made a fateful decision and with my long knife cut through our tow line to* Celeste. *We sprang clear and stopped surfing. Bobbing, oars calmed our balance but there was no use rowing after* Celeste. *The ship sailed away without us.*

"Exhausted and in great anxiety I looked to my left and to my horror saw neither of our other longboats afloat. One had capsized and was torn asunder by the violent tow, her crew one by one falling under whitecaps with cries of mercy never to reappear. Our second, my favorite gig, which was strong and sturdy, also met a sad fate and had capsized. She was dragged, overturned by Celeste heading northwest.

"Three of our boys from the nearer launch could swim and made their way to us. Though overfilled ourselves, we welcomed these men with cheers and encouragement to reach us and climb aboard with our outstretched arms and hands to help them. We sheltered them as best we could with our coats and bodies as the squall hit with full force—a cold and miserable rain eventually stealing the last view of my ship.

"After a restless and cold night, we woke to an empty sea. A man feels never so alone and despondent as when he looks in every direction and sees nothing but water.

"There were no signs of Mary Celeste. *Had she survived? Had she gone down or broached sideways turned onto a shoal? A likely scenario I thought since we had not prepared to hove-to. She would sail on until she lost steerage, eventually succumbing to God's mercy. She was a good ship, true to us, but now likely gone down.*

"I remembered we had sailed past out-islands twelve hours back and thus directed my strong lads to take up oars and get into it. They did with gusto. In a few hours we were as dry and comfortable as ten men and women in a twenty-five-foot boat had rights to be.

"The next day, aided by my spare sextant Providence had induced me to bring along, with water and a bite of biscuit we were on course to an island. Was there a fishing camp or a village? I thought not but dared not offer my opinion. I reckoned we were late for a flood current running four knots westerly. We passed what seemed to be habited out-islands but had not fair winds nor enough oars to deliver us there. So, we pressed onto a

horizon spec in front of us: our landfall or never. Beyond was only Wellfleet in Massachusetts two thousand miles away. My crew long dead by then of course.

"I had my charts in hand and felt confident in this last possible landfall. But I felt far less comfortable about our situation. It was dire…"

Pricilla looked up. Alex stared at the horizon. She turned a few more pages and read quickly to where the writing stopped. She softly gasped and hoped Alex did not notice.

"Alexander. He describes life on this rock-pile. No food or water, no protection from wind and cold. They were scorched all day and froze at night. They came close to burning the boat for warmth, but your father forbade it. I am so sorry…" Pricilla offered her hands and arms. He held her close but never felt such loneliness. Pricilla was stronger. He had failed.

Raca appeared. He looked at the graves without comment and turned to Alex with fury in his eyes. "Where'd he put it?" he spat out. "Buried? Tell me where or I'll cut you for bait!"

Isaiah approached slowly from outside Raca's peripheral vision. Alex saw he also had a gleaming knife in his hand poised not for a stab but for a slice: an ear, an arm, or a hand holding another knife.

"You know where it is," Alex said coldly. He looked past Raca. The cook threw Alex a look of concern.

"What?" Raca asked confused, looking around the desolate shore.

Alex shouted, angry and hurt to make sure everyone heard. "*You* know. We *all* know where it is! My father wrote it *right here*: the damned strongbox sits someplace on the damned *Mary Celeste*! And when our British friends find it on their voyage home, they'll have a hearty laugh at our expense. You understand, Mr. Raca, *right*?" He angrily mocked the mate making no attempt to hide his contempt.

Raca was not sure what he understood. But he heard the boy's hatred. As he also remembered the boy's intent to push his head underwater the night prior. This would be a good time to end it. He stood and started to walk toward Alex and Pricilla sobbing in each other's arms. As he came near, he looked up to see the cook staring at him with a knife in one hand and a rock in the other. The mate turned back to the beach and rowed back to the ship. He would repeat Alex's words as his own. The captain would follow the logic. *Wasp* would sail back to Sao Miguel as fast as the wind carried dashed dreams and lost hope.

As Alex had anticipated… back to the *Mary Celeste.*

Isaiah watched Pricilla soak salted cod in fresh water to make it edible for the evening meal. She had been unusually quiet since they left the island. He watched her hands shake. He had waited to speak to her alone.

"Were these the same islets we passed on our approach into Sao Miguel?" Isaiah asked.

"I'm not sure. I'd have to look at our charts…"

"Aye." It was clear she did not want to say more. "Captain Briggs' log, Miss. I noted you didn't read his last entries out loud…"

"His scrawl was becoming difficult to read…"

"Hmmm?"

"I didn't want to cause Alex any more pain."

A more honest answer, he thought. "Miss, you read aloud starting from his first entry. But when I found the logbook by his body, I read only his last words." She looked up, eyes open and aware. She remained silent. "It was hard—was it not—" Isaiah persisted, "to read Captain Briggs' handwriting as he weakened in his final hours?" She said nothing. He pressed on knowing he must. "But I could read what he wrote, Miss. We both could. He made sure to carefully record the dates he was still alive."

She sighed then sobbed, "Those poor people, Isaiah! Please don't tell Alex."

"He should know."

"If I tell Alex he'll try to kill my father! One of them will die. I cannot make that decision. He's my *father*. He's cruel but he wasn't always. He taught me about life before the mast and how to survive on a ship filled with scoundrels. He paid for my education other girls don't receive. I can't send Alex to murder him!" Hard hit by the reality of her impossible situation, she could not stop her tears—flowing like blood in an interminable stream toward death. "My father will kill Alex instead. Or command Raca to do it."

"Perhaps you're right. Your silence about this may save Alex. But silence can't save your father's soul."

Wasp sailed back to Sao Miguel carrying a crew in foul dispositions. Those who had clung to hope during the many long weeks at sea now despaired. Alex wandered the decks absently absorbed in grief and anger. Pricilla's kindness was only small relief. *Father is dead. Mama dead. And dear Lizzie… so unfair. He would have seen the approaching storm. He would have climbed back on board. He should have found them sooner. How long ago did they die?* He would read his father's log later. Held back for weeks, an urge to strike out raged unleashed.

Pricilla was shaken. She had seen the young Briggs girl recently in Rochester Village. Now the little girl lay under a small mound of rocks on a pile of sand in the middle of nowhere. Pricilla was greatly relieved Alex made it back to *Wasp* unmolested by Raca. The dead-cold look in Alex's eyes frightened her, however. It was a look different than grief. She knew. She must keep him away from the mate and her father.

Gant strode his quarterdeck beyond anger and disappointment. Cheated *again*. Taken by the thieving Navy man. Blocked by a foul Portuguese minion and his corrupt British ally. And now this: a foolish and dangerous search risking his ship and his life. A *total* waste of precious time. Why had he listened to the boy? At least he had one small comfort: Ben Briggs was dead. Once they had been mates and comrades. He recalled lazy days when the two men courted the same young beauty from the estate on Great Hill. But the Briggs family was respected and part of the fabric of the south coast and so she chose the solid standing of Ebenezer Briggs over his privateer passion. Though he married Pricilla's mother a short time later, the bitter taste of a scorned first love never left him. He was not part of Emma Hammond's world and would never be. It was easier to hate Ben Briggs after Emma spurned Gant's final offer. Over the ensuing years fierce competition turned to a manic desperation to beat Briggs and Sons on every voyage, win or steal every cargo, use stolen information to gain every edge. But he had planned the couple's demise too well; now she lay dead alongside him. It was small comfort to know she died before he might have had an opportunity to save her. He had no blame in the matter of her demise—it was Briggs who brought her out here. *Damn them both!*

Only one opportunity to live a satisfied life remained: recover Ben Briggs' strongbox, still hidden aboard *Mary Celeste*. He knew he could not take the ship by force without his full crew so he must use guile. Gant stared at Alexander Briggs standing close to his daughter by a windward railing. He recalled the chest the boy discovered on *Celeste*. The girl had read the papers inside. Immediately after that they had rushed off on this foolish escapade. As he watched them now, he noticed how close they stood, like lovers. He shook his head and clenched his fist. He had sailed too far to be outwitted. Gant would sail *Wasp* back to Sao Miguel faster than a shooting star.

Gregor Raca was exhausted from his near death in the bilge and confused about the futility of the search. He seethed and his feeble brain foamed like a Bedlam inmate. His hatred found a new depth and he fantasized about whom to punish first, when and how. *Stupid Gant!* He brought them on this damned search and listened to the boy. *Gant will die first.* Raca had waited many years and hard voyages and had earned his place. Captain Gant, with his dirty crew, once owned every soul on board including Raca's. But without protection everything has changed. Gant had his chance. He failed and had gone too easy on the boy. Now Raca would get answers his way. Rats and molasses take too long; instead, he'd use sharp blades red hot from a roaring galley fire. And Gant would feel his blade—late at night looking into his killer's eyes... as his blood empties overboard through the scuppers. And the girl, too—the girl who despises him, refuses him, laughs at him. *She will suffer most.* He licked his lips and strode the slippery deck with a renewed purpose.

A northeast breeze was steady from abeam. Despite her shortened-sail, *Wasp* liked Gant's trim and responded well: gliding over swells, dipping into troughs, and rising back up again smoothly. Her empty hold let *Wasp* skip and dance on gentle, thousand-mile-long rollers forming off Nantucket that would wash ashore onto the ancient white beaches of North Africa. Gant had collapsed into his cot. Deck watches were set between the five crewmen and Pricilla. Pierce Harrison had the spokes of the wheel firmly in hand. Raca watched him carefully and pretended to ignore Pricilla busy coiling a heavy, recently trimmed jib sheet. The boy had disappeared below, dead exhausted, angry, and pathetic. Cook and Willy were asleep in their hammocks forward. It was a fair evening sailing fast through a moonlit ocean. Raca looked back at Pierce and nodded: Raca owned the deck.

"Are the lines too heavy for ya?"

"Go," Pricilla said as little as possible to the mate; always the same: *Go.*

"We're alone tonight, eh?"

They were not alone; Pierce was nearby at the wheel but did not look in their direction. Curious. She looked down. Raca held a knife in his dirty hand. "Is your bastard orphan hiding below? Dead *tired*, eh? Ha—dead *dead*, he's gonna be!"

"Leave me alone or I'll call for my father…"

"Ah yes. Your dear Papa. After his draught of Medford rum, I don't think you'll see him this watch. I know your father admires your looks. He tells me when we enjoy our drink you remind him of your dead mother. Reminds him *too* much. He says he'd rather see her alive than you. Ha! Your loving Papa who beats you like a puppy. And yet you turn from me when I offer you my kisses?"

Pricilla did not know how to respond. Was he threatening her? Should she cry out for help? She could not possibly be in danger with Pierce Harrison looking on… He *was* watching, wasn't he? *Oh, dear God…*

"Yes, such a pretty face. Even burned from the sun your face shines clean and smooth, yes." As she turned away, he ran a dirty finger along her cheek; his finger stopped and stayed on her lips. "But you hate me, don't you? But you see I *welcome* your hate. And your father hates me too, right? So, he'll suffer too. But you first. He'll see what I've done…" He held his hand close to her neck and she turned her head the other way, repulsed as his rum and tobacco-breath spewed past blackened teeth and poured over her face. "Your father says you'll not have me. He tells me now I ain't gonna *never* get you despite his promises. Do I got it right? Not in marriage or in bed? You gonna refuse me forever?"

Unlike previous attacks, Raca held a knife in his right hand, and she could not slide away to her left without feeling its blade. She could, however, reach with her right hand behind her back. Isaiah had shown her how to sharpen a knife. He had given her a butcher's knife from his satchel and had shown her the difference between a deadly stab and a mere cut. She learned a defensive thrust to slow or stop an assailant, as well as a stab at a neck or heart meant to quickly end a life. The cook had practiced with her, and she had received small cuts demonstrating her initial lack of skill. He taught her how to lash her new knife to her hip under her shirt so she could reach for it with one hand. He warned her she must display her knife boldly with ample room to move or an opponent might overpower her in close combat.

"Oh, you'll fight me? I welcome a fight! I see you got yourself a knife, right?"

Despite her anxiety, Pricilla had pressed her fingers around the handle of her knife and released it cleanly from its sheath. But her arm got no further than her midsection before Raca's practiced eye had caught the shiny blade and grabbed her wrist with the strength of two men. He saw in her eyes deadly intent and hatred without filter. But her anger was without means. *How foolish and wasteful to arm such a hopeless creature*, he thought. He shook her wrist violently. Once, twice, and after three times her knife fell from her hand. At his moment of conquest, he slid his blade near her face. He let her cower, displaying it in front of her eyes so she could memorize its terror as her life ended. He pressed his blade gently against the soft skin of her neck where he ran an edge and cut a thin red line across the first layer of her delicate skin.

"Willy!" she screamed as loud as she could. Pierce at the helm remained fixed on the stars. "Willy!"

With his free hand, Raca pushed her back against *Wasp's* main mast and slapped her hard squarely in her face. She crumpled. He was surprised at her unexpected armed defense but now laughed at his sudden good fortune and her complete vulnerability. He knew Willy was out as cold as her father with the ample drink they all had shared. Raca had no fear of any interruption. He could do whatever he wanted and congratulated himself. *This will be payment in full.*

As he put his knife back in his sheath so he could fondle her with both hands before the deed, his head exploded with violent pain. At first it stung like a burn or a bee sting. Then he felt a dullness followed by explosions of flames a hundred times worse. He felt his skull ripped apart like talons from a raptor swooping from a nest on fire. He fell away from Pricilla and looked up to meet the blazing eyes of the Briggs boy beating his skull and shoulders with a heavy belaying pin. Alex smashed his wooden weapon against Raca's skull again and again. Blood splattered Raca's face and shirt. The *Wasp's* mate was barely conscious as he fought for his life. He forgot about the girl lying dazed and terrified at his feet. Even semi-conscious, Raca was able to grab Alex's club in mid-swing. With his remaining strength, he shook the weapon free. He looked at the boy. *Scum!* This roach he had tortured for weeks fought with fury. Was the idiot boy loyal to Gant's daughter? Loyal to Gant—a man who intended to throw him on a sandbar with a bucket of gruel? *He risks his life for the girl?* Raca smiled even as a steady stream of his blood dripped into his eyes. He found his feet and held Alex at an arm's length and punched back with a terrific power: first the lad's jaw, then his stomach, and his ribs. Raca knew where to aim. He kicked at Alex's legs and swung again; it would be easy to beat Alex to death. Raca would enjoy it. He no longer cared what Gant wanted. After the boy bled out, he would finish with her. *This will be a night!*

Pricilla awoke and silently watched the fight from a prone position, still too weak to stand. Raca made a ferocious slam with his fist and arm, but Alex ducked. His empty punch threw him off balance which he did not regain as *Wasp* rolled in a swell. He slipped, staggered, and fell back hard onto the closed starboard gate. Repeated orders from Gant resurfaced in Raca's mind; instructions to repair rot near the hinges of this gate—commands Raca had ignored. A wave caught the hull and shifted the ship's previously steady motion. The rail and gate on which his entire weight rested groaned. With the next roll of the ship, all support would break away. Muffled by the ocean's sounds, no one but Raca heard the gate rip from its hinge.

On quaking legs, Pricilla stood slowly; she noticed it, too...

Alex saw genuine fear in Raca's eyes. The gate had sprung open and hung by a single hinge. Only a sliver of rotted wood and weakened metal separated *Wasp's* mate from the deep sea. Alex aimed high and launched his body toward Raca intending to heave him off the ship. Alex's approaching blackened and bloody face stunned an unbelieving Raca who realized his impending death would be delivered by the hands of this scrawny bastard. *Wasp* rolled and Alex gained the high side advantage. Raca had no time to do anything but tense his muscles. Alex was only two feet away from shoving the first mate overboard when a blur passed in front of him.

Raca never saw Pricilla rushing at him until she crashed into his chest. Her head and shoulders lowered, she hit Raca hard—her left hand grabbing for a tied line wrapped around a belaying pin. She had expected her impact on the large man to arrest her momentum and was shocked at how little resistance she met. Reaching out for the rope she was horrified her momentum left it beyond her stretched fingers. Where Raca was falling she would follow.

Her feet lifted off *Wasp's* deck as a hand grabbed her upper arm. Her motion shot her like a child's swing over the waves, but the arm brought her back toward the ship. She frantically grabbed the outboard railing with both hands, her feet clawing at any stable plank dangling 20 feet above the ocean. Alex held one of her arms tight with both arms. Her other hand lost its grip. She slipped, about to fall into the deep but for Alex's hold. Her free hand swung through the air and after two failed attempts found the bulwark; she grabbed the rail for all her life and stared at Alex. His coupled hands remained tight around her other hand with the determination of a carpenter's vice, but he was unable to pull her up and over; he needed both her hands and both her arms in his for leverage.

"Let go!" he screamed: she had to release her terrified clutch on the rail to be able to grab his other outstretched hand. Again, he yelled, "Trust me, now!" Her eyes latched onto his and then four arms and hands met halfway between the rail and the devils deep blue and with a loud grunt expending the last of his strength he yanked her waist up and over the rail. Pricilla fell onto the deck on top of Alex. They held each other momentarily disbelieving their survival. Alex and Pricilla then jumped up and swung their attention to where they had last seen Gregor Raca.

The first mate shrieked as his head hit a low hanging block that knocked him dizzy. He flew off *Wasp* into the dark North Atlantic Ocean. The cold water woke him to his senses and instantly he became aware of severe pain from his cracked skull lashed with sea water immediately followed by the terror and severity of his peril. His last screams were muffled by a breaking wave.

"Helm, about!" Alex cried to Pierce. "Raca's overboard! Jibe-ho! We've got to get back before he drowns!"

As Alex turned his attention to the helm, Pricilla could not help herself but to stare at the shrieking, waving hands the ship was leaving in its wake. She covered her face with her hands and turned away.

Raca watched *Wasp* sail east without him, his lungs filling with cold saltwater, and he choked as he tried to scream for help. A leaden pain in his chest and head dulled his senses as he gulped for air but tasted saltwater instead. He sank five feet, then 10. At 50 feet he looked up, his eyes wide. Before they closed for the last time, he saw moonlight shimmering through the grey Atlantic waters leading him down to his cold grave far, far below.

Pierce, blindly following Raca's earlier commands, did not react, nor did he immediately comprehend how the mate's sudden demise had released him. He had seen the fight in the moon's shadow but remained confused at the sequence prior to the outcome. He saw Alex beat their mate and rush at the wounded, bloody man, barely alive and clinging to the rail. But then Pricilla had flown into the *mêlée* and all Pierce could determine was a sudden confluence of bloody hands and legs until there were only two standing near the open gate. Pierce

Harrison had no doubt Alex meant to kill Raca and if he was able, to throw him overboard; it seemed reasonable. Yet now the boy wanted to retrace their course. Why? To find a floating corpse? There was no chance a man could survive long in these waters, nor could anyone aboard the ship find him in the darkness.

Hearing the yelling, Gant staggered onto the deck, groggy from rum and deep sleep.

"Mr. Harrison, what's amiss?"

Pierce froze, terrified of Gant's tone. He had the helm—the only crewman who had the ability to cause the ship to lurch in an otherwise controlled sea, had he so chosen in order to assist Raca's pitch over the side.

"The mate's over the side, sir!" Pierce ventured.

Gant stared at him as if trying to recollect any unusual motion in the ship's passage.

"What now? Mr. Raca, you say?"

"Aye, sir," Pierce confirmed. As Pierce deadly feared, *he* alone might be held responsible for the mate's death. "The boy and him was fightin'. Blood everywhere, sir! He went over!"

Gant looked at the ocean shrouded in darkness punched by a half-moon. The winds in the sails told him there would be no coming about. *Wasp* was sailing before the wind in a confused sea, approaching land with an ebb tide against her. By the time they could return to where Raca fell over an hour would have passed. He was drowned already. A jibe might cost them a spanker boom or a gaff halyard or both. *Raca had been a loyal dog,* Gant mused, *but he was only a dog.*

"Keep your helm steady. We can't help him." Gant ordered, looking at Alex, blood on his shirt and breeches, a belaying pin nearby on the deck.

"Harrison!" Gant turned to yell at Pierce. "You were only twenty feet away—who done it, tell me now or I'll be thinking you're all in cahoots."

"He done it, sir! The boy!"

"You saw him clear?"

240

"Aye, sir. He attacked the mate and hit him powerful on his head and face—"

"Father, that's because Raca was attacking me! He was ravishing me! Look, he cut me with his knife—"

"Enough girl! You caused me enough trouble this damned voyage. Not another word!"

"But, Father, Pierce is lying—!"

"Not another word!" Gant roared. "Pierce, what then?"

Pierce, steering the ship, careful not to lose even a point of their course, stammered what he recalled, trying to fit lies to match his recollection. He did not have the wit to mesh his lies with the event, so he stuck with the lies.

"He shoved the mate, after he stunned him good with a blow to his blindside, he shoved him across the deck and the mate grabbed the gate!" Gant looked at the obscenely broken gate, its rotten wood held by twisted hinges. He was blameless in this; he had issued more than one command. The mate had met a fate he himself caused.

"Then he *fell* over?" Gant asked, laying out a pathway.

Pierce was not sure if this was his escape or not. If he told the captain what actually happened, Gant would not believe him, or worse, blame him for fingering an obviously innocent female who could no more shove a 230-pound brute off a ship than pick him up with her finger. But someone had to own the deed, and Pierce wanted out from under Raca's boot; hence, the mate's drowning was neither due to his helm nor a failure to raise a cry of warning. Pierce had only one choice. "No, sir, the boy, sir. He hit him hard in the face with the pin and then shoved him through the gate."

Gant looked at the bloody, silent, unsteady youth; he had no interest in a further inquisition. As the captain turned away, Alex stammered like a condemned man trying to find words to save himself as he was led to a guillotine. But he would not give up Pricilla.

She realized the futility of Alex's feeble defense and yelled above the waves, "Father, Harrison is lying! I was the one—"

"ENOUGH!" Gant barked in a voice to make the sea tremble. "The boy will hang for this in Boston. Keep to your course, Mr. Harrison."

Gant said nothing more to his daughter. He disappeared below leaving the deck to Pierce Harrison who ignored Pricilla's icy stare. Willy came on deck sheepish in his stupor and took the wheel from his traumatized cousin. Isaiah approached close behind. He had been in a dream state, now bleary-eyed and confused at the commotion. Then he saw the open gate and Alex spattered in blood. He saw the knife he had given the girl; unstained, it lay where she had first fallen. He picked it up and returned to the kitchen. The fight had come to the young woman. The fight had come to Alex.

It was only after Gant disappeared below that Pricilla finally looked at Alex. He stood alone, blood at his feet, and spattering his clothes and face. Then she looked at the broken gate where she had last seen Raca. Unlike on land where death leaves behind a cold, gray body, a plain pine casket, and a lonely granite gravestone in a church field, out at sea when a man disappears over the side one only feels numb, unsure of how to react to the sudden void. One moment a man is alive on deck, a threat to her existence and then in the next instant—gone... for all time. It was good he was dead she knew; it would take a lifetime however to reconcile how *she* came to be the cause of his death when so many others wanted it too.

Pricilla's legs failed her. She slid onto the deck. Crumpled, she sat far away from the open gate. From her vantage point across the ship's deck, she watched the broken gate swing in and out with the rolling waves. It clanked hard, over and again, repeating its reminder of fate and deadly departure. She decided she could never go home on *Wasp.* Not with her father. For Alexander Briggs and Pricilla Gant their only course was to find their way east to wherever the angry grey swells rolled on exhausted, finally spent.

Pricilla sobbed as they sat on a chest below deck. "His eyes had such hatred."

"Forget him. He's gone." Alex held Pricilla in his bloodied arms.

"'Forget?' I just killed a man!"

"I would have killed him. It's all the same," he murmured. Pricilla regarded Alex, unsure if it was Raca's blood or his own covering his face. She searched for bandages, still sniffling, and wiping her eyes and nose. Alex was correct of course; sins of intent equal the deed itself. She wrapped a bandage around his head. He stopped her and looked carefully at her face and bloody neck. "Forget me. You are injured worse than I. Look up, let me see where he cut you... Good God! I'll get Isaiah..."

"Raca would have killed me had you not come." She felt the stinging below her chin. *My injuries will heal. But a man breathing minutes ago died by my hand. Good.* She was suddenly both terrified and angry but did not understand why. She had killed a man who deserved his fate, yet few would understand how she felt, nor would they sympathize. Soon she would face her father's wrath alone. He blamed her for Raca's lust. He will blame her for his death. What would he do to her? Only this young man stood by her, as injured and afraid as she. "Isaiah may help us with our wounds but who will *save* us Alexander? Papa will have you arrested and hanged. He'll lock me below and then... You will die. My life will continue alone and in misery. All because of what I've done tonight..."

"I won't hang. We'll find a way," Alex reassured her.

"I don't think you understand—*anything*. Me. My life. What happened tonight. What it's like to be a woman trapped on a stinking ship filled with violent men!"

"I understand more than you think—"

"*Oh, you do?*" she interrupted, mocking him. "You understand my *father*? Explain to me why he beats me when I speak and beats me when I do not?" She had promised herself to keep the memory of last spring's tragedy locked away forever but the death of the man tonight brought back her mother's death vividly. "He blames me for everything, Alexander. I tried to save her. He was down east and could have paid for a doctor or the midwife to remain close by. But he saved his dollar, found his tide, and sailed away. I was alone when the baby started to come. I ran to the woman's home but couldn't find her even though she promised she'd come at my call. I left word everywhere. The midwife never came all night. I couldn't stop my mother's bleeding. She and the baby... it was awful! They died Alexander, and I couldn't help them. I had to clean and wrap their dear lifeless bodies by myself. The next day there were only a few people at their burial service. Your mother came, Alex. Did you know that? She introduced herself to me as Emma, the childhood name she preferred though everyone calls her Mary. She hugged me. We both cried. I am so sorry I can never know her, Alex. She seemed so strong, and I felt so useless. When my father finally returned weeks later and saw two fresh graves, he wouldn't speak to me. Not a word! He just stood there. He punishes me for their deaths every moment of every day."

"Pricilla, please stop—" Alex stammered, "I will stand by you."

The vision of Raca looking up at her from the depths haunted her. She shook and tried to make his silent screams go away. She grabbed Alex's arm. "Did you see Raca's face under the water?

244

Do you understand what I've done? It's happened again!" She wept and shook her head hard when he tried to reach for her. She did not want a human touch.

"I don't understand many things. But I'll learn," said Alex. "I'm here... for you." At this rare affectionate moment Alex suddenly seemed older. Beyond his bony, wounded body and bandaged cheeks, Pricilla wondered if she could trust him with her life. She tried to smile in appreciation of his kind words and brave action. He had fought Raca unarmed; he knew he probably would not survive. She looked at her hands and he reached for them and held them. "All men don't behave like *them* Pricilla." He thought of the tenderness between his parents.

In his arms Pricilla gradually calmed. His caress helped. "I've only known men who hurt people. I'm not weak, Alexander, and I'm not like the others—" Tears of fear and hopelessness reappeared. "I can't protect myself... I tried. Look what happened..."

Alex sat in silence. He had saved her. She had saved him. But they were alone. She knew she must commit to him now or retreat to her cabin and remain afraid forever. She looked into the face of a youth and recognized the eyes of a man.

Alex gripped her hands tighter and spoke softly, "When you're with me I won't let anyone hurt you. Raca can't hurt you anymore. And your father..." Carefully he picked his next words. "...does not have the courage to fight both you and me. He pretends otherwise but I've watched him, Pricilla. He moves quick to action but suffers from demons. He hides his fears. He cared for you once. Remember those days. I'm here now. I care for you and always will. I'll never leave you. There may be things I don't understand, but I understand *you*."

Pricilla was surprised by his words. She smiled. She knew however, before they could build a life together, they had to escape from *Wasp*.

Gant quickly dismissed thoughts of the drowned Raca—merely a rat kicked back into its corner. But a malleable knife had been lost. Gant realized the other crewmen regarded him with increasingly disrespectful looks. And these were his paid crew. His passenger no longer hid his contempt obviously not bowing to the politics of survival. He must bolster his left flank and confront the danger straight-on.

"Pierce." The captain's thumb pointed to the rail where only a solitary gull might overhear. "We talked before—about what if I needed a mate. You did well, telling the truth about Mr. Raca's murder. I'm making you *Wasp's* first mate. It comes with five dollars a month extra. But I'll cut your manhood off with a rusty knife and throw it to this gull if you cross me or fail to do my bidding. D'ya got that?" A nod was expected. Pierce did so. "We got ship's people talking behind my back, about things I can guess but don't know for sure."

"A mutiny, Cap'n?"

"Of a kind. Your cousin. Do you trust him? You're an officer now."

Too dull to think through an important question carefully, Pierce answered quickly thinking speed was more critical than accuracy. "Willy's a mean one, sir, but he'll do no wrong on this ship." Gant did not believe his new mate but decided this was not the time to press.

"Then you watch him like a sea hawk. And the boy. Whatever they say, whatever they're planning, you come and tell me. You owe me your future. A man what was raised from before the mast has only one allegiance—to the master who raised him. Not friendship, not family, not a woman. Nothing stands in the way of duty. You got that?

Alex maneuvered to speak to the girl as they passed on the lower deck—she, coming from the galley, he on his way up the main companionway. It would be settled then: the how, the where, the timing of it all. But as she swung open the galley door, a cloud parted and bright sun streaked down the hatchway: there he saw a shadow, not moving at work or at rest. A shadow near to where he would soon climb. Someone was watching. He reversed direction and retreated below.

"Pricilla, I have something important to tell you. About Willy," he whispered in a false hush that to any nearby listener might sound muffled. His words, however, were deliberately articulated. Pricilla looked concerned, not for the pending news, but for the volume of his voice. She did not recognize the building confrontation. Alex continued, "I saw Willy throwing his knife into a target. He doesn't miss his spot. I wager he's got something afoot."

"Will is a good boy, Alex. You're wrong..." Missing the tone and the course of the false narrative she launched into a spirited defense of Willy. Alex's placed a finger to his lips. She stopped short. Preventing her from giving away the ruse, he pointed upwards—yes, she too saw the lurking shadow. Alex rushed up the ladder and grabbed the shirt of Pierce Harrison.

"You're tracking me like a hound, aren't you? "

"I'm... I'm your first mate, lad."

"Only because the captain needs another thug. But he'll get no help from you, you rat!"

As expected, the feeble backbone of Pierce Harrison could not take this kind of affront. The first mate forgot about his new authority and did not bring the boy to the captain for insubordination. Instead, Pierce behaved like the lower deck thug he was and swung his fists like he had seen in tavern brawls, though he had never actually participated in one. His swing missed as Alex ducked and replied with a careful kick to the back of Pierce's knees. Pricilla by this time had raised her head to the level of the deck. She did not hide her vacant indifference as she looked directly into the eyes of the man who had been blind to her assault. Pierce stood, glared at Pricilla, then Alex, and thought the better of another limp attempt.

"My word against yours, *mate*," Alex spewed out in defiance. "I'll say someone threw a knife from the shadows and hit Raca square between his eyes. The knife was what sent him over. Remember Pricilla *called* for your cousin by *name*. There's only one man on *Wasp* could have hit a moving target square in the face. We got *two* against the word of one. Remember *this* before you try to send anyone to the gallows."

Pricilla said not a word and joined Alex as he walked forward toward the bow. She disapproved of Alex's choice for a convenient suspect. His latest feint, however, would surely neutralize Pierce's zeal to lay blame.

"Alex, you don't know Willy like I do. He'd never murder an officer."

"You don't think? I wager he's regretting his rum. He didn't answer your call, did he?"

For the first time in his life, Pierce wished he had taken Willy's advice and learned the art of knife fighting. *This boy deserves a cut, a deep one.* He thought of what to tell Willy about their precarious position... and how best Willy should retaliate.

The Rochester brig sailed the last miles back to the Azores in uneasy silence. Pierce Harrison would back his captain and confirm a murder had taken place before his eyes. He dared not say otherwise.

Wasp slid quietly into Sao Miguel with a tense, miserable crew fewer by one. They were not surprised to see *USS Bill of Rights* confidently at anchor, her lines taut and all sails properly furled. If the world admires a sailing ship as judged by its fastidiously stowed lines and smart, secured sails, *Bill of Rights* represented the proud standard. Her American ensign flew high above her spanker. She was the taut ship *Wasp* was not. Among *Wasp's* distressed crew, everyone but Captain Gant welcomed the arrival of the United States Navy.

Alex kept to himself while Pricilla rested. He hung onto the rail. Isaiah approached at sunrise as he came on watch.

"Miss Pricilla told me how you saved her," Isaiah spoke softly, "You met the challenge."

"That's not what they'll say in Boston. Will I hang?"

"Perhaps..." the older man said with a whisper of a smile, "...you should travel. If you never return to Rochester Captain Gant can't touch you."

"I don't have any money. I'm alone."

"Perhaps not alone. But don't wait 'til the captain throws you back in chains."

"I won't run without Pricilla."

"As you say. Things have changed," Isaiah reasoned.

"Where did she go?" Alex asked.

"Forward. Avoiding the captain."

Alex found Pricilla curled in a hammock as swells gently rocked the ship. He helped her regain her feet. She wiped her nose and eyes and tried to forget about her attacker and his fate.

"He'll drag you back to Massachusetts, Alex. I think money has passed between Pierce and my father. First mate my arse. No one will question the word of two officers against... a woman. Willy was asleep, everyone knows that, and we all heard you say you'd kill Raca as soon as you found your parents." She spoke the truth. "Alexander, we've got to get off *Wasp*."

"I know… but… Pricilla, I need to ask you something. When Raca attacked you, you called out for Willy. Not me." He had stewed on this disquieting turn. Her choice of a rescuer hurt more deeply than the blows from Raca's fists.

She did not expect this. It was a fair question. Alex deserved a truthful answer.

"Had I called you, I knew you'd come. And Raca would've killed you. I wanted to live but not at the cost of your life. I thought only Willy had half a chance to kill Raca." The truth stung but he could not argue. He felt less than a man. She smiled tenderly and took his hand to soften her words. He pulled his hand back; there was much yet to reconcile between them. She did not take offense—it had been a long voyage. She too was thinking ahead. "You proved me wrong."

Isaiah approached along the dark, lower deck ducking his head.

"If the court awards *Celeste* to the British," he spoke firmly but softly, "…they'll sail away with her, and *Wasp* must return home. Captain Gant does not have the men to take *Celeste* by force. You…" He pointed at Alex. "…must get off *Wasp* the minute we drop anchor."

Alex nodded.

"Could Alex and I find refuge on *Bill of Rights*?" Pricilla asked hopefully.

"The Navy will not take you." Isaiah shook his head in her direction.

"But she's still in danger," Alex protested.

"No Naval officer will kidnap a captain's daughter. If *you* want to get on *Bill of Rights* as an able-body crewman, you must leave Pricilla here with her father."

"I'm not going to do that," Alex said without hesitation. He brightened and outlined his new plan, "I'll slip onto *Mary Celeste* before she weighs anchor. Only need a few minutes. I have a good reason to ask the port-warden to allow this. You must trust me."

"Then you may need these." Isaiah opened a satchel and displayed two stolen pistols and bags of powder and shot.

"With any luck, we won't need guns, Isaiah. Where's Willy?" asked Alexander Briggs.

Wasp anchored. With a slip knot Gant rigged a mooring ball made from a watertight barrel so *Wasp* could abandon their anchor and escape without notice. Alex recognized the smuggler's ruse; he anticipated Gant's next move.

Wasp's crew ate the last of their fresh provisions. Gant told Alex and Pierce Harrison to row him ashore where he and Alex would show the captain's log of *Mary Celeste* to Port-Warden Gabriel and validate their claim. If the Portuguese allowed them to board *Mary Celeste* one last time, Gant would force Alex to produce the strongbox. For this last-ditch attempt he changed tactics.

"Once aboard, you'll hand over the gold." Gant said through his pipe.

"I looked already. You find it."

Gant thought a bit as the boat eased its way inshore.

"Do as I say, or you'll never see her again." Gant nodded in the direction of a British ship, a transport no doubt, watering before the long voyage to New South Wales with the desperate and condemned. "By the time the noose breaks your worthless neck, she'll be on the other side of the world." Alex did not give Gant the satisfaction of a retort or even a nervous look. But he knew the captain's words were not gamesmanship.

They rowed to shore in belligerent silence, Gant holding fast to Captain Briggs' log detailing the accident. Alex tried to think past Gant's latest threat, needing to find an answer to his imponderable choices. They passed *Halifax*. Alex looked up at the English ship. Earlier in the week she had been moored in the outer harbor; now she had surprisingly moved her mooring and was rafted menacingly alongside *Mary Celeste*. Had a ruling arrived? Alex unconsciously looked at Gant: *Not good*. Alex was deep in thought when a British sailor hung over and yelled to them from *Halifax's* stern.

"Hey-oh, *Wasp*! Captain Breton invites you aboard. He has good news! We're away!"

"Good news for whom?" Alex asked nervously half to himself, half to his jailer.

"Don't know," Gant barked, avoiding the boy's eyes.

"Perhaps word came from London. The port-warden will know." Alex wanted desperately to get to shore.

"We'll hear the British first." Gant needed to find a way to board *Celeste* after dark unseen. How many men were on watch? Where were they posted? What view did they have of the *Mary Celeste*? This unexpected invitation might provide a solution. *Wasp's* longboat slid up to the side of *Halifax*. Alex watched as Gant climbed up the side with *Mary Celeste's* logbook clenched under his arm. Pierce sat distracted, expecting Alex to follow. He never saw Alex's punch.

"Boy—get back here, you scum!" Gant ordered from halfway up the *Halifax's* side.

Pierce grabbed onto the captain's offered hand and was hoisted out of the water as Alex furiously rowed away. Alex decided the only 'good news' he would believe was to be found on shore.

Willy Harrison had watched *Wasp's* longboat row away from *Wasp*, his cousin on it to guard Alex. The younger cousin was glad to be exempt from the turnkey role. Willy turned to Pricilla who stood on deck close by Isaiah. Willy had noticed her recently lacerated and hastily bandaged neck, her many bruises and scratches, and how badly she limped. Willy told himself he could no longer stand aside; his anger neared its breaking point. He only needed an opportunity to show his valor. He, Pricilla, and Isaiah had been tasked with making the ship ready for an immediate return to Massachusetts; they were not warm to the idea. Willy considered the remaining long boat. He and the girl could escape *Wasp* and find refuge ashore, damn the smuggler and his bloody ship.

"They stopped alongside *Halifax*. Why?" Willy asked, alarmed at the unexpected turn.

Pricilla frowned at the unplanned delay. Alex had promised he would return for her. "I—don't know…"

"Pricilla," Willy interrupted. She turned to him, and he smiled. "You must get away. I have no respect for this ship or your father. I only have allegiance to protect my kin. And you."

"Your words are generous, Will. But how can you help me? I am quite the prisoner."

"I have made no promises in Rochester than cannot be undone. My heart has found another." Fondly, she remembered their passionate moments together. She then thought of Alex who had promised to protect her '*always, forever*'. Willy on the other hand, offered his heart, unabashed and open. A man both honest *and* passionate. She wanted both.

Willy looked at *Halifax* flying signal flags commanding the three remaining *Wasps* to join their captain. He put his spyglass down on the rail and turned to Isaiah. "He wants us over there, Isaiah. I wager Gant has learned we've got *Mary Celeste* returned to us!" He looked at Pricilla "And you and I will speak further…" Willy tried to take her hands and kiss her like before. She took two steps back.

"Willy, you're more than kind. You're a wonderful, exciting man. And yes, I need your help. But after what happened to Raca, I will follow Alex. He came to protect me knowing he'd probably be killed. But you shall always have a place in my heart, please believe that."

Willy backed off, wounded but sober to the realities. He knew she and Alex had not been apart for a moment since Gregor Raca's death. He also knew she was right. Alex Briggs had suffered in her defense while he had stayed above the ugly fray—his cousin's squalid counsel. He chose the wrong path and he knew it; it hurt—a pain to last forever. However, Alex might hang as Gant had promised. Willy told himself he would do what he could to protect Alex from that fate; Pricilla deserved as much. He made her a final offer.

"Let your hair down if you need me to come to you—it will be our private signal, Pricilla. But you must ask," Willy said with his last dram of hope. She nodded hesitantly and kissed Willy quickly and tenderly on his lips.

She turned and headed below to gather a few things for the short row over to *Halifax* and *Mary Celeste*. Unaware she was leaving her father's ship for the last time she had a strangely comforting sense Willy Harrison would forever remain a part of her life.

"You've lost someone, I see," said Captain Breton with folded arms over his thick belly, his contempt curiously in the open for a host, as sailing ship captains often entertained each other with a generosity of spirit and shared meals. Breton nodded in the direction of Alex's escape as the two Americans boarded *Halifax*. Gant dropped his offered open hand. Breton continued to openly mock his Yankee visitors. "Seems your lad has run off to town or perhaps the hills, eh?"

"He's left something he cares for on the ship." Gant looked over Pierce Harrison who caught his meaning and nodded. "I told the crew we're off with the evening's ebb. If the boy misses the tide, he'll lose it forever. He'll be back." *But will he return with Portuguese muskets or U.S. Navy Marines in tow?* Gant did not feel nearly as confident as he sounded. He thought of ways to keep the boy quiet; before, with the port-warden, he had used his young captive's clear thinking and artful diction to his advantage; but now, his elocution might turn the day. Captain Gant determined if the boy returned, he would silence him. *Not a single word will spill out,* he promised himself. Gant stared at his counterpart. The English captain had a familiar air about him. It finally came to him: this man Breton reminded him of another captain he had encountered years ago—the man who sent him to a prison of misery, pain and depravity; wet walls of lost souls he could never wipe from sleepless nights. Both Englishmen flaunted an air of distracted arrogance coupled with abject ferocity when facing a foe. But the British officer from 1814 had gone down with his frigate in a hurricane off Antigua in the year '16, or so Gant had been told. Still… he stared at the other man's belly and into his eyes searching for a clue. "So, London has ruled…?"

"You Yankees get to it directly, eh, yes, we received news from our speedy packet *Ariel* yonder. She's bound for New South Wales with convicts." The English captain motioned toward the ship newly arrived in Sao Miguel during the week *Wasp* had searched for the castaways. "Come, take your leisure, sir. Won't you share a brandy?" Breton asked with decorum but without any genuine enthusiasm.

Gant shook his head and ignored the liquor. "What did they rule?" he demanded, not sure how hard to push. He was quite alone except for one half-drowned, poor excuse for a mate.

"*Halifax* weighs anchors on the afternoon ebb. We leave *Celeste* to you, as we found her, no worse for wear-and-tear. Better in fact. We tidied her rig." Captain Breton waved at her sails and lines.

"You intended to take her, I wager—until the United States Navy anchored under your lee," snorted Gant. The British captain did not respond to the accusation; he turned and seemed uneasy. Gant looked for a pattern through a thickening fog of deception.

Without warning a man in a shiny blue American naval uniform emerged from the cabin below. Lieutenant Matthew Barker, U.S.N. smiled. Gant was surprised to see him again, but not shocked. It would stand to reason the rooster visited the hen house.

"Ah, Captain *Gant*—see, I got it right this time—was your search successful?" Grinning, he looked around the deck. He did not wait for an answer. *What would an American naval officer be doing below deck on board a British merchant ship?* Gant's stomach churned. He regretted not keeping Isaiah and Willy with him. "I understand *Halifax* leaves with the tide and *Mary Celeste* will be turned over to your care? Splendid! Then this unfortunate episode between our nations has been resolved without further… tension," said Lieutenant Barker, dismissing the entire situation with a wave. Gant thought he heard the sound of swords sliding from their scabbards someplace on deck. *And why are all the English sailors on watch at the same time? Why no shore leave?* "Captain Gant, did you find your missing people?" Lieutenant Barker asked again.

"Dead, all of'em. Castaways on a sandbar."

"The boy must be crushed," Lieutenant Barker surmised. "I see he has rowed away with your gig." Gant did not give him the satisfaction of an answer. "Did you ascertain why the crew *of Mary Celeste* found themselves so tragically adrift?" Lieutenant Barker asked while admiring his uniform sleeves which he adjusted and brushed with manicured fingers.

"I have their log. Fire aboard. They abandoned ship." British sailors nearby nodded: an uncontrolled fire deep in the ocean on a wooden sailing ship with its tarred shrouds and canvas sails usually turned into a disastrous conflagration.

"…and so, all this unfortunate, misguided talk of murder and piracy can be put to rest, Captain Gant?" Gant stared noncommittally in Captain Breton's direction. "And, Captain, I have learned you failed to deliver the letter I entrusted to you. For the Portuguese authorities? Did my instructions slip your mind?" Gant stammered. A rare occasion, words escaped him. *Where'd the girl put the damned original?* Lieutenant Barker smiled at Gant's discomfort in full display of the British sailors. Then he moved on to his visit's purpose and filled the void. "The *USS Bill of Rights* has determined no danger to American shipping exists from North African pirates, so we're to sail briskly for New York." Speaking causally to Gant, Lieutenant Barker turned to the companion ladder leading down to the *Halifax's* captain's cabin, "Captain Gant, I will examine *Mary Celeste's* log—to verify your account. Please follow me."

Lieutenant Barker looked over his shoulder as he spoke toward Captain Breton who stood on his deck grim-faced. Gant started to climb down the ladder. After two steps, he hesitated. He turned and observed *Halifax's* crew had conveniently completed their chores at the exact same moment. Glancing beyond the deck of *Halifax* Gant also noticed *Celeste* displayed repaired yards and rigging, her sails newly stitched, loosely reefed: the ship had been made ready for sea. All the while he had wasted his time looking for a dead crew. *Damn!* He should have stayed here!

In *Halifax's* dark cabin, Gant opened his satchel to retrieve Captain Ebenezer Briggs' log of his final days. He felt confident it would play in his favor, though this had been a day of surprises. In the gloom, Lieutenant Barker spoke first.

"That won't be necessary, Captain Gant." Gant's eyes adjusted to the dim light, steeled for whatever might come. "You and I will reach an understanding." Lieutenant Barker looked at Gant with a wispy smile, his thin lips barely moving. "I have the rest of your misfit crew aboard the *Bill of Rights*."

Gant caught himself, waited a moment and asked, "Have they honored us?" *I will play his game.*

"They have." Barker looked out a stern window. "Would you like them returned?"

A direct question deserved a direct answer. "Aye…" Gant said but let the affirmation linger. He was no fool.

"Three dollars per head. Payable now in gold."

There. He had it. Now he understood how the Lieutenant could afford the gold buckles and silk ribbons adorning his fine woolen great coat. How he had paid for the expensive eagle feathers stuck in his ornate hat.

"What if the British change their mind, fight us for *Celeste*? Will *Bill of Rights* remain in port?" Gant fenced in the agreement. He stuck his hand in his trousers pockets having noticed it shook with the excitement of this unexpected turn; he could not control his fingers from twitching.

"We have orders to leave. Signal if the English present you with any difficulties. Your men look like they can handle a skirmish. I will leave a lookout watching aft."

"I only have enough coin for two dollars each. I must provision two ships for a long voyage home." Gant spoke the truth wondering if he was the only one.

"Quickly here." Lieutenant Barker found a quill and paper. "List what you need, and I will send over stores. But I will have my three dollars a head or you will sail two ships across an ocean with only four men and a girl!"

Captain Gant had no choice. He reached for his purse he had brought to enrich the port-warden. Gant added, "For three dollars each, you return my crew, and come to our aid if the British fight us. And take the boy."

"Ah, yes, the poor orphan Briggs. He must be desperate to return home. You *do* intend to return the Briggs' ship to Rochester do you not? Or do you have other plans for *Mary Celeste*? If the boy disappears, no one will ever know what happened here… will they?" Gant's silence said everything. "For

258

an extra twenty, I'll make sure the boy *never* finds his way home."

Gant did not hide his disgust at the extra charge for the troublesome mongrel. But he felt privately relieved—a pittance to suffocate the boy's lies forever. He emptied the generous purse Ezekiel Briggs had so thoughtfully provided. *I'll get my fighting boys back. I'll get the* Mary Celeste, *and at first light we'll tear her apart from stem to stern.* He hoped to find the strongbox, then run east or south around the Cape with his gold, his men, his two ships, and his daughter.

Ah, she comes aboard. Gant could hear the commotion above his head as sailors happily made way for Pricilla. The last of the *Wasps* had rowed over as instructed joining the *Halifax* crew for an amiable parting of ways. He craned his head to gaze out the aft port and saw Willy Harrison, the cook, and the girl still dressed as a sailor. *Once these ships are secured, I'll drag her ashore by her hair if necessary for a proper dress.* She had ignored him their first visit to Sao Miguel; those days of disrespect were over. He was about to turn his attention back to the smirking, self-satisfied Navy scrub counting his blood money when a flash of light peaked through the port. Gant glanced at Willy climbing up and over the bulwarks with his weapon hanging loose. Without Raca, Gant was relieved he was not alone. From the moment they were hailed by *Halifax*, Gant had suspected trouble. Even now with the tide shifted in his favor, his edge had tensioned like a hurricane-taut windward shroud: events were moving too smoothly. Nothing fit. Gant even had the United States Navy's unwitting assistance—that by itself should be a warning. He felt the British ship twist on her cable, lifting his fortunes on the outgoing Atlantic tide. But he understood as well as any seaman the tide turns in any sea, against any fortune. He must keep Willy and his knife close.

Alex ran up the dock to the port-warden's office.

"Master Briggs," called Port-Warden Gabriel who had watched him row ashore. "What did you find?"

"Everyone was dead. Captain Gant has my father's log. He can show you the proof you wanted, Sir! There was a fire... and a storm. The crew went into ship's boats... tried to re-board... but could not. Will you... can you write to London this account? Have you heard of a decision on *Halifax's* claim?"

"Catch your breath, son. Mail came with the transport but nothing from the court."

The port-warden saw Alex's desperation. He thought of the English captain's generous offer. Torn, he offered the admirable American youth a suggestion he hoped might affect events in the American's favor, while leaving his reward safely in place.

"Master Briggs, tell your captain to carefully watch the British. I saw an American naval officer board *Halifax* not long ago. He went below alone with the British captain. Whatever they're talking about cannot be good for *Wasp*."

"A deal?"

"*Bill of Rights* has forty-four cannon. They can point in any direction."

"But the American Navy will protect *my* rights!"

"Sí. But you saw their young Lieutenant? He has expensive tastes. He spent freely yesterday on fine *porto*, Bordeaux clarets, and cakes for his galley. How does he afford this...?"

Alex could easily run past the docks and disappear into the nearby mountains, precipitous and dense. He could hide and escape from Gant and his thugs. Instead, he thought of Pricilla. He had promised her he would return for her. He turned to look at the three merchant ships sitting in the harbor. He stared at his father's taut ship and remembered the strongbox hidden below—*his* legacy, *his* future. He then peered to see a crowd of sailors gathering on *Halifax's* deck close alongside. Finally, he turned his attention to the disheveled *Wasp*, sitting alone near to shore. Would the girl do as they had agreed and jump into his skiff when darkness descended?

Port-Warden Gabriel admitted to himself he had contributed to the boy's present misfortunes. And having set these events in motion, he had a sudden burst of regret—not enough to weaken his resolve and nothing to lessen the pleasure of his reward. But he thought the boy deserved to know what he could not change.

"And one last thing lad... when Captain Breton saw *Wasp* race back into Sao Miguel today, he came and stood where you stand now. He offered me gold to allow *Celeste* to leave unmolested on this afternoon's tide. He intends to cut her on the last of the ebb. He cares nothing for courts. Nor does he seem concerned your Navy might prevent his thievery. One can guess why."

Alex nodded his thanks and sprinted down the quay to retrieve *Wasp's* longboat. The port-warden watched Alex row furiously back to the moored ships and thought of his lengthy, stilted negotiations with Captain Breton, about his seedy offer and a comfortable villa up the coast where he would soon retire. He knew *Mary Celeste* and *Halifax* had both been provisioned, ready to weigh anchor and sail east with hardened men, Azores goats, and weapons.

Alex rowed the heavy longboat with every ounce of strength he had, thinking of his rash plan to row ashore with Pricilla and hide on Sao Miguel with the weapons Isaiah had provided. But the further he rowed the angrier he got. After all this, they would not steal his father's ship! The *Mary Celeste* and the strongbox belonged to *him*. He rowed to *Halifax* with the thinnest of a new plan: to turn his hated oppressor into a necessary ally. Frenzied by anger, desperation, and hope, Alex banged the rowboat alongside *Halifax* and climbed aboard with the speed of a squirrel up a tree. He met faces of curious British sailors, their stern commander, and the full, uninhibited hate of the two men from *Wasp*.

"Captain…!" Between the hard row ashore, the fast, heady conversation with the port-warden, and an impossibly fast row back to the middle of the harbor, Alex was quite out of breath, barely able to spit out even key words of his discovery. Gant strode toward the rail where Alex stood gasping for breath. "Captain," Alex repeated. "…these two… got a deal… to steal—" Gant's fist slammed into Alex's pleading face before his words finished forming. Blood spurted from his split lips, mouth, and nose. Alex collapsed from the blow onto the deck, his eyes filling with a dark night of billowing clouds formed under a northern sky. He forced consciousness to return. *No dammit, you fool, let me speak!*

"Mr. Harrison, sit on the boy and bind his mouth with your bandana! I'll have no further insubordination!" Gant cried out with a captain's affectation.

Pierce heard the fragments Alex attempted to spit out. Even his feeble mind was able to place them into their unnerving context. Unused to bravery of any sort he nevertheless had a strong, ulterior sense of self-preservation. He forced a whisper into his captain's ear. "Cap'n. The boy's tryin' to tell you—"

"Shut your mouth, Mr. Harrison, or I'll dis-rate you before the sun sets! Not another word!" Gant commanded in his loudest quarterdeck voice. More focused on retaining some semblance of respect in front of the British sailors, Gant ignored the bleeding face he had silenced and watched Alex Briggs struggle as Pierce stuffed his dirty cotton neckpiece around the boy's bloody mouth. Alex had collapsed into a sitting position, dazed in a prize fighter's last repose—one more blow would send him flat onto the deck. Gant let him be, *quiet now, good*. It was only then the boy's squealing words and horrible shrieks echoed in his brain: Alex was trying to tell him something *important*. He felt a sudden chill in the humid afternoon and was about to reconsider his options when Lieutenant Barker claimed his arm.

"Ah, I see your pugilist has returned, Captain Gant. Son, we're planning to exchange ships…" the naval officer said with a joyless smile as he looked at the bound and bloody Alex Briggs.

As Alex struggled against Pierce's attempt to bind his arms and shoulders with ropes, Lieutenant Barker announced the *Bill of Rights'* imminent departure, "…before we lose the tide…" Barker eyed Alex with a cold gaze.

"Lieutenant Barker." Captain Breton spoke quickly through his thick white beard. "Captain Gant has graciously accepted my invitation to a hearty repast with all hands of both ships on deck of the *Halifax*—a small gesture of British good cheer. We'd be honored if *Bill of Rights'* officers would endeavor to join us as well."

"Thank you, Captain, but *Bill of Rights* must depart as soon as we transfer Captain Gant's crew," Lieutenant Barker answered.

"But we have roasted mutton and a fine Madeira and… 'eh, what crew is being transferred, sir?" the British Captain asked with his last bit of control.

"The United States Navy has determined we no longer require the extra hands recruited from *Wasp*. They're not deserters after all. Thusly, we will return these men to *Wasp*. Captain Gant needs his full crew to sail the two ships home, of course."

Captain Breton stood mute, stunned. Gant would now have as many fighting crewmen as he. Lieutenant Barker—the snake—had double crossed him. He felt the professional enmity of the nearby American Marines with their long guns, sharp bayonets attached. He looked anew at the frigate, ports open, her starboard cannon run out.

Captain Breton mumbled, "…of course."

"We shall transfer them to *Halifax* forthwith so they may all enjoy your munificent meal." Lieutenant Barker looked at Gant who nodded—he wanted his fightin' boys back aboard *Celeste, fast.* Still dazed, Alex did not take particular notice of the two U.S. Marines who stood behind him until they yanked him to his unsteady feet. "And you, Mr. Briggs," Lieutenant Barker turned to Alex. "Your Captain and I have agreed you shall be transferred to the *Bill of Rights*… to return home to stand trial for the murder of Wasp's first mate… what was the name?"

"Gregor Raca," Gant answered.

"…Gregor Raca." Lieutenant Barker smiled broadly while his hands felt the heavy bag of coins in his great-coat pocket. "Corporal Meade?"

Lieutenant Barker walked to the rail to climb back into the launch for the cross-harbor row back to the *Bill of Rights*. Despite a new open wound and vision obscured by sweat-drenched locks, Alex shot a long last look at Gant accompanied by a loud, desperate scream.

"*Nooo!*"

Gant and the entire crew heard Alex clearly despite his gagged mouth. He approached Alex who had been bound by two Marine guards. The captain considered removing the gag until snickers from *Halifax's* able bodies changed his mind. Reconciliation of any kind would appear weak in front of the British crew; Gant squelched his lingering concern as to the boy's interrupted attempt at a final communication before his permanent incarceration. *A plea for amnesty no doubt. Briggs murdered Raca and every man on deck has heard the charge and seen his arrest.* Gant was within his rights. He had lost an officer, murdered on his own deck. He reached back and slugged Alex with the full force of his back and shoulders into the boy's stomach. Air rushed out and the boy toppled into the arms of his turnkeys who dumped him without ceremony into the frigate's longboat.

Satisfied, Gant turned away to see Pricilla climbing up from below deck where she and Isaiah had been helping in the galley. Only then did the boy's final jumble of broken words rekindle Gant's recollection. But he needed confirmation.

"What was he was saying, Mr. Harrison?" he whispered.

Pierce locked eyes with Alex, now in the longboat, bent over but alert, no longer pleading.

"Ah, Captain, he said these buggers got a deal," answered Pierce.

"What now?" Gant asked noting the English sailors had lost interest in Alex's arrest and turned their attentions to him.

"They aim... to steal something, Cap'n. Them two." Pierce shrugged casually toward Captain Breton still standing in an angry stupor, then toward the boat taking away the duplicitous Lieutenant Barker.

Gant's stomach heaved. "Why didn't you say something?"

"Father? What on earth...?" Pricilla reached him from across the deck. "I heard Alex's cry." Pierce spoke over her, attempting to make a defense for himself to his captain built upon following orders. Before Gant could recalculate what had happened, before he put the pieces of the puzzle together, Pricilla's scream intercepted his focus, "Father, damn you! Alexander! Father, what have you done?" She turned on Gant with fury in her face, her arms shaking by her side, her eyes wider than a topsail.

"The boy has been arrested."

"What will become of him?"

"He'll be tried and executed. You'll never see him again."

"No!" she shrieked and hung far over the rail. "Alexander!"

Alex loosened his gag enough to shout, "Pricilla!"

But his attempt to break free from the Marine's steely clutch met with naval discipline. *Even if he could free himself, what should he say to her? Why had he not said it before?*

265

Pricilla burst into tears and clung to the rail as nearby sailors retreated awkwardly to their meal. Slowly climbing up from the galley, Isaiah had followed Pricilla, and watched in horror. He looked to Willy who held a hand near his hidden knife. Willy returned the cook's look with wide eyes fearing the overwhelming odds. He stared at the girl, hoping she would run to his side for consolation and protection, but she never looked in his direction; the tide had changed. Instead, Pricilla stared after the launch as American sailors rowed their prisoner to the warship taking Alexander Briggs away from her forever.

Isaiah glared at the priggish Naval Lieutenant and the two duplicitous captains. As the sun went down, he wondered what other promises had been broken and what dishonorable terms had been renegotiated aboard a ship reeking of cheap wine and mutton overcooked with deceit.

Captain Coughlin of the *USS Bill of Rights* had chosen a fortuitous afternoon to remain sober. Once again on this voyage Lieutenant Barker had pressed 15 men from an American merchant brig. And now having returned them—no doubt filling his pockets in the process—Barker had somehow acquired a new unwilling passenger. Standing on deck near the taffrail Captain Coughlin watched the ship's pinnace come alongside, hoisted onto its davits for storage on the main deck in preparation for the voyage home. The frigate's forestaysail was hoisted tight with alacrity and sheeted home. Her large main course was loosened from its harbor furl and dropped down where the breeze filled the cotton canvas new this commission. A gang of boys and men forward sang in unison as they wrapped her anchor cable around the topside capstan, working in partnership with another team below deck, and winched each of her two heavy anchors out of the water. Freed from the bottom, and with a full set of sails, a fresh breeze, and a lively crew, *Bill of Rights* boasted a taut ship sailing fast for home.

Captain Coughlin's view of the organized competence was disrupted by his first officer clad in finery and felt. The Lieutenant led two Marines who flanked a tall young man, detaining him roughly by arm and shoulder as the ragged youth continually tried to free himself to speak. The young man limped with a pained gait and his face betrayed having suffered severe beatings.

"What's this Lieutenant?"

"Sir," Lieutenant Barker posed imperiously. "Captain Quartus Grant of the brig *Wasp* has asked us to convey this ruffian to Boston to stand trial for the murder of their officer."

"Who beat the lad?"

"He was handed over as you see him, Sir."

"Let him speak."

"Sir, he's a known brute—"

"Now!"

"Aye... Captain." Barker sensed a change in the weather. He indicated for the Marines to remove Alex's gag but keep him bound tightly.

"And the ropes."

"Aye... Sir." Barker's face bore a look one could not confuse with any other than contempt. *Damn, but I should have made sure the captain was passed out before I dragged this bloody scab aboard!*

Finally free to talk, Alex considered his words carefully as a Marine released him from his ropes. "Thank you, Captain."

Coughlin did not expect such a respectful tone from one so clearly abused. Clearly the lad understood probity and decorum on a warship's quarterdeck.

"What's your name son?"

"Alexander Briggs, of Rochester, Sir. That's our ship to weather, the brig *Mary Celeste*."

"Briggs? Is your father Ben Briggs?"

"Aye, sir, Ebenezer Briggs. We are—" Alex choked a moment before he could continue, "We were shipbuilders. He's dead, sir."

"I am sorry to hear it, son. We heard the *Mary Celeste* was found abandoned. We were sent to search for pirates who might have been responsible."

"Sir, thank you for that. But I haven't much time. I see you've slipped your cable. I must return. The British are planning to steal my ship. Your officer was paid to cooperate—"

"Ahh… not exactly. Sir…" Lieutenant Barker stammered, smiling contemptuously, and continued without his superior's permission. "Seems the lad came aboard the brig as a simple seaman and didn't take to the rigid life before the mast. A rich man's son, you see. He was arrested for heaving his mate overboard."

"Is it true, Mr. Briggs?"

"I wanted him dead, I won't deny it. But I didn't have the ability, or the strength to kill him. I speak the God's truth, Sir. He was attacking a young woman."

"I'll strap him in irons, eh right…" Barker waited too long for the rest. "Captain?"

Deep in the fermented soul of Captain Stephen Coughlin the scales finally tipped. Lieutenant Barker had added 'Captain' with a tad too much hesitation and his words dripped with affected insolence. Barker mistakenly presumed he could continue to bully the man who had captured 12 English merchant ships in the year '14—a fearless fighter who suffered cutlass slashes to his thighs and splinters in both legs and face. Coughlin heard his subordinate's unvarnished meaning needing no translation.

"Thank you, Mr. Barker. Leave us. You may continue to get the ship underway. Corporal…" Captain Coughlin's attention turned to the more senior of the two Marine guards. "Dismissed, both of you. Mister Briggs walk aft with me."

"But, Sir," stammered Barker, "He's a dangerous criminal, a mur—"

"You have your orders, Mr. Barker."

"Captain, Sir, he's lying," Alex pleaded when alone with Captain Coughlin. He had remembered his father's natural respect for a man in a uniform, a captain no less. He would not meet the Lieutenant's lies with interruptions, threats, or oaths. Ben Briggs' son was a gentleman. He spoke to the older man as an equal. "They're stealing the *Mary Celeste*, Captain. She belongs to my family. I must go back. I didn't kill anyone. You must believe me."

Captain Coughlin looked at *Celeste* and *Halifax* astern of the *USS Bill of Rights* with hungry crews gathered on deck. "If I allow your return... what will happen to you? It appears you have overstayed your welcome."

"I will not sail with either ship. I will find other passage home. Captain, you've been misled! No ruling has arrived from any court—*Halifax* aims to steal our ship. Your lieutenant has been paid to allow this. Ask the port-warden." Coughlin rubbed his chin, glad once again he could think straight on this hazy afternoon. He knew Barker was a prissy, graft-grubbing coward but would he stoop to this level of corruption right under his captain's nose? "Sir, I've lost my family but I... I met a girl— her father holds her against her will. She's in great danger. If I don't help her no one will. Please, Sir, let me go!" Alex was also thinking about the strongbox and his future, 200 yards away, hidden where he alone could find it.

Captain Coughlin looked at the son of a man he once knew. A man he had sailed with in their daring youth before he joined the Navy. A man he owed. Ben Briggs had been a brave young man whom Stephen Coughlin had deprived of his due.

Captain Coughlin had noted Alex's awkward walk and wounded, bleeding face as soon as he came on board; injuries he had not seen in a lad since the year '14 when he lost a midshipman brutally maimed by a well-aimed broadside. He mulled over the disparate pieces of the lad's account.

"*Wasp* you say."

"Yes sir..."

"Gant still her master?"

"Aye."

Captain Coughlin made no further comment about Alex's pronounced limp or recent, raw wounds.

"Son, I have strict orders to return with haste to New York after two sweeps off the Tripoli coast. We have captured our anchors." He paused. "Your father and I fought together. He was a master seaman. I venture *Celeste's* fate was not his fault."

"It was not. Sir, please, go and inspect your foredeck. No one will see what happens."

"It's twenty feet down, lad. And if you miss the sandbar, you'll be swept out to sea in the last of the ebb." He looked at his timepiece and the harbor moorings still leaning seaward. Alex's plan might have time to work. "Godspeed." He took Alex's hand into his. "For your father. He was a fine man." Captain Coughlin turned his back on Alexander Briggs and walked forward on his stately frigate. "Find me if you return to Boston," he said over his shoulder.

Alex smiled his hurried gratitude and ran to the frigate's taffrail, climbed up and dove far and clean. *Bill of Rights* shook out her lower sails and gained sudden headway.

Lieutenant Barker came running aft jingling and squeaking, "The boy went over, Sir! Did you not *see* him?"

"What boy, Mr. Barker? Mind your trim. And attend to me in my cabin once we're on our course."

Helpless, Lieutenant Barker looked aft. "Aye, Sir."

"And send the quartermaster."

Again, "Aye." Barker hesitated before departing from Coughlin's presence.

Moments later, Captain Coughlin spoke quietly to his trusted quartermaster. "Search Mr. Barker's seachest and bring me his purse. Say nothing to the other officers." As his master touched his cap and walked away, Captain Coughlin added, "And tell Sergeant Collins to post two Marines outside my cabin."

"Aye, Sir," replied the quarter master and, looking ahead, thought, *This'll be an interesting watch tonight.*

As *Bill of Rights* sailed away Alex Briggs struggled in the saltwater. Swimming hard against an outgoing current felt like dragging a cart up a steep hill. His injuries made swimming difficult; he swallowed harbor water and feared he could not make it. But after 10 strenuous minutes, he finally found a bottom of hard sand and small rocks.

He staggered ashore and half ran, half walked two-hundred yards to a beach where small boats were littered about, some tied to the pier others dragged above high water. He stole a small, brightly colored rowboat and rowed earnestly back towards the two rafted ships. This time he carefully considered his options and their likely outcome. He forced his anger down and away and thought about the girl. He thought about the gold and what the port-warden had said: What was the American Officer doing aboard *Halifax*? Was the Navy conveniently leaving so this thievery might go unchecked? Was violence about to erupt between two heavily armed and motivated crews thirsting after the same valuable prize?

Yes, the answer! In the violence sure to explode on the decks of *Halifax*, he would find her amidst the confusion, escape together in the rowboat, and hide in Sao Miguel's sharp mountains. But first he had to climb aboard *Celeste* and recover his father's strongbox. He had lost everything—his family, his freedom to return home, his ship, and his reputation. He would not lose his fortune, too. Alex rowed deliberately to the far side of the *Mary Celeste*—out of sight from *Halifax's* crowded deck—hoping he had not been sighted. A pungent smell of roast mutton filled the humid afternoon air. He relaxed a bit when he realized no British sailors were standing watch on *Mary Celeste*; his father's ship appeared empty. He secured the rowboat loosely and, grabbing the hand-holds, climbed onto *Celeste's* abandoned main deck. He glanced over at *Halifax* tied tight alongside and was surprised to see a larger than expected number of men eating and drinking. *Gant's impressed men must have been returned to him. Gant has fifty men to scour the hills looking for him and his kidnapped daughter.* But Alex also noticed something he suspected Gant had missed: a few British sailors were staying back and out of sight of the American's feasting on *Halifax's* forward deck. They held muskets and swords by their sides and carried pistols in their belts.

Alex noticed a sailor's everyday working-knife forgotten near a hatch. He slid it down his belt, took cover behind the mast and watched and waited, ready to duck and run forward and below for the chest. From his hidden position on *Celeste's* deck, Alex watched as Captain Breton stood to speak to *Halifax's* revelers. In the confusion and violence, he was sure would erupt Alex's fast-evolving plan was to run below and recover the strongbox then signal to the girl he spotted dishing out roasted meats to the assembled crews. Her face was beautiful but as still and gray as granite; her father stood close.

On *Halifax* Captain Breton observed *Bill of Rights* departure as she loosened her sails and headed northeast, sailing away with the vigor he had paid for. A fully rigged ship with all sails hoisted, including studding sails on lower yardarms was a glorious site—a cloud of beauty and speed unmatched on the ocean or by any machine yet built by men. She was away fast with a determined purpose. For Captain James Breton it was a sight guaranteeing his fortune—his moment had arrived.

"Captain Gant! Miss, Lads of *Halifax* and *Wasp*! I have important news. There has been a change. Listen up now!" Captain Breton bellowed above the din of 50 gathered men. The deck quieted. Gant did not like Breton's sudden authoritative tone, when moments before he had been courteous and obligatory despite poorly masked enmity. Gant belatedly realized the British sailors drinking with far less enthusiasm than their American counterparts, suddenly and stealthily had surrounded his crew. Glistening in the sunlight, he saw steel blades unsheathed, held by British sailors. *Damn to all hell!* He turned and stared at Breton who addressed Gant's unarmed American sailors, surrounded by equal numbers of armed *Halifax* crewmen. "Our Portuguese friends insist *Mary Celeste* remain quarantined waiting for the bloody court to rule on our honorable claim of salvage. However, United States Naval officers and I have come to a more equitable agreement…" He paused. "The American naval authorities *support* our claim…" British sailors cheered. "…so, we need not wait for a ruling. We are free to deliver *Celeste* to Gibraltar where our agent will sell her at auction!" The men cheered wildly; caps flew about the deck. "…and every *Halifax* man will get his share in *gold!*" The armed British sailors roared and prodded each other eagerly, smiling broadly. They raised their swords and muskets and pointed them at the stunned Americans. "And lads from *Wasp*—you can sail home! Fare well." Captain Breton waved toward an open gate.

Gant froze. *The Briggs boy was right, damn it to hell.*

Wasp's crew enjoyed full stomachs, many of them drunk from full-strength rum and port enjoyed with relish under a hot sun. They sat confused. No man dared move without a command from Gant. A threat of a bloody battle hung over *Halifax's* crowded deck, a fight the unarmed Americans would lose.

"You boys shall jump into the harbor," Breton ordered, "On your own or with an English blade up your arse! One by one, over the side!"

It suddenly came back to Gant in a rush of wounded pride and pain: 20 years before during the war, this same man had arrested Gant. Quartus Gant had been imprisoned in His Majesty's penal system where he learned the finer points of hate. Now he met his enemy a second time; how was it possible by any odds? Captain Gant brandished his pistol; he might die this day, but it would be worth seeing the other bleed like a pig. The British Captain, however, had been watching his antagonist. He too had earlier recognized the former privateer who had without mercy or warning fired a helpless British ship, killing a score of British sailors and officers, including the captain's treasured young nephew. From the experience of fighting dogs like Gant on sloping decks slippery with blood, he had anticipated an attack. He turned, dodged, and ducked with more dexterity than his girth would seem to have permitted.

"You lying, cock-sucking piece of—" Gant screamed as he let the shot go. But a British sailor smashed his face with the butt-end of his musket and Gant's shot missed.

Another sailor was about to thrust a pike into Gant's chest when Breton put up his hand. Blood spurted from Gant's mouth, and he fell to his knees. Breton kicked Gant's spent weapon along the deck, his false smile a distant memory. He studied Gant's bloody face, his successful hunt for the murderous privateer finally concluded.

"We have met before, have we not?"

"Damn you to hell…" Gant could only sputter through blood and a broken face.

"I am flush with kindness today, Captain. Instead of sending your dead carcass over the side, I'm sending you home. I trust you enjoyed the King's hospitality in Mills Prison, eh?" Breton turned to his men nearby. "Throw these Yankee bastards over the side!"

Ten ready muskets were raised and leveled at the corralled Americans. Other sailors pointed cutlasses ready for hacking and thrusts. The crew of *Wasp* was surrounded.

Pierce mumbled, "Can't swim, Your Lordship…"

"You won't drown. Look over—I've loosened barrels and flotsam to drift your way to shore. We shall fire on no man in the water. OVER!"

Pierce looked to Willy for support, but Willy ignored him. His eyes were searching for Pricilla.

The Americans retreated. One man after another jumped off *Halifax's* deck and into Sao Miguel's quiet harbor. A few men needed the active encouragement of sharp British bayonets because *Wasp's crew*—like sailors everywhere—knew enough never to step off a deck at sea unless the ship was sinking.

From his crouched pose on the deck of the *Mary Celeste* Alex considered his diminishing options. He frantically struggled with a decision. Staring at *Mary Celeste's* open, unguarded main hatch—a mere 30 feet away—he figured he could run for it, rush below, retrieve the chest and perhaps row back to the town unseen. Find the girl later. Then he caught sight of Pricilla. Her eyes were wide with terror. Gant held his bloody face in one hand and her arm tight in the other; his fury and pain barely masking his humiliation. Alex realized that, from any one of multiple threats, Pricilla faced grave danger: she might drown; Gant would drag her back onto *Wasp* and continue to beat her or worse. And not for the first time, Alex noted with increasing discomfort how Willy and Pricilla seemed a match. From the empty deck of *Mary Celeste*, he watched *Wasp's* crew queued at the open gate. Gant pushed Pricilla harshly and she glared back at him and shook her arm free. Alex watched Isaiah wait patiently for the others, then stoically take his turn; the cook dove and disappeared.

Alex, frantic, had made a promise—Pricilla needed him. He realized he did not have time to retrieve the strongbox *and* pluck her from harbor waters swarming with angry men. He knew she was strong and hoped she could swim well enough to reach shore; or so she had once reassured him. He glanced forward on *Celeste's* deck and then back to where Pricilla stood backing away from *Halifax's* gate. He must decide—now. Again, her father pushed her crudely toward the opening. She screamed, hands to her face, and disappeared into the water.

Captain Breton wasted no time. As the last Americans queued, he hollered commands for both ships to simultaneously get under way. The ships had tied slip knots on their moorings, their anchors abandoned; sails were ready to catch the building wind, holds provisioned, and armed delivery crews assigned to each escaping ship.

"Mr. Levy," ordered Captain Breton, "take your boys and slip *Celeste's* cable. Fast now! Follow *Halifax* out with a full press on and stay on my line until darkness. Remember your orders!" He turned to another officer. "Drop our cable! Lively now! Release our main course and make way. Helm—steer to the north side of the channel where the currents run hardest." He watched the last of the American prisoners disappear from his deck. He congratulated his men now in control of both ships. "While they're swimming ashore, they'll miss the ebb, boys! We'll be ten leagues away heading for the abundant fruit of the Mediterranean before they can set a sail. Well done, mates!"

Alex heard the command and responding cheers. For the last time, he looked down the deck of *Mary Celeste* and shook his head. Climbing off his father's ship he abandoned the skiff and dove clear into the water as the deck suddenly swarmed with Englishmen readying *Celeste* for sea. Hiding under the stern overhang in the warm harbor waters, Alex narrowly missed being seen. He swam around the sterns of both ships where *Wasp's* crew was making slow progress into the rocky shore a few hundred feet away. At first, he had trouble identifying the half-submerged swimmers. Then he saw Gant, bleeding, his belly over a floating barrel, kicking with fury and to his left, a small swimmer trying to swim away from him. Alex swam far to the left around struggling sailors. He came up behind Pricilla, but waited to speak until they were close to shore, well ahead of Gant.

"Psst!" Alex finally whispered. She turned. Crouched low in the water, he held a finger at his lips. She ignored his warning and ran splashing through knee-deep water and grabbed him in a tight embrace. He spun her around in his arms, "Shhh... shhh. It's good, it's good."

"I didn't think I'd ever see you again..." She was laughing and crying at the same time. She hugged him tight, her face inches from his own, surprising them both, but then suddenly she let go. Her joy was replaced by terror, and she glanced frantically behind.

"He'll kill you, Alexander."

Gant's crew was scattered over 100 yards of shoreline. Most stood slack-jawed and drenched watching *Celeste* and *Halifax* escape under short sail with skeleton crews.

"Here." Alex reached for Pricilla's hand which she gave willingly as they waded through rocks to the shore. His grip was firm, and she clasped it intending to never let go.

"No!" she cried, "He's coming. Run!"

"Pricilla. I have a plan."

Gant stomped up. Alex thought he would pounce like an animal.

"I lied," Alex said to the captain before Gant could utter his first oath. Gant pulled up, astounded at what he saw. "How the devil did *you* get *here*?" Shocked and confused, Gant spat blood out from his wounded mouth. "I lied to you," Alex repeated.

"About many things, I am sure!"

"You remember I led you to a hidden chest on *Celeste*. I said it held nothing valuable—only worthless paper, invoices, and bills?" Gant recalled; he nodded absently. "In fact, the chest we found *was* my father's strongbox. And those documents weren't bills. They were redeemable stock certificates. Letters of credit to every major banking house in Europe—Antwerp, London, Lisbon, and Venice. Introductions from my father to his traders and agents. Open lines to draw upon his foreign banks. He bought government bonds from the Federal Bank in New York. His chest contains the entire assets of Briggs and Sons. He emptied his American banks—all our family money is in the strongbox." He pointed to *Mary Celeste* sailing away.

Gant looked to his daughter. "Is this true, girl? You read it. Raca read it!"

"I did. What Alex says is true." Her eyes did not back down.

"How, how…?" Gant recalled Alex—not Raca or himself—carried with no effort what appeared to be a medium sized, lightweight chest from its hiding place. He remembered looking for a large, heavy chest packed tight with gold and specie. "Tell me!"

"My father loaded gold and silver coins plus stacks of currency—American dollars, British sterling—into a false bottom. I'd wager there's enough gold in the strongbox to buy ten ships and pay a crew for twenty voyages. He intended to have a new merchant fleet built in Brest." Gant looked at his men slowly assembling on the beach, abandoning the flotsam the wind had driven ashore. They watched their captain and waited for orders. Alex Briggs continued. "There's enough gold on the *Mary Celeste* for a man to live like a king. Unless she sails away tonight and disappears forever. *Wasp* sails faster, I assure you. And we both know how high to the wind she climbs. *Wasp* can slip her mooring and get away fast—but you have only fifteen minutes before the flood starts in earnest. And if you miss the last of the ebb, you'll be stuck here for four hours. But with your full crew and all her sails set, *Wasp* can catch up to and take *Celeste*—but only if you make your tide. The three of us are the only ones who know where my father hid the strongbox. You can be on and off *Celeste* before *Halifax* can sail back to stop you. The British may accuse you of piracy, but everyone heard *Halifax's* captain renounce his claim. The Navy will back your account. You're only fulfilling your obligation to retrieve private papers of *Celeste's* captain—which you were not able to do because of your involuntary departure this afternoon." Gant did not need more encouragement. Nevertheless, Alex added insurance. "But if you waste precious time trying to drag me back aboard, I'll tell the entire crew about my father's treasure you plan to keep for yourself. They'll mutiny. And likely kill you... so, I won't have to." Alex removed his knife and faced the older man with undisguised deadly intent.

Gant, for a second time this hour, feared for his life. "Daughter, we're leaving." He said as he spit blood from his broken face.

"No." She stared back flatly.

"Now!"

"Father you're a wicked man! You left me alone with Raca and you knew he'd hurt me. What did you promise him to get his loyalty—me?"

Gant did not answer. *I don't have time for this.*

"Father, *I* pushed Raca overboard. Not Alexander! *I killed him!*"

Gant remained silent. *She killed Raca? No! She's protecting the boy.* He shook his head.

"I don't believe you. Briggs will hang." Silence drifted over them for a painful moment until Gant commanded weakly, "Daughter, come. We shall go back on board."

She kept her gaze steady on her father and stiffened. "Papa those people, the crew of *Mary Celeste*, were still alive."

"What's this nonsense?"

"Captain Briggs, his wife, and daughter… little Lizzy. We sailed right by the island where they were stranded as we approached Sao Miguel. But you refused to stop." Pricilla looked at Alex and said sadly, "I am sorry Alexander. I didn't tell you everything your father wrote in his log. I was afraid of what you would do." She looked at her father with cruel vicious eyes Alex had never seen in her before. "Captain Briggs' final entry was written in his hand dated October 22. We passed those islands on October 18. We could have saved Alex's family, but you sailed by. *Mary Celeste's* crew was still alive."

His stomach suddenly queasy, Gant was reminded of his indifference to his enemy's survival and his passion to reach Sao Miguel before the frigate. He remembered his own orders. *She* was there, waiting. *I could have saved her.* He tried to blot Emma from his memory but failed. He stared at the boy and saw the kind of face he well recognized: a man bent on retribution. He felt for his knife and looked around for his men.

Stunned at the revelation, as if he needed another reason to kill Captain Gant, Alex stared at Pricilla, then back at Gant. Alexander Briggs had many reasons to plunge his knife deep into Gant's throat, now one more. But Pricilla's eyes pleaded, hoping her desperate revelation did not prove a mistake. She knew Alex would lose this fight; Alex understood her look: '*There will come a time. Not here, not today.*' So instead, he focused on his one final advantage. Gant's men stood dazed in the Azores' sun waiting on his commands, some 30 yards away. "If you miss the tide, *Celeste* will be too far away to catch before nightfall. After dark you'll never find them again. You got time to fight me for your daughter or you can run and steal my father's strongbox. But you can't do both."

Gant glanced over his shoulder and saw *Wasp* twisting with the turn of the tide. Alex was right. *Damn him to hell!* "I'll return in two days. You got no place to hide. No ship will take a girl without a purse."

"GO! Steal your gold. You'll never see me again!" Pricilla's eyes had a fury Gant had only seen once before in a woman. And like her mother, she was lost to him for all time.

"You'll be here. And if not, when you come crawling back…" He pointed at his daughter, and with a cold voice he snarled, "not a scrap from my table, not a rag from my refuse pile…" He turned. "And boy, I'll make it my life's purpose to see you hang."

Alex took a deep breath. "My family's dead because of you. I'll never forget that."

Gant looked foolish, dripping and cold, threatened by a boy he had had smothered in chains only two weeks before. A fortune was sliding through his fingers for a second time.

"Damn you both to hell!" Gant stormed off. "Men of *Wasp*! We're after them!" he bellowed, pointing at the two brigs catching the ocean breeze outside the harbor. His war-cry repeated along shore by tired and somewhat drunk men. *Wasp* would make her tide.

Willy too had reached shore and stood not far behind Gant, Pricilla, and Alex. He appeared alert and waited for her signal; unlike Pierce and the rest, he had not been drinking. His eyes remained sharp, his knife ready. Gant strode toward him without a word and jerked his head backward to look at Isaiah, still wading awkwardly and slowly into shore. Alex and Pricilla, exposed and apart, stood close together on the windswept beach. Willy stared at her intently and smiled hopefully, waiting. Gant walked up to him; Willy appeared ready to cut the old man down. Pricilla reached up and played with the bun in her hair. She tightened it and her long sun-streaked strands remained firmly in place. She gave Willy a genuine, tender smile but without doubt, it was a smile of farewell. Willy understood, not completely surprised. He let Gant pass unimpeded and with a heavy heart turned away from Pricilla and retreated toward the various commandeered small boats ferrying stragglers back to the ship. His cousin Pierce beckoned him to hurry but Willy longed to join the young couple's flight. He could not, however, abandon his kin despite his increasing antipathy toward Pierce and his cousin's shameless lack of temerity. He would ensure his cousin found his way safely to another ship forever free from Gant. Then as a free man find Pricilla Gant again. With a sad wave, he bade her farewell and swiped away an unseen tear.

Alex watched Pricilla's eyes as Willy turned down the beach. Some secret communication had occurred between the two. The young man who had so recently lost everything he valued realized the importance and the joy of what had just taken place: the girl had decided for *him*; she was his for all time.

As Gant marched down the beach his boots squeaked as he shouted commands to ready the ship to weigh anchor. Alex turned, finally noticing Isaiah—still waist-deep, and struggling. The cook sloshed awkwardly toward shore, slowly stumbling over rocks and seaweed. He seemed to proceed with greater difficulty than the others had had wading ashore minutes before.

"Are you injured?" asked Alex.

"Cook! Come along!" Gant ordered from down the beach as he stepped into a small boat.

"Aye, Sir," Isaiah yelled back, staggering weakly.

"Hurry, damn your soul!"

"Aye, but I've injured my leg…"

"To hell with you if you can't keep up," yelled Gant abandoning Isaiah, too.

Sitting on a small boulder at the waters' edge Pricilla watched her father rush away, arms waving, oaths booming. Like a thunderstorm's last distant echo, he was suddenly gone and out of her life. She was left alone with Alexander Briggs and the cook. She had neither close family nor friends. She could never return to Rochester.

Alex ignored both *Halifax* and *Mary Celeste* as they rounded the headlands. Instead, he eyed *Wasp's* crew to make sure they did not double back along the beach. But the smuggler's crew followed their captain, gathered small boats tied along the harbor, rowed to *Wasp*, and got her underway with the alacrity of a privateer come upon a merchantman.

Pricilla and Alex looked at each other.

"Where to, Alexander?" she asked. "I have no purse… no clothes. We need shelter."

"I don't know," he admitted.

Closing in behind him, Alex heard splashing and heavy breathing. He looked over his shoulder as Isaiah approached, picking his way through the remaining rocks separating shore from harbor.

"Isaiah, are you injured bad? Can you make it to *Wasp*?" Pricilla asked sensibly.

"I am well, thank you, Miss. But *Wasp?* I think I shall not return. See the transport…?" Isaiah pointed to a British ship *Ariel* moored close to the wharf. "Heard from *Halifax*'s cook, she's bound for New South Wales—Australia—to unload transported criminals from London, then on to Macao and Hong Kong to buy spices and silks. She'll also load tea and sail home to try and set the market-price in London." All three looked at the merchant ship. "She needs able-bodies," Isaiah added.

"So, you'll join her?" Pricilla asked.

"No. I'll wait for a west-bound packet. I must return to my family. I was more thinking of you two."

"Yes! We'll go to Australia! They'd never look for murderers there, eh?" Alex beamed. He turned to Pricilla as if sailing to a prison colony halfway around the world was an attractive option for two destitute criminals.

"What do you know about Australia?" Pricilla demanded softly. "Only thieves and crooks there, a sorry lot my father says..." She stopped, thinking how ridiculous it sounded coming from her father.

"Nothing, for sure," Alex answered honestly.

He looked at her tenderly. Although Pricilla was wet and shivering even in the warm sunshine, a smile began to form on her tender lips. After all this, she appeared happy simply sitting quietly next to Alex on a sandy shore. He knew she was all the future he would ever need. He took her hands tenderly and rubbed his thumb along her soft, bruised palms.

"We'll *both* go to Australia!" he said confidently.

"We will?" She smiled.

"Yes. Will you come with me?"

"To *Australia*?"

"Yes, to Australia!"

She looked to the west. The afternoon ended without a sunset of orange and purple skies. The sun simply hid behind a dark cloud and disappeared.

She touched his arm gently. "Alex—"

"I will take care of you." Alex interrupted her and she smiled. She had hoped he would say something more.

"Yes, I believe you will. But I'll need more than *care* from a young man who's taking me to the other side of the world." She smiled hoping to hear from Alex the words that reflected not only his bravery and his noble spirit but how he felt about her after their weeks joined in peril.

Alex looked at *Wasp* swinging at her anchor. Her crew had climbed to drop yardarms and loosen her topsails. The bow pointed east as the slack current turned to flood. He understood what she was asking; he did not know how to answer. The language of the sea came easily to him, but the language of the heart was new.

"Will you give me time?" he asked.

She wrapped her arms tightly around him and stared into his eyes. "Yes," she replied. A brief interlude passed. "Time's up."

Alex did not lose his moment. His lips opened and met hers for a long salty kiss. He realized for the first time what the future could bring—so much more than he had ever imagined. He squeezed her and did not let go until she laughed softly and pushed him away. They both knew this would not be their last embrace. Disoriented and deliriously happy, Alex finally looked to Isaiah whose gaze had been elsewhere, fiddling with something underwater near his ankle, allowing them their bit of privacy.

"Isaiah," Alex tried to breathe again. "Do you think *Ariel* would take us?"

"I suppose... you bein' payin' passengers."

"Ha. Mister Cooper, you're rich," Pricilla said kindly. "Look at us! Wet and without clothes or money." She finally let her hair down to wring out the saltwater before tying the long strands back in a tight wrap. Brine dripped over her red cheeks and nose. She wiped her scratched face with a soggy sleeve and smiled, happy to be alive here with these people.

"Master Briggs and Miss, well... I have things to tell you..." Only then did Alex notice a stout rope in Isaiah's hand leading into the water. "I knew your father well," Isaiah continued, "Many years ago, he saved my family and I from a life of unimaginable hardship. I owe him my freedom, I owe him my life, as I owe you."

"I don't understand," interrupted Pricilla. "You mean when Alexander saved *Wasp* by going aloft?"

"That too, Miss. Ha! Twice I owe him!"

"Remind me of the first time, Isaiah?" Alex asked, perplexed.

"The accident in the work shed." Isaiah undid his collar and showed Alex his ugly wound—raw even after a month at sea.

"It was *you* caught underneath the workboat?" Alex cried.

"Aye. Your double hoist saved me." Isaiah winked. "He 'saved my neck', Miss."

"I'm glad you survived. I've often wondered," Alex replied with a wide grin.

"Before he left Rochester, Captain Briggs told me to watch over you. He feared what your brother might do. He also told me to safeguard the secret of his family's future—his strongbox—in case he didn't return. He had me build a secret compartment... and I was shocked you found it and gave it up to Captain Gant..."

"Gant had to believe there wasn't any gold on *Celeste*. He'd only search if he thought they had kept the strongbox with them. It was my only hope."

"I believe you were right," Isaiah agreed.

"Pricilla," Alex said, taking her hand. "I never thanked you for what you did the day we went aboard *Celeste*." She smiled. "'*Newton Ice and Coal*?'" he asked, remembering the list of vendors she had invented. The deception had sent Gant to search for *Mary Celeste's* missing crew.

She laughed from the gut for the first time in many weeks. "*Wasp* double-crossed a schooner captain last February and stole half his cargo. For days on end, I had to clean coal dust—it was everywhere! I'll never forget the name."

Pricilla wondered if this was the time to reveal to Alex her sordid role in her father's devious plot to arrange for all Briggs and Sons' obligations, loans, and debts to be called in, with the intent—sadly, tragically successful—to cause their utter ruin: family, business, reputation. If so admitted, how could she not admit to her own duplicitous undertaking in the long process: the letters she wrote, the private arrangements she made, the hand delivered pleas, and the fulfilled handouts. How could she deny her father was an unhinged malcontent never resting as long as Ben Briggs breathed? No, sitting on a wet rock on a distant shore she hardened her resolve, this was not the right time for an open disclosure. Today was a day to live, not recriminate nor add more painful revelations onto the shoulders of the man hers now and forever. Let him rest easy. Someday, there would come a time for the other. Someday she would confront the instigators of these events whereby an entire family was left to die, starving and alone. But not today, today was one of joy and relief. They were alive, and free!

Alex grinned and looked to Isaiah. "Apparently my father wrote me a letter—but I never got it. I learned someone called '*T.S.*' would return his strongbox to me if Father died..."

Isaiah asked, "Did you have a favorite Bible story as a child?"

"I did..."

"Was it not the parable of the Good Shepherd?"

"How could *you* know that?"

"Your father said to tell you I was *The Shepherd. 'T.S.'* So you would trust me."

Alex smiled. "It's good I didn't know you were '*T.S.*' They'd have killed you..."

"Aye they might have tried." Isaiah chuckled; he knew his strength. *They'd have failed.* Isaiah rested his weary body on a rock and thought of Captain Briggs. "I was a slave. But because of your father I'm a free man with a free family. I met your father in Charleston where I worked the docks. My job was to clean the filth from the ships as they unloaded my people from the middle passage. I was barely alive, if you could call it living. Your father had sailed south. It's a long tale, but he bought me because he needed crew. He gave me my freedom—he would only hire free men to sail his schooner. I begged him to buy a slave girl I loved. He did not need a woman on board but your mother, who on occasion sailed with him, turned his mind. She being a church-going lady insisted the slave girl right then and there should become my wife. I shall never forget their kindness..." Isaiah looked away for a moment as Gant's crew worked furiously to get *Wasp* to sea. "I knew Gant would not return to Rochester once he got *Celeste*. With you on board, I decided to join the crew. On the day when you located the strongbox in the forecastle after everyone else left, you remember I stayed behind—"

Alex interrupted. "I asked you to return the chest to the compartment."

"You did. But instead, I quickly placed your father's chest into a second satchel I had brought. It had a thick seal-skin lining. I figured our odds of gettin' back on board weren't good. I tied a knot with a strong line and lifted the satchel through the forward hatch, tied it to a loose halyard, and let it fall overboard into the water. It looked like another careless line lying about. All the while *Celeste* was anchored, my satchel hung below the water and out of sight."

"But *Celeste* has just sailed away..." Pricilla pointed out.

"Aye. But I cut the satchel loose just now when I dove over the side." Alex and Pricilla looked at each other. Isaiah laughed. "The chest was heavy. I was lucky the harbor shoals up fast near where we're anchored. I had to drag it along the bottom for fifty feet while swimming until I got my feet down. That's what took me so long..." Isaiah turned and pulled a line and dragged the heavy sealskin satchel from the water to the shoreline. He picked up the satchel and set it on the rock and loosened the top. Inside they saw Captain Briggs' strongbox. Isaiah smiled broadly at Alexander. "So, I figure it belongs to you now."

Captain Coughlin called his quartermaster to the taffrail where he had been observing sails east by southeast.

"You see our three friends?"

"Aye, Sir. Sailing hard from Sao Miguel."

"*Halifax* leads. She's not our concern. Behind her, however, follows *Mary Celeste* in full flight, admirably how well she sails. But she should be anchored in Sao Miguel under Portuguese quarantine. Her unauthorized departure will cause us difficulties in New York."

"Aye, Sir. And she's pursued."

"Indeed. By *Wasp*. Captained by a smuggler who I suspect plans to overtake the *Mary Celeste* and board her with the additional crew Mr. Barker has so generously supplied."

"I have the account of our missing stores you asked for, Sir. And Lieutenant Barker claims those purses of gold do not belong to him. He complains of his confinement, Sir."

"Where he shall remain until his court-martial," Captain Coughlin added, "...and where he'll soon have company."

"Sir?"

"Plot a course to intercept *Mary Celeste* and *Wasp* before we lose our light. Signal them hove-to for boarding."

"Aye, Sir."

"Gather a delivery crew to return *Mary Celeste* back to Sao Miguel with our apologies to the Portuguese for our role in her unlawful departure. Make room for *Wasp's* crew but arrest her captain. Throw him in irons."

"Aye, Captain." Captain Stephen Coughlin hoped to find Alexander Briggs and his young miss with no further injuries. "What about a delivery crew for *Wasp*, Captain?" the quartermaster asked.

"That won't be necessary. It has been too long since Lieutenant Barker has fired a broadside in anger. Load our starboard guns with heavy iron. We shall conduct target practice this evening." The captain jerked his head toward *Wasp* sailing away fast from justice and gave his quartermaster a sober, knowing eye. "My orders regarding captured slavers or smugglers are unambiguous."

"Aye, Sir."

"You may take in our stuns'ls and bring the ship about. Set topsails only," the captain ordered with a calm competence he had not felt for many leagues. He smiled so faintly to be nearly imperceptible. "Prepare for action."

As the sun disappeared, four sailing ships raced east. The three merchant ships had set all their sails but could not out-pace a frigate's clean, copper bottom and a captain bent on a seamans's justice. Each ship was filled with violent men armed for battle but only one would escape safely through Gibraltar's strait, her angry crew forever telling sad tales of abandoned dreams and lost advantage.

THE END

Glossary of 19th Century Nautical Terms

Able-Body (sea man): a sailor who "knows the ropes" or what all the lines are called and how they operate; a higher-paid sailor than a 'common' sailor; able to jump from one ship to another with ease

Batten: wooden straps around canvas covers that protect hatch openings on deck from sea water coming in; 'batten down the hatches' basically means 'close the windows!'

Beam: a ship's width; a *beamy* ship is generally heavy and slow; beamy ships included large naval man-of-wars and merchant ships

Belay: To secure a line (tie it); also used to say, "stop what you're doing"; that is—stop adjusting sails

Below: down ladders to a lower deck; a brig has one deck 'below' the open main deck

Belaying Pin: a wooden bar about 15 inches long that slides into a hole along the side of the ship, and, around it, sailors tie ropes; it can be removed, and therefore used as a weapon—e.g., a club

Bilge: the bottom of the inside of the ship's hull below the cargo hold; into the bilge water often leaks and must be pumped out daily; as a result, the damp bilge tends to attract rats

Brace: ropes used to move the yardarms so a ship can change direction relative to where the wind is coming from and where the captain wants it to go

Brig: a sailing ship with two masts and a combination of square sails and fore and aft sails and jibs; see diagram

British East India Company: a quasi-private/government company whose large, slow ships carried spices, tea, and commodities from Britain's Far East colonies, particularly India. **Indiamen** were ships of the Company and were often convoyed by the British Navy during war and were attractive targets of Britain's enemies—including privateers, pirates, and naval ships

Boat: a watercraft small enough to be brought onto a ship

Companionway or companion ladder: an opening through the main hatches where sailors can climb down to the deck below; in the companionway opening there is a steep wooden ladder

Capstan: a mechanical device that makes it easier to raise a heavy anchor

Come About (or 'about' or 'tack'): to change direction by losing wind from sails; a ship's bow comes across the direction of the wind

Course: another name for a large 'square' sail; also, the direction a ship is sailing

Ease: to loosen a line attached to a sail; this makes a sail lose its wind and power; a ship will slow down when sails and lines are eased

Frigate: a medium size warship with between 28 and 50 cannons; fast, so used to carry fleet messages

Gaff top wooden support for the spanker; heavy to hoist

Jibe (or jybe; also, to 'wear'): to change direction quickly away from the direction of the wind; the wind remains in the sails; requires more sea room to execute than a tack; safer than tacking and so preferred by captains whose ships are far out at sea

Lines: ropes that are attached to a sail and have a particular function—e.g., a jib sheet is a line (a rope to trim a jib sail) or a spanker halyard is a line (a rope to raise a spanker sail)

Lubbers Hole: an opening in the platform high on the mast through which a sailor can climb avoiding the near upside-down climb over the outside of the platform which is quicker; stands for "land lubber" or a non-sailor (e.g., only non-sailors would chicken out and use a "lubbers hole")

Mooring ball and **slip knot**: in the event a ship must depart quickly—perhaps escaping an enemy ship or a smuggler trying to sneak away with stolen goods—she can leave her anchor in the water tied with a slip knot to a floating mooring ball

Orlop: the lower deck on a multi deck ship such as a frigate or ship of the line (a man-of-war)

Peak: top of the mast; also called a 'truck'

Port: a window in a ship; also: a harbor in a town; also: a type of wine with added hard liquor (brandy) made in Portugal; also, after the time of our story—'larboard' was changed to 'port' meaning left looking forward toward the bow—so commands were not confused between larboard and starboard

Larboard: left-hand side of a ship looking forward (to the bow) (renamed 'port')

Longboats, gig, pram, pinnace, jolly boat, etc.: all different types of rowboats on a ship

Privateer: a converted merchant ship—light and fast—approved via a 'letter of marque' issued by a government to attack, burn, and sink enemy merchant ships; also, the name attached to those sailors on board a privateer—also referred to as "privateersmen"

Mid: short for "midshipman" a young officer, as young as 10 and as old as 30; often sons of high-born families looking for a naval career; also called "young gentlemen" in the British Navy

Ratlines: a rope ladder on a ship—how sailors climb up the mast; attached to shrouds or stays—heavy lines that keep the mast in place

Rip: an underwater cliff; the water driven by currents hits a wall of a rip and rushes to the surface creating waves and violent seas; any ship caught in a rip can be turned sideways and pushed on its side which, of course, will cause it to fill with water and sink

Scuttlebutt: a barrel or bucket on deck with a ladle wherein fresh water is stored for sailors to drink during their watch; this is the rare place sailors are allowed to talk to each other while working the ship thus the term: 'that's the scuttlebutt around the office'—rumors at the proverbial water cooler

Ship: in the time of our story a ship with three masts of square sails, for example warships like *USS Constitution*, '*Old Ironsides*'

Ship of the Line: larger warships (bigger than frigates, cutters, or brigs) with two or more decks of cannon

Smuggler: a merchant ship that avoided paying taxes, tariffs, tolls, or fees to the government and carried stolen or illegal/forbidden cargos (contraband)

Slaver: a merchant ship that carried slaves from Africa to other places—especially the U.S. and West Indies (Caribbean); a despised trade

Shoal: a shallow underwater island right below the surface; you cannot see clear evidence of a shoal—unlike a rip which when currents are running hard can be seen by wildly disturbed water and waves on the surface—but they are shown on charts; quite dangerous

Spanker: a large sail at the back (stern) of a ship that is easy for a short-handed crew to trim and sail, although the gaff (top wooden support for the spanker) is heavy to hoist (raise)

Starboard: the right-hand side of the ship looking toward the bow **

Stays or shrouds: firm permanent heavy ropes or cables that support the masts

Tack: to change direction by losing the wind in your sails; sailing too slowly and without enough wind a large ship might not reach the new course; see 'Come about'

Trim: to tighten a sail to better catch wind and sail faster

Weigh anchors: to raise anchor(s) by wrapping an anchor line (cable) around a capstan and turning the capstan with 10 or 20 sailors; difficult to do with a short-handed crew

Yardarms/yards: wooden poles that hold sails, and that turn side-to-side by braces

**Both starboard and larboard originated from Viking/Norse terms when their ships used a wooden board that went down into the water along the sides of the ships—one was called a 'star' and the other a 'lar' (board).

Author's Historical Notes

Most Americans or their descendants (noteworthy exception: indigenous peoples) including those forcibly enslaved and transported from Africa and the West Indies came to America by ship.

Most trade, until the building of the highway system in the mid-20th century, was done via watercraft: sailing ships large and small, barges along canals, skiffs, and dories. The American economy was built on merchant sailing ships and the armed naval ships that protected them.

The U.S. government raised money primarily from tariffs on traded goods until the 20th century, which resulted in a huge industry of smugglers, thieves, and privateers.

Women often accompanied their husbands or fathers on sailing voyages. Entire families sometimes lived on board for years on end.

Sailing ships were wrecked on a regular basis—sailing was hazardous and in places like Vineyard Sound and Wellfleet in Massachusetts, Long Island, Sable Island, and the treacherous Cape Hatteras, thousands of ships were sunk, many with all hands. To this day—all along the East Coast of the United States—ships' ribs sometimes stick out of the beach sand.

Pirates of all nationalities were common on every ocean—not just in the Caribbean Sea.

Many powerful and respectable New England and New York merchant families owned and operated slave ships as well as ships that traded opium into China that caused wars and addicted millions. Britain expanded both trades, but Americans also played a major supporting role as Britain's leading competitor in illicit global trade.

Recommended Reading

Some of the best American and British novels were written about or influenced by our common sailing heritage:

- ☐ Moby Dick (Herman Melville)
- ☐ The Heart of Darkness (Joseph Conrad)
- ☐ Two Years Before the Mast (Richard Henry Dana, Jt.)
- ☐ The Aubrey/Maturin Novels (Patrick O'Brian)
- ☐ Captain Horatio Hornblower novels (C.S. Forrester—Winston Churchill's favorite)
- ☐ The Lively Lady (Kenneth Roberts)
- ☐ Non-fiction books about Admiral Horatio Nelson, the *USS Constitution*, Captain Paul Jones, or Commodore John Barry
- ☐ Non-fiction books by Nantucket's Nathaniel Philbrick

Look for Book Two in the Age of Sail Trilogy

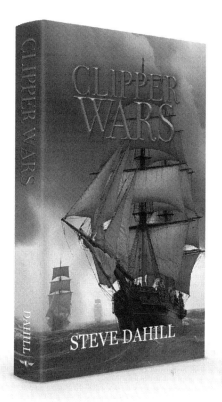

The thrilling sequel to SECRETS OF MARY CELESTE, CLIPPER WARS is the second book in Steve Dahill's Age of Sail nautical adventure trilogy. SECRETS OF MARY CELESTE's key characters continue their adventures alongside the barons of 19th Century industry in New York and Boston, competing for prominence in the world's greatest sailing race. At the height of the California Gold Rush, they race from New York to San Francisco aboard 'extreme' clipper ships, the largest, fastest sailing ships ever built. CLIPPER WARS follows the lives of unscrupulous captains and their wives, ruthless pirates, and honorable but flawed sailors. The ultimate prize of gold and renown awaits the lucky winners who reach the Golden Gate after a 17,000-mile voyage around the notorious Cape Horn. Who among them will sacrifice everything to win in CLIPPER WARS?

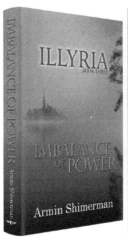  

About the author

Steve Dahill is a direct descendant of the privateer Brother of Revolutionary War hero John Barry cited as the "Father of the United States Navy". Steve is also a direct descendant of revered rebels hanged by the British during the Irish Rebellion of 1798.

Dahill spent many years as an executive in the software industry in Boston, Massachusetts where he lives, overlooking the *USS Constitution* in Boston Harbor, and sails *Riva*, his racing sailboat, along the southern New England coast with his family.

Made in the USA
Middletown, DE
30 June 2024